The Freshman Fifteen

by C. Jules

Chen, Julia 1981-
The Freshman Fifteen: a Novel About College / by C. Jules

Printed in the U.S.A

1 2 3 4 5 6 7 8 9 10

Author's Note

When I was applying to universities, I searched unsuccessfully for a novel that would describe what going to college was really going to be like. Older friends and relatives gave over-simplified and unsatisfactory responses to the questions I could actually articulate. What would it be like to live on my own for the first time, with strangers? How I was going to manage my money? And how I was going to "find myself" in these mystical four years? Never mind the questions I couldn't even bring myself to ask around drinking, drugs and the enormous playing field between first and home base. I was also not prepared for how the relationships in my life were going to change with my old friends, new friends, parents and myself. In the end, everything turned out fine, but I think a lot of people forget the angst and the amusement after they pass through the gauntlet of their freshman year.

The frustration from this experience stayed with me long after college and compelled me to write the novel that I always wished I'd had- a humorous, but realistic preview of college. The Freshman Fifteen is about a starry eyed college freshman who courageously navigates the college minefield of tough decisions and changing relationships in wobbling high heels.

I laughed and cried as I wrote the ups and downs of Amy's chaotic freshman year. She picks up wisdom and perspective the way we all do, through overanalyzing her mistakes. And she gradually realizes, as I did, that college is less about finding yourself than defining yourself in the face of uncertainty. I sincerely hope this novel will make a new adventure less daunting for all college freshmen of the past, present and future.

The Table of Contents

1 Move-In Mayhem

Have you ever had an out-of-body experience that came from being so humiliated you just couldn't process what was happening? You wondered how the hell that poor person (you) wound up in such a predicament and you wanted to tell people, "That's not her at all. You've got the wrong idea about her!"

I was having one of those.

It happened so quickly, I didn't see it coming. It was just past midnight and I was dancing precariously on a giant, thumping speaker, trying to look as if I'd spent every Saturday night shaking my booty in skin tight jeans and three inch gold stilettos. Meanwhile, I kept an eye out for Jeff, the cute guy who lived the floor above me. He had invited me to this party at his frat.

Just minutes ago, he had lifted me up and placed me on top of the speaker, yelling over the music that he was going to get us some drinks and be right back. I tried to look nonchalant. and was comforted to see that a few of the other girls in the room looked as self-conscious as I felt. They had probably exhausted their arsenal of pre-rehearsed dance moves as I had, and were now glancing about uneasily to make sure no one was on to them.

I saw him come through the doorway, his broad shoulders filling most of the door frame. We made eye contact. *Be sexy.* Emboldened by my cover of smoke and dancing lights, through which everyone surely looked surreal and glamorous, I winked at him. He grinned. *Perfect.*

He fought his way through the crowded room towards me, his face mottled by the tiny reflections flashing off of the disco ball, a plastic red cup in each hand. Not terribly classy, but definitely very "college." He handed one of the cups up to me. As I bent over to take it, I felt something heavy fall from my body. A gelatinous mass bounced off Jeff's arm and onto the beer-sticky floor, where it flopped several feet before one of Jeff's drunken frat brothers with frosted tips picked it up, puzzled.

Horrified, I realized what it was.

Earlier that evening, my roommate Casey had loaned me a slinky black sequined tank top meant to highlight curves that I didn't really have. She also armed me with her trusty adhesive bra cups, which she swore by. They looked like raw chicken breasts without the slime. I had tucked them gingerly into the tank top's built in shelf bra. My shape improved dramatically, but I was concerned that they would move around or stick out oddly when I danced.

"They're fine," she reassured me. "I go clubbing all the time and I've never had a problem."

I should have bet on it.

The frosty tipped frat boy realized what it was just moments after I did, delight diffusing across his face.

"A boob!" he yelled, waving it around. "Whose boob is this?" He tossed it halfway across the room to another guy, who threw his head back and howled with laughter.

"Someone's doing some false advertising!"

I watched helplessly as a game of toss-the-boob ensued. Jeff stared, unable to look at me. Suddenly, I caught my breath and scrambled off the back of the speaker, away from Jeff, as fast as I could. Like a trapped squirrel, I searched for the nearest exit. Thankfully, it was a door just a few feet away. I pushed and fought my way through the sea of scantily clad bodies, trying to block out the crescendo of laughter that was roaring in my ears.

I burst into the alleyway outside the frat house and stumbled back out to the street, nearly tripping over a couple engrossed in making out, they didn't stop for one second. I didn't either.

I walked rapidly back up the hill towards my dorm, a molten streak creeping up my cheeks and my temples pounding.

30,000 students, I thought to myself, in a desperate attempt to be positive. *I may not see any of those people ever again.* But I wasn't fooling anyone. At the very least, I would see Jeff again. He lived upstairs. What a way to start college.

Sixteen hours down, four more years to go.

*****

My college experience started in disarray earlier that day. In the weeks leading up to Move In Day, I'd made packing lists with the help of my Mum, and grouped related items into plastic bins and suitcases.But at seven o' clock on Saturday morning, as we got into the line of packed-to-the-brim cars waiting to pull up to the dorms, it became apparent that no amount of planning, labeling and organizing could quell the chaos.

It was anti-climactic in a way. I had expected to walk to my new dorm room with my parents, and let it soak in that I was finally at college after a long summer of anticipation. I had imagined that Mum would help me put away my things and decorate my room. Normally, this level of involvement would have frustrated me, but I wanted to make her happy on the day that her baby left the nest. Dad would want to give me some last minute advice. And we would have the long, tearful goodbye that would mark my becoming an adult. That seemed to be how I remembered Meagan's send off to college, and while I'm generally not in favor of overt parental mushiness, I could see how The Send Off was an important college ritual for the parents. It marked closure.

It didn't turn out quite that way. When we finally pulled into a parking space in front of my dorm, a militant looking man in a blue uniform with a

"Campus Security" badge wrote a ticket and slapped it on Dad's windshield, leaving his palm print on the glass. Dad wouldn't like that.

"This pass is good for fifteen minutes," the security man barked. "We have to get 500 kids moved in today."

"Fifteen minutes!" Mum said as Dad pulled into the parking space. "That's not enough time to get all this stuff into your room. Ame, you're going to have to do the unpacking yourself then."

We all looked uncertainly on the hordes of parents and students, rushing to throw boxes, suitcases and computers onto dollies, or just doggedly carrying them into the building in their arms. Dad went in search of a dolly, while Mum came with me to check in. In front of the cream colored building that I was going to call home, the school had set up a registration table. I waited in line impatiently, stealing a glance at my watch. *Fourteen minutes.*

When I got to the front of the line, a cheerful looking gal, not much older than myself, asked me for my driver's license or some other form of photo ID. I handed her my driver's license and she thumbed through a card box, produced my student ID, my dorm keys, and a stack of paperwork. While she was getting that together, I looked around anxiously for Dad. He was at the car with a bright orange dolly, starting to pile my boxes on it.

The check in girl handed the pile of stuff to me. "My name is Kate. I work in the residence hall. Let me know if you have any questions. Welcome to UCLA, Amy!"

I smiled. I was here. After painstakingly cultivating my transcript, enduring hours of asinine SAT practice tests, and filling out mountains of college applications, I was finally here. I sincerely hoped the hardest part was behind me now.

Somehow, we managed to get through the throngs of nervous students and parents into an elevator that screeched as it neared the third floor. Dad and I were carrying boxes, while Mum pulled the dolly along behind us. We struggled along the hallway towards room 307. The thump of a falling box being caught caused me to turn around abruptly.

A very good looking guy was holding my box, labeled "Toiletries". His tan, muscular arms bulged.

"Your box fell off the top and I caught it before it hit the ground," he said, almost apologetically, as if he'd caused the box to fall.

"Thank you so much!" Mum exclaimed.

"This is Amy," she continued after an awkward pause. "She's our little Bruin."

As if I were starting my first day of kindergarten again. I cringed .

"I'm Jeff. I live upstairs. The elevators are always impossible on moving day, so I take the stairs," he explained, pointing at a door we'd just passed.

So he was not a freshman. I guess I could have figured that out from the calm way he stood in the hallway, in sharp contrast to the move-in madness all around him.

"Hi Jeff, I'm Amy," I said, putting down my box and extending my hand. He did the requisite handshakes all around.

"Listen, if you have any questions or anything about classes or books or whatever, let me know. My screen name is jeffers56," he said, smiling as my parents looked bewildered.

"I'll IM you as soon as I'm set up. Is May sixth your birthday?" I asked.

"Naw, 56 is my football number," he replied, "from when I played in high school. Listen, I need to go help my roommate move his stuff up, but it was nice to meet you all!"

He gave a wave before he disappeared through the door to the stairwell.

"Look, you've made a friend!" Mum was pleased.

I rolled my eyes.

"Mum, did you think I'd have a hard time with it?"

"Well no, Amy. I just mean he seems like a nice boy. Good manners."

"OK, Mum. Noted."

I didn't bother telling her that the fact that he was hot was more relevant.

We continued to walk down the hallway of identical wooden doors. The only things that distinguished one door from the next were the names that were written on large paper stars taped to them. I stopped in front of my door. "Amy", "Casey" and "Erin". All simple two syllables names. Nothing froo-froo. I already liked that about us.

I opened the door to my new home in a significant, sweeping motion. This would be my nest, my home base, my refuge for the next nine months. My expression must have changed from hope to despair quickly because my Dad took one look at me and asked, "What's wrong, honey?"

"It's *tiny*!" I exclaimed.

I had no illusions that it was going to be a presidential suite, but this bordered on ridiculous. They somehow expected three people to live in a room not much larger than my parents' walk-in closet. We faced a large window as we walked in. On the wall to our right, there was a metal framed bunk bed with an upper and lower bed. At the head of the bunk bed, there was a desk. On the wall to our left, there was a wooden framed lofted bed, with a desk and a dresser beneath it. And at the head of that bed, there was the third desk. On either side of the door, there were two very narrow wardrobes. They had utilized every last bit of vertical space in the room with the wardrobes extended all the way up to the high ceiling.

"It *is* a bit small," Mum empathized. "But you won't be spending that much time in your dorm room, right?"

I was too shocked to speak. Where was I going to put everything?

"Amy, we have to move the car," Dad said, interrupting my thoughts. I looked down at my watch. *One minute.*

"OK, thanks Daddy," I said, giving him a hug and a kiss on the cheek. He liked it when I did that. I turned to Mum and did the same.

"Want me to come down with you?"

"No, it's we're fine. Stay here and unpack," Dad said, looking like he wanted to get away quickly before we got emotional.

"OK, I love you!" I said, feeling tightening in my throat. "I'll call you night."

"We love you too, honey," Dad said and began to retreat.

Mum was already getting teary eyed. I waved as they walked down the hall with the empty dolly and around the corner to the elevator. . A few hot tears splash down my cheeks before I wiped them away.

I tried not to think about the permanence of this abandonment. They were leaving me here in an unknown place to fend for myself. Part of me wanted to run after them. Looking at all of the uncertainty ahead of me was like looking up the sheer face of Half Dome in Yosemite. It was a seemingly impossible climb. But that was silly, I told myself. I wanted to be here. I was all about having The Great College Experience.

I shook my head and turned away from the door to look at my suitcase and boxes full of supplies.

They could wait. First, I pulled out Franklin, the trusty brown teddy bear that I'd had since infancy. His fur had long since clumped into little tufts and I'd rubbed most of the fuzz off of his nose with my own. After tucking him under my arm, the comfort was immediate. Then I pulled my laptop out of the box. I considered all three desks and selected the one beneath the high lofted bed. From the cardboard box, I produced the brand new blue Ethernet cable that Dad and I had bought just yesterday. Getting down on all fours, I found the socket for the cable just behind my desk. I plugged one end into the wall and the other end into my laptop. While it booted up, I contemplated which bed I should claim.

Erin, Casey and I had exchanged a few emails before we got to school. After the first few introductory emails, where we covered important topics such as our dating status and our taste in music, we started talking about our room. Erin had written that she was deathly afraid of heights and would prefer the lower bunk bed. So this left Casey and me the top bunk or the lofted bed above the desk. The lofted bed was higher above the ground than the top bunk bed. There were no guard rails on either bed. Falling off would not be a trivial ordeal.

11

" I walked over to the bunk bed and pushed firmly down on the top mattress.

Creeeeaaaaaaaaaaaaaaaaaaak.

When I'd stopped shuddering,, I decided that the lofted bed was meant for me. If I rolled off the bed in the middle of the night, death would be swift and painless. I threw my navy fitted sheet, flat sheet, comforter and pillow up on the bed. ⟍

Finally, from the bottom of the box, I took out a stack of photos that I'd brought along with a box of thumb tacks. Above my bed, there was a small strip of cork board on the wall for hanging up photos. This would be a good way to cheer myself up and personalize the room.. I climbed up the wooden ladder at the foot of the lofted bed and sat down Indian-style on the mattress, facing the wall, photos in hand.

The photos did little to comfort me. In fact, they brought the lump back to my throat. I looked at the first photo. It was a picture of Mum, Dad, Meg and me in front of our house, looking ecstatic. We had the neighbor take the photo when Meg came home for the summer after her first year at college.

The next photo was of Lauren and me after our first all-nighter as co-editors-in-chief for the school paper. We were in her kitchen editing and rewriting articles until six in the morning. Her dad snapped the shot when he got up to go to work and found us laughing deliriously at their cat Mittens for walking through her water bowl. I would miss those nights with her. I wondered if one of us would find a better friend than the other. I shook off the unpleasant thought and turned my attention back to the photo. The problem with this photo was that we both looked like hell. There were dark circles under our sleepy, blood-shot eyes and we looked like one of those exaggerated "before" photos for a make-up commercial.

The next photo was the formal group photo we took at Prom. Everyone looked so beautiful with curls piled high on our heads and floor sweeping gowns in all different colors. I don't consider myself to be very girly, but even I felt like I could turn heads that day. I remembered our last get-together, when we talked about all the ways college was going to be exciting. Total freedom to do whatever we wanted whenever we wanted, discover our calling in life, meet new and exciting people, and party like it was 1999 all the time.

The sound of voices shook me from my reverie.

"Mom, it's fine!" an exasperated voice insisted from down the hallway.

"I just don't think it looks very sanitary." An older woman sounded skeptical.

"This is a college dorm, not a country club!" a male voice retorted. "I'm sure it's fine."

Casey and her parents burst into the room, looking like they just stepped out of a Ralph Lauren catalogue. Casey was more beautiful in person than her profile picture online. She was wearing white capris and a V-neck cable knit blue sweater that made her eyes a brilliant blue. Her blonde hair was pulled back in a ponytail. Her legs went on forever. You didn't have to look far to see where her good looks came from.

Her mother was exquisite. Her highlighted blonde hair fell in fashionable layers around her shoulders and she had the same large blue eyes, framed with long dark lashes that were hypnotic to look at. Her father looked older than her mother, but was definitely a handsome man in his sixties. His silver hair was combed back neatly and he seemed to see everything with his dark, deep set eyes. They were all carrying boxes and bags. It looked about as natural as a goldfish carrying a fork.

Casey immediately spied me up in the loft and dropped the bags she was carrying. She held out her arms.

"*Amy!*" she cried, as if we were best friends that had been forcibly separated for years.

I was thrilled at this welcome and looked for a way to get down to the ground quickly. I backed clumsily down the ladder of the bed, trying to make an awkward long pause a little shorter. I missed the last step and banged my knee in the process, but I managed to catch my balance long enough to give Casey a big hug.

"Mom, Dad, this is Amy," Casey said proudly.

I shook hands with Casey's dad, who was nearest to me.

"Amy, it's *so* nice to meet you, " Casey's mom said. "You should feel free to come home with Casey any time. We live right across the street."

"Thanks!" I replied. "That's so nice of you!"

"Amy, where are you from?" Casey's dad asked.

"I'm from Irvine," I replied.

"Great place," he said. "Good schools."

"Alright," Casey said. "How much time do you have left?"

"However much we need," Casey's dad replied.

"What do you mean? I thought we only had fifteen minutes!" Casey looked at him suspiciously.

"I gave the guy a little something," Casey's dad said, smiling with one side of his mouth. Casey rolled her eyes.

"Well, everything is up here already. I think I can take it from here," Casey said, looking at her parents expectantly.

"Don't you want us to help you set things up?" Casey's mom asked , pushing a perfectly curled wisp of hair out of her eyes.

"No, Mom, it's *fine!*" Casey insisted. She gave the air near her mom's ear a kiss and did the same with her dad.

"OK, well call us if you need anything," her mom said, looking uncertainly around our room.

"Sure Mom," Casey said. "If I forgot anything, I'll just come home and get it! I need to come back to get the car anyway after I get this permit thing all sorted out."

"Right," her dad said, pleased with the situation. "Let's go then, before the waterworks start."

"Bye bye! I love you! I'll be home soon," she repeated until they were out the door.

Casey turned to me with a huge grin on her face.

"We're in *college!*" she said, clasping her hands together. "This is going to be *so* amazing! Oh my God, who have you met so far? Are our neighbors cool?"

"No, you're the first person I've seen so far on this hallway." Her enthusiasm was contagious and I felt thrilled again. "I did meet a guy from upstairs who seemed really nice," I added, remembering Jeff.

"Why don't these people hurry up and move in? I hope we have cool neighbors! Tell me about this guy."

"Well, he's pretty cute," I admitted. "He is not a freshman and he used to play football. That's all I know about him."

"Go for it!" Casey said, giving me a perfect toothpaste-ad smile.

I laughed, self-consciously. For some reason, I felt the need to impress her. She had "stage presence," as my senior English teacher would say. I couldn't take my eyes off of her.

"This room is *tiny!*" Casey exclaimed, looking around.

"Yeah, there's a lot of vertical space, but not a lot of square footage," I concurred. We both looked up at the lofted ceiling.

We both looked at our collective boxes and luggage.

"Do you think it will fit?" I asked her.

"Depends on how much stuff Erin brings. What do you think she'll be like? I looked at her profile online and it sounds like she's kind of nerdy. Like, she's into these multi-player text games online. She has an avatar, whatever that is. And she's going to be an engineer."

"You e-stalked her?"

"Hey, you gotta do your research," Casey said. "You don't have a lot up on *your* profile."

"Yeah, so creepy people can't stalk me!" I teased.

14

"We're going to be good together," Casey laughed. "What do you do for fun?"

"Lots," I replied, not knowing where to start. "I guess I haven't had a lot of free time the last few years. I played basketball, I swam one season, I try to read on my spare time and I like to write."

"Do you party a lot?" She cut to the chase, as she started unpacking one of her monogrammed suitcases.

"Some," I replied, vaguely. The truth was, I wasn't a big partier in the traditional sense. I mean, I liked hanging out with my friends a lot, but this usually entailed the movies, the mall, the beach, In 'N Out late at night or somebody's house.

"What about you?" I asked her. "You said you were from Beverly Hills High School. Did you go to school with celebrities?"

"Yeah," Casey replied, matter-of-factly. "But I hate celebrities. They act so *entitled* sometimes. I'm not impressed by them."

I nodded, appreciatively.

"What do you like to do for fun?"

"Party," she replied, smiling. "Can you tell? I wonder what good parties there will be this weekend," she wondered outloud. I didn't have a clue.

"I don't know. Maybe I can ask Jeff," I replied, glad for any excuse to talk to him again.

Casey nodded, but looked engrossed with her unpacking. I turned to my computer which had finished booting.

I checked my email. I had a new message in my Inbox from Lauren.

From: "Lauren Avery" <<u>lavery@princeton.edu</u>>

To: "Amy Callaway" <<u>acallaway@ucla.edu</u>>

Subject: You're there!

a,

how was moving in? met any cute guys yet? there's a really cute guy that lives down the hall from me. his name is mike and he's a soccer player from nyc who volunteered for doctors without borders over the summer. would blow any of the guys from back home out of the water. he talked to me for awhile in the hallway and said it was cool when i told him i wanted to be a writer.

that's one thing i'm already loving about college. i can actually be cool. it's so liberating! being a pretentious, obnoxious jerk who went to elementary school with other pretentious obnoxious jerks isn't the prereq for being cool here! people actually seem to care about substance! anyway, i'll stop ranting; you get the picture.

what are your roomies like? tatiana says i can go back to russia with her this summer. i'm going to see if i can bring you along! talked to eric yet? i miss you!

love, L

I grinned. Lauren had always had a chip on her shoulder about how popularity at our high school worked. There was a group of kids at our high school who had been dubbed "the cool kids" since freshman year. It was a title that most of them had brought in with them from middle school. One or two "chosen" individuals, usually transfers from other schools, joined the group each year, but for the most part, entry into that club was strictly limited. All attempts at understanding what made them the cool failed .

They were good looking, but definitely not traffic-stoppers. They weren't particularly smart, interesting or talented in any way. A few of them played sports. They certainly weren't nice. In fact, they were very cliquey and exclusive, so no one liked them, though everyone was fascinated by them. The only thing we could think of was that their parents were wealthy and they were always in trendy clothes and cars. But that couldn't have been the whole explanation either. There were wealthy kids who weren't in that crowd.

We just knew that they had an unfounded confidence and a charisma about them that made you envy them though you didn't know why. It was always beyond us who on God's green earth was voting them into student council and the Homecoming court. Lauren pointed out the paradox that they couldn't be popular unless the rest of us let them be popular, but most of us resented them, so how could we?

It was all very puzzling, but I didn't let it bother me too much. I only engaged in these conversations because it was an interesting paradox to think about and to humor Lauren, who was very principled about earning things. After all, it wasn't as if we were unpopular by any means. The first two years of high school were a bit awkward socially while various groups formed, shifted and reformed like the little oil globules in lava lamps, but eventually we found a great group of girlfriends. I figured that's what college would be like too. I just hoped it would be quicker this time around.

Tatiana was Lauren's roommate at Princeton. She sounded brilliant. She

16

was a figure skater from Russia, who was apparently aiming to be a mathematician as well. I was happy that they were getting along, but I couldn't help being a little jealous. Lauren and I have been best friends since middle school, but I'm sure that living with someone for a whole year can bring you closer in other ways.

There was a faint tapping at the door. Casey and I both looked and two dark eyes in a pale, meek face, framed with long, black hair peered through the half open door.

"Come here!" Casey cried, throwing down the shiny shirt that she was about to hang up in her closet.

She held her arms out and Erin walked uncertainly forward and gave Casey a timid hug. I was about to climb down when Erin's parents and younger brother walked in behind her. Suddenly there was nowhere to stand, so I stayed on my bed.

Erin's entire family was small and frail-looking. The boxes that they were carrying seemed disproportionately large and heavy. Erin's father was shorter than Casey. He had graying hair and matching bushy eyebrows. Her mother's hair was still jet black and cut short. She looked anxious and shifted from foot to foot nervously, but tried to smile. Her little brother must have been ten and he looked between Casey and me with a bewildered countenance.

"Hi!" I said, leaning over and extending my hand. "I would come down and give you a hug, but…"

I looked around the room. Everyone chuckled. Erin shook my hand carefully, barely touching it. There was an awkward silence. Casey's smile was frozen on her face, but it looked like she was trying hard to keep it there. Erin's parents looked somewhat uncomfortable. I wondered how much English they spoke.

"My name is Amy!" I said, offering them a hand.

"Nice to meet you," Erin's dad said slowly, in a thick Chinese accent, shaking my hand in the same timid fashion as Erin.

Erin's mom shook my hand and bowed her head at me slightly. I didn't even try with her brother. He continued to goggle at all of us. Casey followed suit and shook hands with Erin's parents.

Finally, Erin's mom opened the box she was carrying and began laying things on the lower bunk. Erin said something to her mother in what I assumed was Chinese. Erin's mom responded brusquely. Erin insisted something and pointed at her watch. Erin's father said something in agreement with Erin. And after several rapid fire exchanges, they moved towards the door. They waved at us.

"Have a good year!" her mother said with less of an accent than her father. Casey and I both smiled and murmured "Thank you." Then they were gone. Erin went into the hallway to see them off. When she came back in, she looked around the room.

"This room is really small!" she said, hesitantly, as if afraid to offend the room.

"Yah, we talked about that," Casey said.

"Do you think we'll have a problem with space?" she asked, looking between me and Casey. Our boxes, suitcases and bags took up nearly all of the floor space and some on the bunks as well.

"I think we'll be ok," I said , trying to be optimistic.

Casey climbed up on her bunk bed which creaked loudly in protest.. We all cringed .

"What a sick sound," Casey noted. "Anyway, I think if I stand up on my bunk bed and you hand me stuff, I can put them in the cabinets up here." She stood up and wobbled precariously. Erin covered her eyes and scrunched her shoulders up.

"Be careful!" she cried.

"You're so cute!" Casey said "Look how cute she is, Amy! She looks like one of those Japanese cartoons when she does that!"

The enormous dark eyes in the small peeked face did indeed make her look like a very cute Japanese animation.

"So why don't we unpack all of our stuff and whatever we can't fit that we don't need all the time, we can put up in those storage cabinets along with the boxes," I suggested.

"That sounds right," Casey said. After a pause, she looked down at us and said, "We're in *college*! Oh my God, it's going to be the best year! I'm so excited, you guys."

Erin broke out in a huge smile.

"I totally agree," I said enthusiastically.

"What are you looking forward to the most?" Casey asked me, sitting down on her bunk bed and looking across the room at me expectantly.

"Meeting all kinds of different people from different places. The high school scene was... getting kind of old. It was the same old people doing the same old things. I'm excited to get hear some different perspectives. And how cool will it be to learn from someone who is so passionate about their field that they devoted their whole life to studying it?"

Casey nodded appreciatively.

"What about you guys?" I asked.

"Wow, I think you hit them all," Erin said slowly. "I hadn't even thought that far. I'm just excited to be living away from home for the first time."

"What about you, Casey?" I asked.

"Dating and making friends. The rest of it is just gravy."

We laughed. I was feeling very good about our living arrangement. We all began unpacking in earnest.

"Here, what are you unpacking first?" I asked. "I think that I should put my suitcase here, and then you can put your box on your bed and Casey can start unpacking her desk stuff first?"

"Uh oh. Are you one of those super organized activity planners?" Casey asked me suspiciously.

I laughed. "No. I'm just trying to make it so that we can all unpack at the same time in different parts of the room."

"OK," Casey said. She carried a few of her boxes to her desk. "Because super organized activity planner people stress me out."

"I will try to remember that," I laughed.

I considered myself to be pretty organized. I had to be! I was the editor-in-chief of the school newspaper and I had so many extracurricular activities that I had to keep track of aside from that. But I would have to tone it down. I didn't want to annoy Casey.

I filled one of my drawers with underwear and socks. I filled the next drawer with school shirts. And I filled the last drawer with pants. I found my hangers in my toiletry box and used them to hang my coats, sweaters and a few "going out" shirts in my wardrobe. The whole time, we heard commotion further down the hallway, but just as I was finishing the last of my party shirts, we heard a noisy ensemble unlock the door next to us.

"Amy!" Casey called from her desk.

I looked up at her.

"Who is it?" she mouthed, pointing to the wall between us and our noisy new neighbors.

I tiptoed to our door and peeked out. I saw two guys and their parents. Boxes, bags and suitcases hung off of all limbs.

"Two guys and their parents," I reported under my breath.

"Cute?" Casey mouthed hopefully.

"Couldn't get a good look. There's a tall white guy and a shorter Hispanic guy. We can go over and introduce ourselves."

"Let's wait until the parents leave. It's always so awkward with the parents," Casey said.

I thought I saw Erin flinch, but I wasn't sure.

We continued to unpack in silence until the commotion on the other side of the wall died down. We heard parents say goodbye. I continued to unpack my toiletries and arrange them in the cubby above the drawers in my wardrobe. Everything was bright and shiny from my sleek blue toothbrush to my stiff new shower pouf. I lined the plastic bottles up by height. New shampoo, new face wash, new moisturizer… everything was symbolic of starting over. Well, except for Franklin and the photos.

"What's happening?" a gruff voice asked from outside the door.

I looked around the cabinet door to see our new neighbors standing awkwardly in the doorframe. One was tall and lanky, with dark hair and dark eyes. The crotch of his jeans was halfway to his knees and he wore a baggy black t-shirt that had across it in plain white letters, "Whatever". There was defiance even in the way he his hair stood up and how he slouched like he didn't give a care what anyone thought. The other was a shorter, stouter Latino fellow, who was wearing a buttoned down Hawaiian shirt over khaki shorts. His hair was slicked back and he looked around at us eagerly.

Being closest to the door, I felt like it was my obligation to introduce myself first.

"Hi, I'm Amy," I said, putting down my contact solution and knocking the other bottles over like bowling pins.

"Sean," said the "Whatever" guy, tugging up the waistband of his jeans with his left hand while extending his right hand.

At once, everyone converged and shook hands all around. We went through the requisite introductions: where we were from, what high schools we went to, what majors we chose (or didn't, in my case). I began to feel a little like a broken record. Sean's roommate's name was Chris. They went to the same high school in San Diego and asked to be roommates. Chris was a history major and Sean was going into political science, which I found to be odd for someone who didn't seem to care about anything.

"Are you in a double?" Casey asked.

Chris shook his head.

"No, a triple," he explained. "The third guy is random. We talked to him a couple of times. He seems pretty cool. He's from Fresno."

"Did you guys know each other?" Chris asked us. We all shook our heads.

"Nope, totally random," Casey said. "But we're going to have an awesome year, I can tell."

"Should we take bets on that?" Sean asked, devilishly..

"Hey now!" Casey protested. "That's no way to have a positive attitude."

"Who's trying to have a positive attitude?" Sean asked her. "You look like trouble."

"I don't know if I like you," Casey said with a flirty pout.

"No skin off my back," Sean replied.

"OK, Buzz-kill, let's go unpack." Chris sauntered back towards the door. "I apologize for this jackass over here. It was nice to meet you. Want to go get lunch later?"

"Sure," Case replied. She looked and Erin and me. We both shrugged and nodded.

"Half an hour?" I suggested.

"Cool," Chris said. "Pick us up on your way out."

"You got it," I replied, turning back towards my fallen toiletries.

As I stood them up again, I thought about how odd it was that these unlikely strangers were going to be a huge part of my world for the next year. I didn't know what to make of them. I wondered if we were going to have great times together or if we would just sort of coexist.

On our way down the hall to the elevator, we ran into a red headed girl lived on our floor and was also heading down for lunch. Her name was Sarah. She looked exactly how I imagined Anne of Green Gables to look, down to the pert, freckled nose. I would find out later that she had Anne's temper to match.

"I'm a bio major," she said . "Pre-med."

I envied the clarity she had in her life. Sarah was from San Mateo, which was somewhere in Northern California. I didn't know much about Northern California. I'd been to San Francisco twice on family road trips, but I didn't remember much except for the Golden Gate Bridge, the Monterey Bay Aquarium and the luxuriantly creamy clam chowder at Fisherman's Wharf. When she asked where we were from, she was equally puzzled.

"I live in Irvine," I told her.

"Where is that?" she asked. "I mean, I know UCI is there, but where is that in relation to here?"

"You take the 405 South about an hour," I told her.

She burst into laughter. I was puzzled. Apparently, Casey was as well.

"What's so funny?" she wanted to know.

"Why do you call it *the* 405?" Sarah asked.

"What do you call it?" I asked, confused.

"I would just say, 'take 405 south for an hour,'" she explained.

"That's ridiculous!" Sean piped up. "The 405 is a proper noun. Of course you would say 'the' in front of it."

"Yeah," I added. "You take *the* car and you take *the* train. Why wouldn't you take *the* 405?"

"I don't know," Sarah said. "No one says 'the' in front of freeway names in Norcal?"

"It's like a different country," Erin observed and we all laughed.

When we arrived at Covel Commons, we walked down a spiral staircase with an enormous large mosaic compass at the bottom. The savory smell of hot meats and cheeses wafted towards us as we waited for the dining hall attendant to swipe our cards through the beeping reader. Then I walked into food heaven.

I grabbed a tray and some silverware and took a lap around to see what sort of goodies I had to choose from. One station served sizzling hot dogs, chicken, hamburgers and French fries. The station next to it was serving single slices of different kinds of pizza with cheese oozing off of them. The station after that was serving some sort of bright orange sweet and sour stir fry over jasmine rice. On the other side of the room, there was a full salad bar. I decided that this was probably the least interesting option to me. Next to that was a station serving bubbling enchiladas straight out of the oven with tortilla chips. And finally, there was a station serving pasta with your choice of sauces.

I had no idea where to start. I wanted a bite of everything. It was a pity I couldn't take a quarter of a slice of pizza or half of an enchilada.

"I hear they have pizza and burgers every day," Sean said from behind me. I started and my silverware created dull metallic clatter as they fell back onto my plastic tray.

"You scared me!" I said. He grinned and made his way to the enchilada station. I followed him and got a small ceramic casserole dish with two enchiladas smothered in spicy smelling red sauce. Then I headed to the Chinese station where I took a plate of sweet and sour. After a bit of deliberation, I grabbed a slice of pizza rustica. The smell of the sweet mozzarella mixed with tangy ricotta made my stomach growl. I went to the end of the food area and filled a cup with pink lemonade. Then I scanned the rotunda for my… friends? Was it too soon to call them that yet?

I saw Casey and Erin sitting at a long table along the edge of the room inner round room. I made my way past tables of people conversing politely towards them. Sean, Chris and Sarah were not far behind me.

"This food looks *sooooo* good!" Casey said, taking a big bite of pepperoni pizza. "No wonder everyone gains fifteen pounds their freshman year."

"I'll say!" Sarah had opted for a large salad, covered with tomatoes, olives, mushrooms, peppers and sunflower seeds. She also had a plate of pasta.

"I wonder if it's like this everyday or if they're just being nice to us at the beginning of the year," I said.

"It's so healthy," Sean noted, in disgust. He had opted for a cheeseburger, fries and a slice of pepperoni pizza.

Chris stopped shoveling fries into his mouth long enough to say, "Ebery day. My friend's brudder is a third year here."

Erin's expression was as sweet and sour as the stir fry she was poking with a fork.

"What's wrong?" Sarah asked her, looking concerned.

"Nothing," she said and continued to poke at her food.

Sarah was not convinced.

"You don't like it," she observed.

"Well…" Erin said slowly. "I'm just not used to it."

"What do you mean?" Sean asked, accusingly. "Don't you eat Chinese food at home?"

She held up a deep fried piece of battered meat covered in orange sauce so bright it glowed. "This… is not Chinese food."

"What is it then?" Sean asked, through a mouth full of pizza.

"This is an American adulteration of Chinese food," Erin declared. "No one in Asia would even recognize this stuff."

"They're missing out!" Sean replied, eating the battered piece off of Erin's fork. "Nothing like good wholesome fried crap to clog up those arteries!"

"Ew!" cried Erin, recoiling from Sean and dropping her fork.

"What?" Sean asked innocently, through his mouthful of Erin's chicken. I couldn't help laughing.

"So if you join a fraternity, can you still eat in the dining halls?" Chris asked Sean.

Sean shrugged. "I'm sure as hell not going to join a fraternity."

"Why not?" Chris asked.

"I'm not convinced I'd get anything out of it," Sean said. "It seems like they just hang out a lot and get drunk. I don't need to pay dues for that."

"I think you make some pretty good friends," Chris countered. "You go through a lot together."

"Oh that's *right*," Sean replied. "They conjure up some weird ways to torture you so that you bond with your pledge class… no thanks, I don't need to pay dues for that either."

What Sean said made a lot of sense. I was struggling with whether or not to join a sorority as well. But when he put it that way, it seemed like a no brainer.

"Well, *I'm* joining a sorority," Casey said. "My mom says that some of her best friends are girls from her sorority."

I felt the mental pendulum swinging the other way.

"I'm surprised by that," Sean said. "I've heard that lots of women in close quarters is a shit show."

"What do you mean?" Casey demanded.

"A whole bunch of PMS-y girls together, stabbing each other in the back, stealing each other's boyfriends..." Sean began.

"That's not true!" Casey was indignant.

"Do you think they cat fight?" Chris asked, hopefully. Four pairs of female eyes swung around and glared at him.

"Naw, they don't cat fight," Sean continued. "They're just passive aggressive. If one girl does something bad to another girl, the victimized girl won't confront her, she will just start a nasty rumor about the first girl and then there's all this love-hate tension going on."

"Well, whatever," Casey said, seeming to grow bored with the conversation. "Amy is going to rush sororities with me, aren't you?"

"Sure," I said, with more certainty than I felt. "It doesn't hurt to rush."

My mind drifted as we headed back to Sproul after lunch. Sean and Chris were quoting *Top Gun* and other guy movies, but their chatter faded into the background of my thoughts.I kept feeling like I was away at summer camp and that my parents would come pick me up at the end of the week to take me home. The idea that this *was* my home for the next four years was still beyond my comprehension. And who would be my friends at the end of this odyssey? Would it be these five?

When we got back to the room, the three of us stopped in the doorway. The place was still a mess of half-unpacked boxes, bags, suitcases. We all sighed in unison. Then we looked at each other and started laughing. It was hard to imagine we would get the room in order any time soon and even harder to imagine that this sterile looking box would somehow become home. Casey and Erin resumed unpacking. I sat down at my laptop to see who was online. Jeff and Lauren didn't disappoint me.

Amyable7: hi jeff, this is amy	**Amyable7:** laur, r u there?
Amyable7: thx for helping with the box earlier	**LoreNsMyth:** hey babe
Jeffers56: any time	**Amyable7:** got your email- thx
	LoreNsMyth: how was moving in?
	Amyable7: good- almost done; cute guy helped; good start to school
	LoreNsMyth: can i call u?
	Amyable7: not yet- room is tiny and roommates r here... no privacy
	LoreNsMyth: k, let me know when
	Amyable7: k
	LoreNsMyth: tell me about this cute guy
	Amyable7: lives upstairs.

There was a knock at the door and I looked up to see Jeff in our doorway. Hurriedly, I finished IMing Lauren.

	Amyable7: omg, u made him appear- bbl
	LoreNsMyth: go get him, tiger

"Hi!" I said, still caught a little off-guard. Since this morning, Jeff had changed out of his dingy white t-shirt into a collared blue shirt. He had combed his hair and shaved, which is probably why he looked even handsomer than I remembered.

"Hi!" Jeff said. "Thought I'd come see if I could help with anything else."

Casey looked up from her desk, where she was setting up her computer. I had to suppress the instant envy that sprang from the dark recesses of my mind. It wasn't her fault she was beautiful.

"I'm Casey," she said. Was it my imagination or was she *trying* to gaze at him seductively?

"Nice to meet you," he said. "I'm Jeff. I live upstairs. I helped Amy with a runaway box this morning."

I smiled. I tried to make it charming, but I probably just looked like a doofus.

"This is Erin," I said, looking over my shoulder at her. She was putting her pillow in its floral print case.

"What are you ladies doing tonight?" Jeff asked, looking at each one of us in turn.

"No plans," I reported.

"We're having a little party down at my frat tonight, if you want to come."

"Awesome!" Casey said enthusiastically. "What house?"

"SIE. We're the white house with the columns about halfway down Gayley," he explained.

"What time?" I asked.

"We'll probably start around 9pm or 10pm, but come over whenever," Jeff replied.

"Great! We'll be there!"

"I'll look forward to it," Jeff said, holding my gaze for just long enough.

He turned and walked out of our room. After we heard the door to the stairwell open and close, Casey let out a low whistle.

"Hey, I saw him first," I said in a mock warning tone.

"All's fair in love and war," Casey retorted.

I raised my eyebrows.

"Just *kidding!*" she cried, throwing an arm around my shoulder. I grinned at her.

"What did you think of him, Erin?" Casey asked.

"I have a boyfriend!" Erin replied, astonished.

"What's that got anything to do with it?" Casey said. And we all started laughing.

It had all started out so normally....

2 The After-Party

When I made it back to my dorm, limping like an injured animal in those wretched stilettos, I was calmer. I swiped my badge at the front door and was astonished at how many people were still milling about at half past midnight on a Saturday night. Groups of students were coming in and out of the front doors at various levels of dressiness. I got in the elevator with my arms crossed across my chest to avoid drawing attention to my unbalanced figure.

I pushed the number 3 on the keypad.

"You're taking the elevator to *three*?" a disagreeable looking girl asked me.

I blinked at her, not understanding why she was upset and not really caring.

"You should take the stairs!" she instructed, as if I were an idiot.

I shrugged, but made a mental note. I stepped off the elevator into the hallway- my hallway- and headed toward my room.

Standing outside of Sean and Chris's room was a tall, dark haired guy with a bath towel wrapped around his waist and water dripping off of him onto the carpet. He looked at me, clearly embarrassed, and stuck out his hand awkwardly, trying to hold both his towel and shower caddy with his other hand.

"Hi, I'm Brian."

"Amy," I offered, shaking his hand quickly so that I could cross my arms again. "You're Chris and Sean's roommate?"

"Yeah," he said. "I just got in. My parents' car broke down outside of Fresno, so we were late."

"How long have you been locked out?" I asked, concerned.

"I dunno- ten minutes. No one seems to be around…"

"Oh no!" I murmured, trying to be empathetic.

"Could I borrow your phone to call the front desk? I thought about going down there, but…" His voice trailed off.

I chuckled."No, you can't go down like that. Here, you can use our phone. Hold on a minute."

I yanked my keys out of my pocket and let us into the room, silently cursing all of the bras and shirts that didn't make the cut tonight, slung over bed frames, desks and chairs. Stepping carefully over Casey's pile of shoes in the middle of the floor, I grabbed the cordless phone and handed it to him.

"Thanks. Do you happen to know the number of the front desk?"

"Yeah, it's in here somewhere," I replied. I flipped through the pile of welcome materials Kate had handed me during move in earlier in the morning. "4000".

"You're a life saver," he said with a lopsided grin.

He dialed the number "Hi. I'm in room 309 and I've locked myself out. I was wondering if someone could let me back in...."

He listened for a second and laughed sheepishly at the response.

I took this time to study the specimen. He was tall and lanky, built like a runner. His abs were cut, but you could still count his ribs. His dark hair stuck up in all different directions. While he wouldn't be classified as hot, he was cute in a quirky sort of way. He handed the phone back to me.

"They're on their way up. Apparently I broke the record. Usually the first lock-out doesn't happen until the day *after* move-in. Thanks for the phone," he said, backing out of the room, tripping on one of Casey's heels on the way out.

"No problem. Hey, we're all meeting in the hallway at 10am tomorrow morning to go on a campus tour with the RA," I said, trying to be helpful, and trying to keep him around for a few minutes to postpone being shut up alone with my misery.

Brian stopped in the doorway and smiled.

"Awesome! That sounds like fun! We'll hang out tomorrow then. I promise to wear more than a towel. This was totally embarrassing."

Yours was nothing, I thought.

"Have a good night, Brian."

Attempt charming smile again.

"Goodnight, Amy."

As soon as the door shut, I shed my outfit and wiggled into my jammies. I thought for a second about washing the makeup off my face and brushing my teeth, but decided against it. I might run into someone in the hallway and I didn't really feel like interacting with anyone who might have been there. I scrambled up the ladder and jumped into bed, scooting myself as close to the wall as possible to avoid adding injury to insult this evening by falling off my bunk and cracking my head open.

As I lay in bed, I reflected on the evening. I was mad at myself for not following my gut. First of all, I never went through this much trouble for a boy. Out of all of my friends, I exerted the least amount of energy talking, stalking and thinking about them. Second of all, I knew those damn bra cups wouldn't stay put! I felt like a total idiot for trying to act all sexy and flirty. I was trying to be chic and sophisticated like Casey, but it wasn't me and I shouldn't have done it.

Someone's false advertising. The words rang in my head. Argh! What would I give to do it over again? Well, it was a moot point. What would I say to Jeff if I ran into him again? I definitely would. He lived upstairs.

I tried to think of ways to play it off. *Did you like my party trick? It gets people every time.* No. *I was doing some product testing for a company. Obviously it doesn't work.* No good either.

I pretended to sleep and heard Erin come home, change into her jammies and go to bed. Then, Casey came in and I felt her looking at me for awhile, probably trying to figure out whether she should wake me up or just talk to me in the morning. I laid perfectly still and tried to breathe deeply. Finally, she went to bed as well.

When enough time had passed and I was convinced Casey was asleep, I turned over onto my side. I tossed and turned for the greater part of the night.

Nothing was as it should be. My new sheets were stiff and scratchy. The mattress smelled like plastic and I missed the familiar scents of my room back home. I was painfully aware of the two other girls in the room, and wondered how they could sleep in an alien space in such close quarters with perfect strangers. As I was turning from my side to my stomach, I was careful to stay clear of the edge of my bed. How could they not put any rails on the bunk beds?

Just when I thought I wouldn't get a wink of sleep all night, I awoke to the clacking of a computer keyboard. I opened my eyes a sliver to see Erin's slender figure, sitting straight and tall like a sentinel meerkat, typing away on her computer. It took me a minute to remember the incidents from the night before. I turned and faced the wall, hoping to delay having to pick up where I left off yesterday by retreating back into slumber. Try as I might, I couldn't get back to sleep.

I heard a big sigh from across the room behind me. Unable to contain my curiosity, I turned over and found Casey blinking back at me. She didn't say anything, but continued to look at me.

"Did you see?" I asked. She nodded sympathetically. .

"I'm sorry I lost your… er… adhesive cup. I promise to buy you another one," I mumbled.

"No, *I'm* sorry," Casey replied, hugging her pillow to her chest. "I can't believe it came out. That one was a little older. It must have lost some of its stickiness."

Erin looked at us inquisitively..

"Do you want to tell her or me?" Casey asked.

"I'll do it," I said. I didn't really want to relive it so soon, but I'm also big into not being a coward. "You have to promise not to tell anyone," I prefaced.

She nodded.

"So last night, remember how Casey dressed me up for the frat party?"

"Yeah. You looked hot!" Erin said, in her sweet, soft-spoken way.

"Thanks," I replied. "Well, Casey let me use her stick-on boobs so that the shirt would look better on me. They worked really well until about midnight. I was dancing with Jeff. Then he lifted me up and put me on a speaker. So I was dancing on this gigantic speaker. And he went to go get us beers. When he came back with the beer, I bent down to get it from him and…"

"One of the boobs fell out," Erin finished my sentence. Casey and I nodded.. Erin looked adequately horrified.

I pulled my covers over my head for dramatic effect. I could hear my roommates giggling.

"It could have happened to anybody," Casey said.

"Don't lie," I groaned, emerging from under my covers. "It could not."

"Fine, maybe not anybody, but whatever. Everyone was drunk. No one will remember it."

"You're lying again," I shot back, emerging from under my covers and staring up at the ceiling. "*You* remembered."

"Yeah, but I'm your *roommate*," she explained. "If it had happened to some random drunk girl, I wouldn't have thought about it for more than two seconds. I wouldn't have enough brain cells to spare if I remembered every stupid thing a drunk person did!"

We stared at each other for several seconds.

"OK, let's talk about something else," I said.

"Do you have a list of your books?" Erin asked. "It's almost 10am. We have to go book shopping with the RA."

"Oh yeah!" I said, sitting up. "I need to print mine out."

I flipped over onto my stomach and crawled backwards until I could no longer feel the bed. Then I felt around with my foot for the first rung of the ladder. I hoped that I would get good at this because clutching at the ladder and feeling my way down was going to get old. The three of us got dressed and cleaned up. There was a line for the sinks in the women's bathroom. In my morning stupor, I couldn't process much besides the wide variety of shapes and sizes of my female neighbors and their sleepwear.

At one sink, there was a tall, brunette who could have been a model. You could see her hip bones jutting up through the waistband of her super short shorts, which accentuated legs that went up to my chest. Then there was a girl next to her with strawberry blonde hair who was shorter and plumper, also wearing short shorts. You could see the crease where her legs and her pillowy tush met out the bottom of them. Note to self: revisit the length of my shorts. I opted to brush my hair back in our tiny bedroom.

After pulling on jeans and a tank top, I joined my hallmates in front of the elevator. Brian, Chris and Sean stood on the opposite side of the crowd, talking to some other guys. Desiree, our RA and fearless leader, stood up on the couch so we could all see her.

"Hey!" Desiree said loudly, waving her arms. She bounced up and down on the couch until we quieted down. "Hey! Listen up! I think I've met most of you, but in case I haven't, I am your resident advisor. I live in this room right here." She motioned to the room nearest the elevator. "My door is always open. Feel free to come talk to me any time about classes, roommates, life, whatever you want. I am here to be your advisor and your friend. But, I also have to enforce a few rules. Have a seat."

After some groaning and shifting, everyone managed to find a spot on the floor. Casey sat in front of me and leaned back so she was leaning on me. Her fluffy blonde mane smelled like a rose garden.

"First of all, this hall is going to be our neighborhood for the next year and it's not exactly Bel Air," Desiree explained. "Because we live in close quarters, it's really important that we keep it clean and learn to respect each other so that we can all live together without killing each other."

Casey turned around to smile at Erin and me. I smiled back.

"So there are some rules that we have to live by," Desiree continued. "And this may seem totally obvious to you, but we're always surprised by how common sense isn't so common actually. First of all, between the hours of midnight and six in the morning Monday through Thursday, there is no loud noise in the hallway. For that matter, you should not be talking loudly or playing loud music in your rooms either. Everyone here will be sleeping at different times and if we don't enforce any sort of quiet period, there would be noise 24/7."

"You're oppressing the nocturnal people," Sean piped up. We all turned to look at him. He leaned back on his hands, looking cocky. "Why can't quiet time be between 8am and 5pm?"

"Because we want you to go to class," Desiree shot back, waving a finger at him. "I can see who the troublemakers on this floor are going to be this year."

Sean beamed.

"No open alcohol anywhere that I can see," Desiree continued, keeping a wary eye on Sean. "I can't stop you guys from drinking, obviously. But if you drink with your room doors open or in the hallway, then I or another hall monitor, will have to bust you. After three violations of any sort, you will be asked to leave the residence hall."

We considered this threat soberly.

"If you make a mess anywhere, clean it up. I have a vacuum cleaner that you can borrow. If you're having any trouble with classes, professors, counselors or each other, come talk to me about it. And if you have any questions about anything, I will do my best to answer them."

She paused to look around and be sure we were all still with her before continuing.

"Now, we're going to go to Reiber for breakfast. Then at eleven o' clock, we're going to meet in front of Reiber and walk down to Ackerman student union together. From there, you can either buy your textbooks or come on a tour of campus with me. I think that some of you haven't had a chance to yet. Are you ready?"

We stood up and let the blood get back in our feet. Then we filed out of Sproul, around the turnaround and up the stairs to Reiber. I looked around, but saw no sign of Jeff anywhere. Whew!

No one had mentioned Sunday brunch in the dining hall as something they were excited about, but it certainly merited *at least* that. There was an omelet bar, a waffle station, a pancakes and sausages station, a bakery station with pastries and cakes, a fruit bar, a cappuccino maker, a dessert bar, and cereal.

"I *love* brunch," Casey sighed, scrunching up her shoulders and letting her eyes flutter shut as she inhaled all of the soulful smells..

I nodded and made a quick dash for the omelet bar. The line was already five people deep. Erin followed me.

"There's so much food here!" Erin exclaimed. "I don't need this much food!"

"I know," I admitted. "I usually eat cereal and fruit for breakfast. But this is a special occasion! It's our first Sunday brunch at college!"

Erin looked skeptical as one of the chefs threw a generous fistful of shredded cheddar on the omelet she was making.

"Does anyone *not* gain fifteen pounds?" she wondered aloud.

"I'm sure once we get used to the food, we'll eat less of it," I reasoned. "The second years don't look fat."

"Yeah, that's true," Erin said, looking unconvinced.

We found Casey at a table with the long-legged brunette and the stouter strawberry blonde that I saw in the bathroom this morning.

"This is Amy and that's Erin," Casey said.

"Hi!" I said, setting my tray down carefully on the table.

"This is Lindsay," Casey said, looking at Ms. Long Legs. "And this is

Autumn," she said, looking at the shorter blonde.

"Nice to meet you," Erin said.

Lindsay was in the middle of telling Casey a story and she continued as Erin and I sat down.

"So I didn't sleep at all the *whole* night. I called the front desk three times. The first time, they asked me if it was poisonous. I was like, 'How the hell should I know?' and they told me that they don't usually send people up for that. I was like, 'What should I do then?' and they said to try to get someone on the hallway to do it. But what am I going to do? Walk next door and say, 'Hi, my name is Lindsay! Could you kill a spider for me?'"

She made eye contact with each of us in turn. You know how there are those people who can make anything sound dramatic? Clearly, Lindsay was one of them. These types of people fascinate me. They speak like they're on stage with a spotlight on them and it totally works. Everyone stops to listen. It's only after the spell has worn off that you realize they were telling a story about nothing. Again.

"So then I called again a few hours later, hoping that they'd changed shifts at the front desk, but the same chick picked up, so I hung up. By then, it was, like two o' clock in the morning and this spider and I were just staring at each other. So finally, I called again and said that I had arachnophobia, which I probably do, and could they please send someone to kill this spider. The chick laughed at me. Can you believe the nerve?" Lindsay slammed her fork on the table for effect.

"Oh my God, you know what I heard?" Autumn interrupted."A girl at my high school had serious arachnophobia and when she cheated on her boyfriend, he left a tarantula in her locker!"

"What did she do?" I asked, horrified.

"She screamed so loud, the kids at PE could hear her on the soccer field," Autumn replied. "Eventually the janitor came to take it away, but I think it took five years off her life."

"I wish we had a janitor that could come take spiders away," Lindsay said."I had to trap it in a cup and flush it down the toilet."

"How did we get started on this?" Casey asked.

"You wanted to know how move-in went yesterday," Lindsay reminded her.

"Oh right," Casey said and they both laughed. "Are either of you going to rush a sorority?"

"*I* am," Lindsay said, tossing her dark hair over her shoulder. "I'm *so* nervous about it. It's such a big deal what sorority you wind up in. You totally get branded by the house that you're in."

"Oh my God, you know what I heard?" Autumn said. "Tri-Os might get its charter revoked because a couple of the girls got caught cheating on their finals this past spring!"

"No! How?" Casey asked. "I thought they were supposed to be a good house. Everybody knows the Tri-Os are hot!"

"A couple of them were in a class together and it was a multiple choice final. Someone saw one of the girls texting the answers to the other girls in the sorority."

"Well how dumb can you get?" asked Casey. "Of course you're going to get caught if you keep picking up your phone during an exam."

"I think they were a little more discreet than that," Autumn said. "My friend told me that they had the phone between their legs during the exam, so it just looked like they were looking at their laps. The girl that was doing the texting got caught."

"I wonder if the Tri-Os are just too used to having things between their legs," Casey said and laughed.

Erin's jaw dropped. I felt the same way, but everyone else at the table laughed.

"Well, *I* don't want to be associated with cheaters," Lindsay said, pushing her scrambled eggs around on her plate with her fork. I noticed that she hadn't eaten very much.

"That's weird- I heard that Chi-Delt was a good house, but a little spacey. Gamma A's are a bunch of nerds," Lindsay said. "I think that Alpha Pi are the nice girls. I have mixed feelings about that. I obviously don't want to be in a slutty house, but I'm worried that a 'nice' house might be boring. There has to be a house where the girls are hot and fun, but not easy. This whole matching process is so stressful.."

Erin and I exchanged glances. This was getting to be too much for me. Every sorority had a reputation that I would have to be worried about? And there was a matching process? The whole thing was beginning to sound more complicated than it was worth.

Casey, Autumn and Lindsay continued their sorority analysis for the rest of brunch. Erin and I listened ,but mostly, I continued to scan the dining room for Jeff or anybody else that I knew from high school and orientation. No one familiar appeared and we finished our meal in time to join Desiree and the rest of the floor outside at eleven.

"Follow me!" Desiree said. Brian was standing just behind Desiree and as I was looking at her, he caught my eye. We both smiled. He walked over and we followed the RA down the stairs.

"Did you find your keys?" I asked him.

"Yeah," he laughed. "I didn't *lose* them. I just forgot to bring them to the bathroom with me."

"Yeah," I sympathized. "It feels weird to have to carry these keys around everywhere."

"Did you sleep well?" he asked.

"Eh," I replied vaguely. "I think it will take me a few days to get used to sleeping in a new place."

Brian nodded. "Are your roommates cool?" he asked.

"Oh yeah, I need to introduce you," I said. "They're both really nice. Yours?"

"Well, Sean is a character."

"There's a euphemism!" I laughed.

"I'm glad I'm not the only one who thinks so!" he said. "Well, honestly, I think he just likes to shoot off his mouth. Deep down, I think he's a pretty decent guy. It's like that book- a lot of sound and fury…"

"Signifying nothing," I finished with him in unison. We both looked at one another for a moment. The boy knew his literature.

"Hey, who's your friend?" a voice asked from behind us. I turned around and saw Casey, Erin, Lindsay and Autumn. I did introductions all around.

"*You're* Sean's roommate?" Casey asked, shaking her head. "I'm *so* sorry!"

"Hey, I heard that!" Sean said from behind them. Today he was wearing a black shirt with the word "Anarchy" on the front of it. "Should he *be* so lucky to have me for a roommate! Isn't that right, buddy?"

"Ask me again in nine months," Brian called back to him.

"That's only if you're worthy of talking to me in nine months," Sean said

"Whatever." Brian chuckled.

"Damn straight," Sean said. All of a sudden Casey stumbled, but caught herself.

"Ow!" she said, turning around to face Sean. "You stepped on my heel!"

Sean tried to look innocent. But he had one of those faces that had held a mischievous expression for so long that it stuck.

"Don't look all cute like that!" Casey play-snapped. "I don't believe you for one second, Mr…. Anarchy. What sort of a shirt is that anyhow? Who wears a shirt with 'Anarchy' on it? You're being conventional in your anti-convention."

Sean pointed to himself and pretended to look puzzled.

We marched down the broad sloping hill from the dorms to the student center. We passed the tennis courts, at the bottom the grand valley created by the stadium on our right. On our left was the entrance to the track stadium.

There were a few recreational joggers on the track, but the team wasn't out practicing. I made a mental note to go down there for a jog to work off the excesses of the dining hall. Finally, we wove between the trees and the Alumni Center to emerge in front of the Ackerman student union.

Desiree turned to face us, tour-guide style. At that moment, a very obese squirrel lumbered across the path in front of her like a bear. The half-disgusted, half-puzzled look on her face made us all laugh.

"The first floor is where all of the apparel is. The textbook store is on the second floor. You probably want to get them now because tomorrow, it's going to be insane."

I got in line with Brian, Sean, Casey and Erin. We all took out our course lists. The line moved and we were in the store within five or ten minutes.

It was not a traditional bookstore. Large industrial metal bookshelves were arranged in long aisles. Each course had its own shelf space in which shiny, shrink-wrapped textbooks were stacked horizontally. The courses were arranged in alphabetical order.

I found the shelf section for my calculus class first. I picked up a textbook and marveled at its glossy cover and pristine pages. In my excitement over the newness of the book, I almost missed the price tag. $179.00! My jaw dropped. What started as a fun shopping trip quickly became the start of Amy's Financial Crisis. My econ book rang up slightly better at $131.00.

Sean knocked into me on purpose as I was looking at the shelf section for my anthropology class. He didn't say anything, but continued his brooding shuffle. I grinnedand turned back towards the bookshelf. It had three different books in it, each about $35.

And there was no bin for my English course.

I spotted Casey in one of the aisles and I walked over to her.

"Casey, I can't find my English class," I said.

"Maybe it doesn't have books," she said. An English class with no books. I tried not to look at her cross-eyed.

"Sometimes the English classes have readers that you need to pick up in Westwood or novels that you can get downstairs. The professor will probably give you a book list on the first day of class," she continued.

We turned around and saw a girl about our age in a blue apron.

"Thanks," I said, gratefully. She smiled and left.

"You'd think they could tell us that somewhere in here!" I told Casey after the girl was out of ear shot. "How would anyone know? If I were running this place, I'd put a sign for every class and special directions for if the class didn't have books yet."

"Super organized planner activity person," Casey chided. I laughed.

"Are you done?" I asked. She nodded. She only had two books. We walked over to the checkout line. My arms were tired and the corner of one of my books was digging into my flesh. As we stood in line, I ran the numbers in my head. My books totaled over $400 and I wasn't even done yet. Sean got behind us with an armful of smaller paperbacks.

"How's it going?" he asked.

I winced. "I wonder if there's some way for me to get these books used or on eBay or something."

"You probably could, but it will be a pain in the ass." Sean said after a short pause.

Sean had a distinctive way of talking. There was always a short hesitation before he opened his mouth, as if he were debating in his mind whether or not the audience's reaction was worth the trouble of speaking. I noticed that the hesitation was much shorter when he knew his words were going to evoke a strong reaction. And he certainly reveled in it. But in talking about mundane things like textbooks, he seemed to deliberate longer before opening his mouth. When he finally got around to saying something, it came out more like a grumble. He was sort of like a big ogre.

"How come?" I asked.

"They use the latest editions of every textbook," he said.

"Well, how different can calculus be from edition to edition?"

"I'm sure the information is no different, but how much money would the publisher make if you just used your grandmother's calculus book?" Sean answered. "They redo the numbering of the questions and stupid stuff like that, so if you don't get the latest edition of the book, you won't be doing the right homework problems that the professor assigns you."

"That's horrible!"

"Well, think about it," Sean said. "Who writes these textbooks?"

"Professors, I guess," I answered.

"Right, and they get paid royalties for every book they sell," Sean continued. I saw his point.

"So they change every edition so they sell more books and make more money," Casey finished for him.

"Look who caught up," Sean observed.

"Oh shut up," Casey told him, but laughed. He looked pleased with himself.

"Next!" a woman called from one of the eight cash registers that were busily dinging away. I walked up to her and dumped my books on the counter. She barely looked up, as she ran the scan gun over my books. The machine spastically coughed out my receipt. I looked at the total and cringed.

Meanwhile, she threw the books into a bag, threw that bag into another bag and handed it to me.

*****

"What's your favorite TV show?" Casey asked, looking across the dinner table at me.

"I love watching reruns of old sitcoms," I admitted. "I haven't gotten addicted to any of the series lately. I couldn't commit to watching them at the same time every week because of sports practices and stuff."

"You are missing out," Casey replied, as if I had missed my senior prom. "My favorite is *Ivy*."

"Is that the one with all of the rich kids at some East Coast prep school?" Erin asked.

"Yeah, it's awesome!" Casey bobbed her head, causing her diamond earrings to sparkle.

"What's it about?" Sarah asked, tying her glossy red hair up in a ponytail after a few failed attempts to drink her tortilla soup without getting a mouthful of locks.

"It's stupid," Sean piped up from the guys' side of the table. "It's about these rich kids who go to boarding school somewhere in Connecticut."

"Why's it stupid?" Casey demanded.

"It's just the same old crap they keep repackaging and showing on TV: bored people lying, cheating, and backstabbing." Sean said. "I guess watching them be slutty is kind of amusing, but the rest of it is just inane. On this show, they do it to get political power. On that show, they do it for money. Whenever it's about high school kids, it's always about getting popular. So lame!"

"Then why do so many people watch it?" I asked.

"I think it's two things," Casey said, defending her unpopular past time. "It's interesting to see how different people live. Aren't you curious to see how rich kids in Connecticut live? You can sort of live vicariously through them. And it's also cool to see how even though situations and people are different, people are still people and they react to things the same way. They get jealous, they plot, they sleep with people...."

"What a glowing commentary on humanity," Sarah scoffed, wrinkling her freckled nose.

"Are our lives so boring that we have to watch other people's lives and live vicariously through them?" I wondered aloud. "Doesn't that just make our own lives seem more boring?"

"Oh yeah!" Chris agreed. "So then, after girls watch that stuff, they create drama in their own lives so that their lives *don't* seem so boring. The girls at our high school were always inventing drama."

"But it is so addictive!" Erin nibbled at her soft serve cone. "It's like looking at a train wreck. It's terrible to see, but you just can't help looking because you're so curious. And once you watch one episode, you totally get hooked and you wind up having to watch the whole series."

"I need dessert!" Brian said, eyeing Erin's cone. He got up and left.

"The worst part of it is that you get desensitized after awhile and they have to do more shocking things every season to get you to keep watching," Sarah said. "So it keeps getting more irreverent and more violent as time goes on."

"It's an endless spiral of depravity," I concluded. "And if we imitate TV, then *we* keep getting worse and worse."

"I don't think people imitate TV," Sean said. "I think that's poor parenting."

"You don't think that watching men cheat on women eight times a week on eight different TV shows doesn't somehow make you feel like it's normal?" I asked him.

He shook his head. "I think that watching it on TV and having your parents either not be around or not say anything when it's happening is what makes you think it's ok."

"That's a good point," I replied.

Brian returned with his dessert.

"It reminds me of the Mojave Desert," I commented. It looked like the tall rock faces I remembered vividly, with multicolored bands of browns, reds, yellows and even dusty colored pinks.

"What *is* that, man?" Chris asked. "It looks pansy! *Strawberry* soft serve?"

"Check it out," Brian said, laying his bowl down and sitting down in front of it. "It's strawberry soft serve, with peanut butter, chocolate sauce and Captain Crunch cereal.

"How did you come up with *that*?" Casey asked, eyeing the concoction askance.

"I didn't. This second year guy told me about it when I was getting soft serve," Brian said calmly. "He says that he and all of his buddies get it every night."

He dug his spoon into the Mojave Mound and wiggled it around to be sure that he got a little bit of everything. We all watched as he plunged the spoon into his mouth with an exaggerated gesture. He worked it around in his mouth and swallowed.

"Well?" Chris asked, trying to sound uninterested, but unable to contain his curiosity. Brian stalled theatrically, holding up one finger and pretending to think very carefully.

"It... is..."

"What?" Chris demanded. "It is what?"

"Delicious!" Brian pronounced, digging in for his second spoonful.

"Bullshit!" Chris cried. "Let me see that!"

Chris picked up his own spoon and made a move towards Brian's bowl. Brian was too quick. He moved his bowl out of Chris's reach.

"I thought it was pansy," Brian said, mocking Chris. "I thought you wouldn't touch strawberry soft serve if someone paid you to."

Brian grinned at me and turned away to take his second spoonful so that Chris couldn't interfere. By this time, the rest of us were laughing.

"Fine!" Chris said. "I don't want any of your girly soft serve. I'll bet it tastes like ballerina Barbie!"

"I'm not letting masculine pride stand between me and good dessert," Sean said, standing up. "I'm trying some."

"Easy for you," Chris said. "You don't have any in the first place!"

Sean looked back at Chris and made an obscene gesture.

"I'm coming, too!" I said, following Sean's lead. One by one, we all stood up and made our way to the dessert bar, leaving a mirthful Brian and a very conflicted Chris at the table.

In no time, we were all indulging in the Mojave Mound, except for Chris, who had decided that he couldn't go back on his original pronouncement that the dessert was pansy. He got himself a brownie and tried not to sulk as the rest of us marveled at the unlikely post-dinner hit.

"This is amazing!" I exclaimed when I'd tasted it for myself. .

"Yeah, who knew?" Sarah said after taking a spoonful from my bowl.

Her overbearing health conscience had gotten the best of her while we were standing in line at the dessert bar and she had refrained from getting her own.

"Mmmm, it's sooo good!" Sean said to Chris. "Are you sure you don't want any?"

"You guys are all asses," Chris muttered, taking a large bite of brownie."I'll bet it's not even that good. You're just doing that to make me feel bad."

We all laughed.

After dinner, we walked back to our rooms. I climbed up on my bed and peered over the edge at my two roommates. Erin had already logged onto her computer and was IMing people and checking her class schedule. Casey was rummaging around in her closet again, pulling out silky, glittery garments from her costume chest.

"Amy, are you sure you don't want to come out with me tonight?" she asked, holding a gold halter top over a pair of black leather pants. The outfit commanded full attention.

"No thanks. I think I'm going to stay in tonight. I have an 8 am Calculus class tomorrow morning and a million phone calls to return," I lied. Well, half of it was a lie. I did have an 8am Calculus class in the morning.

"OK," she replied, shimmying into her black leather pants, jumping up and down while tugging them up her legs. I wondered what life would be like if I looked like Casey. Guys would just drop at my feet. I could almost be happy living vicariously through her. Almost.

A voice called from the door. "I'm going to take a walk on campus. Anyone want to come?"

It was Brian in sweats, his hair tousled.

"No thanks, I'm headed out to a party. Want to come?" Casey asked, through a bobby pin in her mouth.

"Naw, not in the mood for lots of people tonight," Brian replied. "I see that Erin is totally ignoring me. Amy?"

"Oh sorry!" Erin apologized, never taking her eyes off her screen. "I'm talking to six different people right now- can't keep up. Another time, thanks!"

"I'd love to," I replied. "Let me get some shoes on."

It was only 10pm and I wasn't really going to just lie around until bed time, but I hadn't figured out any other plan. A walk on campus with Brian sounded perfect.

After I threw on some socks and shoes, Brian and I made our way outside. It was chilly, clear and starry night, a rarity in Los Angeles. The wind whipped through my hair and I relished my newfound freedom. I could be out wherever, with whomever, any time I wanted to and no one could guilt me into coming home. Of course, we needed total freedom to discover ourselves and to get the whole College Experience. I felt badly for a few of my friends who were still living at home, attending local colleges. I imagined it would be just high school, part two.

"Where did you want to go?" I asked, finally, when we'd reached the plaza at the bottom of the hill with the statue of the bruin bear.

"Nowhere in particular," he replied. "I just wanted to see campus at night. I used to be a Boy Scout and we used to love doing night hikes because everything looks totally different at night. And I wanted to get away from all of the people. I can't even hear myself think in our dorm room."

"Totally," I agreed. "I think better at night anyway.... That's when I used to do my best writing."

"Writing for school or for fun?" he asked, looking at me with interest. The tousled tufts of his hair rippled like water in the wind.

"Both,. I did journalism at my high school since sophomore year, so I was always writing some article or another."

"That's cool! Do you want to be a writer?"

"I think so, but I'm not sure. My journalism teacher always said that writers had to have something interesting to write about, so he wanted us to major in something besides journalism or writing. I'm trying to figure it out. What's your major?" I asked.

"Engineering. There's not a lot of exploring there. They have our whole curriculum laid out for us. I think I get to pick three or four elective classes, but the rest are all required."

"Well, that's kind of restrictive, isn't it?" I asked as we started walking up Bruin Walk towards the Powell Library. "How do you know what you'll like best if you can't try a lot of different classes?"

"I guess it's a leap of faith." Brian shrugged. "The engineering curriculum is so long that we wouldn't graduate on time if we needed to experiment first."

To our right was Kerckhoff Hall, the only gothic building on campus. I gazed at the proud stone tower with stained glass and pointed archways.

"I guess, but engineering is one of the only majors where you can start working with a good salary right out of undergrad," Brian explained. "You have to go to grad school for just about everything else, or get paid peanuts. I think it's going to be interesting. I like figuring out how things work."

"That's cool. Have you always wanted to be an engineer?"

Powell's stately octagonal roof came into view as we started up a small hill.

"Well, no. I still don't know if I want to be an engineer, but I have no idea what I want to be. Engineering is as good a place as any to start. They say that it's harder to switch into engineering than to switch out of it."

"Erin's an engineering major too," I told him.

"What kind?"

"I think she said electrical."

He whistled. "Smart girl."

"Yeah, I think she's got her life figured out better than a lot of us," I said, indignant that being an engineer automatically made her smart. No one would respond that way about an English major. "What kind of engineer are you?"

"Mechanical."

"So will you be able to fix my car afterwards?"

"I hope to be able to design cars afterwards."

"That's cool!"

"It's cool in theory. I'll let you know in four years. The older engineering students told us that it's a pretty hard curriculum during Orientation."

We'd reached the stately courtyard between Powell Library and Royce Hall, the university theater. Both were magnificent brick structures. They looked even more regal at night, with golden light pouring from their windows. I stood facing Powell. Over my left shoulder, I could see the other two brick buildings that made up the first four buildings of the UCLA campus. I looked over my right shoulder and saw the hill where the residence halls sat.

"What are you thinking about?" Brian asked, looking down at me.

"I was just thinking about how amazing campus looks right now," I sighed. "I feel like it expects a lot of us."

"You're *totally* a writer," Brian chortled. "I've never heard anyone talk like that. Want to see if we can get in the theater?"

"Should we?" I asked. "Aren't Boy Scouts supposed to be straight-laced?"

"Shows how much you know about Boy Scouts," he said mischievously.

Interesting....

We walked towards Royce, with its manifold rhyming arches. We climbed the stairs and entered the grand brick archway, which led to three doors. We tried the center front door, which was open. After our eyes adjusted to the darkness, we could see the grand foyer. There was a beautiful medieval looking chandelier above us and we stood on a black and white checkerboard marble floor. We walked up to the theater doors. Brian took hold of the iron ring that served as a handle and pulled. This door was also open. I hesitated, but Brian took my elbow and led me up the stone steps inside the theater.

I crept up one of the long center aisles behind Brian. He stopped halfway to the stage and stepped sideways into a row of seats. The seat creaked as he pulled it down to sit. I sat in the seat beside him, catching my breath. . The darkness was still and silent. If I had been by myself, I might have been scared. But this whole foray was adventurous with someone else. Everything about the theater was impressive: the depth of the stage, the intricate carvings and depictions on the walls, the balcony that wrapped around the three walls and the elaborate ceiling that might have been gold gilded, but I couldn't be sure in the dark.

Brian leaned his head close to mine and my heart thumped in my ears. I sat as still as the viscous darkness, feeling nervous, in a first-date kind of way. It must have been just a gut reaction, because I wasn't really attracted to him. Experience said it was too soon to tell.

"It must be so cool to watch a performance in here," he whispered. His breath was warm on my ear.

"Yeah. We should totally do it," I replied, doing some calculated experimenting.

"Do you write plays?"

"I did one time, for class. We wrote Absurdist plays in AP English."

"What's an Absurdist play?"

"Absurdism is a genre. Didn't you read *Waiting for Godot*?" I asked.

Brian shook his head. He leaned back in his seat and stretched out his lanky legs.

"Well, it has certain characteristics, like themes of playing, exploration of what makes something humorous, mockery of logic, and self awareness of itself as a play," I explained.

"That would be fun, to be aware of yourself as a work of fiction. If I could do that, I would do all sorts of crazy things," he replied, smiling at the thought.

"Like what?" I asked, unable to help myself.

"I don't know- try improv, beat up bad guys... hit on pretty girls." His voice dropped at the end of his sentence so I could barely make out the words.

"Just because you're a work of fiction doesn't mean there aren't consequences to your actions. It just means that the consequences are in your fictional world," I protested.

"Well if it's fictional, it doesn't exist! It's inconsequential!"

"Not true!" I was sure the indignation came through even on the whisper. "Fictional works can have huge impact! What about *Animal Farm* or *1984*?"

"True," Brian admitted. "Well then, I would do all those things to teach people that they should take chances."

"Why don't you do that now?" I asked.

Brian shook his head.

"I'm a chicken," he whispered, leaning towards me again. I held my breath.

"For example, I could never be a writer," he continued, looking into my eyes. "There's too much risk involved for me. Like, what if I couldn't think of anything to write one day? Do you ever get writer's block?"

"Of course. Everyone does sometimes. When I have to sit down and write something about some subject in the next two hours, I might get writer's block. But when I just know I have to get an article out some time in the next month, I'll get inspired randomly and a story starts forming in my head. So when I finally sit down at a computer, it comes out pretty quickly."

Brian contemplated this for a minute.

"College is *kind* of like a big blank sheet of paper. You get to write out your life for the next four years. Do you have writer's block now?" he asked, challenging me.

"What is this, an interview?" I teased, even though I really liked that analogy. He looked at me for several seconds as if trying to read my mind.

If this were a movie, he'd kiss me right now, I thought. But he didn't and I wasn't in a movie. I tried to focus on the question at hand and stop these ridiculous romantic thoughts from running rampant. Who did I think I was? Casey?

"I wouldn't describe it as writer's block," I continued, trying to sound casual. The problem with whispering is that everything sounds important when you whisper.

"It's not like I can't think of anything to write, it's that there are too many interesting topics to choose from. I'm hoping that I get really inspired by one particular topic. My counselor said that I had two years to decide on a major."

"That sounds like a good amount of time," Brian whispered back.

"Two years is too long to be uncertain, I'm giving myself a year to figure it out. I want to start making progress towards a degree sooner than later."

There was a loud creak that came from the back of the stage and I nearly jumped out of my skin. My seat reverberated beneath me after my initial start. Brian reached over the armrest between us and held my seat still, nearly touching my leg. I didn't have time to read into it because with his other hand, he was already motioning me towards the back of the theater, where we had entered. I slipped out of my chair and hurried towards the door. I heard him following behind me. Footsteps crossed the stage .

"Is someone here?" a very stern woman's voice called out. "No one should be in here!"

My pulse quickened and I could hear my heart thumping in my ears again. We continued to move up the aisle. When I reached the top of the aisle, Brian quickened his pace and beat me to the door. He held it open for me, even as we burst out of the theater. I gulped a big breath of air. How long had I been holding my breath?

"Close call!" he said, his eyes dancing. . He looked like he was enjoying himself, and consequently, mocking me.

"You like this!" I accused him, with disbelief. He started laughing.

"You didn't think that was fun?" he asked. I began to laugh in spite of myself.

"I thought you didn't like to take risks!" I reminded him, still trying to catch my breath.

"I guess I like certain kinds of risks," he admitted. "I like physical adventures like this. Here, keep walking. That lady might come out and find us. It would kind of suck to get kicked out before we even started."

I agreed. "Where should we go?"

"What about that fountain that looks like a giant toilet?" Brian asked,.

"The Inverted Fountain," I recited from my memory of the campus tour I'd taken.

"Yeah, I forgot which way it was," Brian said.

"What kind of Boy Scout are you?" I teased.

"Not a very good one."

We walked up the path. My heart had stopped pounding and I was enjoying myself again.

"Some of these buildings are so weird," I commented, as we walked by a black and white building that looked like a piano on its side with giant keys facing us.

"I think that's some sort of library," Brian said, squinting at the darkened building.

"This campus is such a mish mash of totally different style buildings."

"I think it's kind of cool," Brian said. "There's a building for every mood that you're in. You've got your classical ones for when you feel traditional and your funky ones for when you feel kind of alternative and your really weird ones…"

We walked up a few steps to a green lawn with small hills, trees and artwork peaking out of concrete alcoves.

"Oops, this is the Sculpture Garden," I said, making out the silhouettes of several large bronze art pieces. "I think we went the wrong way."

"That's alright," Brian replied, unruffled.

I waited for my eyes to adjust to the darkness. I could make out all sorts of bushes, trees, pedestals and benches on the hills.

"Care to take a stroll through the garden with me," Brian asked, in an exaggerated British accent. He pretended to tip his hat to me and offered me his arm. I threaded my arm through his.

"Lovely day," I commented, in my best fake British accent. "Wouldn't you say?"

"Jolly good!" Brian pretended to twirl an imaginary cane.

I laughed.

We wandered quietly through the garden, the moonlight lighting up the ribbon of concrete that wound itself through the hills. The bronze statues, some of which looked like odd aliens during the day looked less harsh at night. The air was cool on my cheeks.

If I had been by myself, I would have been calmed by this scene. Instead, there was a restless humming growing louder in my mind as I tried to figure out whether he was flirting or if this was just how he rolled. Did I want there to be chemistry? Maybe I was attracted to the idea of him being attracted to me. Or maybe I was just trying to get my mind off of what happened at the frat last night.

Why was I unable to take this moment for what it was- two people making friends and enjoying a stroll through a garden? Part of my problem was that the last time I walked through the Sculpture Garden, the tour guide was telling us how this was one of *Playboy*'s top ten places on a college campus to hook up. That certainly didn't help me think platonic thoughts.

After several quiet minutes, Brian broke the silence.

"I've heard people say that this is one of the best places to..."

"Hook up," I said, finishing his sentence before I could stop myself. I was sure they said it on every UCLA campus tour.

"Well, I was going to say, 'Play laser tag,'" he replied, after a pregnant pause.

I tripped on an imaginary crack in the sidewalk and tried to right myself, Brian caught me by the elbow and pulled me up. He held on to me for a few moments after I'd caught my balance.

"You ok?" he asked, concerned..

I gave him a weak smile and mentally slapped myself upside the head. *Hook up!? For crying outloud!*

"Laser tag would be so fun!" I said, trying to pretend I wasn't totally mortified at my two consecutive trip ups.

"Hooking up would also be fun!" Brian laughed. But he continued walking.

"They told that to us on the campus tour!" I said. "Didn't they say it on yours?"

Brian shook his head. "No, but now I know! You learn something every day." He grinned.

I felt a little better. He wasn't *totally* weirded out.

When we reached the end of the sculpture garden, we headed right and continued walking through campus.

"I feel like we're getting close!" Brian said, rubbing his hands together. "I hear the sound of running water!"

He was right. I could hear the water splashing against the stones at the bottom of the fountain. When it came into view, Brian rushed down the concrete stairs and leaped up onto the thick brick ledge.

"See? I'm not such a bad Boy Scout after all!"

"Good job!" I laughed. I sat down on the ledge beside where he stood. We both stared into the giant circle on the ground. It was lined with round rocks and it slanted down from all sides into a hole in the center. The water rippled over the rocks and rushed to the center of the fountain. I let the sound fill my ears and drown out thoughts of boys, boobs and overpriced books.

Brian looked wistful. "I wish my dog were here," he told me.

He started walking around the perimeter of the fountain, holding his arms out for balance.

"He loves water. He'd be in there in two seconds, making a mess. Then I'd have to go in there after him."

"What kind of dog do you have?" My parents had never let me have a dog.

"A mutt," Brian replied, with obvious adoration. . "He was a rescue."

"That's so nice! You got him from the animal shelter?"

"Actually, I literally rescued him," Brian yelled above the roar of the water from across the fountain. "I was backpacking with my brother in the Sierras and he had his foot caught in a trap. If we had left him there, the coyotes probably would have got him. We put up fliers but no one ever claimed him and he just became our dog."

"Miss him?" I asked. He nodded.

"He sat on my suitcase when I was packing because he knew I was leaving. And he's a pretty big dog. Like, seventy pounds. He's part Australian Shepherd. I had to push him off my suitcase four times. It was so hard to leave him."

He had made his way full circle around the fountain and took a seat next to me.

"What about you? Who are you going to miss the most?"

I considered this question carefully. I let the sole of my shoe dip into the water. I couldn't tell him that I was going to miss Eric the most.

"That's so hard to say right now," I responded after some time. "I feel like there's so much going on right now. I haven't had much time to think about home. I probably won't know until the dust settles. Even then, it's probably not any one person. I think I'm going to miss my whole world back home: my parents, my friends, my teachers… maybe even people I wasn't even friends with, but just were part of my day to day life, you know?"

"Yeah," he agreed. "I mean, I couldn't wait to get the hell out of there. But you're right. Once the novelty wears off, I'm probably going to miss everything about home."

"Right now, I miss Lauren the most," I said. "She's my best friend. She's at Princeton now. We talk about everything, but it's going to be harder now with the time difference and roommates and stuff. I think I will miss being able to just call her any time I need to."

"You can come talk to me any time you need to," Brian offered. "I'm probably not as cool as Lauren, but I can try."

"Thanks! I'll take you up on that. Isn't it weird to think that in four years, we're going to have best friends from college? And at this moment, we don't even know who they are going to be?"

"A lot of things are going to be different in four years," Brian added. He kicked up a sparkling arc of water into the air. We watched the droplets make expanding targets in the water as they fell.

"We're going to have degrees, and jobs, and four years worth of *ridiculous* stories to tell our grandkids."

I laughed. "It will be an adventure."

"Will you write about it?"

"In fact, I've already been asked to," I said, continuing to stare into the rushing water.

"Oh really?"

"My high school journalism teacher asked me to write an article about what to expect in college. It'll be for this year's seniors. It's a tradition at our school that the old editor-in-chief writes an advice piece for the next year's graduating class."

"What are you going to say?"

"Don't know yet. I have a couple of months to write it. But first, *I* need to figure out what the hell this whole college thing is all about."

"Well, what did the last editor-in-chief write?"

"I can't even remember." I scrunched my eyebrows together, trying to summon back that memory. "It wasn't that good. I felt like he wrote it the night before he emailed it to us. It was some generic piece about having a lot of freedom and discovering yourself. Oh yeah, now I remember. He was a big partier, so he wrote about getting laid and wasted. Laur and I had to cut that part out because the school wouldn't let us endorse that."

"You'll write a better one," Brian predicted.

"I wish I were as confident in my writing as you are," I sighed. "I just want to be more... thoughtful about it. I mean, I really want to touch on all facets of the college experience, like what you learn in classes, what it's like to live with roommates, the social dynamics, that sort of thing."

"That's awesome! I want to be the first one to read it. Promise?"

I felt like he was flirting again.

"OK," I agreed. We sat in silence for awhile longer and I continued to have thoughts about what we would do if we were in a chick flick. Brian glanced at his watch.

"It's almost midnight. We should probably head back."

He jumped off of the ledge and offered me his hand. I let him pull me up, even though I was perfectly capable of getting up on my own. We headed back towards the dorms.

"Isn't it funny how we *really* do have to walk uphill both ways?" I observed, as we started first down hill to the student center before turning uphill to the dorms.

"Yeah!" Brian replied, enthusiastically. "I was thinking that this morning too. It's so weird that they built the dorms on one hill and then built the rest of campus on another hill. They should have just built a zipline across the two hills so that we wouldn't have to do this dip in the middle."

"That would be so fun!" I said, delighted. "Well, I guess it's good in some ways to keep us in shape."

Brian chuckled. We plodded the rest of the way back to the dorm in a comfortable silence. When we reached the top of the hill, he opened the door to Sproul for me and we swiped in with the security guard.

"After you." Brian held the door open for me to start up the stairs to our floor. I really liked how he was like this big goofy kid, but he was also polite and thoughtful and... sort of on my wavelength.

Everyone seemed to be wide awake. Almost everyone's door was open and people were talking in the hallway, talking on the phone, talking on their computers or playing video games. It might as well have been the middle of the afternoon.

"And I thought it was getting late!" I told Brian.

"Seriously!" he agreed.

We reached his door first. Sean and Chris were playing video games and didn't even see us.

"Have a good night!" I said, cheerfully, proceeding to my own room.

"You too." Brian hesitated for a moment, as if he were trying to make up his mind about something.

Finally, he said, "I had a really good time tonight."

"Me too!"

I tried to come up with something else to say that was witty or cute, but nothing came to mind. I gave him an awkward wave and walked back to my room.

To my surprise, Casey was already home in her red silk pajamas, preparing to climb into her 1000-threadcount-Egyption-cotton-spread bed. She looked out of place in our little hovel of a dorm room. Erin was at her computer, typing rapidly, exactly as I'd left her.

"I thought you were partying tonight?" I said to Casey.

"I was, but the party was lame. I couldn't get into it, so I just came home."

"Hi Erin," I said, turning to the other one.

"Hi Amy!" she said, after a few seconds of delay. "Did you have a good walk?"

"Yeah. Campus looks really cool at night!"

"That's cool," Erin said, distracted by her computer again.

"Anything going on with Brian?" Casey asked, raising an eyebrow over her shoulder at me.

"No!" I replied, a little too quickly. "He's a cool guy. I'm glad he's our neighbor. But… he's not my type."

"Yeah," Casey agreed, over the loud creaking of her bed. "He's the friend type. Just doesn't have that Casanova thing going for him."

There was an email from Eric in my Inbox. For the umpteenth time tonight, my heart skipped a beat.

From: "Eric Wolf" <ejwolf@berkeley.edu>

To: "Amy Callaway" <acallaway@ucla.edu>

hey amy,

how's it going? excited to finally be @ UCLA? everything is ok here. classes have been interesting, though it's easy to fall asleep in some of the bigger lectures in the morning and after lunch. i've been up late every night. we're playing this game called assassin with some people in my dorm and its awesome, but we do most of our plotting late at night. i shd probably get on a better sleep schedule.

i'm thinking about walking on to the water polo team here. if i do, i'll have morning practice and that'll probably fix my sleeping habits. remember how i didn't want to play because i was burned out on it and i thought it would be too much with adjusting to school? classes don't seem to be that bad yet and i already feel like i'm getting out of shape.

i miss u. write soon.

Seeya, Eric

I've known Eric since freshman year in high school. He sat behind in me World History. He was skinny and gangly back then- a total class clown, but a good student. We didn't really think anything of one another until senior year, when we became lab partners and spent at least one day a week trying not to blow the place up. By that point, four years of water polo had filled out his wiry frame and turned the tips of his dark hair blonde and soft like chick fuzz. He looked like the guys you see in surfing competitions on TV.

I started wearing my favorite shirts on lab day and trying to look as cute as one can behind clunky lab goggles. He also started to be extra goofy on lab days and we were often laughing uncontrollably by the end of class with an over-titrated beaker of something toxic. At the end of the year, he asked me to Prom and we decided to have a "fling" over the summer before going to college.

Those were happy summer days. It was the first summer that I wasn't booked with enrichment classes, sports camps, music classes or volunteer activities. Eric was always thinking of fun ideas for dates. People didn't really date at our high school. You were either *very* single, or you were in a long term relationship. *Dates*- real dates, the kind where you still get butterflies and buy a new outfit- were rare.

Eric and I went out all the time: to the movies, to the beach, to the theater, to fun restaurants, out with friends, and even ocean kayaking. He was the perfect mix of a boyfriend and a best friend. We would have discussions about books, classes, human nature and future ambitions between kisses and cuddles. We would joke about friends, mock our high school teachers and laugh at each other all the time. And at the end of the night, he would put his coat around my shoulders, open the passenger side car door for me and make me feel like a princess. In short, it was the perfect relationship that came abruptly to end when he left for Berkeley a few weeks ago.

I'd entertained the idea that it was perfect precisely because it had been cut short by his going away to college. Maybe if we'd dated longer, we would have let personality quirks and diverging life goals fray the fabric of our adoration.. I'll never know. At the end of the summer, I was ready to start college committed to a long-distance relationship. But Eric made us stick to the terms of the agreement. We were going back to "just friends" and we needed to date other people in college. I was disappointed, but I could understand his rationale. Four years of being away from one another were bound to be painful. So, I came to school on the look out for someone to distract me from daydreaming about Eric.

"Hey, do you guys mind if I use my sound machine?" Casey asked. "I tried to sleep without it last night and it was so hard! I use ocean sounds- it's really soothing. You'll love it!"

Erin shrugged.

"Go for it," I said.

Casey hit a button on her alarm clock and filled the room with sounds of waves. I exchanged a look with Erin. The sound machine was loud. I don't know how Casey could sleep with it right next to her ear.

She snuggled blissfully beneath her silky duvet. "*Much* better!" she said.

I decided to give it a chance. After all, it could have been worse. She could have grown up falling asleep to heavy metal. Before I headed off to bed, I fired off a quick email to Meg.

From: "Amy Callaway" <acallaway@ucla.edu>
To: "Meagan Callaway" <mcallaway@excelsior.com>
Subject: Hi Meg

Meg,

How's it going? Mum said not to call you because you're working all the time. Are you OK? Should you be killing yourself in your first job out of college?

I'm doing great! Mum and Dad dropped me off yesterday. The room is a shoebox. My roommates are cool. Casey is this really pretty tall blonde girl from Beverly Hills. She's a partier- it's going to be interesting. Erin is this petite Asian girl who is majoring in engineering. They're both really nice, so I'm hoping for smooth sailing.

I met two cute guys already. One of them lives upstairs. He invited me to his frat party last night and my fake boob fell out of my shirt. Don't ask. I'm still humiliated. So I think I blew that one. The other guy is my neighbor Brian. We took a walk on campus tonight and he seems like a really nice guy. You're not supposed to date neighbors, right?

Mr. Ives asked me to write an article about what a freshman should expect from college to run for the seniors in the spring. Any ideas?

Stop laughing about the boob.

Love, Amy

I had a hard time falling asleep with the waves crashing ten feet away from me. When I finally drifted off to sleep, I dreamt that I was drowning. Maybe this was a sign from a greater power that I was going to be in over my head at college.

3 First Day of School

From: "Meagan Callaway" <mcallaway@excelsior.com>
To: "Amy Callaway" <acallaway@ucla.edu>
Subject: Re: Hi Meg

Amy,

Work has been insane. They put me on a case with a really tough client who wants to see progress every five minutes. If I don't kill myself in my first job out of school, when am I going to do it? There isn't a high paying job out there that doesn't require you to bust your ass. I'd rather pay my dues now than later, when I have a family.

I'm not laughing. Totally sympathetic. Maybe over Thanksgiving you'll feel good enough to tell me about it. Worse things will happen to other people during your time at UCLA. I still can't believe some of the random nonsense that happened to me and my friends during college. Don't worry about it. Besides, I'm sure everyone was drunk and no one remembers anyway.

Don't date your neighbor! If things go badly, you'll have to live with him every day for the rest of the year! When classes start or you get involved in other activities, I'm sure you'll meet other cool guys.

From college, I think you should expect to gain 15 lbs, make new friends, experience new things, consider new ideas (both in and out of class), and begin to figure out what you want to do with your life. The thing about college is that there are no rules, no structure, no expectations, nothing. So anything goes and you can do what you want to. Some people let the freedom get to their heads and they totally go off the deep end with drinking, drugs, sex, being stupid, etc just because they can. But I figure you know better =)

Love, Meg

I smiled at the implicit maternal warning at the end of the email. What would I do without Meg? If she said something was going to be ok, it usually was. That was the power of the big sister. Supposedly, she'd learned all the rough lessons so I wouldn't have to. Supposedly.

*****

Casey and I had breakfast together on the first day of class, since we both had 8am classes. My schedule for the   quarter looked like this:

	Monday	Tuesday	Wednesday	Thursday	Friday
8-9	Calc	Econ	Calc	Econ	Calc
9-10					
10-11	Anthro	English Dis.	Anthro		Anthro
11-12			Anthro Dis.	Calc Dis.	
12-1	Lunch	Lunch	Lunch	Lunch	Lunch
1-2	English		English		English
2-3		Econ Dis.			
3-4					
4-5					
5-6					

I'd purposely put all of my classes earlier in the day to force myself to get up at a decent hour and still have the rest of the afternoon up until dinner to study on campus. Attempting to study in my room after dinner would be a challenge. And I didn't like the idea of trekking back to the dorms after class for dinner and then trekking out to campus again to study.

Casey and I walked down to campus, retracing the steps that I'd taken with Brian. I wondered if he would be thinking of that when he walked down to class today. In front of the student union, we parted ways. She went left towards North Campus, home of the arts, humanities and sculpture garden. I went towards South Campus, home of math, sciences and buildings that were ugly as sin.

I walked up the stairs of Boelter Hall, the engineering building. The green and white tile on the ground, next to the sterile white walls made the inside just about as exciting as the outside. The elevator doors were just closing when I hopped inside and looked at nothing in particular until the elevator doors opened on the 3rd floor. Apparently everyone was headed to the same lecture. We filed into a lecture hall that looked like a movie theater, with those seats that are kind of like clams. You pull the seat part down and sit on it. Then you pull the little paddle-like thing out from next to your seat, rotate it and bring it down across your lap. This serves as a desk.

There were about 300 seats that were steadily filling up, at ten minutes to the hour. There were three large chalkboards across the front of the room, and a white screen that you could pull down over the center chalkboard to show overhead transparencies or movies on. I found the projector mounted onto the ceiling, along a row of stage lights, shining on the front of the room. Further inspection revealed large speakers mounted on the ceiling in the four corners of the room. It seemed more like a theater than a classroom. I half expected the professor to come out singing show tunes.

When the professor materialized at exactly 8:03am, it became clear very that there would be no show tunes. Professor Zalawi was a very serious man who looked like a lost lumber jack. He was wearing a plaid shirt with suspenders. He was also so focused on math, he had forgotten to cut his hair for several years. The salt and pepper mop on the top of his head matched his shaggy beard. He came into the classroom with a notebook and calculus text under his left arm and an orange juice in his right hand. When he reached the front of the classroom, he clipped on his wireless microphone and tucked his chin down so he could survey us over the top of his glasses.

"Welcome to multidimensional calculus," he said. "Let's get started. Pass the syllabus around. Good. Let's get the housekeeping done."

He wrote his name, office number, email address, office hours up and the URL of the class website on the board. I copied them in my notebook.

"You have every homework assignment written down on the back of your syllabus and it's also on the class website. Homework is due every Friday in class. If you need help with any of it, ask your TA first and if they can't help, come see me at office hours. Homework is 20% of your grade. Your midterm is 30% of it and the final is 50% of it. Any questions?"

He paused for a minute and absent-mindedly tugged at one of his suspenders. Exams were worth 80% of our grade? No pressure or anything!

"Right," he continued. "As most of you know, the quarter goes by very quickly and I've had to take a semester's worth of material and cram it into ten weeks. The university somehow feels like you guys learn more if we cram three quarters into every academic year instead of having two longer semesters. I will refrain from telling you what *I* think about this. But let's not waste any time getting started. Taking derivatives with respect to multiple variables is not that different from taking derivatives with respect to a single variable…"

And away he went. To his point, he did not waste a single minute of lecture, but pushed forward at breakneck speed so that by the end of the class, my hand was cramped. I was a bit intimidated. I'd spent most of my attention copying what was on the board, and when I could manage it, I would also write down some of the professor's commentary, but I didn't always follow the examples all the way through. This class was not going to be a cakewalk.

I stood in the traffic jam of people filing out of class at 8:55am and was thankful for the hour that I had before Social and Cultural Anthropology to walk up to North Campus. On the way over, I stopped into Kerchhoff Coffee Shop and bought myself a caramel latte. To celebrate the first day of school, I told myself. I couldn't push out the thought that it was also to comfort myself after the first lecture. I savored my sweet treat in small sips and moseyed my way between Royce and Powell towards North Campus, checking my campus map like a dork.

Anthropology was in an even bigger lecture hall and I was glad that I'd gotten a seat near the front of the room. I didn't even know how anyone could see the whiteboard from the back. My Anthropology professor was as different from my calculus professor as day from night. He was in his thirties, had a healthy tan and wore a blue button down shirt over khakis. Aside from knowing how to dress, he also had a different approach to class.

"My name is John Brenner," he said, as if he had all the time in the world. "Please call me John. I'm a new professor here in the Anthropology department and I'm very excited to introduce you to the world of Social and Cultural Anthropology. Here is the syllabus. Please pass it around. You can get all of your readings at the bookstore and I've put some books on reserve at the library as well."

"What is anthropology?" he asked. Up until that point, there had been a nominal level of whispering, paper rustling, and people shifting in chairs, but after he asked the question and paused, it became so quiet you could hear a pin drop.

The professor laughed at us.

"What happened? Everyone became quiet. Do you think this is a natural behavior or do you think that this is behavior that is somehow linked to our society or our culture? What do *you* think?" he asked, stopping in front of a poor kid in the front row.

"Um, natural," the kid stammered. I could barely hear him. He was about six rows in front of me.

"Why?" asked the professor.

"We all sensed danger and so we froze… like animals being hunted." The class laughed,.

"I hope you don't view me as a predator," the professor said. "That's a good answer, but what if I told you that I posed the exact same question to a class of this size in Iceland and they were all waving their hands to answer me?"

He gave us a minute to ponder this.

"Why did you view it as a threat?" he asked.

We thought again. Or, at least, gave the appearance of it. He must have sensed that he wasn't going to get anything more out of us, so he continued.

"This quarter, we're going to open our minds and debunk some of the myths we've grown up with, like what is inherently 'natural' and what is a societal construction. For example, what do you think when you see this picture?"

He flashed a picture up on the screen of two men standing very close to one another and looking intensely at each other's faces. Their pants were just a little too tight- something that only male models could get away with in a catalog but not something you would wear out on the street. These fellows were not good-looking enough to be models though.

"They're gay," someone piped up from the middle of class.

"Actually, they're not," the professor told us. "I know both men and they have wives and kids."

"They could still be gay," the guy persisted.

"Well, they could be, but let's say they're not. What do you think about it now?" he asked.

No one said anything, but everyone clearly felt like something was not right about the picture.

"You're all feeling uncomfortable," the professor stated, reading our minds. "And the reason why you feel uncomfortable is that you've been raised in a society that has invented a notion called 'personal space.' What's more, 'personal space' is especially important between men, who keep a lot of distance between one another. Extensive eye contact has been deemed inappropriate and signals sexual attraction. This photo was taken in Spain, where this idea of 'personal space' has not taken root and these two men are buddies and perfectly comfortable talking like this."

He paused a minute to let it sink in.

I scribbled down notes as he highlighted the different units we would be covering in the course. Besides kinship, we were going to be talking about family units, societal units, money versus value, and discrimination based on race, ethnicity and gender.

"We're going to read some really backwards articles written by scientists a hundred years ago, who were trying to argue that African Americans were less intelligent than Caucasians and failing miserably at it," he told us. "It goes to show you how people go to great lengths to protect their biases."

My jaw dropped.

"We're also going to talk about how our society today views men and women differently," he continued. "I'll give you a little teaser. There was a study done that asked a large group of people what the ideal man's body looks like and what the ideal woman's body looks like. The respondents were asked to choose between cartoon bodies. Then, the study went on to show that a much higher percentage of men have the ideal man's body than women who have the ideal woman's body. I mean, orders of magnitude more. And, the ideal man's body is much more achievable than the ideal woman's body if you don't already have it. A man can build abdominal muscles, whereas a woman cannot really build a larger chest or longer legs in a non-invasive way. What are the societal implications of this?"

He paused and looked around.

"American women, as a whole, have body image anxiety. Much more than American men. Companies have a field day with this, selling weight loss products, make up and clothes to insecure women. When we get to that unit, we can talk about how this is a self perpetuating cycle. Little girls see advertisements for these products and caught up in this trap too."

I was fascinated. This bit about body image was something that I'd read about in magazines and seemed sort of fluffy, but hearing it in an academic setting, spoken by a male professor somehow validated it as a real, quantifiable, scientific problem. This class was going to be awesome.

"If you take only one thing away from this class, I hope it's this: I hope that you will question what seems 'normal' or 'natural' or 'right' from now on. Really think about what shapes your perceptions and be open minded because cultures and societies don't always have it right. As I mentioned, it can't possibly be right to have a large percentage of our society's women fall victim to body image related low self-esteem. And when we talk about cultures and societies, we don't mean countries, necessarily. Your dorm has its own culture and norms, that may be different from the dorm across the street. Sorry, I ran over time. See you on Wednesday!"

I left Anthropology feeling enlightened and I made a beeline for Powell Library, where I knew I could get on a computer right away and email Lauren. I missed her a lot just now. I wish that she could have attended that lecture with me. She would have been as excited as I was about the prospect of turning everything that we knew upside down. When the next available terminal opened up, I jumped right on it.

From: "Amy Callaway" <acallaway@ucla.edu>
To: "Lauren Avery" <lavery@princeton.edu>
Subject: First Day

L,
    howz it going over there? i just got out of the most amazing lecture on social and cultural anthropology. totally smitten! the prof is hot. but more importantly, he spent the whole lecture talking about how we are influenced by culture and society to think that things are right, wrong, normal, or weird. i wonder how come they didn't teach us this stuff in high school? we probably could have used some mind-opening classes.

    i was inspired. ever thought about being a prof, laur? it would be awesome to change the way people   think or what they know. i'll bet he gets to study whatever the hell he wants! i totally wish i could be as charismatic and engaging as that guy was today! spout off brilliant and profound observations...

how's it going with that guy? he sounds like a hottie. but meg says we shouldn't date our neighbors, in case it doesn't work out. too bad i'm already crushing on two of mine. well, one is my next door neighbor and that's really bad. his name is Brian and he's cute in a nerdy kind of way. i met him a few nights ago when he was locked out of his room and he was just in a towel. ;) the other one is this guy named jeff who lives upstairs from me. he's a frat guy. i went to a party with him and acted like a total klutz so it may be over before it even starts.

k, this is getting long. just wanted to tell you about anthro. i miss you! wish you were here!

love, a

After I sent the email off to Lauren, I saw that I had a new message in my Inbox from Sean.

From: "Sean Alexander" <sealex@ucla.edu>
To: "Amy Callaway", "Erin Chen", "Casey Brown", "Brian Robertson", "Sarah McAdams"

hey yall,

im having lunch @ reiber @ 12:00pm and im in a good mood, so i am willing to grace u w/ my presence. i know uve got nothing better to do. c u there!

-sa

Sean was something else. Living next to that guy would not be dull this year. Lunch at the dorms sounded good. I was already hungry. I glanced at the bottom right hand corner of my computer screen. 11:15am. What could I do in forty-five minutes?

I logged off the terminal and wandered outside into the brilliant sunshine. Campus was quietly busy at this hour. The trees rustled as I headed towards Bruin Walk. I rounded the corner and saw Kerchhoff, and remembered the newspaper office was in there. I hesitated for a second because I didn't have any writing samples to leave with them just now. On the other hand, the sooner I got the introduction over with, the better.

I entered through the arched stone doorways of the medieval looking castle and followed the signs for *The Daily Bruin* to the back of the building.

The *Daily Bruin* office greeted me with the comfortable chaos of a newspaper office. Along the walls, there were makeshift cubicles- the kind with beige carpet on the divider walls. There were stacks of papers on every horizontal surface that an outsider might dismiss as random or disorganized. A tall guy in a plain white t-shirt and corduroys lay on the beat-up leather couch in the corner, reading something on a clipboard, a red pen in one hand, coffee mug in the other. An editor. A girl in jeans and a sweatshirt lay on her stomach by his feet sketching a layout. The guy in the cubicle closest to me was on the computer reading an article, sitting in what looked like the aftermath of a tornado. Everyone looked so relaxed. I knew straight away that this is where I needed to be.

The guy on the computer looked up from his screen when I walked in and watched me take in the room.

"How's it going?" he asked. He tousled up his curly red hair. I walked over to his cubicle and leaned over the counter.

"Great," I replied. "I'm a freshman and I was wondering how I become a staff writer here."

"Well, there an online application that you fill out," he replied, turning back to his computer to pull up the webpage for me. "If you're selected, there are these training sessions you have to go to. Then you can be a staff writer. It's this whole long process."

Of course there would be an application process, but I guess I had hoped it would be less formal. I swung my backpack off of my shoulder to get out a sheet of notebook paper so that I could write down the website. He looked up at me and must have seen the disappointed look on my face.

"But honestly, the best way to get involved right away is to send us articles. If we like your stuff, we can publish you as a guest contributor, and it really improves your chances of being selected as staff."

"How do I submit my articles?" I asked, pen in hand.

"Just send them to dailybruin@ucla.edu," he told me.

It was so generic. This is probably what they told every hopeful freshman who wandered into this office. I wrote down the email address and stuffed the paper back into my backpack.

"Thanks," I replied. "What kind of articles are you looking for?"

"Whatever you've got. We like sports, opinions, political commentary, news. You know, the usual."

"Right," I nodded, heaving a big sigh. "Thanks."

I turned towards the door.

"What's your name?" the guy asked from behind me. This was promising. I turned back around. The guy had stood up and walked out of his cubicle.

"I'm so sorry," I apologized, walking back toward him. "My name is Amy Callaway."

"Matt Baker." He offered me his hand. I shook it.

"Thanks again for the info," I said.

"No worries," he replied, with a smile. "I hope we see you in here soon."

I tried hard to give a big smile as I turned to walk out the door.

*****

"Anyone have any exciting classes today?" Sarah asked, as she sat down at the table with her tray. She was wearing a turquoise shirt, which made her skin look paler and her freckles more prominent than usual.

"I had Physics and Computer Science this morning," Erin volunteered. She tied her long black hair up into a ponytail before she sat down to eat.

"She asked for *exciting* classes," Sean pointed out. He pulled up the waistband of his jeans before he sat down at the table and tucked his knees under it. Then, he started on his lunch, which consisted entirely of fried meats and starches.

Erin shot him a dirty look.

"Physics *is* exciting," Brian said, in Erin's defense. "Erin can calculate how much force she needs to knock your teeth in."

We laughed. I swallowed my mouthful of chicken taco.

"My Anthro class was pretty cool this morning," I said.

"What's cool about it?" Sarah asked, putting down her veggie burger.

"The whole class is about separating what is true and universal from what is a societal construct," I replied. "For example, something that is true is that people feel closer to their blood relatives than to other people. But what is a societal construct is how people feel about their friends or spouses relative to their blood relatives. That's dictated a lot by culture and society. Also, different cultures treat men and women differently.

"What's the point?" Sean asked, unimpressed.

"The point of the class is to recognize when our beliefs are shaped by culture and not truth." I paraphrased my professor's words, which were still fresh in my mind. "Because what we think of as normal and right could just be societal constructs and other societies might have more productive ways of thinking of them. Take women, for example."

"My favorite topic!" Sean injected. Sarah rolled her eyes.

"In America, we have this societal idea of what the perfect woman's body should look like," I continued. "And it's very rare and pretty much unattainable if you aren't born with it. So we have all these women who have body image problems and low self-esteem. But it doesn't have to be that way!"

"Sure it does," Sean replied. "If girls had high self-esteem, how would boys ever get laid?"

Sarah threw a pickle slice at him from across the table.

"You are *unbelievable!*" she cried. "Do you have a mother?"

Sean looked at his fried chicken drumstick, smothered in gravy and back at Sarah.

"I don't think you want to start a food fight with me, Missy."

Sarah glanced at the drumstick and capitulated.

"Go on," Brian told me. "Don't pay attention to him."

I smiled at him. He was such a sweetheart.

"Anyway, the whole class is about challenging assumptions and being open-minded, which I think, was such a good thing for me to hear on the first day of college," I finished.

"Totally," Brian agreed. "That sounds like a cool class. Maybe I'll come to one of your lectures one of these days."

"Absolutely!" I agreed.

"Being open-minded is overrated," Sean countered. "Open-minded is just a euphemism for not having your own thoughts."

"I see both sides," Brian said. He paused a moment as he squirted ketchup on his burger. "I think you have to listen to other people's ideas, especially if they're different than yours, so that you can decide which ones work better for you. But, at some point, I think that you have to decide who you are and what you're about."

"Yeah," Sarah chimed in. "Or else, you don't stand for anything. I mean, the ultimately open-minded person has no identity, values or beliefs if they're always open to other ones."

"On the flip side," I argued. "The person who didn't stay open-minded long enough was the slave-owner before the Civil War or the German Nazi."

"Maybe before they were slave-owners and Nazis, they were being open-minded and after hearing lots of ideas, decided it was better for them to believe in slavery and eugenics," Sean pointed out.

"That's a good point," I conceded.

"Anyway, this seems like pretty heavy conversation for North Campus," Sean observed.

"Are you saying that there aren't serious conversations in the humanities and social sciences?" Sarah asked.

"Maybe," Sean replied.

"If it *were* a South Campus conversation, there wouldn't be this many girls at the table," Erin pointed out. "It's really weird. There don't seem to be very many girls in South Campus. Did you guys notice that?"

"Come to think of it, there weren't as many girls in my calculus class as boys," Sarah said, casting her eyes ceiling-ward, as she tried to recall.

"Well there aren't as many *hot* girls in South Campus, that's for sure," Sean asserted.

"What do you mean by *that*?" Sarah asked. As a Biochem major, she was solidly a South Campus girl.

"I thought it was a well-known fact that beauty and brains are inversely proportional," Sean replied, as if it were obvious.

We all looked at him, aghast.

"There are *definitely* exceptions to that!" Brian pointed out, playing peace-maker.

"So one way or another, you're insulting us," I observed, trying hard to suppress a smile. "We're either stupid or we're ugly."

"Hey, don't shoot the messenger," Sean said, holding up his hands. "There's a lot of empirical evidence out there. And it makes sense, right? If you're a girl and you're beautiful, you really don't have to work hard at much else to get the attention that you want. Ugly girls have to try harder."

"You *did* say you had a mother at some point, right?" I asked, when I recovered.

"Leave my mother out of this." Sean grinned. "Weren't we talking about being open to other people's ideas, especially if they're different from your own, or some shit like that earlier?"

"Suppose that in some universe, that logic were right. Then it should apply for guys too then," Sarah pointed out.

"I don't know." Sean shrugged. "I can only assess whether girls are hot or not. I don't check out the guys."

"Just eat your lunch," Erin said, in mock irritation. "You're ridiculous. I hope you gain *more* than fifteen pounds. Keep eating that fried crap."

"By my theory, that will make me smarter," Sean said, unruffled. "But the theory doesn't even pertain to me because I'm special. My mom told me so."

"So you *do* have a mother," I noted. "And this is all her fault."

Everyone laughed, except for Sean. He made an obscene gesture and took a giant bite of his drumstick.

*****

I left lunch with plenty of time to get to my English class, so I took my time strolling and thinking about ideas for articles. This was fairly natural for me, as I'd spent most of my free time over the last few years doing exactly that. Ideas popped in and out of my head as I shuffled down the giant concrete hill leading to campus. The track team was out practicing and I admired how effortlessly they covered the length of the straightaway. I marveled at the amount of free time I had now that I only had three classes a day. College was great!

The two thoughts that popped into my head were of the article that I had to write for Mr. Ives for the high school paper about what to expect in college, and of the Freshman Fifteen. I wondered if gaining fifteen pounds was really something to worry about or if it was an urban myth. On one hand, the dining hall food was delicious and abundant. But I *would* get tired of it at some point, right? The Freshman Fifteen seemed to be the one thing that most people agreed that one should expect from college. Maybe that was the case because it was a lot less complicated to explain than "Find yourself" or "Discover your life's mission". The alliteration was certainly cute.

An idea began forming in my mind. What if I titled my article, "The Freshman Fifteen"? It could be a list of the fifteen different things that freshman could expect from college. I wasn't sure if there were really fifteen universal things that a freshman could expect, and I generally disdained top ten lists in which people had to scrape the bottom of the barrel to complete the list, but the title was too perfect to pass on.

I was one of the first to arrive at my English classroom. There were thirty students in the class, and the classroom looked disappointingly similar to a high school classroom. There was a chalkboard at the front of the room and there were thirty desk-chairs lined up in five straight rows from the front of the classroom to the back.

I wrote "Freshman Fifteen" at the top of a sheet of notebook paper and began to brainstorm.

- **gain 15 lbs**
- **find yourself**
- **explore new ideas**
- **make new friends**
- **party and drink**
- **date**
- **find your life's purpose**

By this point, all the seats were filled and the professor strode into the room. This one looked more professorial than the other two I had earlier in the day. He was a tallish man in his late fifties, with a full head of white hair, combed neatly over to one side of his head. In tan dress pants, a dress shirt and a navy suit jacket, he was smartly dressed and stood up very straight. I was trying to decide whether I thought he could be considered good-looking or not for a man of his age, but I deferred the decision to after he started talking for a bit.

"Let's get started then," he said, all-business, in a British accent.

I decided he was good-looking.

He began pacing at the front of the classroom, with a silver pen clasped in one hand. He periodically stopped abruptly, looked intently at the class and clicked his pen when he wanted to emphasize something he was saying.

"My name is Professor Barnard and I have been teaching here for twenty <click> years. This is the introductory English Composition class which will lay the groundwork for all other classes in the department. As such, it will be fairly basic <click>. We will discuss elements of good composition <click>, rhetoric <click> and language <click>, as indicated by the course title. I know some of you think this is subjective, but at the very least <click>, there are definitely elements of bad <click> writing that we can identify and avoid. We will also review literary devices that writers use to add nuance <click>, reality <click> or emphasis <click> to their work, such as metaphors, hyperboles, and local color."

The clicking of the pen was distracting, but when I blocked that out, I liked what he was saying. We listened quietly as he told us what to expect this quarter. We had writing assignments every other week in addition to a final paper. There were books we needed to pick up at the reader store down in Westwood. He went on for awhile about people who wanted to add, drop or audit the course. And soon enough, it was done.

As I slipped my notebook into my backpack, it occurred to me that this English professor might have connections with the *Daily Bruin*. If any subject was close to journalism, it was English composition. As the last few students filed out of the room, I took a deep breath and walked to the front of the classroom, where the professor was packing his briefcase.

"Professor Barnard?" I said.

"How can I help you?" he asked, peering over his glasses at me. His grey eyes were pale under his bushy eyebrows.

"My name is Amy Callaway and I am interested in writing for the *Daily Bruin*," I explained. "I was wondering if you knew anyone that I could talk to who could help me out."

The professor took off his glasses and stuck one end in his mouth. He stared and the ground and thought hard, heaving a big sigh.

"I'm not that connected to the paper, but I'll do my best. Did you visit their office in Kerchhoff?"

"Yes, I went earlier today. They said I had to apply and they gave me a generic email address to send articles to for now, so they can publish my work as a guest contributor if they like it."

Professor Barnard continued to look at me. He nodded, but didn't say anything.

"I guess I was hoping for an actual contact on the staff, you know, to increase my chances of being read," I added, looking at my feet.

"What sorts of articles do you write?" he asked.

"Well, mostly news and personal interviews in the past, but I'm hoping to do some op ed pieces on college life and society and stuff," I stammered, thinking about my "Freshman Fifteen" article.

I had not expected to be put on the spot like this.

"Really, I'm open to anything right now.   I expect to do some experimenting. I just want to write," I added.

Professor Barnard nodded slowly. "Give me your email address. I'll see what I can do."

"Thanks a lot!" I said, smiling. He handed me a spare syllabus and I wrote my email address on it.

"See you next class," he said. Then he went back to packing up his briefcase, as I walked a little lighter out of the beat up wooden door.

After class, I toyed with the idea of getting started on my homework on campus before dinner but then realized that all of my textbooks were in my dorm room. So I headed back up The Hill towards Sproul. I was very eager to transfer my scribbles into a proper document on my computer and begin developing the idea. My first article as a college student! I had to think about what angle I wanted to take. I knew I didn't want to be condescending. No one likes articles that sound like their mothers. But I hadn't yet decided if I wanted it to be light and humorous, down-to-earth and serious, or witty with some sophisticated irony sprinkled in.

A little dart of doubt entered my mind. Was college something that could even be described accurately to a high school student? Perhaps it was meant to be experienced and not explained. Well, it wouldn't hurt to try.

There were two major topics on which I hadn't yet taken a position-drinking and sex. I would have to establish them before I finalized the "Freshman Fifteen" article. My experience with booze was limited. The "cool kids" at my high school sometimes came to school on Monday mornings, bragging about their weekend binge drinking adventures. But this didn't make me particularly inclined to do it. They weren't exactly human beings I wanted to model myself after. Over the summer, I went to a couple of beach bonfires and house parties where my friends, gleeful in their guilt, produced beer and wine coolers that they'd smuggled from their parents or coerced siblings to buy for them. We usually reached the stage of slight teetering in our gait and excessive giggling. None of us had the guts to actually get smashed. There wasn't a single parent among my circle of friends who wouldn't skin us all if we were caught drunk anywhere in town.

In a way, it was a relief. Deep down, I was afraid to meet Drunk Amy. What would she be like? Would she learn to throw caution to the wind and become the life of the party? Somehow I doubted this. Would she be flirty and promiscuous? Worse, would she just be quiet and withdrawn? I had no idea and I wasn't sure if I was ready to find out yet. Teetering and giggling worked just fine for me. Plus, the idea of drinking to the point of vomiting sounded disgusting to me. How long could I stave off the pressure to drink a lot here at University of California Party Central?

I was unsure of whether I should send the socially responsible message, "Don't drink if you don't want to" or the slightly less socially responsible message, "Get wasted once and decide after that." Of course, I'd have to walk the walk if I was going to write it *that* way. The words of my Anthro professor drifted back into my mind. I had to suspend judgment. I had to be open-minded to get the most out of this college experience.

I felt similar on the topic of sex. Eric and I had never gone past second base. And judging by how awkward I felt then, I was just fine staying right there for awhile. This probably made me a total prude. I would have to think about how to present that topic and whether I endorsed experimenting.

I let myself into our room and booted up my laptop. The responsible thing to do was get started on the Calculus problem set or maybe knock a few pages off of my Anthro reading, but I was just itching to get some words down on the screen before I lost my inspiration. As I waited for my word processor to open, a window popped up.

Jeffers56: hi pretty girl

I froze, fingers a few inches above the keyboard, not knowing how to respond.

What do you say to the guy who watched your fake boob bounce across his frat house floor? I wasn't quite sure whether I should be talking to him or not. In fact, I didn't know if I could ever look him in the face again. And why would he ever want to talk to me ever again either? He could never take me back to his frat house. It would be so embarrassing! I drummed on the keyboard without pressing any of the keys.

69

> **Jeffers56:** u there?

ARGH. What to say?!

> **Amyable7:** hi jeff! howz it going?
> **Jeffers56:** good! just 1 class today- pretty chill
> **Amyable7:** that's good! what have you been up to?

Don't bring it up, I thought frantically. *Keep it friendly. Keep it cool.*

> **Jeffers56:** trying to think of an excuse 2 talk 2 u again

Double take. The man had lost his mind. This was the equivalent of befriending the kid who picked his nose in kindergarten. It was social suicide. *Save yourself!* I wanted to tell him. *Don't go down with the ship!*

> **Jeffers56:** ive never seen anyone run that fast in high heels :)

I had begun squirming on my hard wooden chair. Avoiding the topic wasn't going to work. Well, he was the one who started down this path. Out with it!

> **Amyable7:** jeff, i wouldn't blame u if u didnt want to hang out with me again. i totally understand.
>
> **Jeffers56:** what r u talking about?

I blinked at the screen. This was just cruel. He wanted me to spell it out in writing?

> **Amyable7:** u know- about the "wardrobe malfunction" at your frat the other night
>
> **Jeffers56:** hahaha. that was nothing!
>
> **Jeffers56:** crazy shit like that happens all the time. it was no big deal. after u left, some girl threw up all over the d.j.

I didn't know how I felt about this. On the one hand, I was relieved that he didn't view it as a big deal. On the other hand, he was belittling one of the most catastrophic moments of my life. In a twisted sort of way, I felt like I deserved a little bit of notoriety for it.

> **Amyable7:** well thats a relief- i thought id be the laughing stock of SIE
>
> **Jeffers56:** naw. and if u were, i wouldnt care
>
> **Amyable7:** thats sweet of u- thx for the support
>
> **Jeffers56:** any time
>
> **Amyable7:** how was the rest of the party?
>
> **Jeffers56:** normal- drinking, hooking up, sleeping in. skipped hooking up

I couldn't tell what he was after. He was flirting, but I didn't know how seriously to take him. He didn't even really know me. I decided to proceed with caution- see his bet, but not raise him any.

Amyable7: thats too bad

Jeffers56: naw, too much of that stuff going on

Amyable7: a romantic!

Jeffers56: i wouldnt go that far- im just not into random hooking up

Amyable7: me neither

Jeffers56: yah, overrated

Amyable7: i like the way u think

Jeffers56: good! we should hang out again some time and ill tell u more about what i think

Amyable7: sure, sounds fun!

Jeffers56: this week, i have rush stuff every night at the frat but after we should

Amyable7: u got it- lemme know

Jeffers56: k, c u

Amyable7: c u

And as abruptly as it had started, it was over. I saved the conversation.

*****

Promptly at 6:30pm, Casey stood up from her desk and announced, "I'm starving, let's get dinner."

Erin and I murmured in agreement. We stood up and grabbed our sweatshirts, cards and keys. The guys' door was open, so I peered inside to see everybody staring at their computer screens. I was amused to see that it didn't take them long to trash their room. Dirty sneakers were already peaking out from beneath furniture, shirts were slung over chairs and bold colored comforters were dangling over the edge of the beds. This entire mess was presided over by the bare women on the walls whom I tried not to stare at. Casey went further down the hallway to get Sarah.

"Dinner?" I suggested. They all stood up and there was general chaos as they tried to get around the room without running into each other to gather their things and put on their shoes.

"I don't know how people live like this," Sean commented, after bumping heads with Brian when they both tried to sit in their chairs and tie their shoe laces. "I wonder who's bright idea it was to cram three people into this *cell*."

"It's not *so* bad," Chris said. "My brothers and I share a room about this size at home. You get used to it."

Sean didn't look like he believed Chris.

After everyone had retrieved their food and sat down, Chris got down to business.

"Who is going to the football game on Saturday?" he demanded to know.

"I have the season tickets package!" Casey said. "Doesn't everyone?"

The rest of us shook our heads.

"I was going to see how I liked the first one before I committed to any other ones," Erin said.

"Me too," Sarah agreed. "It seemed like a lot of money to put down right away. I didn't know if I would find people who wanted to go or what. Plus, later on in the quarter, if I'm swamped with work, I might not have time to go, so it would be a waste of money."

"Oh, you can always sell your ticket," Casey replied. "Are you serious? None of you guys bought season tickets? Why did you come to UCLA if you weren't going to buy season football tickets?"

We all laughed.

"Well, are you going to go?" Chris asked us. "It's supposed to be a really good game against Ohio State!"

"I was going to go," Sean replied. "Can I still get tickets?"

"Yeah," Chris nodded. "But you'd better get them soon or they might sell out of student tickets. Just go down to that ticket office on the back side of the Alumni Center. Are the rest of you going to go?"

"I think I will," I said, making up my mind on the spot.

I had never been much of a football fan. To me, it had always been a bunch of meat-head guys running into one another, pretending to be macho. Many an indignant male friend had told me, "There's a lot of strategy involved!" But judging by the football players I'd known in high school, the strategies couldn't be that intellectually taxing. Still, even if I didn't like the football, it would be a good bonding day with everyone who went.

"Yeah, I guess I'll go too. I won't have *that* much work yet after one week of classes," Sarah said.

"Oh my God!" Chris cried, rolling his eyes. "Show some enthusiasm, woman! It is straight up offensive that you're coming just because you don't have that much work yet. Would it kill you to show some loyalty to our illustrious institution for the next four years?"

"Fine." She sat up tall and cleared her throat. "*Of course* I'm going to go! *Nothing*, not even a huge stack of work that could potentially determine my future, would stop me from worshipping the mighty Bruins."

We laughed at her exaggerated enthusiasm.

"If you guys go, I'll go," Erin said.

"Now we're talking!" Chris said, clapping his hands together and sitting back in his seat.

"Now about the tailgating," Casey began, leaning towards us in preparation for disseminating important information. "The game starts at four o' clock, which means we should try to get there by one. So we should leave here by eleven thirty so we can stop at the grocery store and pick up tailgating stuff."

"Who has a car?" Sean asked.

"I have an SUV," Casey replied, waving her hand. "It will fit everyone, no problem."

"Brian, are you coming?" I asked, trying to be quiet, but immediately, all eyes swung towards us.

"I can't," he said, looking down at his food.

"Why not?" several of us asked at once.

"I have to go home for the day. A friend of mine is sick."

"Oh no!" Erin said. "Is it serious?"

"No, nothing serious. I just said I'd go hang out."

"Bummer," Chris replied. "Will you be back in time to party with us?"

Brian brightened up at the idea that he wouldn't be missing the entire college football experience. "Sure! When do you think you'll be back?"

"Probably nine or ten," Casey said. "The game will take around four hours and then there will be crazy traffic getting out of there."

"Where are we going to get the booze?" Sean asked.

"I can bring some back from my parents' house," Brian offered. "My brother has some stashed in his closet."

So then it was settled. I wondered who he was going to see at home. Was it a girl? Boys don't go over to each other's houses when they're sick, do they? Who knew? They were like a different species anyway most of the time. One of my regrets in life was not having a brother to help me understand the oddities of the male mind.

"Wait a minute!" Casey said, pausing dramatically to give us all a chance to look at her. "I think sorority rush starts on Sunday! That was kind of bad planning for them to do that right after the first home football game. Everyone is going to be hung over!"

"Are you guys all rushing?" Sean asked, looking amused.

"I think I am," I said,. "It's worth checking out."

Erin and Sarah shook their heads.

"Maybe in the spring," Erin said.

After dinner, I added "Get pumped about college sports" to my Freshman Fifteen list, and I climbed up onto my bed to call my parents.

"Amy?" Mum said, delighted. "Hold on, let me put you on speaker phone so that Dad can hear too."

There was a beep and then I heard background noise.

"How's school, Ame?" Dad asked.

"It's good!" I was trying to keep my voice low so that I wouldn't disturb Casey and Erin, who were sitting at their computers.

"Today was the first day, right?" Mum asked. "What are your classes like?"

"They're all interesting, My calculus class and my Anthropology class are huge. There are at least a hundred students in each. My English class is thirty students, so it's more like a high school class. All of the professors seem fine."

"Is it going to be a lot of work?" Mum asked.

"It's too soon to tell," I answered. "I can't imagine it's going to be busier than high school. I had every class every day. Now I only have each class twice or three times a week."

"But they could give you a lot more work for each class," Dad pointed out.

"True. I don't know. I'll see."

It felt odd, talking to them on the phone. Until now, I spoke to them on the phone when I needed them to pick me up from practice or if I was away on a trip. It was strange to think that this would be my primary mode of communication with them… forever?

"How are your roommates?" Mum asked .

I cleared my throat. "Yeah, I'm in my room right now with my roommates." .

"Ohhhh," Mum replied, catching my drift.

"We're having a great time though," I continued. "We're going to the football game on Saturday. Casey and I are rushing sororities on Sunday."

"Be careful," Mum admonished.

"OK, Mum," I replied. She couldn't see me roll my eyes, but I knew that she knew I was doing it.

"I can't stop being your mom just because you went off to college!" Mum pointed out.

"I know. How are you guys doing?"

"We're fine. Dad went to work and I had a bunch of errands to run. I got groceries, went to the dry cleaners, picked up Dad's prescription from the drug store and had to mail Meg her passport at the post office. Then it was time to cook dinner and talk to you!"

"Great," I murmured, laying flat on my back and putting my feet up against the wall. "Did you have a good day, Dad?"

"Same old," he replied. I smiled. Dad had never been much of a talker.

"Ok, I'm going to go do some work," I told them.

"Study hard!" Mum said. It sounded awkward to me.

I realized that it would take us awhile to develop phone mannerisms and routines with each other. I tried to start one of my own.

"I love you!" I said. going out on a limb.

"We love you too," Mum replied after a moment of pleased silence. I could imagine Dad looking at the phone with a puzzled, uncomfortable expression. We're not a very "I love you" kind of family. I mean, we do love each other, but we rarely say it.

When I got off the phone, I climbed down off of my bed. Casey and Erin were glued to their computers and didn't even notice me. I sat down at my coarse oak desk and wiggled my finger on the scratchpad to wake it up. Upon checking my email, I was delighted to find the following message in my Inbox.

From: BruinPoet@gmail.com
To: "Amy Callaway" <acallaway@ucla.edu>

Amy,
    Please send your Daily Bruin article submissions here, so that an actual human being can read them.
'Night!
John

This was encouraging. It would be helpful to have a personal connection with an insider at the paper. I wrote down the email address in my planner for later. Then I took out the notes and handouts that I'd collected during the day. I had planned to do some homework before dinner, but Erin and Casey had come home soon after I did, and we fell into chatting about our day, so no homework got done.

I glanced at my Calculus syllabus. It looked like I already had ten problems due on Friday. I hefted my calculus book onto my desk and flipped to the section that contained the first few problems. Derivatives of functions with multiple variables. I could theoretically get started on that now because that's what today's lecture was on, but I wasn't sure I had the mental energy to do it. I wearily pushed the book to the corner of my desk. Then I pulled out a blue sheet from my Anthropology class. For Wednesday, I had a reading assignment from a case study, which seemed much more palatable. I was about to put the handout down when the page numbers caught my eye. "Pages 4 to 101."

He doesn't mess around! I thought to myself. Lastly, there was also a reading assignment for my English class, but I needed to go down to Westwood and pick up the reader for the course first. I made a note to myself to go into town after class tomorrow.

I decided to try a bit of the calculus before launching into the long Anthropology assignment. With a sigh, I pulled the calculus textbook back towards me and began to skim the text. It seemed to make sense. When I started the actual problem set about twenty minutes later, I found myself struggling, revisiting the text, and consulting my class notes for help.

About halfway through the few problems I was going to attempt tonight, Casey flung herself back in her chair with an exasperated sigh. I looked over at her.

"What's up?" I asked.

"This guy," Casey replied, jutting her chin at her computer monitor, where there were several instant messaging windows open and flashing. "He won't let it go."

"What?" asked Erin from behind us. Casey and I turned our chairs so that Erin could be part of conversation.

"I hooked up with him at a party a few weeks ago, and now he keeps trying to ask me out, but I don't want to go out with him," Casey complained, combing her golden hair with her fingers.

"Why not?" I asked.

"He's too serious," she said. "He's some sort of engineer and I can tell that he doesn't want to *date* me. He wants a relationship."

"What's wrong with that?" Erin demanded.

"I just started college. Why would I want to trap myself a relationship? There are so many hot guys here, just waiting to be dated!" Casey pointed out.

"No, I mean with the guy being an engineer!" Erin clarified. I grinned.

"I guess I just don't think of them as being very sexy," Casey replied. "Except you, of course."

Erin batted her eyelashes at Casey and we all laughed.

"Anyway, he's got other problems," Casey continued. "He's my friend's brother too. I probably shouldn't have hooked up with him in the first place, but since I can't take that back, I shouldn't let it go any further. She would kill me when I broke it off."

"So why *did* you hook up with him?" I asked, curious.

Casey shrugged. "Drunk? Bored? He was the hottest guy at the party and I couldn't help myself?"

Erin shook her head. "I can't even *begin* to imagine your problems."

"What?" Casey cried, indignant that now she was being branded as odd. "You've never hooked up with someone you shouldn't have?"

"Not really," Erin admitted. "I've never hooked up with someone I didn't want to have a relationship with."

Casey considered this for a moment.

"But how do you know if you want to date them if you don't hook up with them first? How do you know if you have, you know, physical chemistry?"

"I can usually tell from far away," Erin replied. "I mean, I can tell if I'm attracted to them by hanging out with them and talking to them."

"Yes, but how do you know if they're a good kisser if you haven't kissed them?" Casey persisted.

"I guess it doesn't matter to me that much if he's a good kisser," Erin replied. The two of them looked at each other as if they were different species entirely.

"Amy, what do you think?" Casey asked, turning towards me.

"You can train a guy to be a good kisser," I replied.

"That's a lot of work," Casey commented. "But I guess you're right. OK, this guy is waiting. Let me blow him off real quick and get the whole thing over with."

She turned back to her computer screen and I turned back to multidimensional calculus. It was about ten o' clock when I couldn't do anything analytical anymore. I began to prepare for bed.

"So soon?" Erin asked, when I grabbed my shower caddy and pajamas.

"I'm not going to bed yet," I told her. "I have over a hundred pages of Anthro to read, so I was going to read in bed for a few hours. I figured it would probably put me to sleep, and I don't want to have to come back down to get ready again."

"You're so efficient," Erin observed, with admiration. I beamed.

When I was done showering and brushing my teeth, I climbed into my bed with my Anthro reading and snuggled under my cream-colored, down comforter. I tried to read a case study on the Dobe Ju/'Hoansi. These are the people of the African bush, the ones you see on the Discovery channel, who use clicks in their speech. The case study was pretty interesting. The Dobe Ju/'Hoansi would name their children after other people in their tribe, not necessarily related to them. And then the child would have this lifelong bond with the person they were named for. That person would take special care of them. The pairings were sort of random, in a way. The naming of the child was enough to obligate the one to the other. This was their way of creating an extra level of kinship or care within the tribe.

College was sort of that way too, I realized. We all lived next to each other totally randomly, just because the housing office set us up this way. But that was enough to obligate us to watch out for each other and become friends. It was strange to think that if the dice had landed differently, I would have a whole different set of friends and may never have met these people.

I was lying on my stomach, skimming page 40 when Brian came through the door, whistling.

"Hey Brian," I heard Casey greet him from below me.

"Hey ladies!" Brian said. "What's the word?"

"Just bumming," Casey replied. "What about you?"

"Don't want to do anymore work," Brian said. "So I wanted to come in here to see if anything interesting was going on in here. Amy, you're not going to bed already, are you?"

I sort of wished I wasn't in my jammies with my hair a wet and wild mess. But I supposed I would have to come to terms with occasionally being caught looking sub-optimal, being Brian's neighbor. I couldn't be dolled up at every hour of every day just because he might wander in from next door.

"I have a lot of Anthropology reading," I explained, looking over my shoulder at him. "So I thought I would do it in bed and be prepared to fall asleep any moment."

Brian came over and put his chin on edge of my mattress and grinned at me like a little kid.

"What?" I asked, and I couldn't help smiling back.

He shrugged.

"Nothing," he replied. "Why can't I just smile?"

"You can. I was just wondering."

"What does it say?" he asked, tilting his head sideways to read the cover of the case study.

I explained what I'd learned about kinship in the Dobe Ju/'Hoansi culture. He listened.

"Cool," he replied. "If *I* lived in that society, I would get myself named

Bill Gates, or whoever the richest guy in town was. Then he would take care of me."

I laughed.

"But everyone would have that plan and he would eventually not have enough money or attention to give to everyone," I pointed out.

"True. Hey look, I brought a picture of my dog for you to see."

He held up photo of a scruffy looking shepherd, with his head cocked quizzically to one side, but a happy grin across his furry brown face.

"He's so cute!" I couldn't help cooing.

The easy grin on his face grew wider. He was like a child showing his mom his first finger painting.

"No wonder you miss him. What his name?"

"Bobo," he replied, somewhat sheepishly.

"Bobo?" Casey echoed.

Brian looked embarrassed.

"I love it!" I said.

He beamed as he put the photo down.

"You look so comfortable, all tucked in. Just like the kids I used to babysit," Brian said.

"Did you sing to them?" I asked, feeling silly.

"Yeah," he replied. He thought for a moment, then a look of resolution came over him.

"OK, are you ready?" he asked. "Now this song isn't about you, it's just to an imaginary person, ok?"

I nodded, shutting my book, already amused. He cleared his throat.

"Mimimimi," he sang. I had to choke back my laughter.

He glanced at me and suppressed a smile. Then he continued singing.

"Doooooo your ears hang low?

Do they wobble to and fro?

Can you tie them in a knot?

Can you tie them in a bow?

Can you throw them o'er your shoulder

Like a Continental Soldier?

At this point, Casey, Erin and I were doubled over. Casey's face was bright red and she laughed in spurts. Erin had a tear running down her cheek.

"I didn't know you were supposed to throw Continental Soldiers over your shoulder," I gasped, when I could finally speak.

"Sounds kinky!" Casey commented from below.

"That was awesome, Brian!" Erin said, clapping.

Brian took a little bow.

"Glad to be of service," he said. "Have a good night!"

"Goodnight!"

After I finished most of my reading and got Casey to shut off the light, I lay in bed and thought about boys some more. Brian held doors open for me, said all the right things and was adorably goofy. I could never tell if I was imagining things or not. You know how when you like someone, you pay extra special attention to everything that he does and every gesture becomes exaggerated in your mind? Sometimes, I was sure there was some chemistry between us, but other times, I'd remind myself that he'd never crossed the friendship line and I was just inventing signs that weren't really there. Did I even want something to happen between us? I still wasn't sure, but I knew that I liked having him around.

Jeff was miraculously still flirting with me, and he was definitely a hottie. He was more aggressive, more confident and very... masculine. I could tell by the way he IMed me and the way he interacted with his frat brothers. He was commanding. They respected him. Many came up to us before "the incident" that evening to knock knuckles with him and to say hi to me. It was very attractive.

Of course they both paled in comparison to Eric. I fell asleep to memories of carefree summer days.

4 "Get Pumped about College Sports"

Saturday morning, I woke up to a beautiful day. It's funny how just about every day is a beautiful day in Southern California, but it only occurs to you that it's a beautiful day when you're anticipating something important. The sun was streaming into our room and I lay blinking in my comforter cacoon. I rolled over and glanced at my roommates. Casey had pulled her pillow over her head. Poor girl- the sun was streaming right onto the part of the pillow where her face would have been. The only part of her that I could see was a tan arm hooked lazily over her comforter. Erin was curled up on her side like a little dormouse, with her shabby floral blanket half on the floor. I looked at my alarm clock. 10:03am.

The game started at 4pm. Today, the mighty Bruins were playing the Ohio State Buckeyes. This still meant very little to me. *But* it was hard to not get excited when the first question out of everybody's mouth over the last few days was, "Are you going to the game?"

Clearly, this was a college experience not to be missed.

I heard the deep inhalation of someone about to wake up. Casey yawned and opened her eyes.

"Morning!" I said.

"Morning, Sunshine!" she said, mocking me.

She leaned over the edge of her bed to look at Erin.

"Wake up, Sleepyhead!"

Erin groaned, turned over to face the wall and continued her slow, heavy breathing. Casey motioned me to come down from my bed. I threw the covers off and climbed down from my bed. I met her on the floor. She acted out pouncing on Erin. I stifled a giggle. She put up her pointer finger... two fingers.... three.... JUMP!

We both leapt onto Erin's bed. Casey was shaking her and I was on my knees, bouncing up and down on the mattress, causing the rusty springs to squeak.

"Skee- skawwww... skee ... SKAWWWW."

All of the racket and the motion jolted Erin out of her sweet slumber.

"*Oh my God!*" Erin cried, pulling the blankets over her head. "You guys are *crazy!*"

"Wake up! Wake up! Wake up!" we chanted, laughing.

"You guys are *awful*," Erin groaned, through her blanket. We continued bouncing and laughing on the bed.

We heard rapid knocking on the door and looked at one another. Who would be knocking on a Saturday morning? Casey swung her long legs over the edge of the bed and got up to answer the door. Sean and Chris were standing there in sweatpants and ratty t-shirts, looking over her shoulder at Erin and me.

"What the…" Casey asked.

"We heard you guys jumping on the bed and thought you might be having a pillow fight in… your lingerie," Chris announced. "We wanted to watch."

Sean guffawed. "Chris was hoping you were having a pillow fight *naked* and he wanted to *participate.*"

Chris grinned, showing all of his teeth.

"Whoa, boy! We're going to have to drain some of that testosterone out of you," Casey said, rolling her eyes and pushing them both out into the hallway.

She shut the door.

"We'll meet you for brunch in half an hour!" she yelled through the door. "Don't go back to sleep!"

"Wow! They can hear everything through these walls!" I said, after we heard their door shut again, suddenly feeling very exposed and self-conscious.

"No, I think it's only early in the morning," Casey said. "I never hear them playing video games or talking on the phone at night. I think it's because we're doing stuff in here too."

I nodded. "What are you guys wearing to the game?" I asked.

"Duh! What else would I wear?" Casey paused for dramatic effect, hands in her closet. "The craziest UCLA clothing I own!"

She pulled out navy sweatpants with gold-embossed "UCLA" letters down one leg, a gray UCLA t-shirt and a white UCLA sweatshirt with baby blue felt letters.

"Won't it be too hot to wear a sweatshirt?" I asked, motioning to the window.

"No, it will get cold at the Rose Bowl when the sun goes down," she said. "I've gone with my parents before."

I was envious of Casey the same way I was of Lauren's childhood friends. There were stories that they would share with Lauren that I would never be a part of. In this same way, Casey and UCLA went way back. I could see the allure of attending the same college as your parents- being a part of the school and having the school be part of you even before enrolling.

I didn't have nearly as much UCLA paraphernalia as Casey, but I did have a baby blue T-shirt with "UCLA" written in gold script across the front. Mum and Dad bought it for me when I sent in my Intent to Register. I laid it on my chair. I noticed that Erin looked troubled.

"What's wrong?" I asked her.

"I don't have any UCLA stuff yet," she said slowly. "I haven't had time to stop by the student store."

"Borrow mine!" Casey offered.

She tossed Erin blue t-shirt with a Bruin baring his teeth on the front and "UCLA" on the back. And everything was happy again. The three of us gathered up our bathroom caddies and headed to the girls' bathroom to wash up. I was very cheerful. We were all getting along so well and having a great time. Wouldn't it be perfect if we wound up being the best of friends? I felt a little guilty about betraying Lauren and my high school girlfriends this way, but wasn't that part of college? Making new friends?

On the way back to the room, Casey slammed on the boys' door.

"Wake up, lazy asses!" she shouted through the door. "Or else we'll leave without you!"

We heard a bed squeaking and some incomprehensible muttering as someone climbed out of bed. Further down the hall, a door opened and Sarah waved at us. She was already dressed and ready to go.

On the way into our room, we stepped carefully over Casey's shoes, which outnumbered mine and Erin's put together at least five to one. I thought I heard Erin sigh.

"We're going to get so wasted tonight!" Casey announced.

"What if we lose?" I asked.

"What do you mean?" Casey looked at me blankly.

"I mean, we'll get wasted if we win, but what will we do if we lose?" I clarified my question.

"If we win," Casey explained, "we drink. If we lose… we drink. So really, it's not that hard. It just affects how happy we are when we drink."

"How did you celebrate when you were a kid though?" Erin asked. "You guys didn't drink when you were five, right?"

"Well, no," Casey replied, looking like she had to drag memories out from the very far reaches of her mind. "I think we went out to dinner after games whether we won or lost. Same idea."

I laughed. "Was it *that* long ago that you started drinking?"

"I think I started drinking when I was fifteen, maybe fourteen."

"*Fourteen?*" Erin and I said in unison.

"Yeah! When did you guys start drinking?"

"Just in this past year," I said, leaving out the fact that you could count the number of alcoholic beverages I had had on one hand.

Erin just shrugged. We both knew that she hadn't really drank prior to coming to UCLA. She was too straight-laced.

"It's going to be so fun tonight!" Casey paused a minute and looked at us like toddlers going to Disneyland for the first time.

"I'm *so excited* for you two!" she continued. "Your first UCLA football game! You're going to love it! I can't wait to see the looks on your faces when you go into the Rose Bowl. UCLA football games are awesome! Everybody gets so amped!"

I couldn't help smiling at her enthusiasm, though I was a bit nervous about getting wasted tonight.

"It'll be great!" Erin agreed with, what I sensed was also, reserved enthusiasm.

We met the boys and Sarah in the hallway. They were still yawning and rubbing their eyes. We hiked up the stairs to Reiber for brunch. The electricity in the air was palpable. The cafeteria was already filled with blue and gold. The boys and I went straight to the omelet station. Casey and Sarah headed for the waffle iron. Erin went to the fruit bar. I ordered an omelet with ham, mushrooms, tomatoes and cheese- my favorite. I could feel myself salivating as I watched the chef flip my omelet.

"So how much do you know about football?" Chris asked me.

"I don't know. The basics," I replied, disinterested.

"What does the linebacker do?" Sean challenged me.

"I don't know. Do I *need* to know that?"

"Yes!" Chris insisted. "We have to teach you *everything* or you're just going to embarrass us."

I snickered. "You guys embarrass me all the time, but *I* don't try to teach you to behave better."

"That's because you like it," Sean said, proudly. "You think we're funny."

"I do not," I replied, cursing my lips for twitching as I tried not to smile. "You're just beyond reform."

"She loves it when we embarrass her," Sean told Chris.

To my horror, he started doing some sort of jig while standing in the omelet line, lifting his knees up and kicking his heels.

"I luuuu - uuuvv Ammm-mmmmy," Sean sang out, completely off-key. "I luuuuu-uuuvv Ammm-mmmmy."

Chris laughed. He put his index finger on the top of his head, crossed his eyes and staggered around in a circle, singing along with Sean.

I covered my face in mock humiliation. How did I wind up living with these two goons? When my omelet was finished, I thanked the chef and fled the scene, looking for the girls. They were already sitting at a long table, watching the guys throw any last shred of dignity to the wind in the middle of the crowded cafeteria.

"Did you dare them to do that?" Sarah asked, looking mortified , between bites of whipped cream drenched waffle.

"No. They said I had to learn about football or else I'd embarrass them today and I told them they embarrass me all the time and then they started... *that.*"

I motioned towards them with my fork.

"They're like the little brothers we never had," Erin observed, also smiling.

Chris and Sean reached the table and put down their trays. Chris ran around to all the tables around us and grabbed salt and pepper shakers.

"Oh no," I groaned.

Chris wasted no time. He set up a line of salt shakers on one side of the table and an army of pepper shakers on the other. He bunched a napkin up into a little ball.

"Pay attention," he instructed with mock sternness. And he launched into his lecture on "The Art of Football."

I pretended to be exasperated, but I actually thought he did a pretty good job of explaining it.

Afterwards, we brought our dirty dishes and silverware on our trays to the conveyor belt of tray holders and deposited them there. Then we followed Casey to her car in the parking structure beneath the suites. We piled into her black SUV. I smiled at the sticker splayed across her rear bumper that read "Beverly Hills Princess," in hot pink script.

"OK, first the grocery store," Casey announced, peeling out of her parking spot.

We stopped at the neighborhood Ralphs, where we had to take a parking ticket to display on our dashboard for as long as we were parked in the Ralphs parking lot.

"Only in Westwood," Erin muttered.

We got hotdogs, bratwurst, buns, ketchup, mustard, potato chips, Gatorade and cookies. When we got up to the checkout line, everybody looked at one another uncomfortably.

After a pregnant pause, Casey said, "I can put it on my credit card and you guys can pay me back."

We agreed to this. Then, we were on our way again.

The ride to the Rose Bowl went by quickly. Sean wanted to hear girl gossip.

"Who is everybody dating?" he demanded.

"Nobody," Casey replied from the front seat. "I'm still looking around, but I'll let you know when I find someone interesting."

"I have a boyfriend at MIT," Erin said. "We're high school sweethearts."

"For now," Chris muttered, under his breath. Erin hit him.

"What?" Chris exclaimed, rubbing his arm ruefully. . "A long distance relationship is not much of a relationship at all, especially if you're across the country from each other."

"That's not true!" Erin cried. "We tell each other everything and…"

"Can you make out?" Sean asked. He didn't even wait for a response. "If you can't, then you're just friends that say sappy things to each other."

Erin sputtered but couldn't formulate a response.

"Are you saying that a necessary condition for a relationship is being able to make out?" I asked, also appalled.

"Look, I'm just saying that I think long distance relationships are doomed from the start," Sean said. "What's the point? If you love each other after four years, then get back together after four years, but at least have normal relationships with other people during that time."

"But what if I don't want to have a relationship with anyone else because I only want to be with him?" Erin asked.

"That's such a chick thing," Sean said, leaning back into his seat. "Dudes would always prefer to have more options. What about you, Red?"

He looked at Sarah.

"I have a boyfriend at UC San Diego," Sarah said. "He was supposed to come up this weekend, but he decided to rush a frat and I think they have some sort of event tonight."

"Aren't you worried that he's going to sleep around," Sean asked.

"No," Sarah replied, defensively.. "He's not like that."

"Why'd he join a frat then?" asked Sean.

"He likes the guys in the frat," Sarah insisted.

"Sure… 'he likes the guys in the frat,'" Sean repeated sarcastically.

Sarah shot him a warning look. Sean shrugged.

"Do you really think girls are that interchangeable?" Erin asked, recovering from her initial shock.

"I never said you were 'interchangeable'," Sean replied. "We appreciate each and every one of you for the qualities that are unique to you. Isn't that right, Chris?"

Chris looked scared to enter the conversation, but he jutted his chin out as a non-committal agreement.

"Men are not meant to be monogamous. We're supposed to try to 'spread our seed,'" Sean continued, putting quotes around the last phrase with his fingers. "To be monogamous would be to admit that one girl is so much more attractive than all of the other girls that I'd be willing to forego... encounters... with all of them for her. I haven't met that girl yet."

I looked around. Casey looked amused, but didn't say anything. Sarah was turning beet red. It was probably a lot of work to refrain from smacking Sean. Erin's scowl was uncharacteristic in her otherwise sweet, shy visage.

"So does this mean *you're* not dating anyone?" I asked Sean.

"Why would I limit myself that way?" Sean asked. "She'd have to be a goddess for me to give up my chance at all you other fine women."

Sarah snickered loudly at this. I could hear Casey chuckling.

"I haven't met any goddesses yet," Sean continued, ignoring Sarah. He looked over at me.

"Are *you* dating anyone?"

"Not really," I replied cautiously. "I've been talking to this guy Jeff, but we're just kind of flirting online right now."

"How can you tell if he's flirting?" Sean asked. "The problem with IM is that you can't tell if he's joking, sarcastic or serious."

"That's true," Sarah piped up. "Before we were officially boyfriend-girlfriend, I hated talking to my boyfriend online. I would put myself out there. You know, say something kind of suggestive. And then he would just not reply for awhile. It used to drive me nuts! I didn't know what he was thinking. I didn't know if he was talking to someone else, if he left to go to the bathroom or what! It's so cryptic!"

"Yeah, it's so ambiguous. Makes it hard to tell if someone likes you that way," Chris said in a way that made me think he had experience.

"And, it makes it too easy for him to *sort of* like you," Sean said.

"What do you mean?" I asked, trying to dam up the flood of doubt that was about to be unleashed by my over-active imagination.

"Back in the day, if you liked a girl, you had to take a big step and pick up the damn phone. But now with IM, he can like you enough to IM you or leave a message on your wall, but not enough to call you. And he can be doing this with a lot of people at once," Sean pointed out, matter-of-factly.

"Great," I sighed. "I'm feeling real good about this…."

"Yeah," Casey added, not really addressing my comment. "And you can play all sorts of games on IM. I was away-message flirting with this guy that I met at soccer camp for weeks before I found out he had a girlfriend."

"You mean you guys were leaving up suggestive away messages?" Chris asked.

"Yeah!" Casey said.

"Well then he was flirting with *everyone* on his buddy list!" Chris hooted.

"No, we were playing this game, where we would leave song lyrics up on our away messages, but the song lyrics that he would put up would be in direct response to the song lyrics that I put up," explained Casey.

"And he had a girlfriend?" Sarah cried. "The nerve!"

"Whatever," Casey said. "I wasn't that into him. If it worked out, it would have been fun, but I had plenty of other interesting fellas around."

"Yah," Erin said. "I think IM is a terrible medium for starting a relationship. It's good for keeping up with a lot of people at once. And for keeping up with people you wouldn't call, like Sean was saying."

"It's also good for stalking people," Sean said, devilishly. . Sarah studied him warily.

"Note to self: don't leave locations on away messages," Sarah said and we all laughed.

I grew quiet. Was Jeff really playing me? It was true that I didn't know how many other people he was "IMing". Maybe I was being optimistic. I mean, what would a good looking, confident guy like Jeff want with a clueless freshman like me? I was mad at Sean for sullying my memory of our IM conversation. Then I was mad at myself for misdirecting my anger at the messenger.

Traffic got worse and worse as we approached the Rose Bowl and by the time we exited the freeway, we were barely moving. When we finally pulled into a parking spot, it was already 2pm.

"Wow! We don't have much time to tailgate!" Casey exclaimed as we all sort of fell out of her SUV. "Chris, will you grab the little propane grill in the back and fire it up? Girls, start unwrapping the meat. Sean, there's beer on the floor of the backseat wrapped in a towel."

"Yes, ma'am!" Chris yelled, saluting her like an army general. "You are so damn organized!"

"That's my kind of woman!" I added, not mentioning the state of our dorm room. We all marveled at the great planning. She had brought foil to lay over the propane stove. She had even brought a pair of tongs to turn the meat with.

Casey beamed. "I don't joke around when it comes to partying and UCLA football games."

"Where did you get the beer?" Sean asked, perplexed. "You didn't get it when we were at the grocery store!"

"I keep an emergency stash of it," Casey replied.

Erin and I exchanged a glance and grinned. Of course! Who didn't keep an emergency case of beer in their backseat?

Casey handed out the meat. Sarah shook her head when Casey got to her.

"I'm vegetarian," Sarah declared, confirming what I'd suspected. "I'll just take grilled cheese."

In record time, we were chowing on the hot dogs and bratwursts, drinking beer at varying rates. Sean and Chris were guzzling it. Casey and Sarah were drinking it casually, as if it were a soft drink. I noticed that Erin was sipping hers, as I was.

Beer just didn't taste good to me. It was bitter and sort of washed out tasting. But this is the sort of observation that should be kept to oneself during a tailgate.

As Casey and the boys got into the details of which players had experience and which ones were likely to buckle under pressure today, I looked around, soaking in the whole tailgating experience. It was a merry scene. There were cars in every direction, as far as the eye could see. Groups of people were clustered around grills and ice chests, laughing, talking, eating and drinking. Many of the groups had a very simple set up like ours- a blanket or two on the ground, one mini grill and a case of beers. Other groups, especially alumni groups, had incredibly elaborate set ups. Folks came with RV's, tents or canopies; lawn chairs; tables; full-sized grills; banners and flags; and even some TV's! The people who were watching TV or listening to blaring radios tuned into the pre-game coverage on ESPN. Between clusters of people, guys were throwing footballs and frisbees around, enjoying the day. Nearly everyone in sight was wearing some article of UCLA clothing including hats, jerseys and foam gloves with the huge #1 finger. Even the unsuspecting babies of alums, bewildered at all the hoopla, contributed to the fantastic mosaic of blue and gold.

At 3:30pm, Casey declared it was time to pack up and get moving towards the game. We started walking towards the colossal stadium , looking for the entryway stamped on our student tickets. Our search took us through enemy territory.

"Wow!" Sarah exclaimed as we waded through the sea of cars, trucks and RVs regaled in red and white. "These people live around here right? They didn't *all* drive here from Ohio, did they?"

"Actually, I'll bet a lot of them drove," Chris said. "Look at their license plates. They all say 'Ohio' on them."

"What about class?" Erin asked, unbelieving.

"Some things are more important than class," Casey told her.

Erin shot her a look.

"To *some* people, not me," Casey added. We all laughed.

Just as we spotted our entryway, we ran into a throng of Ohio State frat boys that wouldn't let us by. They were drunk from the looks of it. The pack leader was this very broad looking blond frat boy, wearing a string of chestnut-like beads around his neck.

"BUCKEYES! BUCKEYES! BUCKEYES!" they chanted, pumping their fists in the air.

"We are going to *kick* your *ass!*" the leader said, pointing at us. The Midwestern twang was heavy in his drunken voice.

"Those are some fighting words," said Chris, stepping up. You could feel the tension shoot up between us and them. I held my breath. I didn't want Chris to get into a fight. Casey pulled him back by his shirt collar.

"Let's see if your team can walk the walk," she told them, with a fake smile. "See you in the stadium."

The frat boys considered this for a moment, then moved to one side to let us pass.

"What the hell is a buckeye anyway?" Sarah asked them as we walked by. The question threw them into confusion for a minute.

"It's a nut," one of the guys piped up, rather stupidly.

"A nut?" Sarah scoffed. "Your mascot is a *nut*?"

"Yeah, this nut," the leader informed her, holding up his necklace. "Wanna know how we win?"

He glanced sideways at his buddies, who began to snicker and laugh.

"The girls rub our nuts... and then we score! Wanna rub my nuts?"

Without warning, Sarah lunged at him, a flash of fiery red hair and freckles. Sean caught her arm before she hit the guy and he pulled her back.

"Let me go! He just insulted me! That was *totally* inappropriate!" Sarah yelled, squirming to get loose so that she could run after the crowd of laughing frat boys.

Sean held on to her, repeating, "It's not worth it," until she was calm.

We continued walking towards our entryway, our moods having shifted in the last five minutes from good natured hope of winning to fierce competition.

As we passed through security and guards were confiscating anything that

91

could remotely be used as a weapon or vessel for carrying liquids, I was reminded of Meg's first year in college. My parents wanted her not to go to any football games because they were afraid of terrorism. After the September 11th disaster, my parents were concerned that a huge crowd of people would be a target for biological or chemical warfare. I tried to put the thought out of my mind, but I could see why they'd be worried. As soon as I entered the Rose Bowl, I knew that I was in the largest crowd I had ever experienced. After pushing and shoving our way into the student section, I finally looked up at the huge screen at one end of the oval stadium. The broadcasted attendance was 75,231!

Our marching band and cheer squads were out in full force. The leggy cheerleaders came out, doing cartwheels, high kicks and that spastic thing they do with their pom-poms. They were glowing. I wondered how it was that I could envy and scorn them at the same time. Beside me, I saw Chris leaning in towards Sean and pointing at the cheerleaders.

"Yeah, that one has the nicer ass, but the blonde one has the nicer rack *for sure!*" I heard Chris insist.

"If you want to talk about just cup size, the one on the end wins," Sean pointed out.

"But her face isn't as cute," Chris retorted.

I leaned away from them towards Sarah and Erin.

"The guys are comparing the cheerleaders according to cup sizes!" I reported.

"Ugh, boys!" Sarah sniffed. I nodded, disgusted.

"Please stand for the National Anthem," a voice boomed over the loudspeaker.

I marveled at the vastness of the rustling all around me as 75,000 people stood up from their clam chairs. On the other side of the stadium, a lady walked onto the field, dressed head-to-tow in gold sequins. She looked no bigger than my thumbnail.

As the sacred words, "O'er the land of the freeeeeee, and the home of the braaaaaaave" reverberated off of the stadium walls, I felt chills, followed by pride swelling up in my chest.

Soon after, the Buckeyes came running out onto the field to booing from all around me, and faint cheering from the other side of the stadium. They got themselves organized at their bench, making a big show of stretching, throwing the football around and strutting about with their chests puffed out like proud roosters. Then, the UCLA marching band played the UCLA Fight Song. Our football team ran onto the field to a heroes' welcome.

The game started with us, the Bruins, kicking off to the Buckeyes. One of the little figures in red caught the ball and began running up the field. We tackled him pretty close to the 50 yard line. An enormous roar rose up from around the stadium. Then everyone quieted down again as both teams set up for the first play of the game.

I couldn't help chuckling when I discovered that I was surrounded by countless coaches for our football team. Any time the team did something well, there rose a chorus of comments.

"That's my boy!" or "That a baby!" in concert with high fives, fist bumps and back pounding.

When they did something badly, the comments changed.

"You should have got that!" or "Do that thing where you put the ball in the end zone!" along with head shaking and swearing.

The Buckeyes failed to make it to the end zone after their fourth down, and so the Bruins got the ball. I watched with interest as the ball was hiked to the quarterback and the players scattered in a seemingly random pattern. Out of nowhere, a blue and gold clad receiver broke away from the cluster and took off for the other end of the field. The quarterback threw the ball heavenward, where it floated for what seemed like ages. 75,000 people held their breath. Red and white clad defenders were in hot pursuit of the quick receiver, but he was several yards ahead of them. He slowed for just a moment to ensure that he'd caught the ball securely and proceed to tear down the field with graceful, long strides into the end zone.

And suddenly, everyone remembered to breathe again. The crowd went wild. A wall of screams and cheers rose up.

I was giving everyone high fives and dancing to the taunting tune of our marching band, when something caught my eye. Someone, in the section right in front of us, was totally facing the wrong way, looking at us instead of at the field. He was backlit in the setting sun, but as I squinted, I could make out "SIE" on his t-shirt.

It was Jeff!

Still intoxicated by the last touchdown, I waved at him and he waved back. He took his cell phone out of his pant pocket and pointed at it. I made a large exaggerated shrugging motion because I didn't have his cell phone number. He pointed at me and held up his phone.

I suddenly caught on to what he wanted me to do. I held up nine fingers. He nodded vigorously and punched it into his phone. I held up four fingers, praying that no one else was paying attention to me. His frat brothers, standing around him looked up to see what he was looking at. I could tell that they were exchanging jokes and head nods. When I finished signaling my phone number to him, I saw him bend over his phone, texting.

Sarah, standing next to me, elbowed me lightly in the ribs and gave me a knowing smile.

"Is this IM Boy?" she asked.

I nodded, grinning from ear to ear, elated at how publicly he'd asked for my number.

I waited for the text message, as UCLA kicked off to Ohio State. The Buckeye receiver made it about 20 yards before one of our guys nearly flipped him onto his head. There was more cheering. I felt the vibration of my phone in my palm and looked down to see the long awaited envelop icon.

I eagerly opened it.

coffee tmrw nite?

I shut my eyes for just one second and reveled in the moment, game totally forgotten. I texted back:

what time, where?

Then I tuned back into the game to make the waiting go faster. The Buckeyes were 4th and 3. My phone vibrated again.

9pm *bux in wstwd?

I looked down and saw Jeff looking up at me with the most charming smile.

Be cute or be clever.

I stroked my chin and rolled my eyes upwards, pretending to be considering it really hard until I thought he'd been kept waiting long enough. Then I broke out into a huge smile and gave him two thumbs up. He gave me two thumbs up back and turned back around to watch the game. The rest of the game was a blur of blue, gold, white and red. Oh, and we won.

5 "Party and Drink"

That evening, all of campus was celebrating. At least, it seemed that way. We could hear the laughter and loud voices from a thousand parties echoing in the turnaround. Brian beat us back to campus because we'd stopped at Inside Out to pick up burgers for dinner. He had called me when we were on our way back from the game to see where we were. I asked if he wanted dinner from the burger stand and received an emphatic "yes!" So I got a cheeseburger with grilled onions for myself and a double cheeseburger for him.

Brian was as good as his word and had brought back huge bottles of vodka and whiskey from home. He hid them under the covers of his bed. Our RA had been careful to warn us not to drink in plain view out in the hallway because the building monitors would write us up if they caught us during their hourly walk-throughs. So after we finished stuffing our faces with the juicy, beefy goodness, we gathered in the guys' room and shut the door.

Seven people were not meant to occupy these dorm rooms at once and we certainly couldn't all stand up at the same time. Sarah and I sat down on chairs, Erin and Casey sat down on the lower bunk bed and the boys scrambled about, putting things away to make more room for us.

This was the moment I'd been looking forward to and dreading for weeks now. When Sean shut the door, I felt very anxious all of a sudden. Despite the levity in the room, there was an air of solemnity. I suspected this was the first "drinking for drinking's sake" event for others as well. Erin had gotten pretty quiet in the half an hour leading up to this point. Chris was trying a bit too hard to act like he knew what was going on, which made me suspect he probably didn't. Brian was cleaning off tables, beds and chairs so that we would have places to sit, with nervous energy. Casey and Sean carried on as if they'd done this every week for years. They probably had. Sarah was the only one who I couldn't read.

Everyone stood around Sean's desk, watching him pour shots of vodka out into red, plastic cups. Chris was putting together a play list on his computer to get us in the mood to party. When Sean finished pouring, he handed them all around and held up his cup for a toast.

"To the Bruins!" he said.

"To the Bruins!" we chanted, lifting our cups.

And then everyone threw their heads back and drank. I couldn't down the whole shot in one gulp. It took me two, so I tasted the vodka acutely. It had a bite and it burned mildly going down my throat. The taste clearly wasn't anything to get excited about. I didn't realize I was making a face until Brian pointed at me.

"That good, eh?" he asked and everyone laughed.

"Who wants seconds?" asked Sean, already unscrewing the cap of the whiskey bottle.

Everybody except Erin and me held out their cups.

"I'm going to pass on this one," Erin said. "I'm Asian. We lack the enzymes to metabolize alcohol."

"She's going to turn bright red in a minute," Casey said, validating her claim, and we all looked at Erin. Her cheeks began to flush and we couldn't tell if it was the alcohol or the embarrassment.

"Stop looking at me," she demanded, sheepishly..

"Amy, you want another?" Sean asked, holding out the whiskey bottle.

I racked my brain for a good excuse not to drink so rapidly, but I couldn't think of anything that wouldn't make me sound like a wuss. Whatever happened, I just didn't want to throw up. I finally lost my nerve.

"Sure," I capitulated, holding out my cup. "Hit me up."

"To college!" Casey shouted. "It's everything I thought it would be!"

"To college!" we all chanted back, laughing.

After a second's hesitation, I downed my whiskey and nearly choked on it. The sting spread quickly from my throat to my sinuses all the way down into my stomach.

A fit of coughing exploded from my chest. I wasn't the only one. Everyone shook their heads to shake off the bite.

"Whew! That burns!" Sarah cried. "Do we have any chasers?"

"Wow, that must have been *bad*," Erin commented, observing everybody's wincing and watering eyes.

"We've got juice next door," Casey said. "Come to think of it, we have OJ so we can make Screwdrivers." She popped out to retrieve them, while the rest of us tried to get the taste out of our mouths.

"So how was the game?" Brian asked us. "I had it on in the background, but I didn't watch all of it."

"Oh man, you missed a great game!" Chris said. He launched into a play by play of the game. It was literally a play by play. Sean interjected when Chris left out a play or didn't give a satisfactory analysis. Brian listened thoughtfully. . Meanwhile, Sarah, Erin and I began our own conversation.

"So, what did IM boy say?" Sarah asked.

"He asked me out to coffee tomorrow night!" I replied, lowering my voice because I didn't want Brian to hear. It turns out, I didn't have to worry about it because Sean and Chris were each trying to talk louder than the other to analyze the plays for Brian.

"That's great!" Erin said. "It's a date!"

"Well, I'm not sure. It *could* be a date."

"A training date!" Sarah repeated, laughing. "What are you going to wear?"

"I don't know. I hadn't thought about it yet." Then I changed the subject because I didn't want Brian to overhear this conversation. "When are we going to meet your boyfriend?"

"Well, he has a car with him at UC San Diego and he was going to try to drive up here every other weekend," Sarah said. "He didn't come up this weekend because of Rush stuff, so I'm hoping he comes up next weekend."

Casey showed up with the OJ. Sean shut the door behind her.

"Who wants a Screwdriver?" she asked.

We all held out our cups. Diluted with orange juice, the vodka didn't seem so intimidating. Furthermore, I could sip it slowly instead of being expected to down it. I was beginning to feel the familiar light-headed, giggly feeling.

"What about *your* boyfriend?" I asked of Erin, beginning to feel better about this whole drinking thing and getting chatty.

"I don't know when you would see him," Erin said, sipping her Screwdriver. "He only plans to fly home over winter break and spring break. For winter break, we'll all be home. Maybe his spring break is different than ours and he'll come visit then."

"How long have you guys been together?" Casey asked, joining our conversation.

"A year and a half," Erin said. "He asked me out after Winter Formal last year."

"Awwwww," Sarah cooed. "Are you worried about doing the long distance thing?"

"Well, a little," Erin admitted. "There's this girl there that's a family friend of his and I think that she likes him, so I'm a little worried. The good thing is that my friend from high school is there and she's going to watch him for me. She's really smart."

"Is she hot?" Sean asked, as the guys pulled up chairs to sit near us.

"That family friend or my friend from high school?"

"Your friend from high school," Sean replied.

"What's that got anything to do with anything?" demanded Erin. "I was just saying that she is really smart."

97

"Well, if she's smart, but she's not hot, *I* wouldn't be interested in her," Sean said, pouring himself another shot of whiskey. "Remember that whole conversation we had lunch about intelligence being inversely proportional to attractiveness?

"That's so shallow!" Sarah said, accusingly..

"Is it?" Sean asked, enjoying the indignation he was causing. "I'm biologically rigged to want my children to be attractive so that someone will want to mate with them and *they* can pass my genes on too."

"Well that wouldn't be a problem if other people weren't shallow as well," Erin shot back. "If everyone valued things other than appearance, it wouldn't be a problem at all. In fact our world would be a better place if people were attracted to smart people and nice people. Men are so shallow!"

"You're not telling me that you don't like cute boys?" Chris said.

"Well I do," Erin admitted. "But I think 'cute' encompasses personality and intelligence as well. I think that an 'unattractive' man is probably more likely to find a date than an 'unattractive' woman in this society. Women are looking for the whole package. They want someone who is attractive from a personality standpoint too."

"Bullshit!" cried Brian. "Look at how girls go nuts over movie stars! You don't see men screaming over movie stars."

"No, they just hang up posters of naked super models in their dorm rooms," I said, pointing at the buxom piece of evidence pouting at us from above Chris's desk.

"OHHHHHH!!!" Casey said, giving me a high five. We clinked plastic cups.

"Actually, I think girls go nuts over movie stars because they confuse actors with the roles they play," Sarah said. "How many women fall in love with movie stars that play villains? And, how many women do you know who hang up posters of male models? Isn't that the epitome of only being interested in appearance? Men go nuts over models because they don't give a rats' ass about whether the girl has any personality or not."

"Maybe that's true," Chris conceded, still a little embarrassed about being called out on his naked girl poster. "I hadn't thought of that. I read a study saying that we're more visual than women are."

"But you perpetuate the problem yourself," Sean said. I noticed that he had trouble with the word "perpetuate." The alcohol was beginning to set in.

"What do you mean?" Erin asked.

"You *like* to be objectified!" Sean said.

"What?!" the four of us cried in unison.

"How so!?" Erin demanded.

"Look in your closet! When you go out on Thursday nights, what do you wear? You wear tight pants and low cut shirts and all this make up! You *want* to be looked at!"

We thought about this for a moment.

"Well maybe we've just realize that we won't get anyone's attention if we don't look like that," Casey said. "If this is how the game is played, I have to play along or I won't get any attention. But that doesn't mean it's not sad."

"The worst part of it is that you don't even look that good with make-up on," Chris said.

"Ohhhh, I don't think you know what you're talking about," Casey said, swaying in her seat a little. "Who looks better without make-up?"

Chris pulled a magazine out from under his bed. He pointed at the cover at a model, wearing nothing a red thong, sitting on a fire-engine red motorcycle. She wore dark, heavy eye shadow.

"This girl has make-up on and she looks *awful*," he said.

He flipped to an inside page at a girl who was sitting in a bathtub with all of her money parts covered in soap suds.

"She is not wearing any make-up and she looks beautiful," he announced. Sarah snatched the magazine from him.

"You think she's not wearing any make-up?" she asked him, her voice growing loud in disbelief.

Chris shook his head.

"This girl has so much make-up on, you could probably scrape it off her face!" Sarah exclaimed. "Look at her lips. See how they're all shiny like that? That's not natural. She's wearing lip gloss. And see her eyelids. Here, look at my eyelids."

Sarah closed her eyes and pointed at her eyelids.

"See how they are skin colored? *Look* at her eye-lids. They are all shimmery and purple. Does that seem natural to you? That's make-up!"

Sarah shoved the magazine back at Chris, who looked as if she had shattered his fantasy world and was grinding the splinters of it under her heel. He tossed the magazine back under his bed.

"Anyway," Sean said "What if we were just attracted to you based on your personality? Couldn't someone say that that was shallow? The mean girls wouldn't get any attention then. No matter what criteria you pick, it could be construed as 'shallow.'"

"That's not true!" Erin exclaimed. "I think it's shallow to judge on something that can't be changed, like appearance. If it's something that you can change, then everyone has an equal chance!"

"Why do things have to be equal in order for them to not be shallow?" Brian asked.

No one could answer him. It just seemed like that's the way it should be. Chris poured himself another cup of vodka and passed it around

"I just thought of something," Chris said. "Aren't women shallow to want men who have money?"

"No," Erin replied. "Money is the result of using your brain. Unless you inherit it, and I'm not interested in that."

"But that's just you!" Chris said. "Plenty of women like men with money, no matter how they get it."

"Well of course there are exceptions to every rule, but I'm just saying the average guy is more shallow than the average girl in picking a mate."

"I have some buddies who are dating ugly girls," Sean said.

"That's a terrible thing to say!" I groaned.

"I'll bet it's because they are putting out!" Caseys voice sounded sarcastic..

"See? So not all men are shallow! Women can help whether or not they are 'putting out'." Sean raised his cup to no one in particular and downed his vodka.

"What?" Sarah folded her arms. "That's a form of shallow too. They just want girls that put out!"

"How's that shallow?" Chris said. "I could call you shallow for just wanting a man that showers you with flowers. If that's the case, girls are shallow too!"

We all sat dumbfounded for a moment. It was a bit of a ridiculous conversation, and we were all a bit tipsy.

"More drinks!" Sean uncapped the whiskey bottle again. "Amy, are you going to nurse that Screwdriver all night?"

I nodded. "I think I am."

"But I thought we were getting smashed tonight!" Casey protested.

"Let her ease into it," Brian said. I gave him a grateful smile.

"Awww, one more all around!" Sean urged us. "Come on, I've had six already!"

"You have not!" Chris challenged him. "You've had five! I've had five too!"

"Who cares? Why are you counting?" asked Sean.

"I've got an idea!" Caseys voice sounded thick. "Let's play 'Never Have

I Ever.'"

"How does that go?" asked Erin.

"Everyone takes turns saying something that they've never done," Casey explained. "For example, I could say, 'Never have I ever been to the circus.' And if you have been to the circus, you take a drink."

"Right on, let's start!" Sean rubbed his hands together. "Everyone have something to drink?"

We all nodded.

"Great, then I'll go," Sean continued. "Never have I ever eaten sushi."

There was general grumbling all around as all of us took a gulp of our drinks. I took a very small sip of mine, while Casey downed her whole drink and poured herself another.

"I can't believe you have never had sushi before!" Brian remarked.

"It's gross," he replied, sparking off a chorus of protests. "Go, Chris."

"OK, let me think for a minute. Never have I ever had my own room at home."

"Wow, another good one," Sarah commented, as all of us took another drink.

"Never have I ever kissed a boy," Brian said.

"Not even your dad or your grandpa when you were little?" Erin asked.

"Fine, on the lips," Brian added. The girls took a drink,.

"Let's not do gender ones," Sarah complained. "It just turns into a battle of the sexes then."

"OK," Brian agreed.

Sarah went next. "Never have I ever cheated on an exam."

Chris and Casey lifted their cups.

"Does it count as cheating if I was the one giving answers?" Sean asked.

"Yes!" Sarah said.

Sean shrugged as if bored and threw his head back. "I'm out," he announced, pouring himself more vodka. "Who else needs some?"

Chris, Casey and Sarah held out their cups for more.

"Amy, go," Sean told me.

I took a moment to think. "Never have I left the United States."

Everybody drank. I suddenly felt very parochial. *Everybody* but me had been out of the country?

"Good one!" Erin paused. "Never have I ever gotten past first base."

This caused a bit of uncomfortable shuffling and downcast eyes. Very reluctantly, I brought my cup to my lips and felt kind of dirty when I saw that Brian and Sarah left their cups untouched.

"You guys have *never* been past first base?" Casey asked, as if they were from a different planet.

"Hey, it's not a race," Sarah pointed out.

"First is just kissing, right?" Brian asked.

"I thought it was up the shirt." Chris frowned as if confused.

"No, it's kissing," Sean said. "Second is up the shirt. Third is down the pants."

"Wai, wha's a blow job?" asked Chris, slurring his words. "I though first was up the shirt, second was down the pants and third was a blow job."

"No no no," Sean said. "That doesn't make sense. This is all about what the *guy* does *to* the girl. There's a whole different set of bases for what she does to you."

"There is?" Casey asked. "I've never heard of that."

"Well, I just mean, you don't mix blow job into this set of bases." Sean clarified, impatiently. "We could google it."

"OK, I didn't mean to set off this whole big long conversation." Erin blushed. "Who's going next?"

We all laughed. I was still feeling self-conscious.

"I have never done it in a public place." Casey swayed in her chair.

She was met by six blank stares. No one drank.

"You know what I need?" Sean said. "A Kookie King cookie."

"Are they still open?" Brian asked. Sean's computer clock said it was nearly midnight.

"Yeah, they're open until one," Casey said.

"Let's go!" I was in favor of anything that would slow the pace of the drinking.

Plus, you could not go to UCLA and not love Kookie King . Even the most awkward and reclusive of math grad students frequented Kookie King . For a dollar, you scored a scoop of ice cream wedged between two fresh baked cookies of your choice.

"Alright, everyone gets one more shot for the road," Sean insisted. He picked up the whiskey bottle and poured everyone a shot, but Erin. I was prepared for the aftermath of whisky shot, so it was not quite as bad.

We all stood up in a tangled mess and made our way to the door.

"Everyone have keys, cards, wallets?" Erin asked.

"Yes, Mom!" Brian replied, grinning.

We walked merrily down the hallway to the elevator, where we shot each other knowing smiles, as if we were in on some big secret together. The cool evening air outside relaxed me, though it didn't stop the spinning of my head.

***

We turned down the street and the bright, inviting storefront of Kookie King came into view. I cowered inwardly as we walked by a homeless man, wearing a tattered winter coat that was worn through in some spots. His sunken eyes seemed to look through us and we ignored his outstretched hand, uncomfortably. The smell of fresh baked cookies wafted down the block. . There was a line out the door half a block long.

We got into line and Sarah returned to another topic that we had left hanging. "The reason why men objectify women is because they're addicted to sex."

"We're not *addicted*," Sean said. "Are you addicted to food?"

"No," Sarah replied.

"Of course not," Sean said. "But you get hungry and you like to eat yummy food."

"Oh my God, are you going to tell me that you need sex to live?" Sarah asked, a bit loudly. A girl and a guy in line before us turned around and stared at us.

"Well, no, but I think that for men, wanting sex is ana... analogous to being hungry," Sean explained. "It's a biological urge that we can't help."

"I don't believe you," Sarah said. "I need a second opinion. Chris, Brian, is this true?"

"Actually, that's a pretty good description of it," Chris said. Sarah looked at Brian.

"More or less," Brian mumbled, trying to keep his voice down.

The smell of cookies was making my mouth water. We edged closer to the front of the line.

"The problem is not that you have urges," Erin spoke up. "The problem is how you manifest them. I hate it when guys gawk or whistle at women in public. You can be hungry, but there are socially acceptable ways to show it. When I get hungry, I don't gawk at food or say, 'I can't wait to get my mouth on *that* piece of steak!'"

She said the last part so lasciviously that we all burst out laughing.

"That's such a good way to put it," I said. "It's ok to have the urges but you don't have to make the rest of us feel uncomfortable!" *Wow, the word "uncomfortable" has a lot of syllables in it.*

"We don't *all* act like that," Brian said.

"That's true." I nodded. "Not all guys are like that."

"But enough of them are," bemoaned Sarah.

"Awww, lighten up," Sean said. "Why's it always a problem with men? I think the problem is with women. They can't separate love and sex. If they could just realize that we are perfectly capable of loving somebody and being attracted to other women at once, I think we'd all get along great!"

"I can separate love and sex!" Casey was drunk. Even as she stood, she was swaying slightly; her words came out slurred.

"Really?" Chris egged her on. "How did you learn to do that?"

"It's not hard, I've had sex with guys that I've just randomly met at clubs, but didn't really care about. And I didn't sleep with the one guy that I was in love with during high school."

"Why didn't you sleep with him?" asked Chris.

"It changes the relationship. It's sweeter before you have sex," she said simply.

"Next!" the guy at the cash register called. Sarah went forward to order her ice cream sandwich.

Cinnamon sugar, oatmeal raison, chocolate chip, white chocolate chip, white chocolate chip with macadamia nuts, double chocolate white chocolate, peanut butter, M&M.

"Wow, I'm in heaven," I said aloud, without realizing it. Brian heard me and laughed.

"What'll it be?" the guy at the counter asked.

"Ice cream sandwich with white chocolate with macadamia nuts, chocolate chip and vanilla ice cream. No, wait, cookies 'n cream ice cream."

"You got it."

It was the best ice cream sandwich I had ever had.

*****

We returned back to the dorm room after cookies. No longer able to sit in her chair, Casey came over to the bed and fell onto Sarah. It was a domino effect. Sarah fell over onto me and I fell over onto Erin and we dissolved into a massive giggling heap.

I was aware that I was thinking more slowly and had to make more of an effort to speak. It felt like everything was slower, simpler somehow. And, I distinctively felt more cuddly. Apparently everyone was. Sean and Chris wasted no time falling on top of the heap.

An upbeat dance song came on and all the girls began belting it out, joyously. Casey freed herself from the people pile and started dancing on a chair. Erin looked worried.

"She's going to bite it," Chris observed, voicing Erin's concern.

"Hey Casey!" Sean said.

"Wha?" Casey tottered on the chair, but regained her balance.

"Can you touch your elbows behind your back?" Sean asked, mischievously.

"Mmm, I dunno!" Casey stuck her elbows out to the side, then arching her back in an attempt to try to touch them behind her back. She struggled with it for a few minutes, with the boys gaping at her before the rest of us put two and two together.

"Stop! They're just trying to get you to stick out your chest," Sarah explained, hitting Sean upside the back of his head.

"Damn." Sean rubbed the back of his head. "She blew my cover."

"Ass," Sarah said disapprovingly, and then giggled. "You're so bad."

"Do you guys want to watch a movie?" Brian changed the subject.

"Yeah! Put on something funny!" Chris shook his rear end to the music.

I fell back in the bed, laughing and clapping.

Brian popped a DVD into his computer and the climbed carefully onto our human heap. We all moved and shifted over the course of the movie in an attempt to get comfortable. Casey fell asleep with her head in Sean's lap on the bottom bunk. Chris, Erin and Sarah climbed to the higher bunk for more space and were lying on their stomachs, all in a row, watching the movie. Brian and I stayed in the lower bunk with Sean and Casey.

Part way through the movie, I rested my head against his shoulder. If he objected, I could blame it on the whiskey. I felt him stiffen for a moment, trying to decide what to do next. And then I felt his cheek rest on the top of my head.

*****

I was cold and my pillow was all messed up. And something was digging into my hip. I reached for my covers, but couldn't find them. Finally, I gathered up the resolve to crack an eye open reluctantly and found myself looking right at Brian, who was a couple of inches from my face, fast asleep. It was not my pillow that was messed up, but rather Brian's bony arm, which I'd been sleeping on. I lifted my head and looked around. Casey was still asleep at the foot of the bed. Sean had fallen asleep sprawled out on the floor.

A freckled hand dangled off the bunk bed above us and I knew at least Sarah was asleep up there.

I had fallen asleep on my left hip, where my keys were lodged in my tight jean pocket. Slowly and carefully, I got out of bed to avoid waking anybody up. I was still a little dizzy, and I nearly lost my balance as I stepped over Sean to let myself out of their room.

Erin had made it successfully into her own bed and was sleeping soundly. Her alarm clock said it was 4am. I thought about changing into my jammies but decided against it, threw my keys on my desk and climbed into the bliss of my own bed, where I could stretch out luxuriously. I slept on and off until morning.

I woke up again at 9am. My throat was parched and the bright sunlight seemed to bore straight through my eyeballs into my throbbing brain. I pulled the covers over my head, hoping to slip back into painless slumber. *So this is a hangover,* I thought, still in a fog. I heard clicking noises and thought that it was all in my head until I peeked out from under my covers and saw Erin typing away at her computer.

"Morning," I croaked.

"Hi Amy!" she said cheerfully.

"How come you're not hung-over?" I asked, holding my head between my hands.

"I didn't drink that much last night. Here," she said, handing a Gatorade up to me in my lofted bed.

"Thanks." After downing the whole thing, I felt a little better.

"Casey's still in their room," Erin said. "Should we go get her?"

"Naw, let her sleep. I'm going to get cleaned up."

I slipped out of bed and grabbed my shower caddy. Now that I had eased the sore throat and headache a little bit, I began to notice all of the other ways I felt completely awful. My stomach was a bit queasy still and I just felt dirty and disgusting all around. Yesterday's make-up rested in a greasy layer on my face. It felt like there were sweaters on my teeth and all of yesterday's sweat and grime were caked on my body. My hair was still pulled into a ponytail and my scalp ached when I took out my scrunchie. The unforgiving bathroom mirror revealed that I looked about as good as I felt. I felt tired and sluggish all over, but I forced myself to get into the shower and scrub down. After brushing my teeth and my hair, I felt much better.

When I got back to our room, Casey had materialized. She was sitting on Erin's bed with her head in her hands as well.

"Are you ok?" I asked, rubbing the top of her back supportively.

"I feel *awful!*" Her voice was raspy. "I'll be fine. Just need to keep

106

drinking water."

Erin handed her a Gatorade and she sipped.

I rummaged through my closet for today's fashion statement.

"Oh no!" Erin yelled.

I wheeled around. Casey had grabbed the trashcan and was vomiting into it. We stood and watched her helplessly. I walked over and held her hair back for her. When she was finished, face scarlet and eyes watery, she fell over in Erin's bed.

"Are you ok?" Erin's dark eyes grew large in her small white face.

Casey nodded, but didn't open her eyes. "I just need to lay here for awhile."

Erin and I exchanged a look. This was exactly what I never wanted to happen to me. How on God's green earth could she drink so much when she knew she had *this* coming in the morning?

The queasiness in my stomach had increased to nausea after watching her puke. I sat down at my computer and tried to calm my stomach.

I will not throw up. I will not throw up.

I kept drinking Gatorade and felt much better. Casey had dozed off on Erin's bed. Just as well. Erin was IMing, probably with her boyfriend, so I just surfed the web, mindlessly, skimming my friends' profiles. Eric hadn't posted to his in days. I wondered what he was up to. Maybe he was getting drunk and romancing some lucky girl out there. It was a sad thought. I probably should have done some Anthro or English reading, but I couldn't bring myself to think just yet.

A knock on the door startled us all. Since I was nearest, I opened it to find Brian standing there, rubbing his eyes and yawning. I wondered how much of last night he remembered.

"We're all up. Wanna go to brunch?" he asked.

"What time is it?" I asked.

"It's 11:00am," Erin said. "I'm starved!"

"I don't think I'll eat much, but I'll go," I said. "Should we wake Casey?"

Brian shrugged. I shook Casey's arm, timidly.

"Case, we're going to brunch. Do you want to come?" I whispered.

She grunted.

"OK, I'll bring you back something."

I grabbed my keys. Erin and I followed Brian out into the hallway.

"Wow, how much did she drink last night?" Brian asked, when we were safely out of hearing range.

"A lot," I said. "I didn't count, but I know she kept on downing whiskey even after the rest of us stopped."

Sarah and the boys were waiting in the hallway. Everybody looked horrible.

"What a night!" Sarah rubbed her temples. "I couldn't get up for my run this morning! Where's Casey?"

"Oh, she's sick," Erin said. "She's still sleeping."

"Poor thing," Sarah said, as we walked down the stairs and towards the dining hall, squinting in the sun.

"I know. I hope she feels better. We have to go to Rush this afternoon. How are the rest of you guys holding up?" I asked no one in particular.

Chris moaned. "My head is killing me!"

"Yah, I need coffee." Sean pulled his hood over his head.

In stark contrast to yesterday, we did not dash off in all directions to pile our plates with food this morning. I shuffled slowly to the bakery island, where nothing looked appealing except for the blandest baked good I could find- a piece of plain toast. I picked up a short stack of pancakes and a glass of water. I found Sean, who really had only gotten a cup of coffee and was staring off into space. Erin was the only one who had a normal breakfast of omelets, pancakes, bacon and waffles.

"Oh my God, do you know what I heard?" Autumn's voice rose from behind me. I turned around with some difficulty to look at her.

"What?" Sarah asked, trying to look interested.

"Do you know that girl that lives upstairs with the pink streak in her hair?" Autumn asked, lowering her voice to a juicy-gossip appropriate level.

Everyone shook their head.

"She thinks she was *raped* last night," she reported with self-importance.

"What do you mean, she thinks?" Sean asked, furrowing his brows together. "How can you not know something like that?"

"She woke up on a bench next to the track this morning and didn't remember anything about last night," Autumn said, seeming to take delight in the horror that was spreading across our faces.

"What happened?" I asked.

"She went to this house party last night and started talking to this guy. Then she got really sleepy. She thinks he slipped her some kind of date rape drug. She says... parts... hurt, so she suspects she was raped. She's going to see a doctor now."

108

Erin, Sarah and I looked at each other, alarmed.

"How do you know all this?" Chris asked.

"I know her roommate," Autumn replied.

"Why was she alone?" Erin asked, in a small, frightened voice.

"She went with some people from her hallway, but they probably thought she *wanted* to spend the night with that guy, so they just left her there."

"That is freaking scary." Sarah shook her head. "Don't you guys ever leave me at a party like that."

"You have to keep an eye on your drink," Sean told her, matter-of-factly. "He wouldn't have been able to slip something in her drink if she had been watching it."

After brunch, we headed back to the dorms. Casey met us in the hallway. I handed her the muffin I snuck out for her.

"You know what we need to do?" she said, between mouthfuls of muffin. "We need to go to Cancun over Spring Break. That's the ultimate college trip!"

"I can see that someone is feeling much better," I joked.

"Seriously! Don't you guys think that would be awesome?" she asked.

"Totally!" Sean agreed. "A week of sex and booze! I can't think of anything better."

Spring break in Cancun! I imagined lying in a bikini by a poolside, sipping pina coladas from a coconut. That *had* to be part of the whole College Experience!

"You know what else we should do?" Brian asked. We turned to look at him.

"We should play laser tag…"

"In the sculpture garden," I finished for him. We grinned at each other, acknowledging the slip up I made the last time I tried to finish a sentence about the sculpture garden for him.

"Brilliant!" Chris yelled. "Let's do it! Sean and I will look into it."

We headed back to our respective rooms for some quiet time. I noticed that Casey had left the trashcan with her vomit in our room and it was beginning to reek. She showed no sign of attempting to deal with it.

"Casey, are you going to clean this up?" I asked.

"Can you help me? I don't do vomit."

I held a plastic bag open as she dumped in her chunky orange-and-white vomit. I sent her to the bathroom to rinse out the trash can, while I walked down to the trash shoot and threw away the bag, trying not to gag the whole time. When Casey returned from the restroom, she looked suddenly anxious.

"What time is it, Amy?" she asked.

"Two, why?"

"We only have an hour to get ready for Rush!" she said, flinging open her closet door. She flicked one hanger after another like someone flipping through a giant dictionary.

"What are you going to wear?" I asked, walking over to my own closet. I tried to remember what nice outfits I had brought.. I had no idea how one would dress for sorority rush.

"It has to be something that you would wear to a country club. A nice sundress... maybe white pants with a cute top. You might be able to get away with jeans if you have really high end ones." Casey pulled out an example of each one in turn.

I frowned. I had a sundress, but I was sure it wasn't right for the occasion. It was something I wore to my cousin's wedding and it was too... floral. I didn't own a pair of really nice jeans or white pants, though I did have a white linen tea length skirt. I'd been afraid to wear it all summer for fear of getting it dirty. But it seemed like now might be the time to bite the bullet and wear it. Besides, how dirty could it get at a sorority meet and greet? I pulled it out of the closet and held it up for Casey.

"Does this work?" I asked her. She stopped just long enough to glance at it with a critical eye.

"I guess that's alright," she said. "It's kind of long. You don't have anything shorter? You want to show some leg. It's really warm out."

"You did *not* just say that! I want to show some leg? Why?" I laughed.

"Suit yourself. You will represent one of these sororities some day. They want to see that you're good looking and a good dresser."

I didn't reply, but I thought this was sort of extreme. I wanted the girls at the sororities to like me, and I wanted them to think that I would represent the sorority well, but was I supposed to feel like a dog at a dog show? Would they want to look at my teeth as well?

I donned the linen skirt and the girliest top that I owned, a fitted navy top with scooped neck and capped sleeves.

Casey was already on to her make-up, moving between her palettes, jars and applicators.

Make-up was still a fairly novel concept for me. I mean, I wore make-up to dances and special occasions in high school, but I didn't like to wear a lot of it, and I didn't really experiment with it. So, I did what I always did. I rubbed in a layer of cover-up to smooth out the splotches in my skin. I gingerly drew a brown line across my eyelid just above my eye lashes. And I slicked on a layer of lip gloss to make my lips shiny. I looked in the mirror and thought I looked alright, like a tidier version of myself. My new clothes were still stiff and bright. I slipped on brand new brown mules that didn't look like I'd gotten them from a clearance rack, which is precisely where I had spotted them.

"How does Rush work?" Erin asked, watching us from her desk.

"Well, today, every girl is going to meet with all of the sororities that have houses on campus," Casey said, pausing to feather up her long lashes with the mascara brush. "Then, we will find out which houses liked us. Next time, we will meet with just those houses.And it keeps narrowing down like that until you find one house that wants you that you like. Then that house takes you out to do all sorts of fun stuff to try to persuade you to pledge. It's awesome."

"How are we going to meet with every house today?" I asked, wondering if I'd set aside enough time this afternoon in my schedule.

"We spend fifteen minutes with each house,.I mean, you're not going to be able to talk to more than one or two girls in each house, but that should be good enough for both sides to get an impression, you know?"

"What if no sorority wants us?" I asked, concerned.

"That's ridiculous. They will *love* us."

"Why are *you* rushing all of the houses?" I asked, remembering something all of a sudden. "I thought you wanted to join the sorority your mom was in."

"I do. But I want to make sure that no other house is way better and I want to check out the competition. Ready to go?"

I nodded. Casey looked amazing. She had changed into a really cute sundress. It was a blue and white striped, empire waist dress that fell just above her knees. She grabbed a white patent leather purse and slipped into matching strappy heels. So this was what an old school Cadillac parked next to a trendy convertible BMW felt like.

"OK, wish us luck!" Casey called over her tanned shoulder to Erin.

"Good luck!" Erin said, blowing kisses and giggling.

Casey and I set off. I didn't have to do much talking because Casey never stopped for a second.

"Oh my God, I'm so excited for Rush. There are girls from my high school in almost every house, so I can get the scoop from all of them. That way, you won't have to worry about them pulling the wool over your eyes. I've totally got your back. I'm wondering if I can not commit to my mom's house right away, just so I get the opportunity to get closer with more girls and go to more events, you know? They're always nicer to you before you pledge officially. It's totally like dating. Once someone commits to you, then you start to take them for granted. Casual dating is much better. They're still trying to get you to commit, so they're on their best behavior. I don't know how realistic it is to pretend like I'm not going to join my mom's sorority though because everyone knows that I'm legacy. I wonder how many legacy girls don't join."

Casey went on and on like this as we made our way all the way across campus towards Hilgard Street on the other side of campus. The sun shined down on the grand buildings of campus. The few souls that we saw were girls dressed in their best daytime "casual wear", also walking east across campus. It dawned on me that to an unknowing observer, we probably looked like well dressed lemmings being drawn magnetically towards... what? Towards instant acceptance, social status, and friendship?

I hoped so, though I recognized that there was something inherently paradoxical about trying to obtain things instantly that should usually take time to build.

Was I was the only lemming whose feet were killing her? It seemed like my heel could not stay in the place that it landed on my shoe and it was rubbing my heel raw. The sidewalk zigzagged unmercifully. Eventually we reached Hilgard Road and could see the beautiful sorority houses lined up along the road, all the way down the hill, like ladies in waiting. There was a white house with colonial style columns in the front, a salmon colored Spanish style house, a charming yellow cottage...

"What house do we start with?" I asked, squinting at the Greek symbols over the door of the house in front of us.

"We start at Iota Gamma Chi," Casey said, walking down the hill. I followed her and took note of the garden of sundresses spread out before us. Casey walked on to the lawn of the Spanish style house, where pairs of girls were already talking.

"We should split up," she instructed me. "That way, we can compare notes later. Go talk to a girl who isn't already talking to someone. I'll come find you when we have to move to the next house."

"OK," I replied, maneuvering around all of the sundresses around me.

A girl in a green and white sundress walked by and handed me a cup of lemonade. I was parched after the trek across campus on a warm day. I hoped there weren't sweat stains under my arms.

I found a slender brunette in a pink sundress with a white scroll pattern on it, standing near a hedge by the side of the house. Her big Audrey Hepburn sunglasses were perched on top of her head and she looked me up and down through long, dark lashes as I approached.

"Hi, I'm Amy," I said, extending my hand. She shifted her cup to her left hand and gave me an awkward, pansy handshake.

"Welcome to Iota Gamma Chi," she said in a voice more enthusiastic than how she looked. "My name is Brooke."

"Nice to meet you, Brooke," I replied. There was a pause.

"So where are you from?" she asked, tucking a wisp of sleek brown hair behind her ear.

"I'm from Irvine," I replied brightly. She nodded, but said nothing. So I added, "What about you?"

"San Diego." She shifted her weight and I noticed that she was wearing strappy white heels that looked like Casey's.

"It must be so nice to live in San Diego! My neighbors are from San Diego. I don't know their last names though. They're from Bonita, I think."

Brooke shook her head. "I don't know anyone from Bonita."

I nodded. "What year are you?"

"Third year," she replied. Another pause. "Are you enjoying school so far?"

I nodded. "It's been kind of crazy, adjusting to everything, but I really like my classes and my roommates."

"What's your major?"

"Undeclared right now," I replied, wondering how much of my life story I should disclose to this total stranger that I would only be talking to for... I glanced at my watch... for thirteen more minutes.

"You have *plenty* of time to decide,"

"What's your major?" I asked.

"Comm." She didn't elaborate, so there was another pause. I nodded and took a sip of water to buy myself some time.

"What's your sorority like?"

"Oh, it's great," she replied. "The girls in the house are really nice. We have so much fun together. The fraternities love us. We're the 'fun girls' on Hilgard. We're super active and... uh oh!"

She stopped abruptly and her entire body stiffened. I followed her eyes to a bee that was flying back and forth between us.

"Oh my God, I hate bees, I hate bees," she said, stepping away as the bee buzzed near her again. It landed on the rim of her cup. She shook her wrist up and down, but the bee was undisturbed.

"Go away, go away, go away!" she said. Without warning, the bee lifted off her cup and flew straight for her face. I would have expected the cup of lemonade to go flying up into the air, or maybe out to the hedges. It would, in fact, have been nice if it fell straight to the ground. But no, it flew straight at me and I watched in horror as it splashed all over my white linen skirt.

"Oh my gosh!" Brooke said, once the bee flew off and she saw the damage. "I'm *so* sorry. Let me get you a napkin!"

She disappeared into the house and came back out with paper towels. I tried to dab at my skirt. There were two problems here. The first was that I was wearing white underwear with blue dots on it, which had previously been invisible to the general public. And the second was that the yellow dye in the lemonade left a clear yellow edge that remained, even as the sun began to dry the wetness.

"What happened?" Casey's voice caused me to look up. I saw her walking towards me briskly, concern written all over her face.

"There was a bee on my cup and I accidentally threw it... on her," Brooke said.

Her initial detachment had melted and now she couldn't be nicer to me.

"You'd better pay for dry cleaning," Casey told her, not in a mean voice, but just as a matter-of-fact.

"Of course!" Brooke stammered. "I can go up and get money. How much will it cost?"

"Don't worry about it," I said, trying to keep things in perspective. "It can't cost that much. It was just an accident."

"Are you sure? I feel really bad about it."

"Badly," I corrected her before I could stop myself. It was automatic these days. Casey shot me an exasperated look.

"Yeah, it's fine," I said to Brooke. "Don't worry about it."

"OK," a girl called from somewhere on the lawn. "Move to the next house!"

Casey linked arms with me and we joined the mass migration up the hill to the next sorority house.

"What are you going to do?" she asked. "Do you want to go home and change?"

"By the time I walk back to the dorms and back here again, it will be half over. And my feet are going to fall off if I have to walk in these shoes any longer than I have to."

"But, it looks like..." Casey's voice trailed.

"I know, it looks like I peed on myself."

Half of me wanted to laugh and the other half of me wanted to cry. I tried to stay positive.

"You know, whatever. It's a funny story that I can tell when I meet girls from the other sororities. They won't forget me now, right?"

Casey looked unconvinced, but we continued to walk on to the lawn of the next house. This is about where Amy's Twilight Zone began. I talked to one or two girls from every single sorority. There must have been nine or ten

114

sororities. I lost count after five. Every single meeting started exactly the same way.

"What happened to your skirt?" the sorority girl would ask me, looking put off.

"One of the girls from Iota Gamma Chi spilled her lemonade on me," I would explain for the umpteenth time.

"That's terrible. Who was it?" she would ask, feigning concern.

"I think her name was Brooke," I would reply, feigning nonchalance.

The sorority girl would respond with either, "I know her. Ugh, she's such a party foul." Or "I don't know her, but IGC girls are horrible like that."

I would try to get on with the inevitable. "Well, my name is Amy."

Then she would play along and tell me her name. She would then follow up by asking where I was from.

Dreading the rest of the conversation, I would reply, "Irvine."

She would either play the, "Do you know so-and-so" game or say nothing in response.

I would attempt to keep the struggling conversation going by asking, "Where are *you* from?"

After we finished flogging that dead horse, we would move on to majors. We would talk about what major she was. She would ask what major I was. In spite of numerous opportunities to come up with a creative answer to this question, nothing satisfactory came to mind.

Finally, I would ask the most interesting question I thought they were capable of answering in this setting, "How is your sorority different from the other sororities?"

The responses that I received were not very encouraging.

"The girls here really take care of each other. No one will make you drink until you puke... Unless we're in Mexico. Or a Mexican restaurant."

"The girls here are so hot. Look at us. We're by far the *hottest* girls on campus. All the other girls know it."

"The girls here are so nice. We're not ho bags like the other houses. Frat guys respect us."

"The girls here are so great. We have so much fun together! And we really *do* community service!"

"The girls here have so much personality. Frat guys love us."

All I could do was pretend to be interested and drink lemonade. I received a new cup at every house. I didn't notice until the fifth or the sixth house when I suddenly had to use the restroom.

115

The petite blonde girl had just finished telling me how their house was the most athletic house when I asked if I could use the bathroom in their house.

"I don't know if we're supposed to let you."

"Please?" I begged, no longer worried about what anybody thought of me. This was an emergency.

"OK, follow me," she said looking around nervously.. I followed her up the stairs of a beautiful Mediterranean style house. The inside of the house was not as frilly as I expected. We walked past an enormous living room with a big screen TV and ample couch space. She led me down and hallway and pointed to a door.

"Thanks," I said.

"I'll wait for you here," she said. "I don't know if I'm supposed to leave you in here by yourself."

"Fine," I said, dashing into the bathroom.

As I was sitting on the toilet, I looked around the bathroom. It was very nicely decorated. There were pearl colored scrolls embossed on the creamy wallpaper. The shower curtains were forest green and matched the hand towels, the soap dispenser and the rug. I noticed a small wicker basket with plastic sandwich bags on the counter. There was a handwritten note on the side of the wicker basket facing away from me. I turned the basket so that I could read it.

In curly bubbly script, the note read, "Stomach acid corrodes the pipes, so please use a plastic bag and throw it in the trash."

Gee, I thought to myself. *One of these sororities should have told me, "The girls here are so normal. We don't throw up our dinners!"*

***

By the end of the afternoon, I staggered home with Casey, completely frazzled. Visions of cookie-cutter sorority girls in crisply ironed sundresses haunted my thoughts. I felt disappointed. Depressed, in a way. I was hoping to find girls that clicked with me, who were excited about school, extracurricular activities, life and me. Everyone seemed so fake.

I listened as Casey analyzed every one of the houses.. It was amazing that she could remember every girl she talked to at every house. She noticed what they were wearing, where they were from, what they talked about and where they partied.

"I can't believe that Chi Delta advertised itself as the athletic house!" she exclaimed. "Who joins a sorority on the basis of athletic ability? That wouldn't get you into any happening parties! If you wanted to play sports, you would just join an intramural sports team. And did you see her shoes? Some flats are ok, but those were *gross*."

I grunted in non-committal agreement.

"What houses did you like?" she asked.

I shrugged. "They were all about the same to me."

Casey stopped dead in her tracks and gaped at me.

"No way. They are so different. What do you mean?"

I understood that they varied in ways that mattered to her. They were all so far off my mark, it was like asking me which insect I wanted to cuddle with at night. But I couldn't very well tell Casey that. She was so enthusiastic about them.

"I guess none of them matched my criteria exactly."

"Well, who was the closest?"

I picked one out of the air, just to appease her and she went on with her analysis.

When we got back to our room, I didn't feel much like staying in there with Casey and her exuberance about Rush. I felt restless and I needed some love. I changed into jeans and a cotton shirt, grabbed my cell phone and keys and put my running shoes on.

"Where ya going?" asked Casey. "We just got back."

"Just need to take a walk. I'll be back in a few!"

I glanced into the boys' room and saw them all at their computers. I wandered down the stairs and moseyed into the courtyard, where a group of skaters were doing tricks that I was glad their mothers couldn't see. I hit "4" on my speed dial. *Ring... ring... ring... click.*

"Amy?" the voice on the other end was excited, which was exactly what I needed.

"Laur, how's it going?" I asked, smiling into the phone.

"I'm great! What's going on?" she asked.

"I'm feeling funny," I admitted straight away.

"Talk to me, babe," she said, sensing my angst with best-friend sonar.

"I don't know what's wrong with me! I think I'm homesick," I began. "I mean, nothing is *wrong* or anything. My roommates are nice. I've been hanging out with this group of kids in my hallway and everyone is cool. We went to the football game yesterday and had a good time. I even drank with them last night, but, but...."

"Everyone is still a stranger on some level," Lauren said, articulating my thoughts. "They're nice, but they don't *know* you. And you feel like you've always got to be on your best behavior so they'll think you're cool."

"Exactly," I said, relieved to hear it articulated. I told her about Rush.

"Wow, that sounds terrible. Don't do it, man."

"I have to think about it,. It's part of the college scene here. I want to be able to write about it in my article for Ives. How's yours coming along?"

"I'm not thinking about it until the end of the semester," Lauren said. "I'm not going to chase down experiences. I'm just going to write about what happens to me this semester."

That was a good strategy. It was very... Lauren.

"I miss you. And the girls. And Eric. And home. Sometimes, it just feels like I don't belong here."

"I miss you too, Ame, But remember how we were *so* ready to get out of there and start college? It'll be ok in a few weeks. It's just rough at the beginning. High school was too, remember?"

I muttered an incomprehensible reply.

"Let's talk about happy things. How was the football game yesterday?"

"Oh, it was fun," I said, feeling a little better.

It's amazing what a dose of well-intentioned sympathy can do.

"That guy Jeff turned around in the middle of the game and asked me for my number. Well, it was too loud and he was too far away to ask, but he held up his phone and kept pointing at me. So I held up my fingers to give him my phone number. And he texted me to ask if I wanted to get coffee with him tonight!"

"That's awesome. Are you stoked?"

"I am flattered. But I still miss Eric."

"I know, but you can't be stuck on him or you will never know what else is out there," Lauren said.

"Yah, I know," I muttered.

She was right.

"How's it going with soccer boy?"

"I think I'm in love," she said dreamily. "He's perfect! He's so cute and so smart. I never in a million years thought that such a guy existed. I get really nervous around him. He's really nice to me. I mean, he says hi all the time and talks to me in the hallway, but I don't think he's interested in me *that* way."

"Well, why the hell not? You're beautiful and smart!"

"Amy, everyone is beautiful and smart here. Even the squirrels."

"My neighbor thinks that beauty and brains are inversely proportional." I laughed.

"Wow, he *said* that to you?"

"He's a piece of work. He totally says these things for shock value, but it keeps things interesting."

"Listen, Ame," Lauren said, guiltily. "We're heading out to go watch a movie on the lawn. Can I talk to you later?"

"Sure," I said, trying to hide my disappointment.

"Are you sure?" she asked, concerned. "I can just meet them out there later, if you need to talk. I know it's hard with the time difference and the stupid daytime cell phone minutes."

"No, I'm fine!" I said, forcing myself to sound upbeat. I loved that she could read my mind.

"OK, love you!" she said.

"Back at you," I replied, as I had at the end of millions of phone calls.

I felt better after talking to her, but I wasn't fully satisfied. I flipped the phone open and held down "5". *Ring... ring... ring... ring... ring...click.*

"Hi, I can't take your call right now, but do your thing at the beep."

I shut my phone with a sigh and didn't know if I felt better or worse. I just needed to hear his voice again. The voice that made me melt instantly a million times over. I probably should have left a message. Now he'd see the missed call and think that I was stalking him. Oh well. Maybe, he'd get curious about it and call me back. I headed back towards my room.

When I got back to the hall, I noticed Chris's brown sauntering figure walking from one open door to the next.

"Whatcha doing? Selling Girl Scout cookies?"

"Do you have four quarters?" he asked, looking desperate and getting straight to the point. I had to think about this for a minute. I *had* four quarters, but I would need them in a day or two to do my own laundry.

"Please?" he begged, sensing my hesitation. "I can go to the arcade tomorrow to get more quarters to give back to you. I've been wearing the same pair of underwear for three days!"

"OK, OK, too much information." I laughed. He followed me to our room, where I produced four quarters from my coin purse.

"Thanks," he said.

"You *promise* to bring me back quarters tomorrow."

"I *promise*! Hurry, Amy! Someone might beat me to the laundry room!"

I dropped the quarters in his eager palm and he scurried out of the room.

A moment later, his face popped back in our door frame.

"Can you look at these washing machine settings for me?" he asked, trying to mask sheepishness. "I think I know how to do it, but I just want to make sure."

I gave a mock sigh of exasperation and followed him to the laundry room. Chris set his mesh laundry bag down on the floor and opened it.

"Whew!" I said in spite of myself. It smelled strongly of dirt and sweat, mixed with a little bit of beer and musky male deodorant.

"I know," he said, not meeting my eyes. "OK, now my mom says I have to separates the colors from the whites and wash the colors in hot water."

"I think you're mixed up," I told him. "Colors will bleed, so you want to wash them in cold water."

"Are you sure?"

"Why would I lie to you? Fine, try washing the colors in hot water and see what happens. Haven't you ever done laundry before at home?"

He shook his head.

"Mom does it," he said.

I couldn't believe it. I had done laundry since I was twelve. I mean, not every week, but once in awhile, Mum would be busy with something and ask me to throw a load in the washer or move a load into the dryer. It never really occurred to me that someone might not have a clue about how to do it. I launched into a quick overview of what each of the knobs did when Sean's head appeared in the doorway.

"Laundry costs a buck seventy-five?!" he said. "That's expensive!"

"Word," Chris agreed. "I've been begging for quarters all afternoon. How can anyone have three-fifty in quarters lying around the room to do a load of laundry? Wait, I have to do two loads, so that's seven bucks! That means I can only do one load today. Amy, which load do I do?"

I was about to tell him that I wasn't his mother and he was old enough to decide which load to do first, but Chris already looked dejected, so I decided to be nice.

"You should probably do whites if you're out of underwear," I told him. "You can throw some of your older colored clothes in there too, if you don't think they will bleed."

"Seven bucks!" Sean exclaimed, still stuck on that fact. "That's freaking extortion! There's no way it costs the university seven bucks for two loads of laundry! They are making a profit off of us. It's not right."

"Well what can we do about it?" I asked him impatiently. I wanted to get back to my reading so I wouldn't fall behind because of my date tonight.

Sean held his index finger up. "I'm on it," he replied. He was already investigating the coin deposit slots on the washing machine. It was a tray with seven narrow ditches in it, where you stood each of your quarters. When it was full, you pushed the tray into the machine and then a little orange light lit up. The digital display on the washing machine then read "Choose your cycle." We chose the warm cycle. The water began flowing into the bottom of the donut shaped cavity around the agitator.

"Where's your detergent?" I asked Chris. He scurried out of the room.

"Get Brian's tool box," Sean called after him. Chris returned a moment later with a large plastic bottle of detergent and Brian on his heels.

"What do you want my tool box for?" Brian asked Sean.

"Imna figure out how to keep the Man from preying on poor students like us," Sean said.

"What are you talking about?" Brian demanded.

"Do you know it costs seven bucks *in quarters* to do two loads of laundry?" Sean said.

"No," Brian replied.

"Yeah! That's ridiculous! There's no way it costs the university that much to do two loads of laundry! They're making a profit on us!" Sean repeated for the benefit of Brian.

"I just want to look at how this coin collection thing works. Maybe we can make it cheaper."

"I'm not going to help you steal from the university!" Brian said.

"What about them stealing from us?" Sean replied. "I'm not going to make it free. I'm just going to make it cheaper, ok?"

Brian looked unconvinced.

"Look, I'll just do the dryer. I won't do the washer. Do *you* have seven dollars in quarters lying around?"

Brian shook his head.

"That's right. Because it's unreasonable!" Sean said.

Brian handed over his toolbox. "I'm not going to be a part of this," Brian said, backing out of the room.

"You already are," Sean said. "Just stand guard out there, will you? If I get caught, I'm bringing you all down with me."

Against our better judgment, we stood around watching Sean. Brian stood outside, trying to look nonchalant, monitoring the hallway. I knew that I shouldn't be condoning this, but it was so fascinating and mischievous, I couldn't help myself. There was hardly anybody around on a Sunday afternoon.

Sean unscrewed the coin collection device and removed it from the dryer. He peered into the cavernous rectangular hole left in the machine. Then he picked up the coin collection device and inspected it all around.

"Brian, you might find this interesting, being a mechanical engineer and all," Sean called out. Brian peeked back inside the room, also unable to control his curiosity.

"Every quarter pushes up against this little skinny button," Sean explained, showing us the seven silver slivers of buttons. There were seven of them right above the seven slots where the quarters went. "When all of the quarters are in the tray, they push up against all seven buttons, this little latch thing goes up and that triggers the machine to start up."

Sean put seven quarters in the tray and pushed it in to show us how a metal arm on the side of the box raised up.

"And after the latch goes up, the quarters fall down," Brian finished, taking the heavy metal contraption from Sean and turning it over in his hands.

Chris looked excited and scared. He poked his head out in the hallway and looked up and down.

"No one is coming," he whispered.

"So, we either have to find a way to tape the quarters into the slots permanently or make that latch go up permanently," Sean said.

"The latch is better," I said. "People will notice if there are quarters stuck in there permanently."

"Right," Sean said. "What can we jam in there to keep that little lever raised?"

"There's some cardboard in our room from moving in," Brian said.

"Awesome," Sean said. "Can you cut me a square of it? We only need a little one."

Brian hesitated.

"It's for the common good of the community!" Sean told him.

Brian disappeared and returned a few moments later with a small square of cardboard.

"Are you going to use tape to stick it under the latch?" I asked. "It won't stick very well."

"String would work better," Sean said, studying the latch. "You're right-tape won't stick for long. Amy, can you find me some string?"

I thought for a minute and then went back to my room, where I pulled some dental floss out of my dispenser.

Erin was typing away on her game and Casey was lying on her stomach, talking on her phone. Neither of them noticed me. I snuck back to the laundry room and handed the dental floss to Sean, who barely looked up at me. Ingrate.

We watched as Sean tied the cardboard to the bottom edge of the latch so that it stuck up permanently. He wrapped the dental floss around it ten or fifteen times before he got to the end of it and then he tied several knots in it.

"Voila!" he announced, showing us his handiwork. He slid the metal coin collector back into the rectangular cavity above the dryer and began to put all of the screws back into it. He had barely finished the first screw when the little orange light on the dryer lit up.

"Well I'll be a monkey's uncle," Brian said in amazement.

"Did you doubt me?" Sean asked disdainfully. "You may now call me Master Sean."

"Well, let's see if it really worked." I shut the door to the dryer and pushed "Start."

The machine roared to life. I shook my head in disbelief. It seemed too easy. We stood around marveling Sean's work when the spin cycle finished on the washing machine.

"Now you can do both loads of laundry," Sean said to Chris, who beamed. He opened the door to the dryer and the machine stopped. Chris began to transfer his clothes from the washer to the dryer.

"What setting?" he asked me.

"I usually use 'Cotton'," I told him. "It gets the clothes dryer. Permanent press is for more delicate things, but you shouldn't need it."

Chris set the knob to "Hot/Cotton" and then he hit the "Start" button. He looked at me.

"That's it," I said, shrugging. "You come back in an hour or so and it should be done."

"Awesome," Chris said, pumping his chin out and in like an ancient Egyptian. He put his fist out toward me and I bumped my knuckles with his knuckles.

"You can thank me by doing my laundry," Sean told him.

"Dream on," Chris said, punching him in the arm. "You get cheap laundry too, so *I* don't have to give you anything."

"Cheap bastard," Sean muttered. He started for the door and we all followed him.

"I'm hungry," Chris announced. "Let's get dinner soon."

"It's only 5:30pm," I said, looking down at my watch. "Give me an hour.

I need to finish my reading."

"Fine," he said, pouting.

I returned to my room to finish my reading with renewed vigor.

*****

During dinner, Sean bragged about his ingenuity with the dryer.

"How did you know what the latch did?" Casey asked, scowling.

"It's just logical that the latch would trigger the machine!" Sean said, tapping his temple. Casey made a face at him.

"What's going to happen when they go to empty the quarters out?" Erin asked. "They will see what you did."

Sean shrugged. "Unless they want to replace the whole coin collecting system, they will just undo it and we can redo it again."

"Aren't you afraid you're going to get caught?" Erin asked, wide-eyed.

"How would they know it was me unless someone ratted me out?" Sean asked, looking at all of us.

"The RA is on to you," Casey said, twirling spaghetti around her fork. "She would totally suspect you."

"Yeah, but she can't prove it," Sean said, unaffected. He took a huge bite of hamburger.

"Did you get your clothes out of the dryer yet?" I asked Chris.

He shook his head.

"When I went in there, the dryer was still going, so I figured it still had a few minutes left," he said.

"Do you need me to show you how to fold them too?" I asked, winking.

"I know how to *fold* laundry!"

I shrugged. "Well I don't know! I would have thought you would know how to work the washer and the dryer too!"

"I don't know how to work the washer and the dryer!" Casey said. I was shocked. But after thinking about it a moment, it made sense that no one in her family knew how to operate a washer and a dryer.

"Amy can show you," Chris said. "She's a good laundry teacher."

"I've achieved my life's aspiration," I joked and everyone laughed.

After dinner, we walked past the laundry room to get to our room. The group stopped in front of the door. The dryer was still going.

"Is that your load still in there?" I asked Chris.

"No one took it out," he replied, pointing at his empty laundry bag still lying on the floor.

"It's been over two hours!" I said, starting to get panicked. "Sean! Maybe you broke it!"

"No way!" Sean cried. "I just triggered the start mechanism. The machine should have its own timer or whatever to make it stop!"

"Open the door!" I told Chris. He pulled on the handle, but it wouldn't open. He used both hands and the door opened suddenly, causing Chris to fall back on the ground, with laundry shooting out of the dryer all over him. There was a moment of stunned silence and then we all started laughing.

I pulled a child-sized t-shirt off of his head. It was still hot from the dryer .

Casey was laughing so hard, she had to lean against the wall. "So much for you being a genius!"

"Hey, he got free drying!" Sean said, but he looked stunned as well.

"He sure got more than he paid for!" Brian laughed.

"What happened to my clothes?" Chris wailed, picking a sock up off of his shoulder and looking at it. "How come everything's so small?"

"You're not supposed to dry clothes for that long!" Erin explained to him. "Cotton shrinks! Especially new stuff. Are some of these clothes new?"

"Look at this one!" Sean said. holding up a shrunken white t-shirt with a pink stain across the front.

"What the hell is that?" Chris cried, alarmed. I took the shirt from him and looked at it carefully. It looked kind of greasy. It smelled faintly of strawberries.

"It looks like lip gloss or lip balm or something," I conjectured. "Did you put it in your pocket?"

Chris looked dejected again. "It was in my jean pocket. Sarah asked me to keep it for her during the football game because she didn't want to carry it around and she didn't have any pockets."

Sean howled with laughter.

"Bastard!" Chris said. He stood up and began gathering his clothes.

"Need help?" I offered. He shook his head. We all left Chris to his laundry and went back to our rooms.

"That was hysterical," Casey commented.

"Poor Chris," Erin said. I agreed, but couldn't spend much more time thinking about it.

I began digging through my closet for the perfect outfit to wear to coffee with Jeff. I wanted to wear my black suede boots because they made my legs look longer, which meant that I *had* to wear the jeans that were slightly too long for any of my other shoes. Those particular jeans sat low on my hips, so I *had* to wear a shirt that wouldn't leave my tummy exposed to critique. It had to be cute, but it couldn't look like I was trying too hard. I tried and rejected a half dozen going-out tops before I settled on a simple black halter top that wasn't too clingy. Casey loaned me some small black hoop earrings and offered to do my make-up. I was afraid she would overdo it and I didn't have the energy to be humor her and then redo it afterwards. So, I just touched up the make-up that I'd had on from rush.

I grabbed my purse, winked at my roommates and tiptoed past the boys' room to avoid provoking any questions from any of them. Once I got down the stairs and out the main entrance, I began to walk normally. It was a windy night and my ponytail whipped around my neck. I walked down the hill towards Gayley and along the street down into Westwood.

It's amazing what nice clothes and a little make-up do for the spring in your step. I wondered why I didn't bother to dress up more often. Oh yeah, because it takes too damn long in the morning and you have to watch what you do for the rest of the day. One accidental eye rubbing and you look like a raccoon.

I glanced at my watch. 9:00pm. Shoot, I was going to be late.

I arrived at Starbuck's slightly winded and flushed from rushing. Jeff was waiting just outside the door. He was wearing a baby blue polo shirt which brought out his glowing tan and blue-gray eyes.

"Hi, Beautiful!" he said, holding the door open for me.

"I hope I haven't kept you waiting," I said, smiling broadly at him.

"It was worth the wait," he said.

Slick.

I felt his hand rest lightly in the small of my back as I walked past him through the door. I noticed how very aware of my body I was at that moment and tried to stand up taller. "Contract your abs, lift up through the chest, roll your shoulders back, extend your neck and tuck your chin," I heard Meg's yoga instructor say in my mind. I was also very aware of how Jeff was arranging the space between us. Once we got into line, he stood close behind me, his hand still on the small of my back. It felt very reassuring without being overly dominant or inappropriate. I studied the menu above the barista.

"What are you going to get?" I asked him.

"Espresso," he replied.

"Are you anticipating a late night?" I asked, puzzled.

"No, caffeine doesn't really affect me anymore."

"Small hot vanilla," I told the barista, and pulled out my wallet.

"I've got it," Jeff said in a voice that dared me to argue with him. I let him get it.

"Double espresso," he told the barista and he paid for both of our drinks. "Inside or out?" he asked once we got our drinks.

"Outside!" I said. "It's so nice out!"

We sat down at a round table just beneath the massive sign of the Fox movie theater, lit up with hundreds of hot little lightbulbs, where numerous movie premiers took place. I drank in the scene. It was a pretty quiet night in Westwood, with a few groups of students and a few couples sauntering about at a leisurely pace.

"So how did you like the football game?" Jeff asked. "It was your first one, right?"

"Yes. It was amazing! There was so much energy in the stadium. I couldn't believe it!"

"I know. Everyone gets so pumped. That's the best part about football games- the atmosphere. Everybody has the same goal."

"Well, except for the lone guy looking the wrong way."

"You should be flattered," he said and laughed. "It takes a lot to distract me from a football game."

I blushed and looked into my drink. "Thanks."

"So what do you think about college so far?" he asked, leaning back in his chair and stretching his legs out beneath the table. He continued to hold my gaze with his intense blue eyes.

"It's exciting! Everything is totally different. I'm just trying to soak it all in. You know, get the *whole* college experience."

"I was like that too last year," Jeff said, chuckling. "I wanted to go to every party, every football game, every class and every late night video game-a-thon. You don't have to do it all this quarter though. Four years is a long time to soak it all in. College isn't going anywhere."

"Well, what have *you* liked best about college so far?" I asked him, taking out a fresh sheet of mental notebook paper.

"I like the freedom. I like doing whatever I want to do whenever I want to do it. I like that we're not responsible for anyone but ourselves right now. "

"So what are you doing with that freedom?" I grinned.

"You know, parties, sports, hanging out with the guys in my frat, taking out pretty girls," he ticked off, nonchalantly.

I smiled.

"What are you going to do with it?" he asked, turning the question on me.

127

I thought for a minute.

"I want to figure out who I am and what I stand for. Everyone that I grew up with thinks a lot like me and I'm ready for some new ideas," I said at the risk of sounding cheesy.

"Cool," Jeff said. "This is a good place to find them. It's a good place to try a lot of things on for size, not just ideas."

"What do you mean?" I asked, not following him.

"Well… for example, people," he said. "You can date different people and see who is most compatible with you. You can try different majors and see which one fits best. There are a lot of things to try out here. College is the only time you can get away with experimenting. If you do something dumb, everyone just chalks it up to you being in college."

"What sort of things have you done that have been dumb?" I was eager for war stories.

"For spring break last year, we went speed boating while were on spring break," Jeff said, after taking a long sip of espresso.

"How is that dumb?"

"We were drunk. One of my bros fell off the back of the speedboat, so we were circling around to get him and almost ran him over on accident. That was a close one."

I shuddered. "Have you dated a lot of different people?" I asked, picking out the most interesting part of his list.

"Not a lot. I've dated a few," he responded. "I'm still looking for that special someone, or special someones."

"Special someones?" I asked.

"Well, one of my buddies is convinced that you can love more than one person," he explained, his blue eyes fixed on me carefully over his drink.

"At a time?" I asked.

"Yes. Well, you love both your parents at the same time, right?" he said.

"It's not the same kind of love." .

"Have you ever liked more than one person at once?"

"Of course, but that's not the same as love either. I think that part of what makes love so special is that it is exclusively between two people." I realized that I was getting too adamant about a topic that was inappropriate for a first date, so I backed off. "But who knows? Maybe your buddy is right."

"It's just an idea. I'm not sure he's right either," Jeff said. "Just trying to be open-minded."

I nodded. There was another pause as we both took sips of our drinks at the same time.

"What's your family like?" he asked me.

I launched into a high level description of my family. There was Dad, the quintessential engineer, who wrote everything in upper case letters that looked like print. He liked us to be tidy, prompt and responsible. It was not an option to be good at math in our household. Jeff laughed at this. Mum was a homemaker, which was wonderful. She was always there for us. We were lucky that way. Meg was my best friend besides Lauren. She was always paving the way and looking out for me. She had always been on the fast track, so after college, she struck out as a management consultant, working 80 hours weeks. Jeff whistled.

When I felt like I had done enough jabbering, I turned it around on him.

"Tell me more about you. What's your family like?"

Jeff launched into a description of his family. His dad was a contractor, his mom was a teacher. He had an older sister and a younger brother. His older sister was in finance, whatever that meant. His younger brother was just starting high school and wanted to play football like Jeff did.

"That must be a cool feeling. To have someone look up to you like that."

"Yeah," he admitted. "I just wish I could hang out with him more. I try to get home once a month or so."

You gotta love a man who is serious about being a role model to his little brother.

"Have you liked being in a frat?" I asked. "What are your frat brothers like?"

"Yeah! The frat has been awesome! The guys at SIE were all really chill, decent guys. So I decided to rush. It's like an automatic group of friends. There's always someone who's willing to throw the ball around with you or go out."

"How come you don't live in the house?"

"I didn't want the fraternity to become my whole life. It's easy for that to happen when you live in the house. I will live there my last year, when I get back from my junior year abroad, but I wanted to live in the dorms one more year."

"Where are you going?" Going abroad for a year sounded so adventurous.

"I want to go to Scotland. They practically invented drinking there."

"There's an important cultural contribution!"

He didn't seem to hear my sarcasm. "Totally," he said. "I can push my tolerance higher. And, my roommate says there are castles all over the country, which is cool too."

"Who's your roommate?"

"Actually, this random dude," Jeff said. "I was supposed to live with one of my buddies from high school, who played football with me. He was going to be a freshman this year. But at the last minute, after we had already turned in all the housing stuff, he got a great offer from Fresno State and decided to go there."

"That sucks!" I exclaimed, imagining that I would be livid if someone did that to me.

"No, it was better for him, "Jeff said generously. "The random dude is fine. He's clean and pretty much keeps to himself. If I don't like it after a quarter, I might move into the frat house. But for now, it's working out. What are your roommates like?"

I told him about Casey, the Beverly Hills princess. She was a party girl with a lot of accessories. Nice, but could be loud and messy at times. Then I told him about Erin, the soft-spoken electrical engineer who looked like a Japanese animation.

He laughed. "You guys are all so different."

"I know, it's great! I feel like we're all going to learn a lot from living with each other. So far, no problems yet."

"It's been a little over a week," he reminded me. "I'll ask you again in a month."

The surrounding stores were beginning to turn out their lights. I glanced at my watch. 11:00pm already!

"Want to get going? I'm guessing you have early class tomorrow," he said, getting up from his chair, and walking to my side of the table.

"How do you know?" I asked, rising out of my chair and chucking my cup into the trash.

"You have a bad poker face," he replied, eyes twinkling. "You got all worried when you looked at your watch."

"No good. A girl's got to be able to have her secrets," I sighed. I took a chance and slid my arm through his. He looked down at me with a smile. We started walking towards the dorms.

"I went to Rush this afternoon. Do you think I should join a sorority?" I asked. "It sounds like you really like your fraternity."

"Well... Fraternities and sororities are a little bit different. I don't generally like to stereotype, but I've heard that girls in sororities can be mean sometimes."

I considered this.

"But, you should check it out if you're curious. I've known plenty of sorority girls to be really nice. Why do you want to be in a sorority?"

"I think it would be fun to have that 'automatic group of friends' that you were talking about," I replied. "I like the idea of having all of these formal social activities set up for me and stuff."

"I think that some smaller schools, a lot of activities revolve around the Greek system. But at a school this huge, you will make tons of friends and be involved with plenty of activities without being in it, if that's all you're concerned about," he said. "Also, sometimes people get so caught up in their fraternities and sororities, they don't make friends are get involved in other stuff as much."

"All good points," I said, drifting into thought. We strolled in silence for awhile. We reached the base of the hill, where we could see Sproul.

"Let's take a detour," Jeff suggested, and I followed him up the stairs of Bradley International Center, a building that looked like it was made of huge red and orange blocks pushed together. He turned into a small covered stairwell and I followed him. Midway up the stairs, he stopped and said, "This is where I go sometimes when I want to be away from people."

I smiled. "I'll know where to look in the future."

"Listen, I had a really great time with you tonight," Jeff said, looking down at me. I felt my heart flip flop in my chest. "Can I see you again?"

I nodded. He lifted my chin with his hand and kissed me on the lips. Everything was still. I looked at him and he looked at me, and suddenly, we both smiled the same euphoric smile.

He held out his hand, and I took it. And we started climbing the stairs again. After some twisting and turning, we emerged in front of Dykstra Hall and then rounded the corner to get to Sproul. We walked up the stairs and I suddenly remembered Brian.

"You don't have to walk me all the way back to my room," I told him.

"OK, let's do this again." he said, holding his arms out for a hug. He gave me a really good bear hug.

"Definitely."

I walked on air all the way back to my room.

***

The door to our room was open. I waltzed in and saw that my roommates were having an impromptu girls' night with some of our hallmates. Casey, Lindsay and Autumn were sitting on Casey's top bunk, while Erin, Sarah and Kate were sitting on the lower bunk. They were just getting to the end of *Bridget Jones's Diary*, one of my favorites. Erin reached over to Casey's keyboard to hit the pause button.

"So," Casey said with the air of self-importance. "How was your date?" Everybody looked at me, highly interested. I felt a little bit uncomfortable to be put on the spot like this, especially in front of a few girls I hardly knew at all.

"It was really nice." I climbed onto the lower bunk with Erin, trying to signal to her that we should start the movie up again.

Casey leaned over the edge of the top bunk and persisted. "Did you guys hook up?" she asked.

"Well, what do you mean by 'hook up'?"

"Did he kiss you?" Sarah asked, blue eyes dancing.

"Kiss you?" Casey echoed. "I don't care if he kissed you! I meant did you guys 'hook up'? You know, do the... horizontal tango?"

"Wait, I thought hooking up meant making out," Autumn said, confused.

"Well, I think it's an ambiguous term," Lindsay said. "I've heard it used both ways. It can mean to make out and it can also mean to go all the way."

I tried to stay as still and quiet as possible. If they continued their discussion of the semantics of "hooking up", they might forget to continue interrogating me about my date. No such luck.

"Fine, whatever," Casey said. "Did you?"

"No, we just kissed," I confessed, unable to get out of it. I was then pummeled with an avalanche of questions from all directions.

"Do you like him?" "Will you see him again?" "Who is this?" "Where did you go?"

I laughed and shook my head, not wanting to jinx myself by telling the whole story to everybody and their mother. "I'll tell you later," I lied. "I'm still deciding what I think about the whole thing. Start the movie, Erin." And I was saved by the antics of Ms. Jones.

6 "Date lots of people"

How does one take the integral of an integral? I stared so hard at the page, I could feel the strain behind my eyeballs. It seemed to make sense when the professor was doing it on the board this morning, but when I started on the problem set, it became painfully apparent that I had no clue what was going on. Well, let me give myself slightly more credit than that. The professor picked an easy, straight forward example out of the book to demonstrate in class. But then he assigned ten convoluted problems to us for homework.

I had been sitting in the basement of Powell Library for two whole hours and had managed to get through only two out of the ten problems I needed to finish. Not even two *whole* problems. One whole problem, and half of two other problems. I was beginning to feel cranky, desperate and, honestly, a bit dumb. Today was Wednesday. Tomorrow was discussion with my TA and the problem set was due on Friday. A planner by nature, it was driving me crazy that I couldn't get my homework done in the time that I was allotting to it.

The problem set was only part of why I was feeling crappy. It was Week Three of the quarter and I felt like my honeymoon with college was coming to an end. The golden veneer of The College Experience had begun to tarnish when I went to Rush. In spite of Casey's best efforts to convince me that sororities were loads of fun, I couldn't subject myself to anymore lemon water, cookie cutter sun dresses or talk about how the girls in every house were "soooo sweet."

It wasn't as though college wasn't fun anymore or anything. Aside from classes and Rush, the first two weeks had been great. I had lunch with some subset of my hallmates nearly every day. The group of us from Sproul 3 North were becoming default friends. We met up at 6:30pm every night for dinner. Then, most nights after dinner, we made the most of our College Experience.

Last Thursday night, we went to Chris's brother's friend's frat to party, where the boys were able to get into the party. We had a great laugh over Sean and Brian, neither of whom was very enthusiastic about dancing. Two nights ago, we took a midnight stroll to Westwood for coffee and a fresh baked cookie at the famous Kookie King . Last night, we felt guilty about the Kookie King and took a group field trip down to the gym and pretended to work out.

My favorite nights were the ones spent sitting in the hallway until the wee hours of the morning, reliving high school stories, mocking the latest current events, and having deep discussions about the meaning of love, life and friendship.

The problem with me was the slow onset of long-term sleep deprivation, which resulted from this nocturnal lifestyle mixed with my early morning classes. When I had signed up for classes over the summer, it had seemed like a good idea to get my classes over with early in the day, so that I could get more done during the day. It hadn't exactly worked out as planned.

The few times that I tried to go to bed early, things always got in the way. Sometimes it was just my lack of will power. I would get ready for bed, then someone would propose something fun, like a movie, and I would falter. I didn't want to miss out on quality bonding time with my newfound friends. Other times, I would actually make it into bed at a decent hour, but then struggle to fall asleep because Erin was clacking away on her computer keyboard and Casey was talking to someone on the phone. She always tried to lower her voice, but no matter how quietly she spoke, curiosity would get the best of me and I would feel myself straining to hear about her latest sexcapade with a lucky member of her myriad suitors. She had even mentioned a date with a married guy one night just as I was drifting off. It wasn't so much that I adored Casey and wanted to know all about her life. I was getting over that. It was more that her life was so different from mine, I couldn't help but to be fascinated.

In any event, the sleep deprivation was beginning to make me do stupid things. Just this morning, I tried to use my BruinCard to get cash out of the ATM. The woman behind me must have thought I'd completely lost it. Sleeping in on weekends helped a bit, but Monday morning was always a shock to my system. By Wednesday, I felt like a zombie. I found myself alternately nodding off in class or forcing my eyes open. I had not realized before college that forcing oneself to stay awake was almost painful. Sean pointed out to me that it is used as a torture device for war criminals.

In addition to being sleep deprived and a little- ok, a lot- of out of it, I was currently on my period, which never makes for a good time. Today, the cramps were especially bad and made it easier for me to pick at the pretty picture of my College Experience compulsively like a child at a scab.

Somewhere, across the room, someone's cell phone alarm began to beep and I saw its owner lift his shaggy head off his desk. I looked at my watch. 5pm. It was time to retrieve my English paper from my TA's office hours. I packed away my calculus book, notes and homework. As soon as I stood up to leave, a very intense looking red-headed boy rushed over and dropped his backpack on the desk. I'd learned that some classes had two midterms per quarter and the first ones started now. Seats in Powell during midterms were apparently as hard to come by as parking spaces at the mall on Black Friday.

*****

I moseyed through the maze of metal book stacks and up the simple staircase to the foyer. Walking in and out of Powell always gave me a little thrill because it was really a grand building.

Bruin Walk was bustling with activity. As I walked down the brick and concrete stairs, under the rustling canopy of dry leaves, I looked at Kerckhoff, to my left. Yesterday, I'd sent in another list of potential stories that I thought were worth pursuing to the email address that I had for the *Daily*

Bruin, but had received no response yet. It was hard on my ego to go from being the editor-in-chief of my own newspaper to practically begging for a position as a staff writer at the *Daily Bruin*. I could appreciate that the university was full of ex-editor-in-chiefs, but even so, I felt like I deserved a little more consideration than some bum off the street.

My high school counselor had called it the "big fish in a little pond" syndrome. I hadn't thought it was going to bother me. After all, isn't that what college is all about? Starting fresh and rediscovering yourself? I guess I liked the idea in theory; but in practice, I found that I really missed the reliability of my reputation and the familiarity of high school. It was frustrating to have to prove myself all over again.

I bumped up against the edge of the crowd of students heading back to the dorms after class. The guy I ran into glanced at me and went on without a second look. So many people. So many strangers.

Anonymity here was a double edged sword. On some days, it was nice to be able to sit in class, and completely zone out or do the crossword, without having to worry about what the professor thought of me. He couldn't tell me from Adam anyway. But other days, my anonymity was troublesome. In high school, I prided myself on getting good grades in honors classes, being a mediocre basketball player, leading a silly, but respectable newspaper staff and being an easy-going, approachable person. People treated me accordingly. Teachers enjoyed having me in class. Fellow students respected me for being an athlete. The popular kids largely ignored me. Freshmen and sophomores hoping to be staff writers were appropriately deferential. Whether people liked me or not, they knew me and treated me in a predictable fashion, in a way that was specific to me. But here, I had none of that.

I could go the entire day on campus and not see a single familiar face. Everyone, including professors, treated me like they treated everyone else. The paradox of being at a big school was that there were so many strangers that could potentially be friends, but you become overwhelmed and don't reach out to any of them.

When I first arrived at UCLA, some of the other freshmen were eager to make friends. You could randomly say hi to a clueless looking person in line at Starbuck's and make a new friend. But now, people were beginning to fill their friendship quotas. Many of the acquaintances made in those Starbuck's didn't progress to full-fledged friendships and were reduced to awkward "Hi's" or aversion of the eyes in the courtyards. The window for meeting people easily was shutting.

I felt my phone vibrate in my pocket and was delighted to see who it was.

"Laur!" I exclaimed into my phone. "How's it going?"

"Alright," Lauren replied, sounding equally glad to hear my voice. "What are you up to?"

"I'm going to pick up my English paper from my TA," I told her. "I'm nervous because it's the first graded assignment that I'm getting back here."

"You'll do fine! It's *English*!"

"I hope so."

"So I have to tell you about soccer boy!"

"Well, tell me!"

"I asked if he wanted to go on a run with me down to the battlefield yesterday. We ran by this *beautiful* lake behind the institute where Einstein used to teach. He said he wanted to stretch for a minute, so we slowed down and started walking around the lake. Then he held my hand and we started kissing. We ended up making out for, like, half an hour by the lake. In our sweaty running clothes."

"Sexy!" I joked. "So you guys are a thing then?"

"I guess. I'm excited, but I'm trying not to let my hopes get too high, in case this is a fling or something. I have to see how it goes. How is your situation?"

"Which one?" I asked, grinning.

"Both."

"Well, Jeff, the frat guy, hasn't asked me out since our date last weekend. He's been flirting with me online and we had lunch together yesterday. But it doesn't really feel like he is in any hurry to be in a relationship."

"Are you?"

"I guess not. Defeats the purpose of the whole dating thing."

"Well, no. Isn't the point of the whole dating thing to find the person you want to be in a relationship with?"

"Beats me," I laughed. "According to Casey, the point of the whole dating thing is to have fun."

"What about the other guy? Brian?"

"He's weird too! We hang out *all* the time. He comes into our room or I go into his room multiple times a day. You know, to say hi, talk about our day or watch a YouTube video online. Anyway, I definitely feel like I am his closest friend in our little group. He totally singles me out to hang out with, but he hasn't crossed the friend line. I'm so confused."

"Maybe he's gay," Lauren suggested.

"No. I just don't get that feeling."

Brian *wasn't* gay. I was sure of it.

"How many gay people do you know?" she asked me, knowing well that the answer was zero.

"But, he talks about girls with his roommates. I mean, he's not crude like them. He's usually pretty respectful."

"Then he's definitely gay," she repeated.

"Laur, just humor me. Suppose he's not gay. What do you think is going on? Maybe I'm just imagining that he likes me."

"Mmmm, if he's not gay, then it *sounds* like he likes you. Does he know about you and Jeff? Maybe he doesn't want to interfere."

"I don't know if he knows about Jeff. I didn't tell him or any of his roommates that I went on a date. Jeff never comes down to our room. He's almost always at his frat house. And when I see him, it's usually on campus or in Westwood."

"Maybe one of your roommates let it slip," Lauren suggested.

"Maybe," I agreed. "But you would think that if he were interested in me and found out that I was dating someone else, he would either confront me about it or stop hanging out with me."

"Or, he's just biding his time and making friends with you. So when you stop dating Jeff, you can date him."

"True. Besides, Jeff and I aren't exclusive. And it's not like I see him more than once or twice a week. I could potentially date them both."

"You go, girl!" Lauren laughed. "Way to be ambitious!"

"Am I terrible? " I asked guiltily. "I only kind of like them both."

"No. It's good to have options."

"Listen, Laur, I'm in front of my TA's building now, so I have to go."

"Good luck! Let's finish talking tonight?"

"You got it!"

I shut my cell phone and walked into the English building. After studying the map by the elevator, I found my way to Ethan's office. The room was stark, with a whiteboard on one wall and four simple, metal desks, one in each corner. Ethan was sitting at his desk with his back towards me, reading a paper. I cleared my throat softly to let him know that I was there. He swiveled around awkwardly in his chair.

"Hi," he said.

"How's it going?" I asked.

"Alright," he replied absent-mindedly. "I finished your classes' papers at 3am this morning and now I have to do the other section by tomorrow."

I grimaced, empathetically. "How long does it take you to read a paper?" I asked.

"These have been taking me about half an hour each," he replied. "It takes me about ten minutes to skim it the first time to get the overall structure, and then I go through it slowly for details."

"Wow!" I couldn't believe he had another ten hours of grading to do before tomorrow. But then again, it was his job, so I guess he was prepared to do it.

"OK, what's your student ID number?" he asked.

I had forgotten that we'd been asked to write our ID numbers instead of our names on our papers. I realized that this was to keep the grader fair, but at the same time, there was something a little disturbing about being reduced to a number.

"002826853," I told him. He flipped through a stack of papers on his desk.

"Here you go," he said, handing it to me.

I glanced at it. Lots of red marks. That wasn't a good sign. On the top of the paper, above the title, was the number "6.5" written in large red writing. I felt my heart skip a beat. Not in a good way.

"Ethan, what was this out of?" I asked, hoping with every cell in my body that it wasn't out of ten. He'd already started reading another paper.

"Hmmm?" he asked, not looking up.

"What... is... the...score... out... of?" I asked, enunciating for him.

"Ten," he replied, glancing at me.

Shit. That was a D.

"OK, thanks, have a good night," I stammered and ran out of the room.

As I walked back through campus and up the hill to the dorms, my chest felt like it was concurrently caving in and bursting open. How did I get a D on an English paper?! English was my subject. It was my *thing*. I glanced down at the first page of my paper.

"Weak argument, need to address counter-arguments" was scrawled in red ink on the right margin.

The Voice of Indignation rose up in arms. *Were we supposed to be lawyers now? What counter-arguments? He wanted us to convince him of our position and so I did!* I felt so slighted that I couldn't bring myself to flip through the rest of it. *He must have been mistaken. Maybe he was distracted when he was reading my paper. Maybe he read my paper last and he was already cranky.*

I felt my breathing become labored as I powered my way up the hill towards Sproul. The Voice of Doubt grew louder than the Voice of Indignation. *Maybe he wasn't mistaken. Maybe I'm really not that good of a writer compared to all of these other big fish from all over the state. Maybe,* I thought, growing increasingly concerned, *English teachers gave me A's because they liked me as a person. Or maybe they gave me A's because everyone else was so bad!*

This was truly depressing. I couldn't shake the thought no matter how hard I encouraged the Voice of Indignation to speak up. *If I can't write, I don't know who I am anymore.* It was turning out to be a truly lousy day.

*****

Moments later, I wandered into our room. I guess I must have looked listless because Erin glanced up from her problem set, and a look of concern came over porcelain doll face.

"Are you feeling alright?" she asked.

"I just have a cramp," I replied, wrinkling my nose.

"Do you need meds?" she asked, pulling out her desk drawer. "I have aspirin."

I shook my head.

"Thanks, Erin. I think I'm just going to lie down."

"Sure?"

"Yeah. Thanks, though."

I set my backpack down and booted up the laptop. While I waited for my computer to boot, I asked, "How was your day?"

"It was ok." Erin sighed. "These problem sets *never* end! Physics is due on Wednesday, Calculus is due on Friday, Computer Science is due on Monday…. I feel like I'm always doing them."

"You *are* always doing them," I sympathized. "You haven't been out with us once since that first week. Your professors are totally unreasonable to be heaping that much work on you."

"Well, the problem is that they forget we have other classes. All of my professors think their class is the most important class. And the other problem is that I really want to do well in case I want to go to grad school."

"Yeah. No one can put as much pressure on you as you put on yourself. I want to be a great writer someday and I feel like it totally consumes me some days."

I left it at that. I wasn't ready to talk about my English paper.

"Totally," Erin said, turning towards her problem set again. "But I guess it's better than not setting goals at all. It seems like the people who don't could get totally lost here, right?"

I nodded and turned back towards my computer. As I did, I noticed a note on Casey's desk in Erin's handwriting.

C, Can you please put away your shoes so I can vacuum tonight? --E

This was the second time Erin was asking Casey. She had asked us both yesterday. I had put away my shoes, papers and books that had been lying around on the ground, feeling bad about my clutter. Casey had been on her way out to a sorority function and promised to do it later. I sensed the beginning of some roommate tension and kept my fingers crossed.

My computer greeted me with a welcome IM window.

Jeffers56: hey cutie

Jeffers56: im looking 4 a hot date 2 the party @ the house tonight. busy?

I screwed my eyes together, completely conflicted. On the one hand, it would be a great way to get my mind off =the damn English paper. Also, I had not seen Jeff in several days. On the other hand, I felt awful and it showed. I was bloated, for starters, and my skin was blotchy and broken out. I wasn't so sure I could forget my English paper which would just make me a mopey date. I made up my mind to stay in,

---

Amyable7: i would love to go, but i'm not feeling well

Amyable7: can i take a rain check? wanna get coffee tom night?

I began opening several other applications on my computer to distract myself as I waited for the response.

Double-click on the internet browser. *What's he thinking?*

Double-click on Solitaire. *Response please?*

Double-click on "Freshman Fifteen". *Come on, come on, come on.*

Finally,

> **Jeffers56:** oh no- anything i can do?
>
> **Amyable7:** ur so sweet. i think i just need to sleep it off. ill be fine by tomorrow night.

Hint Hint. I'll be fine in time for COFFEE.

> **Jeffers56:** awesome. go get some rest. ill find someone else to go.

Long pause. Then his away message went up.

"Crap!" I didn't realize that I'd said it aloud until Erin turned around again.

"What happened?" she asked, her thin black eyebrows knitting together.

"Jeff asked me to go to a party with him tonight, but I didn't feel well, so I asked him if we could go to coffee tomorrow instead. He totally ignored that part and said he'd find someone else to go with."

"What a bastard!"

"Well, no. I mean, he was totally sweet about it and wanted to know if there was anything he could do to help me feel better. I really couldn't expect him to just not go because I don't feel well. Of course he's going to find someone else. It's not like we're boyfriend-girlfriend."

Erin shook her head. "I couldn't handle the ambiguity. It's just so much simpler when you're boyfriend-girlfriend."

I sighed. She was right. The freedom to date other people was only good if you were actually dating other people. Well, maybe I should get on that. I made up my mind to hang out with Brian tonight. My bruised ego needed some male attention.

I changed "Date" to "Date lots" to my "Freshman Fifteen" list.

Sean sauntered into the room, with half a smirk on his face. His cynical, argumentative presence wasn't exactly the male attention that I wanted.

"Sup," I said to him, trying to speak his language.

"Where's that one?" he asked, jutting his chin out at Casey's empty chair.

"I don't know. Why?" I asked, now annoyed that I'd just been ignored.

"Just have something to tell her."

"Well, why don't you tell *us*?" I asked.

He shook his head and walked back out of the room.

"Jerk," I muttered, and felt mildly better.

My inbox indicated a message from Lauren.

From: "Lauren Avery" <lavery@princeton.edu>
To: "Amy Callaway" <acallaway@ucla.edu>
Subject: Raincheck!

A, can't talk tonight- forgot that we're going to nyc to watch Phantom of the Opera on Broadway. pton is subsidizing tickets! sorry! how was the English paper?

Love, L

I was disappointed, but I tried to be happy for her.

From: "Amy Callaway" <acallaway@ucla.edu>
To: "Lauren Avery" lavery@princeton.edu
Subject: Re: Raincheck!

L,

How was the show? I'll bet it was amazing! Who did you go with? Everything is so-so. Got a bad grade on my English paper. Maybe I'm not cut out to be a writer.

Love, A

*****

Casey, Erin and I had just come back from dinner when my cell phone rang. It was Mum. Again.

She had been calling nearly every day this past week, always on some barely legitimate excuse like, "I saw Daniel's mother in the grocery store and she asked how you were doing" or "You got a letter from your high school. They want to know what day you're available for your five year reunion."

After being overly generous with the details of her day, she would get around to asking for the details of mine. Then she would express concern about my health, safety or psychological welfare. She made me feel about nine years old.

Yesterday, I added "Leave the nest" to my "Freshman Fifteen" list.

I picked up the phone. "Hi Mum!" I tried to sound cheerful.

"Hi, Honey, how are you?"

"I'm good. I have a cramp, but other than that, everything is fine."

"Are you remembering to take your multi-vitamins?" she asked, as she did every day.

"Yes, Mum."

"Did you choose a major yet?"

"Not yet. I haven't learned any more about any other majors since I talked to you last night."

"Well, which class do you like the best?"

"I don't know if that's a good way to choose my major. What if I just happen to like that particular professor and I hate all of the other professors in the department? Also, I only have four classes each quarter. Maybe I'm supposed to be a Philosophy major, but I would never know it because I haven't taken a Philosophy class yet."

"You could be a business major, like Meg," Mum suggested.

"Yeah, but she says that she only used a fraction of what she learned in school at her job now. If that's the case, what's the point in having one major?" I wondered out loud.

This was indeed a problem that had been weighing on my mind. How could I go from studying several subjects and liking them all, to loving a single field and abandoning the rest? It didn't seem right. I couldn't think of a field that I loved so much, I would be willing to forego all others for it. I recalled that this was exactly the basis of Sean's argument for not wanting to be in a committed relationship with a girl. No girl was good enough to make him forego the others.

"Well, you can't even get into some professions if you're not the right major. Dad couldn't be an engineer without an engineering degree. You're eventually going to have to pick one profession."

"Yeah," I muttered. "What's new with you?"

"Nothing much," she said, in her chatty voice. "I was over at the dry cleaners. You know, the one by the women's gym that I belong to. And I ran into your old music teacher from elementary school, Mrs. Watson! She retired last year and she's working at the community center, teaching kids and senior citizens now. She asked me about you and I told her you were at UCLA now. She's so proud of you! We grabbed a cup of coffee and she got me caught up on all of your old teachers. Mrs. Naramore is still teaching third grade, though she took two years off after her second baby. Mrs. Belcher has retired now and moved to Canada. Mrs. Belitz and Mrs. Hammeras..."

"Mum!" I interrupted her, unable to contain myself any longer. "Can you tell me all of this over the weekend? I have this huge calculus problem set due on Friday and I've still got a ton of work to do on it."

"Well, alright," she said in a small voice that I didn't know she had.

I felt exasperated. She was calling because she was lonely now that it was just her and Dad in the house. And, of course, she missed me. I understood that. But on days when I was stressed out or feeling off, I just didn't have the patience to chat or entertain motherly questions. I was in college now, a legal adult.

And while I told her that I was too busy to be chatting it up, I knew in my heart of hearts that this wasn't true. I had plenty of time to screw around after dinner, so it wasn't a time issue. Even if it *had* been a time issue, it might have been more effective just to talk to her. The guilt always lingered long after the phone call might have lasted.

Not long after I hung up my cell phone, Casey's cell phone rang. She picked up.

"Hi Mom!" she said. "Good timing! I am heading out on a date in a few minutes."

She listened for a minute.

"No, I told David that I didn't want to see him anymore," she told her Mom rapidly. "He was so boring. All he ever wants to do is make-out in front of the TV. I want to date people who actually want to go out. You know?"

Pause.

"Well, right now, I'm dating two people. Remember that guy that I told you about a few days ago? The tall one that I met at the frat party last week. That's Trevor. He plays volleyball for UCLA. He's really cute and pretty nice. But he's a relationship kind of guy, so I have to be careful with that one. Tonight, I'm going out with this guy named Connor. I met him at a bar on Monday. He's older and works in Hollywood as some kind of set designer or something. *He* is a total bad boy. It's going to be awesome tonight!"

I felt doubly guilty at this point. *I* should be this excited to confide in *my* mother. What was wrong with me?

Casey abruptly changed her tone.

"Hi Dad," she said. "How are you?"

She paused to listen. "That's good. I hope you're not working too hard." Pause. "I'm doing well. My classes have been interesting." Pause. "I'm a communications major, remember?" Pause. "Yes, my roommates are great. We get along really well." Pause. "Ok, Dad. It was good to talk to you.

144

Bye."

She hung up the phone and caught me staring at her. She looked back at me, expectantly.

"You talk so differently to your mom than your dad," I observed to fill the silence.

"Yeah, I'm not as close to my dad as I am to my mom," she said, inspecting her manicured finger nails. "He wasn't around much when I was growing up."

I knew it wasn't my business, but I couldn't help myself. "Why not?"

"Dad's a big entertainment lawyer," Casey explained without any emotion in her voice. "He works a lot of hours. When he's not working, he's hanging out with his clients."

I climbed up into my bed, where I flopped down and winced.

. "What's wrong?" Casey asked.

"Damn cramp," I replied, wrinkling my nose. "It's been one of those days."

"You need meds."

She opened her cabinet, inspected a few of the dozens of medicine bottles on the shelf, and pulled out two brown vials with the child-proof white caps.

"I've got aspirin and Prozac," she told me.

"Don't you need a prescription for Prozac?" I asked suspiciously.

Casey shrugged.

"My friends and I share it all the time," she said. "It totally works. Balances the chemistry up here."

She tapped her temple. I chuckled.

"Thanks. I'm good," I replied. "I just need to lie down for a minute."

Honestly, I tried not to take any meds if I could help it. My family had always been that way. We only took medicine as the absolute last resort.

"OK," Casey said. "But they're in here if you need them. Help yourself."

She threw the two vials back into her sock drawer, glancing up at me to make sure I could see them.

I smiled feebly at her.

"You should think about going on the Pill," Casey told me, sympathetically. "I used to get the worst cramps, but then I got on the Pill and they went away."

"Really?" I asked, interested. "But doesn't it have side effects? Like doesn't it make you gain weight and get all moody?"

"There are all different kinds now," Casey told me, matter-of-factly. "Different ones have different side effects. Some make you gain weight, some make you lose weight. Some make you moody, some make you happier. I think people's bodies respond differently to them. You just have to try a few."

"But don't they mess with your hormones and stuff?" Erin asked, concerned. "I mean, aren't they essentially tricking your body into thinking that you are pregnant?"

"Something like that," Casey said dismissively. "But everyone takes them now and they're not like our moms' Pill. They're super low dosage now, so I think the side effects are minimal."

"I don't know," Erin said slowly. "It seems kind of scary to be taking something that's fundamentally changing your hormone levels and screwing with your natural cycle. What if you can't get pregnant later when you want to?"

"They have fertility drugs for that," Casey replied.

Erin looked unconvinced. Truth be told, I was as well.

"Hey, a girl's got to do what a girl's got to do," Casey said. "Think about how much fun Amy has to miss out on because she has cramps. And because she can get pregnant. It's a trade-off, right?"

Erin shrugged. "I'd rather have the cramp. You don't know what that Pill is doing to you. And you plan to take it for years and years, right?"

"Anyways," Casey said, irritably. She turned to look up at me.

"Will you be alright for tomorrow's Rush parties? They're going to be so much fun! We'll see which houses want us!"

I had been dreading this conversation. I cleared my throat. "I don't think I'm going to go."

Casey gaped at me, her blonde eyebrows furrowed together. "What? Why?"

"I didn't really feel like I clicked with anybody at the first rush event and I just don't feel like I fit in at any house."

"You only talked to each girl for *two seconds*!" Casey pointed out. "And you had that accident with your skirt! I don't think you got a very good feel for how cool the girls are. You can't quit now! Being in a sorority is part of being in college."

I saw Erin shake her head out of the corner of my eye.

"I know," I said, not because I did, but just to appease her. "But I'm feeling overwhelmed and crappy right now. I think I'd better rush in the spring, when I have all of my ducks in order," I told her.

"But you'll miss out on the Winter Formal and two whole quarters of amazing parties! Plus how are you going to become more like them if you don't try?"

It was my turn to gape at her. She was assuming that I was *aspiring* to be like them and was dropping out of Rush because I didn't think that I could cut it. I didn't even know how to respond to this.

"I don't know, Case," I said. "I'm just not feeling it right now."

Casey shook her head. "Alright. Well, it doesn't sound like I can convince you. But you're making a big mistake."

We both stared mournfully at one another.

Casey's phone rang again. She looked at the display screen and cleared her throat before picking it up.

"Hiiii, Trevor!" she cooed into the phone.

Erin and I pretended to stop looking at Casey, though we continued listening.

"I miss you too," she said. "Ohhhh, I *really* wish I could. But I have plans with a … friend already."

She frowned and looked troubled. "Which friend? You don't know her. It's one of my high school friends…. You know I would *totally* rather hang out with you, but I can't blow her off. I haven't seen her in ages!"

There was a knock at the door. We all looked up to see a guy in a black leather jacket and jeans, leaning in the doorway. He looked like he could have been a movie star.

Casey motioned him to wait a minute, and he winked at her.

"Listen, I need to go now, but I'll call you later?" she asked, trying to keep up the impatience out of her voice, as she grabbed a handbag off of her cluttered desk. "I'm excited to see you too!"

Pause.

"I *promise* I will call you after class. Alright, bye!"

"Who was that?" Connor asked, lifting an eyebrow.

"One of my sorority sisters." Casey walked to the door to give him a kiss. "She wanted to go shopping, but I told her that I had better things to do."

Connor looked like he had a good idea of what was going on, but he continued to be amused.

"You certainly do," he said, looking her up and down. "I'll make you forget all about… shopping."

Erin and I exchanged a disgusted look. *Hello*, we were still in the room.

"We'll see," Casey replied, flirtatiously, as if to challenge him. "Alright, let's go! Bye guys!"

"Bye," we replied.

After the sound of their footsteps faded away, Erin turned to look at me. "Do you think she is so interested in guys because her dad wasn't around so much when she was growing up?"

I chewed on my fingernail. "Well, it's not like she's in desperate need of male attention. I don't get the feeling she tries really hard to please them or anything."

"That's true. She's always in control of the situation. It's like they're always falling all over themselves for her."

"She doesn't seem serious about any of them. I think she's just having fun. Remember that whole thing about being able to separate love from sex when she was drunk?"

"But do you think it has something to do with her dad not being around?"

I shrugged. "Maybe it does. But maybe it's just because she's hot. She *can* have all these guys following her around, doing stuff for her. It must be fun."

Erin appeared to think about this for awhile, then turned back to her problem set.

After about ten minutes of indulging my cramp, I climbed back down and turned to my outline.

The Freshman Fifteen
By Amy Callaway

Expect to:
- gain 15 lbs
- find yourself
- explore new ideas
- make new friends
- hang on to old friends
- party and drink (in a safe environment)
- experiment with sex (???)
- find your life's purpose
- get pumped about college sports (but keep it clean)
- date lots
- leave the nest

I clicked over to my buddy list. Jeffers56 was still active. Maybe he decided not to go to his party after all. Maybe he couldn't find another date. Or maybe... he didn't want to go without me!

148

This was wishful thinking, but I couldn't help hoping. If I ran upstairs to tell him I changed my mind, we could still get there in plenty of time.

I hesitated. Would that be a bad move? No. *He* had asked *me*.

I stood up from my desk and grabbed my keys. I climbed the stairs two at a time and arrived at his door breathless. It was shut. I gave myself a few seconds to catch my breath and compose myself, then knocked.

The door opened. A gaunt looking fellow stared at me, his dyed long black hair too harsh against his white face and pale blue eyes. He looked listless, as if he hadn't seen another soul, much less another living thing in a long time.

"Jeff just left," he said, lackadaisically. A little sorrowfully. .

"Oh," I tried to keep the disappointment off my face because I didn't want this guy telling Jeff that I was falling over myself for him.

He began to close the door. Normally, I would have just left. I was pretty much done with the old meet 'n greet routine at this point, but something about his complete lack of expectation or hope for a conversation made me feel bad for him.

"My name is Amy," I said, extending a hand.

He looked startled. He reached out and shook my hand, barely touching me.

"Brandon," he said.

"Nice to meet you," I said, smiling. "I'm Jeff's, err, friend. I live on 3 North."

He nodded. "Freshman?" he asked after a long pause.

"Yah," I was painfully aware of how hard both sides were trying to keep up this conversation. "But don't ask my major. I'm still not sure. Have you decided yet?"

"I'm an English major."

"That's one of the majors I'm thinking about. I love literature and I like to write."

"Really?" he asked, showing a bit more interest. "What do you write?"

"Well, I'm into journalism. I used to write for my high school newspaper."

"That's cool," he said. He deliberated for a moment. "I write poetry mostly."

"About what?" I asked, trying not to be too intrusive.

He hesitated. "About how society is oppressive, trite and superficial," he declared with sudden vigor, looking at me as if to gauge my response.

149

"Social anthropology!" I observed, not knowing what else to say.

"I suppose so," he said. He looked at me expectantly. I was running out of things to say.

"Well, I just came up to say hi. Good to meet you!"

"You too," he said with the closest thing to a smile I saw during our whole interaction.

I didn't hear him close the door behind me and when I turned to walk down the stairs, I caught a glimpse of him looking at me still.

***

When I got back to my room, I saw Jeff's away message up. I leaned over my desk and checked his away message.

Jeffers56: hot date + party

Whatever. I headed next door, hating myself for needing this fix of male attention.

The door was open, but only Brian was in the room, lounging in his chair, reading sports news on ESPN. "What's up, Amy?" he asked, motioning me to come in.

"Had a rotten day. Was hoping for a pep talk."

I stepped over a stack of porn magazines right in the middle of the floor and cringed. My Anthropology professor would have said that I was societally conditioned to find porn degrading and distasteful. And yet, Sean was right. We wanted guys to think we were sexy. So why was I put off by women looking sexy?

I mulled this over as I stepped around clothes, shoes and books strewn all over the ground and looked for a place to sit. My conclusion was that there was a difference between looking sexy and offering sex. There must have been a look of disgust on my face.

"It's Chris's," Brian said, apologetically. .

He kicked the stack of magazines under the bed. Then he pulled Sean's chair out for me.

"What's that smell?" I asked, trying to place the strong, bittersweet odor that was mixed in with the usual smells of dirt and sweat.

"Oh, I keep telling Sean not to smoke pot in here," Brian said, frowning. "We're going to get busted one of these days. "

I shook my head, disapprovingly.

"You'll love this," Brian told me, enthusiastically. "I was walking home after class today and saw this squirrel dragging *a slice of pizza* up a tree!"

"No way!" I laughed. "Was the pizza bigger than the squirrel?"

"It wasn't bigger than this giant UCLA super squirrel."

"No wonder they're so fat!" I commented, relaxing. It was hard to be tense around a goofball.

"So what's wrong?"

"Nothing egregious. The little things are just... adding up."

Suddenly, I didn't know how much I wanted to disclose about my writing, my college woes and my love life. I didn't want him to think I was petty.

"That's kind of vague," he said, encouraging me to elaborate.

"Well... You know how I was telling you that I wanted to write for the *Daily Bruin*?"

He nodded.

"I went into their office and they said I needed to submit a few articles as a guest contributor first before they would let me be a staff writer. So I've been submitting a few copy ideas, but I'm not getting any responses back."

"Are you just sending ideas or full articles?" he asked.

"Just ideas," I replied. "That's how we used to do it in high school. Writers would send me ideas and I would tell them whether to pursue the article or scrap it."

"Maybe they're looking for full articles that they can just pop into the newspaper," Brian said.

That was a good point. Since I wasn't a staff writer, maybe they didn't have time to review my ideas and give me feedback.

"Yah, you're probably right," I sighed. "It's harder that way because I have to invest all this time into writing an article that I'm not even sure they want. If they would give me a thumbs up or down on the copy idea, it would be a lot more efficient."

"It's hard starting over again. You just have to have faith in your talent as a writer and once you get your big break, it will all work out fine."

"See, that's the other thing. I used to think that I was a pretty decent writer. Good, in fact, some days," I added to be cute.

He chuckled obediently.

"But I just got my first English paper back and I did really badly on it. What if I'm a terrible writer, but I was just good compared to other kids in my class? I'm worried because if I'm not a good writer, I don't know what I am!"

The words were out of my mouth. I couldn't take them back. Here I was pouring doubt and pity all over myself in front of Brian. *Really attractive, Amy.*

"Whoa whoa whoa," Brian said, reining me in. "Who says you did badly on it? Some TA?"

I nodded.

"Why would you let one miserable grad student ruin the confidence you've built over the course of your lifetime?"

"What if he's the only person who's been honest with me about my writing?"

"Maybe, but I doubt it," Brian said. "Why would any of your teachers or friends lie to you about your writing? And I think that writing newspaper articles is probably a lot different from writing an English dissertation, which is probably what this jerk was looking for."

I began to feel better.

"I'm sure it was a fluke. You probably need to talk to this guy and figure out what he's looking for. English is so subjective.."

"Really?"

He nodded. "Feel better?" he asked.

"You're the best!" I told him.

"Anything else bothering you?"

His cell phone rang. He glanced at the number and switched it to silent.

"No, that was the big thing." Maybe *he* was the one I should have been hanging out with more.

"*Wassup, homies?*" Sean yelled from the doorway.

Startled, I jumped out of my seat. Sean and Chris laughed as they made their way into the room, carrying paper bags from Puzzles Café, along with cans and bottles of drinks.

I'd had plenty at dinner, so I wasn't hungry, but my mouth watered at the smell of seasoned curly fries. I moved out of the way so that Sean could have his seat back again. He dumped his armful of food on his desk and flicked his mouse to turn his screen on again.

"What are you kids doing?" he asked, checking his away messages.

"Just chatting," I said, moving towards the door. "I was having a rough

152

day and Brian gave me a pick-me-up."

"A pick-me-up, eh?" Sean said, raising his eyebrows. He elbowed Chris in the ribs. "He gave her a pick-me-up, if you know what I mean."

Chris guffawed. Brian rolled his eyes.

"You can make anything sound sexual if you add *that* phrase to the end of it," Brian pointed out.

"That's true!" Sean exclaimed, his whole face lighting up. He elbowed Chris again. "She cleaned my room out, *if-you-know-what-I-mean.*"

Chris roared along with him. I couldn't help chuckling.

"Alright guys, I'm out," I announced, heading for the door.

"What's your rush?" Sean offered me a curly fry.

I knew I shouldn't have, but the smell was too hard to resist.

"You sure know the way to a gal's heart," I said, taking the fry.

"I know the way to a gal's something else too!" Sean replied, naughtily.

I rolled my eyes.

Chris turned on the TV and took his video game console out from behind it.

"There's no better cure for a bad day than a good shooting game," he said, handing me one controller.

"I've got work to do," I protested. I had to finish my Calculus problem set, read for Anthro, start my Econ problem set, think of a topic for my next English assignment....

"Aw, do it tomorrow," Chris said, undeterred. He shoved a pile of mismatched blankets and comforters to the corner of Sean's bed. Then he sat on the edge of it and patted a spot next to him. I sat down. Sean sat on the other side of me, eager to instruct me.

"OK, just one game," I said.

Sean took the controller out of my hands and began moving his thumbs all over it.

"You push this one to shoot, you push this one to make it turbo, you push this one to duck, you push this one to select a different weapon..."

"Wait! You're going too fast!"

Sean went through it with me again. Before I knew it, I was slinking around a warehouse turned war zone, shooting at shadowy figures that randomly appeared. Occasionally, I was shooting at Chris's character, when I could manage to get him in my crosshair. It didn't take long for me to become swept away on the familiar tide of adrenaline generated by competition. My heart thumped in my ears and I was a tense as a bow string. I kept one eye on

Chris's half of the screen, trying to deduce where he was hiding, and the other half on mine. Everything else melted away in the background. It was all about me and him, and who could shoot more people faster. It was downright scary just how therapeutic it was to focus all of my thoughts and energy on blowing things up.

Sean was dumping barrels of fuel onto the fire. "Go right, go right! Get him! Get him! *Thatagirl!*"

Sean clapped me on the back and I took satisfaction in Chris's swearing. Out of the corner of my eye, I noticed Brian smiling at me from his desk. Guys love girls who can be one of the guys, right?

"One more game! One more game!" Chris yelled.

He yelled it after every game. I'd lost track of how many games we'd played.

"Fine, one more game," I acquiesced, vaguely wondering what time it was, then coming to the conclusion that I didn't really care.

Brian's cell phone rang again. He glanced at it and walked out into the hallway because we were being too loud.

"Oh yeah," Chris said, not blinking or taking his eyes off the screen. "I forgot to tell him that his girlfriend called on the land line earlier."

My thumb froze over the "duck" button at a bad time. Chris shot me in the back and my screen went red.

"How do you like *that*?" he yelled, jumping up and doing a little dance.

Suddenly the rest of the world came back into focus again. My shoulders and neck were sore from sitting tensely on the bed through several digital massacres. The clock said it was half past midnight. I had class early in the morning. There was a pile of unfinished work on my desk. Brian had a girlfriend.

I handed the controller to Sean.

"You got me!" I said to Chris. "Good game!"

"One more game!" he suggested.

"I've got class early tomorrow morning. I'm off to bed," I said firmly.

Chris pouted like a petulant child.

"Here, I'll play instead," Sean said, starting the game up again. "I will *own* you!"

Chris leapt at the challenge and sat down to play again. I headed back to my room.

Erin was getting ready for bed.

"Oh there you are!" she said, climbing under her covers. "I wasn't sure if you had your keys and I didn't want to lock you out."

"Oh no! Sorry! I hope I didn't keep you up too long."

"No, it's fine," she said sleepily.

I turned out the lights and shut the door. I checked my email one last time and found that Lauren had sent me a one liner:

From: "Lauren Avery" <lavery@princeton.edu>
To: "Amy Callaway" <acallaway@ucla.edu>
Subject: Nonsense

A, Why do you write? L,L

I thought about this as I brushed my teeth and got ready for bed. Then, against my better judgment, I sat down and wrote a proper response to this question. It was after 3am when I finished.

From: "Amy Callaway" <acallaway@ucla.edu>
To: "Amy Callaway" <acallaway@ucla.edu>
Cc: "Lauren Avery" <lavery@princeton.edu>
Subject:

Why do I write? Writing makes things real for me. It seems like I'm always thinking a dozen half-baked thoughts every second. They're effervescent, bubbling into my mind one second and popping out the next. But the instant I write them down, they become real and permanent. They are my creations to own and commit to. They can't be rejected later. In school, I could read textbooks and listen to lectures all day long, but until I wrote out my notes or equations, I didn't fully understand the information. I didn't own it.

Also, it's so much more satisfying to relive memories as they happened and not as I imagine them in hindsight. Imagining something makes it a daydream and not a memory, and somehow that's cheating. Anyone can imagine a magical evening, but it's entirely different to actually have a magical evening. If the real thing was amazing, I would want to capture the memory while it was still fresh, like flash freezing vegetables right after they're picked. I horde these written memories like my hamster horded seeds, frantically and obsessively.

I started out writing for myself. As it became more natural to me, I began to write as a way of communicating to others. I don't think so well on my feet, but given just a few more moments, I can articulate myself much better in writing. Any time Eric and I had an argument, I would write him a letter to accuse, apologize or explain. It always turned out

155

more coherent and diplomatic that way.

Then I wrote for the newspaper because I liked being the messenger and clueing people in to what they missed. Describing something accurately gives me a thrill. It must be the same sort of thrill that an artist gets when they paint something and it's dead on. I'm hoping that someday, I will write things that cause people to really think about things differently or help them see something they didn't used to see before.

PS. Was mean to Mum on the phone today- want to kick myself. I'm an ingrate.
PPS. Brian is not gay. He has a girlfriend. Which is worse?

Exhausted, I collapsed into bed. Lauren's response was waiting for me in the morning.

From: "Lauren Avery" lavery@princeton.edu
To: "Amy Callaway" <acallaway@ucla.edu>
Subject: You've got it, write

A, Then do it for you. And do it for the benefit of others. Who cares what the damn TA thinks?

L,L

P.S. Phantom was freaking amazing. I cried the whole second half. How long does a girl have to wait for love like that in real life?

P.P.S. Go for the neighbor boy that *isn't* a slut. What a freaking fraud.

P.P.P.S. You know I love you, but you'd better apologize to your Mum. I won't tolerate anyone being mean to Mrs. C, not even you. Talk soon!
xxoo

7 "Get a Job"

Thursday was another average school day. Econ class was uneventful. We were learning about fixed costs and variable costs at the firm level. Then I was able to work out a few more problems on my calculus problem set after discussion with my math TA.

When I got back to my room, I didn't quite feel like doing any more work. So I looked around for a suitable diversion. Something that didn't take too long, but that would be amusing. I found what I was looking for lying face down on Casey's bed. I picked up Casey's latest girlie magazine and scurried up the ladder to my extra long twin bed, six feet from the ground. Flopping down on my stomach, I flipped to the table of contents.

Where to start? "Surprise Celebrity Couples"? *Too gossipy.* "Flatter Abs in Two Weeks"? *Yeah right.* "Ten Ways to Please Your Boyfriend"? *Betty Friedan would be livid.* "Do You Have a Healthy Relationship with Food?" That one sounded somewhat relevant. I flipped to page 56.

"Take this simple quiz to help you understand your relationship with food.

1. Do you
> a) Eat to live
> b) Live to eat"

It took me a moment to understand what the question was asking. Then it was a no brainer. B. Of course I live to eat! Food is easily one of the core pleasures in my life. In fact, last night's BBQ ribs at Hedrick were still very much on my mind.

"2. What is your primary criterion for selecting what you eat?
> a) Nutritious content
> b) How tasty it is"

Another no brainer. B. I mean, once in awhile, I eat something because it's good for me, but not usually.

"3. Do you eat when you are stressed out?
> a) No
> b) Yes"

B. I was beginning to see a pattern here.

"4. Do you use meals, desserts or drinks to celebrate?
　　　　a) No
　　　　b) Yes"

　　B.　It started with pizza parties after sports victories and cake during birthdays. This survey is unreasonable. Who would possibly answer no to this question?

"5　Do you use meals, desserts or drinks as a social activity more than twice a week?
　　　　a) No
　　　　b) Yes"

　　B. Every night, in fact.

　　I didn't look at the rest of the questions but instead looked at the scoring guide at the bottom.

　　"If you answered b) to more than five questions, you have an unhealthy relationship with food. Using food as an emotional crutch is dangerous because it causes you to consume more calories than your body needs. You should talk to a professional and rethink your eating habits."

　　I chucked the magazine across the room in disgust.. It landed, as I intended, back on Casey's bed.

　　Erin walked in, her slight frame slouching under the weight of her disproportionately enormous backpack. She looked flustered.

　　"Hey!" I said.

　　"Hey, Amy," she said, looking up at me and smiling like it took a lot of effort. "How's it going?"

　　"Well, Casey's magazine over there said I had an unhealthy relationship with food," I reported, rolling my eyes.

　　"What does that mean?" Erin asked.

　　"Apparently, I eat for emotional reasons," I told her.

　　"Like what?"

　　"Because I like food and it makes me happy."

　　"Who doesn't?" she asked, still looking confused.

　　"That's what I'm saying!"

　　I felt vindicated in my harsh treatment of the ridiculous periodical.

　　"Who doesn't like food?" She swung her backpack to the ground and sank into her desk chair with a sigh. I sensed that it was more than the heavy backpack that was weighing on her.

"What's up?" I asked her. She looked up at me, troubled

"Jim changed his profile," she said.

"What do you mean?" I asked her.

"His relationship status used to say, 'in a relationship with Erin.'" she told me. "Now it's just blank."

"Wow."

I didn't know what else to say. Nothing good could come of this. Everybody and their mother could see Jim's profile. It was the modern equivalent of yelling it in the town square.

"Did you ask him about it yet?"

"Not yet. He just did it today. I don't know if he meant for me to see it or not. Maybe it's his way of telling me that it's over."

"Were you guys having problems?" I asked, trying to help her diagnose the situation.

Erin shrugged. "I mean, I was sort of suspicious of that girl he knows there who is a family friend and I told him so, but he said I was just being paranoid. Aside from that, I thought we were fine. We talk all the time online. And he always says, 'I love you' at the end of every conversation."

"Wow," I breathed, not being very eloquent today.

I couldn't imagine saying that to anyone at this point in my life. That was a pretty big deal.

"I know, right?" she said, starting up her computer.

"Well he didn't change his status to 'single,'" I pointed out, trying to look on the bright side.

"Come on! Leaving it blank after he had it up that way for six months is tantamount to announcing that he's single!"

"You're right. What are you going to do?"

"I'm going to confront him."

"You should change your relationship status to be 'in a relationship with Amy'," I suggested.

"That would be the ultimate insult," she laughed. "Telling everyone that he turned me into a lesbian."

We both giggled. But the air turned somber again quickly.

"I don't know why he's doing this."

"Well, he's a moron if he gives you up." I said firmly.

"That doesn't help me any," she said, miserably.

Her computer finished booting up. I saw her buddy list pop up.

"Is he there?" I asked.

She nodded and began pounding the keys.

I crawled down from my bed and retrieved my Economics book. It was a bit of a relief to escape to something much less complicated than real life.

When the typing subsided, the silence rang out like a gunshot.

"Erin?" I asked, alarmed.

"It's fine now." The relief was evident in her tone. "He put our relationship status back up on the profile. He said he didn't realize it would bother me so much. He just didn't want people at school knowing too much about what was going on in his life."

This sounded fishy to me, but I kept my mouth shut. "Great!"

"OK, now I can get some work done before dinner," she said, diving into her backpack and producing an enormous physics textbook. I winced just looking at it.

"Cheers," I replied, diving back into my own work.

*****

That night after dinner, I was sitting at my desk, attempting to make up some of the work I'd sacrificed to the video game gods. I'd read the same paragraph about six times on how to integrate 3-D shapes using polar coordinates, but I couldn't get my head around it.

My cell phone spastically came to life, buzzing with self-importance. It was Mom. I took a deep breath. I'd promised myself that I would be good the next time she called.

"Hi Mom!"

"Hi Amy!" she said, the relief palpable in her voice. "How was your day?"

"It was busy," I told her. "I have a calculus problem set due tomorrow. My professor is insane. He puts these easy problems on the board and then he gives us all these hard problems for homework."

"I'm surprised," Mum said. "You've always been good at math!"

Be quiet, count to three. One, two, three... I let the wave of annoyance pass for a second.

"Well, I might have met my match," I said. "Anyway, I had Economics this morning, then my Calculus discussion. Then I came home to work on my homework."

"Sounds productive!"

"I suppose… How was your day?"

"It was good. I went to the gym, stopped by Marshall's to look at what they had on sale, then I had lunch with Mrs. Armour. She says hi, by the way."

"Tell her I said hi," I murmured.

"And I spent this afternoon picking up around the house," she finished. "Dad and I went to Giovanni's for dinner."

"Wow, you are eating out a lot!"

"Well, it's hard to cook for just two," Mum said, a little defensively.

"Are you keeping busy?"

"Well, sort of," she admitted. "I think I may look for a part-time job or a volunteer position somewhere. I don't know who is going to hire me after I've been out of the work force for so long."

"Don't give up, Mum," I said, alarmed.

All of my life, my mother had been busy, confident and in charge. It scared me to hear her sound uncertain all of a sudden.

"You're so smart," I told her. "Maybe you could start by volunteering to build up your resume again and then you could apply for a job."

"By that time, I'll be ready to retire," she laughed. But I could spot the concern trying to hide behind her laughter. "It wouldn't hurt to make a few extra bucks with you in school and Meg paying off her student loans."

I was suddenly struck with guilt.

"And I checked the online bank statement this morning. You've been in school for less than a month and you've already withdrawn $200 from the ATM! What on earth are you buying?"

"Well, textbooks, a sweatshirt…" I started.

"No, those you charged to the credit card," Mum cut me off. "What are you using the cash for?"

"Football tickets, movie tickets, eating out, coffee…" I was beginning to feel cornered.

"Are those really necessary?" Mum asked. She continued without waiting for an answer. "We're paying for your meal plan so you shouldn't be eating out. And why do you need to be drinking coffee? Aren't you sleeping enough?"

"They're social expenses!" I pointed out. "Sometimes I'll meet up with someone for coffee or a bunch of us will go to dinner and a movie."

"Well you need to be more selective about it, Amy!" she said. I could hear the exasperation. "Do you know how much your tuition, room and board cost?"

"Twenty thousand," I muttered. "Minus the two thousand from my scholarship."

"A little more than that, if you count your books," Mum said. "Do you understand how much money that is after taxes?"

I stayed silent.

"After we hang up, I want you to do the math, ok? We can't afford to pay so much for your entertainment. You're there to learn. Socializing is secondary," she reminded me.

"OK, Mum," I said, resigned.

"I'm sorry, Honey. I wish we could afford to pay for all of the fun things that you want to do with your friends, but with only one income and your dad thinking about retirement, we just can't do it."

"I know, Mum," I said, feeling like a spoiled brat. "It's ok. I'll figure it out."

We sat in sorrowful silence for awhile. Then I broke in.

"I should get back to my homework."

"Alright, Amy. Have a good night. I love you."

"Thanks, Mum. I love you too."

When I hung up the phone, I found I wasn't in the mood to integrate in polar coordinates anymore. I gave up and decided to tackle my own Economics problem.

How much could I make doing work-study? Probably minimum wage. Then The Man would take some percentage of it. OK, so let's say I would get to keep about five dollars an hour. I scrawled out the math on the corner of my calculus problem set.

$20,000 / ($5/hour) = 4,000 hours

4,000 hours/ 52 weeks = 76.9 hours/week

I sat bolt upright in my hard oak chair. That couldn't be right. I would have to work 80 hours a week at minimum wage to put myself through college? That wasn't even possible! I'd have to work 16 hours a day, five days a week! Well, obviously I couldn't do that. I tried the math a different way to see how much spending money I could make.

$5/hour x 10 hours/week = $50/week

It seemed like a lot of work for not that much money. I could spend $50 a week, easy. But I already felt like there weren't enough hours in the week. And I wanted to save some portion of it for the trip to Cancun. For the second time that night, I felt defeated. I slumped down in my chair.

"What's wrong?" a voice called from the doorway.

It was Brian. Great. I hadn't felt like dealing with him yet because I still felt hurt on many levels. As a friend, I was angry that he was keeping secrets from me. As a crush, I was mad that he had a girlfriend. And as a human being with an ego, I was mad that I made a fool out of myself flirting with him when he hadn't encouraged me to because he had a girlfriend. Or had he? I might as well be mad at him for the ambiguity in my mind, while I was blaming him for everything else.

"Nothing," I lied, forcing a smile.

I looked at Erin to make sure we weren't bothering her. She had put her headphones on, probably when I started talking to my mom. Casey hadn't come home for dinner and we didn't know where she was.

"You're lying," Brian said, coming in the room. "You look worried about something."

He peered over my shoulder to see what I was doing. I leaned over my paper so he couldn't see it, annoyed that he was in my societally constructed "personal space".

"I'm just making a budget if you must know!"

He backed away with his hands up.

"Sorry!"I could tell he had been well trained. He knew to say sorry even though he didn't know what he was sorry about.

"No, it's fine," I said grumpily, realizing he'd only been trying to help. "Mum just gave me a lecture on my spending habits. I think I need to get a job if I want to continue having any sort of social life."

"Yeah, it's expensive to eat out and stuff," Brian concurred. "I was looking at the jobs posted in Kerckhoff. I was thinking about working at a coffee shop or a bookstore on campus."

"Really?" I asked, becoming very interested. "Maybe I should apply for one of those too!"

"The bookstore is looking to hire work-study students for Winter Quarter," Brian said, relieved to be on my good side again. "You can get the application online. I can IM you the link. I was going to take mine in tomorrow. Want to come?"

I nodded. While I would bemoan the loss of some precious free time, I knew this was the right thing to do.

I took out the "Freshman Fifteen" list and added one to the bottom.

The Freshman Fifteen
By Amy Callaway

Expect to:

- gain 15 lbs
- find yourself
- explore new ideas
- make new friends
- hang on to old friends
- party and drink (in a safe environment)
- experiment with sex (???)
- find your life's purpose
- get pumped about college sports (but keep it clean)
- date lots
- leave the nest
- get a job (if you expect to have textbooks and a good time)

*****

Casey swept into the room just as I was finishing my job application. She always moved as if she had a spotlight on her.

"Our sorority meeting ran *so* long tonight! Amy, are you going to put sex on your list of things to expect in college?" she asked me, as she swung her backpack onto her bed and began taking off her shoes and sweatshirt.

I was flattered that she had even remembered I was writing an article. "Maybe. I have mixed feelings about that one because I don't know if I should be encouraging girls to try sex in college."

"Oh, come on! Anyone who hasn't had sex by the time they've reached college should at least experiment once they get here! What have you got against sex?" she asked.

"Pregnancy and disease," Erin stated, removing her headphones and turning around in her chair to face us. "There was this girl at my high school who was really popular. But then she got pregnant junior year. She had to quit school halfway through senior year to have the baby and take care of it."

"That's rare," Casey said. "She was probably dumb and didn't use protection."

"Well, no," Erin said, craning her slender neck up to look at Casey. "I remember how we were all scared because she was on the Pill and she *still* got pregnant. Oh my God, it was awful. Somehow, her parents worked out a deal with the school so that she could take a few remedial classes and still graduate. But none of them could show their face at graduation. They were all humiliated."

"Oh please," Casey said, exasperated. "What town was this? Colonial Williamsburg? Did they give her a big scarlet letter too?"

"I'm just saying that it's a really big price to pay for a little fun," Erin pointed out.

"I'll bet she wasn't taking her Pill at the same time every day,.And how

164

do you know it's just a little fun? You're still a virgin, right?"

"And proud of it," Erin said.

Casey bristled. "If you're still a virgin, then you have no idea what you're talking about. It's the ultimate natural act."

"It's the ultimate natural way to have babies and spread diseases!" Erin retorted.

"It's also the ultimate natural way to have fun! And it's an intense way to connect with another person."

"It's also the way women hold power over men," Sean said from the doorway.

All three of us started.

"Jeez!" I said, throwing my hands up into the air. "We need to close the door more often!"

"What do you mean?" Erin asked Sean.

"You know, with you guys being the weaker sex and all that, God needed a way to even up the playing field. So he gave us testosterone and he gave you the power to take advantage of it," Sean said, enjoying the indignation rising around him.

"Weaker sex?" cried Erin. "I'm sure any man would die if he had to give birth!"

"Oh, nonsense. It's probably some big conspiracy among women. I'll bet giving birth feels great. They just say it's excruciating so they get sympathy from the men," Sean said, unaffected.

Three jaws dropped simultaneously.

"Are you joking?" Casey said.

"If you're so strong, then why are we always the ones to go to war?" asked Chris, who emerged from his room to join the battle of the sexes.

"Because women don't have the 'mine's bigger than yours' complex," I piped up. "It's not that we couldn't go to war, it's that men care more about it."

"No, you're physically weaker," Chris said. "Ask any army guy."

"Maybe physically, but I don't think we're mentally weaker," I said.

"Oh really?" Sean asked. "Then why are most of the scientific breakthroughs and major inventions done by men?"

"Because for the greater length of history, women haven't been given the opportunity to get an education," Erin said.

"Well, why not?" asked Sean. "Maybe they couldn't cut it in the classroom."

"Bullshit!" said Sarah, who smelled the blood and came running. "I've been the top of my class since kindergarten. I've *smoked* all the boys I ever went to school with."

"Men have historically tried to keep women down by forcing us to stay home and raise the kids," I offered.

"Well, if you were so smart and so strong, why did you let them?" asked Sean.

"Maybe we figured society would go to crap if we let the men raise the kids," Sarah said.

"*Ohhhh!*" Casey yelled, giving Sarah a high five.

"Oh please," Chris said, shaking his head. "How hard can it be to bring up a kid?"

This time, four jaws dropped simultaneously.

"Silence, village idiot," Sarah told him. "Mark Twain once said, 'It's better to be quiet and look like an idiot than to open your mouth and confirm it.'"

"Yeah, I can't believe you said that," Erin said, still recovering from the shock.

"Well, shit!" Sean said, pretending to look concerned. "If they're letting women get an education *and* they still have the power in relationships, we're pretty screwed, aren't we, fellas?"

He looked at Chris and Brian, who was coming out to see what the racket was all about.

"What are you talking about?" demanded Erin. "Why do you keep saying women have power over men? I'd sure like to know about this power I didn't know I had."

"Are you serious?" asked Sean. "Our one Achilles' heel," he continued. "Is sex. We need it more than you do, so you have the power. It's the only thing that overrides our reason. For example, say Erin wants her boyfriend to go to the ballet with her. Any normal, ridicule-fearing man would say no. But say her boyfriend thinks he will get some if he goes to the ballet with her. Then he'll let his little guy override his reason and he'll go to the ballet with her."

"That's awful!" Erin cried.

"Hey, I'm just the messenger," Sean said. "I'm just telling you how we're wired."

"But what if they're not having sex?" I asked, eager to elucidate more of convoluted workings of the male mind.

"Well then all bets are off," Sean said. "She has no advantage anymore. He will tell her that ballet is for fruitcakes and he'll have nothing to do with it! Or, if he's smarter than the average bear, he'll still go with her in hopes of accumulating points towards scoring with her later."

"That's so crude!" Sarah exclaimed, scrunching her nose.

"That's life," Sean said.

"I can't understand how you can have such a one track mind!" I said.

"Don't listen to him!" Brian said, looking at me. "We're not *all* that way. Some of us enjoy the friendship and the romance."

I looked at him coolly. "Your girlfriend got lucky then," I said, before I could stop myself.

He was caught off guard. He stammered for a few seconds, but couldn't find the words, so he looked at the ground.

"How much of your day is spent thinking about getting a girl into bed?" asked Sarah, disgusted, but fascinated.

"I don't know," Chris answered. "But more of my day is spent thinking about how to get *two* girls into bed!"

He high five'd Sean, who yelped like a hyena.

"Whatever happened to good old-fashioned polygamy?" Chris said.

Casey's laughter rang out and surprised us all.

"You think it would be cool to have *two* girls at once?" she said, dimples dancing. "Let me tell you... I pity the fool who has to put up with two women being bitchy at the same time. Can you imagine the horrors?"

"She makes a good point," Sean said to Chris. "One's bad enough."

"I read an article about how polygamy is actually bad for men anyhow," Brian said. He had apparently recovered. "In societies where you can only marry one woman at a time, things are about even. Most men get a wife. But in societies where a man can have more than one wife, the men who can support multiple wives get multiple wives and poor men don't get any. So it's good if you're rich, but otherwise..."

"You get shafted," Casey said, grinning.

We laughed appreciatively at her appropriate choice of words. The conversation dissolved at that point and we headed back to our respective rooms. I sat down with a sigh and hit the space bar to bring my computer back from its slumber.

There was an IM message.

This was interesting. But I was still a little upset at him for going with someone else earlier. My pride was hurt. I wasn't a big fan of boys at the moment.

And I left it at that.

"It's Thursday night!" Casey pointed out, out of the blue. "We *have* to go out! I heard that there was going to be a rockin' party over at Beta Pi. Some of the girls I met at Rush are going."

"I can't," Erin said. "I have three problem sets due tomorrow and I'm not done with them yet."

I suspected that she was also still a little mad at Casey over the sex argument. Casey didn't fight her, but instead looked expectantly at me.

"Come on, Amy," she cajoled.

I screwed up my face as I thought about it.

"Come *on*," she insisted. "It's Thursday night!"

If I couldn't figure out this problem in half an hour more, then I probably wasn't going to figure this problem out at all. Anyway, this is how I justified my admittedly less-than-responsible decision.

"OK," I told Casey.

She looked satisfied and turned to her closet.

When we arrived at the party, it was already in full swing. The uniformed security guard ran his eyes over each of us, not for security purposes, I suspected. There was a line of non-fraternity guys forming outside the house. As far as I could tell, none of them was getting in any time soon.

We walked into the living room, where the dancing had started. On the other end of the room, there was a fireplace. The DJ stood in front of it, holding one side of his clunky head phones up to one ear, his baseball cap cocked over the other ear. Thank goodness we were across the room from his speakers. The music was deafening as it was.

Casey and her friends wasted no time and started dancing like it was their job. I tried to get into it as well, but I found myself distracted by the volume of the music, the writhing bodies clad in skin-tight silk and sparkles, and the random people who kept running into me.

Someone grabbed my ass. I jumped about a mile, but by the time I turned around, I couldn't identify the culprit. Unbelievable!

I saw a good looking guy come up behind Casey and wrap his arms around her waist. She turned her head to see who it was. Then she smiled at him and they kissed over her shoulder. I guessed it was probably Trevor. He was a handsome specimen. Nice bone structure. They proceeded to thrust their hips as one to the music.

All of a sudden, there was a blinding flash from beside the DJ, accompanied by the sound of a tremendous crash.

The music stopped. For a moment, everyone froze. Then, there was wholesale panic.

People began screaming and running towards us. Everything was dark. The last thing that I saw was the DJ slumped over his turn table and smoke billowing from one of the speakers.

As a wave of people tried to shove their way to the front door, I felt people closing in on me from all sides, pushing, pushing, pushing.

I couldn't breathe because I was being crushed from all sides.

I began to throwing my weight towards the front door as well, to get out of this pack of bodies so I could breathe again. The smell burning plastic permeated the air and there was shouting all around.

Where was Casey? Ahead of me, I saw one of the girls we came with. She was almost through the door. The smell of burning grew stronger and I gasped for air, continuing to struggle forward in the dark and the smoke.

The doorway was nearing. With one immense push, I broke through the doorway, taking a clump of people with me. I tripped and fell down the stairs, onto the lawn, where several people were laying or kneeling in the cool night air. The absence of a deafening roar rang in my ears.

When I caught my breath, I looked around and found Casey hanging on Trevor's arm, panting at the edge of the lawn. Her face was red and her eyes were watering. I made my way to her. She held out her arm and I tucked myself under it.

"My God, what *happened*?" I asked, still very tense. My heels were sinking into the lawn. I didn't know if that was mitigating or exacerbating the wobbling in my knees.

Casey shook her head. Her normally fluffy hair was stuck to her sweaty neck.

"I don't know!" Casey replied. "It sounded like an explosion."

"Maybe the DJ's equipment broke," Trevor suggested. We both

169

looked at him and saw a trickle of blood dripping down his jaw.

"You're hurt!" Casey cried, alarmed.

He wiped the side of his face and looked surprised to see the blood on his hands.

We heard the wail of sirens grow steadily louder behind us. Everybody moved away from the sidewalk as paramedics rushed up to the house with stretchers. Wisps of smoke were escaping from the front door.

"I should go in there," Trevor said. "I don't know if any of my bros are still in the house."

"Don't go in," Casey begged. "Let the firemen do it."

Trevor obeyed.

We watched silently as the paramedics brought out a girl, whose arm looked burned and blistered. She was crying hysterically. Then they brought out a guy, who had streams of blood running down his face and arms from several lacerations.

"Uh oh, that's my little bro," Trevor said, letting go of Casey and walking towards the stretcher.

Finally, they brought out the DJ, who was completely unconscious, but covered with burns and cuts. I had to look away.

As the police arrived on the scene, many people, some of whom were bleeding and injured, fled into the night. Firemen and paramedics began walking amongst those of us on the lawn, bandaging our cuts and scrapes.

A policewoman approached us with a pad of paper, muttering under her breath. I thought I caught the phrases "spoiled kids" and "mixing beer with electronics". She stopped in front of us and looked disapprovingly.

I suddenly felt ridiculous in my skin tight outfit.

"What happened in there?" she asked, jerking her thumb towards the house.

"We were dancing, and then there was an explosion," Casey told her, lifting her chin proudly.

"Did you see anyone suspicious around the DJ's equipment?"

Both of us shook our heads.

"Was it one explosion or multiple explosions?"

Casey and I looked at each other. I couldn't remember.

"I think it was one," I told her. "But I can't remember."

"Can I get your name and number in case we have further questions?" she asked, eyeing the people she wanted to question who were beginning to walk off the premises.

Casey and I wrote down our contact information.

"Alright. Go home, girls," she ordered.

We obeyed and began walking back to the dorms.

"Do you think we'll get in trouble?" I asked, when we were out of earshot.

"Naw," Casey said,. "We hadn't started drinking yet, which was lucky. They'll probably just decide it was an accident and that will be that."

"Someone probably spilled beer on the speaker," I suggested, paraphrasing what the policewoman had been muttering.

I blanched at the memory of myself dancing on a speaker with a beer not that long ago. For the first time, the rollaway boob didn't seem like the worst thing that could have happened in that situation.

"That's so scary," Casey commented. "I've been to so many parties with beer and sound equipment. And this is the first time something like this has ever happened."

"I know, it's totally scary."

When we arrived home, Erin saw the looks on our faces and sprang up from her desk.

"What happened?" she asked, alarmed.

"A speaker exploded at the party," I told her. "It was crazy. One minute, we were dancing and it was a normal frat party. And the next minute, there was this flash and an explosion. There was smoke, and everyone started pushing to try to get outside. I was worried that I was going to get trampled."

I dug my heel into the rough carpet and wrenched the shoe off of my foot. I was glad to be rid of the painful constriction of the plastic straps.

"Was anyone hurt?" Erin asked.

"Yeah, the DJ and a few people close to the speakers," Casey replied.

She stood up straight, picked her right foot up behind her daintily and removed her shoes. Boy, I had a lot to learn.

"Are you guys alright?" Erin asked, sitting back down at her desk.

"Yeah, we're fine," I assured her. "I mean, I think we're fine. I'm still trying to make sense of it."

"Yeah, I'm just weirded out," Casey added. "This is the first time I've ever felt physically unsafe at a party. Even when the guys get into fights, you never have to worry about your own safety, you know?"

I nodded, as I grabbed my shower caddy and jammies. I tried to let the rushing water drown out the ringing and lingering sounds of sirens in my ears.

They persisted far into the night.

*****

"Listen to this," Sarah announced at lunch the next day. She cleared her throat and read us a section from the *Daily Bruin*. "There was an explosion at the Beta Pi fraternity house last night around eleven-thirty during a regular house party. Three people were seriously injured, two of which are undergraduates of the university. Preliminary investigations show that there were charges planted in one of the DJ's speakers. The detonation device has still not been found. If you have any information regarding this incident, please contact campus security..."

"I knew it!" Casey declared, relieved. "I knew it couldn't just be spilling beer on the sound equipment! I've spilled beer on sound equipment before and nothing exploded."

"But who would do this?" I asked. "Why would anyone want to blow up sound equipment at a party?"

"I can think of a million reasons!" Sean replied. "A rival fraternity could have planted it. Maybe a jealous ex. It could have just been some deranged sociopath who was bored."

We chewed our lunches in silence.

After lunch, I found myself retracing last night's nocturnal promenade to Beta Pi's frat house. I don't know why I went there other than the fact that I felt unsettled. I wanted to see the crime scene for myself to make sense of what had happened last night. It all just felt like a bad dream. It's too bad you can't vomit out a bad thought like an excess of libations. I hoped that seeing the room cleaned up and quiet might expel the sounds of screaming and sirens from my head.

The house looked decidedly less glamorous in the afternoon sunlight, paint chipping, drapped in yellow plastic tape, like a poorly wrapped gift that no one wants. A police car was parked out front, with two policemen leaned up against it, discussing the contents of a plastic bag. I tried to look casual as I swung around the back of the house, my thoughts racing.

You shouldn't be here. You look suspicious. You're trespassing on a crime scene. Don't touch anything.

I decided just to peek in the window to see the living room where the accident took place. As I crouched in the bushes beneath the living room window, I made out some letters scrawled in the velvet dust blanketing the window.

"F Elitists"

Elitists? I was puzzled. What could this mean? Who would think of frat guys as elitist? I caught my breath when I heard the voices of the policemen coming through the house, and I quickly made my way back to campus.

8 "Learn to live with roommates"

Midterms literally started with a bang. Some of us fared worse than others. I counted myself among the lucky, as I'd actually been attending classes. But that didn't mean that I was as prepared as I should have been.

We were eating dinner on Sunday night, leading into Week 5, halfway through the quarter, when Sarah asked Sean if he'd tried the practice test for chemistry. Sean froze, his BBQ chicken halfway between his plate and his mouth.

"What practice test?" he asked, looking wary.

"The one that the prof handed out in class last week! Out of the kindness of my heart, I brought you an extra copy, remember?" Sarah replied. "The midterm is in two days- it's on the syllabus that we got the first day of class!"

Sean groaned and began to look worried. The rest of us were sympathetic. Well, to a point. How sympathetic could you be to someone who had not been to class since the second week of school? Some mornings, when I dragged myself out of bed in time for 8am class, his door would be open and he'd still be up playing video games or computer games from the night before.

I was terrified of my Calculus midterm. This past weekend, I had tried to go back through the textbook and redo all the examples again. I saved the harder homework problems for tonight and tomorrow. It seemed like a reasonable plan over the weekend. Now I was kicking myself for not doing more over the weekend.

The Economics exam was less intimidating. I generally understood the main concepts that the professor presented in class. I was worried about two things. The first involved any sudden, unpredictable moves by my professor. My Economics professor had a tendency to lecture about one thing, then turn around and assign us homework on a completely different subject. My second worry was what the curve would look like in that class. I'd heard that in easier classes where the curve was not well distributed, a stupid mistake, like an arithmetic error, could be the difference between an A or a C. And I was prone to stupid arithmetic errors, especially when I was sleep deprived. To top it off, in all of my classes, I was generally unsure about what sort of competition I faced.

I sighed and distracted myself by thinking about a way to work study habits into "The Freshman Fifteen."

When we got back to the room after dinner, Erin and I took our seats at our respective desks. Casey began looking in her closet again. I wondered vaguely what her midterm schedule looked like, or if she cared.

"Who wants to go out with me tomorrow night?" she asked in a sing-song voice, looking between Erin and me. It was the same voice I used to use when I was baby-sitting and was asking who wanted a cookie.

Erin shook her head.

"I don't know why I even bother to ask you," Casey sighed, wrinkling her perfect button nose. "You *never* want to go out!"

"That's because I always have problem sets due the day after you want to go out!" Erin pointed out. "And I'm not really into drinking either, but you always go to drinking parties."

"Amy, you'll come out with me, right?" Casey cajoled, turning to face me.

"Can't,I have a calc midterm on Wednesday that is going to kick my ass. I have a study group I need to prep for on Tuesday night."

"You guys are so lame!" Casey pouted, evidently put out. "What about this whole College Experience you keep talking about, Amy?"

I smarted when I heard my own words being thrown back in my face. Part of me wanted to just forget my midterms and party with Casey. After all, you only live once, right? On the other hand, I knew I would pissed at myself for a long time if I bombed my midterms.

"Midterms are part of the college experience too," I replied, trying not to be bothered by her cruel pronouncement. "Plus, remember what happened at the last party we went to?"

Still pouting, Casey took out her phone and began scrolling through her address book.

I took out my calculus textbook and notebook and began to look over homework problems.

I noticed that Erin had a pile of Skittles on her desk. She finished doing what looked like a physics problem, then flipped to the back of the book to check her answer. She nodded her head in approval. Then, she carefully picked out a red Skittle and ate it. Maybe I should devise a reward system.

Chris strolled in with a small red container of Chef Boyardee in his hand.

"Can I use your microwave?" he asked. Erin gestured towards it, without taking her eyes off her physics book.

"Thanks," he said, and popped it in.

"Hey, I was looking through Casey's 'Physics for Poets' book," he said, and then paused to be sure we were all listening. Casey was taking the less rigorous Introduction to Physics class for humanities majors, nicknamed with the aforementioned nickname. "There's a problem in there that stumped me," Chris continued. "It said, 'You fire a 10 pound cannon ball at a height of 3 feet off the ground at a 35 degree angle with a velocity of 100 miles an hour."

He paused a minute, as Erin drew a diagram out on her scratch paper and began writing out formulas.

"How do you feel about that?"

He burst out laughing and we all broke into smiles, except for Casey, who would normally have been very good natured about it.

"F you!" she said, irritably. "Why does everyone treat me like I'm dumb?"

Sean strolled in. He'd clearly been listening to the whole conversation up to this point and could smell a provocative discussion from miles.

"It's because you're a Comm major," he said, as if it were the most natural thing in the world.

"Why does that make me dumb?" she asked.

"It doesn't make you *dumb*, per se," Sean clarified. "Your classes are just less rigorous than other people's classes. Everyone knows it. Don't feel bad about it."

Don't feel bad about it. Those words always have the opposite intended effect. Or maybe, they have exactly the intended effect.

"My classes are as rigorous as anyone else's!"

"Then how come you can go out while everyone else is studying? What classes are you taking?" Sean asked.

"Whatever, Mr. Champion-Video-Game-Master," she sputtered. "Maybe my classes aren't as time consuming as other people's, but that doesn't mean they couldn't be difficult!"

"What classes are you taking?" Sean repeated.

"Comm Studies I, English and Physics 6A," Casey replied, defensively.

"Hm," Sean replied. He didn't need to say anything more. I know we were all thinking the same thing. First of all, she was taking three classes while some of us were taking four. And second of all, none of her classes were considered very difficult.

"Whatever!" Casey said. "Everybody generalizes around here. I hate it!"

Feeling the need to defend my roommate, I chimed in, "Yah, college majors live in the world of stereotypes. At least you've picked a major. Everybody looks at me like I'm developmentally disabled because I can't pick a major."

"I've noticed that too," Sean said. I gave him an exasperated look.

"No, not that you're developmentally disabled!" he clarified. "That people don't take undeclared majors very seriously!"

I rolled my eyes and tried another angle.

"Erin, I'll bet you're sick of being stereotyped as an engineer."

Erin thought about this for a minute. "Actually, I kind of like it! Everybody thinks that I'm smarter than I probably am."

"Bullshit!" cried Chris. "You *are* smart!"

"Case in point," Erin said, smugly.

"But don't you think it's bad that people do that?" I asked, because I could see Casey getting angrier out of the corner of my eye.

"I think some stereotypes take root in reality," Erin said calmly.

Casey bristled.

Suddenly, there was a loud sound that startled us all.

"BANG!"

We all jumped about a foot into the air and then started freaking out. I stood up, knocking over my chair.. Everyone looked frantically in different directions, trying to determine the source of the noise. I had visions of exploding speakers in my head.

"Oh my God, *get down!*" Sean cried, dropping to his knees and curling into a ball. He didn't need to tell us twice. We all dropped from where we were sitting or standing.

"What the hell was that?" Casey cried from under her desk. I was sure she was thinking what I was thinking.

"You're closest to the window!" Chris yelled. "You look!"

He had no desk to crawl under. He and Sean were curled up on the open floor.

"Are you crazy?" Casey yelled back. "I'm going to get killed!"

"It totally sounded like a gunshot!" Sean said.

"How do you know what a gunshot sounds like?" Erin asked.

"I'm from the 'hood," Sean said, condescending even in his state of fear. "Trust me, I know what a gunshot sounds like."

He began crawling on his elbows, GI style, towards the door, dragging his legs behind him.

"Where are you going?" I asked, panicked. There was strength in numbers.

"I'm going to get help!" he said, continuing to crawl out. "Besides, we stand a better chance separately if someone is running around shooting."

Every muscle in my body was tense. My pulse was pounding against my ribcage and thoughts were flying through my mind. Was it some psycho sociopath like the shooter at Virginia Tech? If so, where would we go? I

176

frantically tried to think of alternative ways out of the building should the shooter come up the main stairs. We were sitting ducks should the shooter come into this room. Casey had barricaded herself beneath her desk, using her chair as a shield. I tried to think about how hard it would be to jump out of our window and land in a planter.

"What's going on here?" a voice demanded from the doorway.

Sarah was standing there with her hands on her hips.

"There was a loud bang from in here."

"What do you mean?" asked Sean, looking up at her from the floor, where he was still creeping on his elbows towards the door.

"There was a loud bang from in here," Sarah repeated. "What have you guys done?"

"Beep... beep... beep... beeeeeep." The microwave stopped its humming to announce the end of its kitchen detail.

We all ignored it, except for Erin. A look of understanding spread slowly over her face. She crawled out from under her bed and opened the microwave oven. Smoke was coming out of it and there was a smell of burnt plastic.

"You know what a gunshot sounds like, do you?" she said to Sean, a smile tugging at the corner of her mouth. "Does it sound like metal discharging in a microwave?"

She began to giggle. By the time Casey and I emerged from under our respective desks, she was sitting on her bed, laughing until tears were running down her face.

"I don't understand," I said. "What happened? Why did Chris put metal in the microwave?"

"I didn't!" Chris objected. "I thought the container was microwave-safe. Isn't it made of plastic?"

"Yeah, but usually there's a metal lid on it that you have to remove before you put it in the microwave," Sarah said, laughing as well. "Didn't you read the directions on the label?"

Chris looked sheepish. He pulled the sleeve of his sweatshirt over his hand like a mitt, reached into the microwave and pulled out his midnight snack. There was a hole the size of a dime in the red plastic lid of the container that was burnt along its ragged edges. Casey and I began to chuckle.

"I'll just... take this back to my room," he said, backing out the door. "Thanks for letting me use your microwave." He rushed out, stepping around Sarah, who was still standing in the doorway laughing. Sean was close behind him. By this point, Casey and I were laughing out of sheer relief.

"Little boy from the 'hood," Casey called out after Sean. "Where are you going so fast?"

177

"Midterms... you know," he called from next door. We heard them shut their door behind them.

"Never a dull moment," Sarah said, wiping laughter tears from her eyes. "There's never a dull moment with those clowns around." She left with a cheerful wave.

"Hey," Erin said. Casey and I looked at her expectantly. "Can you two clean your stuff off the floor so I can vacuum tonight?"

I had at least three separate stacks of papers on the floor along with my backpack, tennis shoes and pajama pants. I began gathering up my papers and shoving them into one of my desk drawers.

"I'll do it before I go to bed," Casey said "Hey Amy," she said, turning towards me.

"Yeah?" I replied, looking up from my cleaning.

"What are you going to wear to the Halloween party at SIE?"

"Haven't had time to do anything about it. Got any ideas?" I asked.

"Well, I was thinking we could take a study break and head down to Zoey's to have a look!" she suggested.

"Right now?" I asked, glancing with some concern at the double integrals in polar coordinates on my desk.

"Well yeah. They close in an hour!"

"Well..." I said, chewing on my pencil, conflicted.

"Come on!"

"Alright, let's do it!" I sighed, giving in. I stood up and looked around for my sweatshirt. Casey's cell phone began to ring. She picked it up.

"Hey, what's going on?" She paused. I pulled the sweatshirt over my head.

"Yeah, I'm game," she said. "I'll be there in half an hour."

She hung up the phone and looked at me.

"Can we go tomorrow?" she asked.

"Why?" I asked, trying to keep the disappointment out of my voice.

"We're having a slumber party at my sorority tonight. They just called it. My big sis just got engaged," she explained.

"Uh... ok, Does 5pm work for you?"

Casey nodded and began packing up her Louis Vuitton messenger bag. As she packed, a piece of paper fell out of one of her books next to my chair. I picked it up and saw that it was my English professor's reading list. There was a phone number scrawled across the top. No doubt, it belonged to some hot

178

guy.

"Case, I didn't realize we had the same English prof!" I exclaimed.

"Oh, you have Grandpa Grumpy too?" she asked, taking the paper from me.

"Yeah, that's a great name for him," I said still struggling with the conflicting goals of trying to stay in Casey's good graces and letting her know that I was annoyed at her for dropping me like a hot potato when her sorority friend called.

"He has a terrible rating on uclaprofessors.com," she said. "Check it out-people have written horrible reviews about him. Apparently he's sort of distracted and not into teaching at all. It's a wonder he's still around."

"Tenure," Erin piped up. "Once he has tenure, there's pretty much nothing the university can do to get rid of him."

"That's a medieval system," replied Casey. "CEO's get fired all the time if they do something bad, even if they're really senior."

She threw her toiletry bag, a shirt and her make-up into her bag. When she was done, she shut off her computer.

"See you guys tomorrow! Good luck on your midterms. Amy, I'll meet you at Bruin Plaza at five then."

I nodded.

Erin turned around in her chair and complained. "Why does she have time to go to all of these social functions, but she can't spend five minutes picking up her stuff so I can vacuum?"

"She'll do it eventually."

I hoped I wasn't lying. We turned back around to continue studying. I stared at the 3-D donut on my paper and began to feel like I wasn't doing a good enough job being the peace keeper between the two of them.

"Hey, after midterms, the three of us should go out for dinner or to see a movie or something," I suggested. "I feel like we've been so busy lately, we haven't spent quality time together."

"Maybe," she said. I sensed hesitation.

"Or, we could just do the two of us," I offered quickly, hoping that it didn't seem like I was trying to force her into being friendly with Casey.

"I'm just not big into going out," Erin said, sounding a little bit tired. Seeing the disappointment in my face, she added, "I really appreciate the invitation though. Want to have lunch tomorrow?"

"Sure!" I relied and penciled it into the already brimming schedule. I decided to take a short break to clean up my mess, as Erin had asked. I threw my shoes in my closet and noted that they looked very tired next to Casey's stack of crisp looking heels in this fall's popular colors. I snatched my pajama pants off the floor and threw them on my bed. Then I picked up the stack of books on the ground and lined them up on the bookshelf above my desk. Finally, I took the remaining stack of papers and put them carefully into my backpack, which I also tossed up on the bed. It was astonishing how those few little actions suddenly made the room look much tidier.

Erin turned around and noticed that I was cleaning.

"Thanks, Amy," she said.

"No, sorry it took so long," I replied. We surveyed Casey's mess, which was everywhere. She had at least eight pairs of shoes just strewn about the room, mixed in with a few belts and handbags that were gaping half open. Her clothes were all over: on her bed, on her chair, on the floor. It was like her closet exploded. Her schoolbag lay slumped against her desk, next to a pile of binders with papers oozing out of the sides.

"What a disaster," Erin said, shaking her head.

"Maybe you should leave her a note," I suggested. Erin pulled Casey's pad of stickies out from under a fuchsia patent leather handbag. She showed it to me when she was done.

Casey,

Could you please pick your stuff up off the floor? I need to vacuum.

-Erin

I took a look at it and nodded, then forced myself to work until I could feel sleep tugging at my eyelids.

On nights like tonight, when I was exhausted and stressed out, I missed my bathroom at home the most. Thinking about what sorts of sweat, germs and other bodily fluids were splayed on the bathroom and shower floors stressed me out more. I was careful to keep my flip flops on at all times to avoid stepping directly on the tiny, grimy tiles. I set my shower caddy on the wooden bench directly outside of the shower and was careful not to let my clothes fall onto the wet floor, where clingy strands of hair floated in questionable puddles.

I had to brace myself for the pitiful trickle of unpredictable temperature coming from this dorm showerhead. It didn't have to be this way. Back home, showering was such a pleasurable experience. I would have paid a lot for a hot, high pressure shower in a clean tub tonight. The kind that you could just space out in, reveling in the heavenly clean steam.

Erin had just shut down her computer when I came back in the room and climbed up into bed.

"Good night!" she said, shutting off the lights and heading to the bathroom with her plastic bag of toiletries.

"'Night," I replied drowsily, setting my alarm clock. I flopped indulgently into bed and drifted off quickly in the absence of the infamous noise machine.

I'd like to say that I slept soundly until morning and woke up feeling rested and refreshed, but I would be lying. I was awakened by someone turning on the light. I cracked an eye open and craned my neck to see my clock. 3am. I tried to go back to sleep again when I heard the shuffle of uneven steps.

"Oh shit!" Casey gasped.

I heard her stumble a few steps and deduced she'd tripped over her shoes, which she frequently did in broad daylight as well. I could hear her moving around the room, probably in search of her pajamas. Erin had also been rudely awakened. I could tell by the impatient creak of the bunk bed as she turned to face the wall and go back to sleep. Casey turned the light off again and then climbed into her bed, which gave a squeaky groan. About five minutes later, her cell phone rang.

"Hello?" she whispered. Pause. "Yeah, I got home ok." Pause. "You're kidding. What did she say?" Pause. "What a dumb-ass. I *told* her that he was playing her." Pause. "What do you mean how do I know? He totally came onto me at the party last week." Pause.

I thought about whether I should say something. This was totally out of line. How was anybody supposed to get any kind of rest around here? But if I was going to say something to her, I would start a scene and it would wake Erin up again, and it might be a long time before any of us got back to bed. I decided to pick a different battle a different night.

"Yeah, he's screwing around. It's too bad she fell for him so hard." Pause. "Totally, let's talk tomorrow." Pause. "Ok, lunch?" Pause. "No, I'm in North Campus. Let's go to Northern Lights!" Pause. "Fine, let's just do Ackerman." Pause. "Later."

And then, there was sleep.

*****

The next morning was typical in the lives of Amy, Casey and Erin. You see such a different side of people when you live with them.

Take Erin. Everyone thinks she's totally got it together. She's always punctual to class, lunch, dinner and any appointment you set with her. She is organized, to the point of compulsiveness. The only reason Casey and I remember what our desks look like at all are because we can actually still *see* Erin's desk. She just has an air of preparedness about her all the time.

But, I'm one of the privileged few people who knows that first thing in the morning, Erin is a disaster. Her radio alarm clock will go off at 7:00am because she always plans to get up early to look over her notes before class. All three of us will wake up momentarily and then blissfully return to a state of slumber.

At 7:05am her alarm clock will go off again. She will hit snooze again.

The same thing will happen at 7:10am, at which time, I wake up because I need to get ready for 8am class, and I secretly enjoy watching the scene that unfolds on the days that Casey is planning to sleep in.

By 7:20am, Casey has her pillow over her head and is groaning in a state of half-sleep, half-consciousness.

Around 7:30am, when I'm getting dressed, Casey will usually lean down from the upper bunk without actually opening her eyes and beg Erin to turn her alarm clock off.

Erin, making a sincere effort to wake up, will open her eyes a fraction, lift her head off the pillow, mutter, "OK, five more minutes" and inevitably collapse once more onto her pillow.

At 7:40am, after Erin has snoozed twice more, Casey will begin chucking stuffed animals and pillows at her, croaking, "Turn it off. Pleeeeeeeeeasssssssssssseeeeeeeeee turn it off!"

Usually, right when I'm about to leave for class, Erin will finally wake up enough to turn off her alarm clock, and apologize to Casey in a disoriented fashion, and flop down on her bed, returning to her prior comatose state.

I feel badly for Casey on these mornings, but the sight of her firing misaimed stuffed animals at Erin is priceless. If they'd been at the same high school, they never would have given one another the time of day. Casey would have been too popular for Erin, and Erin wouldn't have had any use for a party girl anyway. She was too intellectual. But here, their lives were so intertwined that they at least had to give each other the time of morning. I wondered where else in the world a glamour girl would be begging a nerd for anything.

Now take Casey. Everyone who knows her thinks she's just exquisite. And she is. She's tall, statuesque and always looks like she stepped out of the pages of a fashion magazine. But you should see *her* first thing in the morning.

Her straw colored hair sticks flat to her head. Her skin is splotchy and her eye lashes are tangled together. The retainer she wears most nights causes her to wake up with froth and drool all around her mouth. Lovely.

Then we get to the bathroom, where I'm almost embarrassed on her behalf. First, she goes into the toilet, where she generates noises and smells that I try to drown out by brushing my teeth vigorously and inhaling the minty fresh smell of my toothpaste. Then, she jumps into the shower, where she proceeds to snort and cough up phlegm. It's not a pretty picture. And I try not to over-think it. We're all people, right?

After all this, Casey will blow dry her hair and put on her make-up. Then the rest of the world sees her and thinks she's delicate and beautiful. By the time I get back to our room, Erin will be just forcing herself out of bed.

This morning, she was sitting up already by the time Casey and I got back to the room. Her silky black hair was tousled and covering half her face and she clearly was still trying to make sense of which way was up.

"Morning, Sunshine!" I said, teasingly, as I turned to my closet.

Flinging open my shirt drawer revealed an unhappy situation. All of my "good" shirts were already in the laundry bag. I flipped through the B string. Nada.

Damn me! When was the last time I'd done laundry? I tried to remember and couldn't.

I yanked out a navy blue t-shirt I'd picked up when I signed up for a credit card I would never use on Bruin Walk. It still smelled like factory and it was way too big. I put it on and looked like a large blue potato sack. I *had* to get some laundry done. And I shouldn't have left it to midterm week. The sock situation was much worse. There were no socks in my sock drawer.

I threw a glance behind me so that my roommates wouldn't notice as I furtively opened my laundry bag and began digging around for the cleanest pair of dirty socks I could find. In the crumpled, sweaty mess, I found one black sock that was not overly wrinkled. I remembered that I'd only worn it out to the movies one night, so it wasn't even a whole day old. It took me considerably longer to find its mate. When I turned back around, I found Casey looking at me with a concerned expression in the mirror, where she was applying the final touches on her make-up.

I shrugged. She went back to applying her make-up. I threw on my socks and jeans. My planner was lying open on my desk. I quickly glanced through the schedule for the day.

<u>Monday:</u>
8-9	Calc class
9-10	Ch 3.2, 3.3 hw
10-11	Anthro
11-12	Ch 3.4, 3.5 hw
12-1	Lunch w/ Erin
1-2	English
2-4:30	Ch. 3.6-3.9 hw
4:30-5	See Ethan about paper
5-6:30	shopping w/ Casey
6:30	dinner
7:30-?	Ch. 4 hw

Do Laundry!!!! I scrawled across the top of the page. There was no time for laundry. Moreover, there was no time to find a time for laundry in the planner. I threw the planner in my backpack, grabbed the banana that I'd taken from the dining hall last night and headed out the door.

"Have a good day, guys!" I called over my shoulder. I heard two grunts and smiled.

I was worried in class all day. During calculus, I resented the way our professor never stopped his breakneck pace to ask if we had any questions. Usually, I could get one or two of the easier homework problems myself. I would attend discussion section and the TA would help us with another two or three of them. Then I would go to office hours and get one more elucidated, maybe two if I were lucky By the time I got the homework back, I was usually too busy on the next week's homework to really understand what I did right or wrong on last week's homework. I'd spent the last few afternoons after class in the library, trying to work through old homework problems. This is when I realized that I didn't understand some of the harder problems, even the ones that I got right with outside help.

On top of that, I sank low in my chair so that as little of my ugly, shapeless Smurf shirt was visible to the general student body. I didn't know what was worse: people knowing that I hadn't done laundry in weeks or people thinking that I was just fashion-challenged.

While I sat through Anthro, I wish that I had skipped it to study for my math exam. But there was no point in that. I was already here. Besides, when the Anthro exam rolled around, I'd be wishing I hadn't.

*****

Campus had a somber air about it now that we were solidly into midterms. There were fewer people sitting on the steps of the various buildings socializing these days. The people that I saw today were all walking very purposefully towards class, discussion, office hours or review sessions. *Wow, I am halfway through my first entire quarter of college*, I thought, striding quickly towards the English building. *Where the heck did all the time go?*

Ethan glanced up at me when I strode into his office. He was in the middle of penciling notes in the margin of some play. I couldn't see the title of it.

"Amy," he said. He'd never said my name before. I didn't know that he even knew it. "How can I help you?"

I took a deep breath. "I was wondering if you could tell me how you graded our last paper. I was, um, disappointed in my score and I just wanted to know how I could have done better." There. I had done it.

"Do you have your paper with you?" he asked.

I nodded and pulled it out of my backpack.

He skimmed it over. "I remember this one. What's your question

184

specifically?"

I stared at him for a minute. Hadn't I just stated my question? "Well, what was wrong with it?"

"Nothing was wrong with it, per se," he said, choosing his words carefully. "The problem was that there was very little right with it."

I continued to stare at him. You know how sometimes you react instantly to something and get upset or insulted? Then there are those times when you're not quite sure how you feel and you can decide to get upset or insulted, or be fine. This was one of those times.

"The purpose of the paper was for you to convince me of your point. In this case, you were trying to convince me that the author was using various literary techniques to underscore his actual resentment for the main character. But when I was done reading your paper, I wasn't convinced. What's more, I wasn't even sure that *you* were convinced of your position. You weren't passionate in your argument, and you didn't address any counter arguments. Does that make sense?"

I nodded, but I must have not been very convincing... again.

"As I said before, there's nothing wrong with it. But to be a college level paper, you have go above that. You need to be really thorough in your argument and your analyses. You might have to cite other works or other authors' critiques. You have to find several examples that support your points in the text. And you have to think about any counter arguments anyone might have to your theory and nullify them."

I was beginning to get it. Conveying ideas was no longer sufficient. I needed to actively convince a non-believer. The professor had mentioned this when he gave us the assignment. I just hadn't internalized it.

And then I said the unthinkable. "Can you help me with our next paper? Can I bring you an outline or a draft before it's due?"

He smiled. "Totally. I'm glad you're being proactive in improving your writing."

"OK, thanks," I replied and felt better.

"Amy?" he called as I was halfway out the door.

I turned around to look at him again.

"The same thing happened to me in my first college English class," he said. "You're going to be fine."

I felt a little more light-hearted as I made my way to the Bruin statue in front of the student store to meet up with Casey. The method was beginning to come out of the madness.

*****

Casey was on time, and waiting for me in Bruin Plaza. I felt conflicted when I saw her. Part of me was excited to spend time with her. But part of me was still very annoyed at how she had treated me last night. Then again, it was a rare occurrence and I shouldn't judge, right? Maybe I just didn't understand what was involved in being a social princess.

"Ready?" she asked. I nodded and we turned towards Westwood.

"Did you have a good day?" I asked, making small talk.

"Well, I'm exhausted today because of that slumber party I went to last night at the sorority. There was all this drama."

She paused to step over a section of inlaid brick in the concrete.

"One of my pledge sisters is seeing this guy and she's totally in love with him," she continued. "He's hit on me and some other girls at parties that I've been to recently. So I was trying to tell her not to get too involved, but she said I was just jealous. *As if!*"

I chuckled at the reference to the high school classic, *Clueless*.

"So then last night, my big sis called me and told me that this girl walked in on the guy making out with another girl and went ballistic!"

"So now you can say, 'I told you so!'" I finished for her.

"Exactly!" she said, smugly.

We walked in silence for about a block.

"What's with the ugly t-shirt?" she asked, glancing at me with the same look I've seen on little kids when they first see someone who has a deformity. It was a mix of curiosity, sympathy, fear and disgust.

"Need to do laundry."

"Need to go shopping," she corrected me. I laughed and more of the anger dissipated.

We arrived at Zoey's, the funky costume and novelty store in Westwood that catered to adults.

It turned out to be a fun excursion. A very realistic, life-sized witch stood outside of the store, stirring a cauldron of bubbling, green goop.

"Awww," I cried, picking up a tin lunchbox with Lucille Ball stuffing chocolates in her mouth off of a conveyer belt. "I *love* 'I Love Lucy'! Remember this episode?"

Casey grinned. "My favorite episode was when she did that commercial for that health syrup and got drunk."

"It *would* be," I replied, laughing.

"Hey!" she said, in a mock warning tone, pointing a sparkly magic wand at me.

We walked into a section of scented candles and smooth rocks with words like "Love," "Tranquility", "Power" and "Happiness" carved into them. The next section had various soaps and lotions.

"Do you need any edible, flavored massage oil?" I asked Casey, in jest.

"Actually..." she said..

"No no no!" I said, holding my ears. "I don't want to know!"

She shrugged.

"You asked," she said, dropping a bottle of it in her shopping basket.

"Hey, why don't you be a fairy?" Casey asked.

I shook my head. "That's not me- it's too froo froo."

"That's the idea of a costume. It's not supposed to be 'you'."

"I know, but I don't want to be a fairy. I want to be something with a little bit of an edge. How about a pirate wench?"

"Now you're talking. I didn't think you had it in you."

Upon looking at the pirate wench costume, I decided against it. The front dipped so low, I'd be arrested for indecent exposure on my way to the frat house. We continued strolling past lava lamps, shot glasses and inappropriate wall hangings.

"Who would eat this?" I held up pasta shaped like little penises. "Ew!"

"Yeah, that's pretty bad," Casey admitted. She held up a T-shirt. "Should I get this for Erin?"

It said "One tequila, two tequila, three tequila... FLOOR!" on it.

"That's giving her too much credit, don't you think? For her, it would be 'One tequila... FLOOR'."

We both laughed. I was pleased that she was still in a good enough mood to be thinking about buying things for Erin. Things were becoming steadily more tense between them. Their priorities in life were just so irreconcilably different. Could someone who aspired to be a brilliant scientist ever be on the same wavelength as someone who aspired to be a glamorous socialite?

Something caught my eye. I walked over to it, took it off the rack, held it up against me and turned to show Casey. .

"That's it!" she cried. "It's perfect!"

It was a French maid costume that was made out of a stretchy material and was, therefore, form fitting. But it had a high collar. The little black dress, covered with the requisite small white apron was very short, but there was a layer of ruffly tulle beneath it that extended out longer than the skirt. .

"Is that your size?" Casey asked me, some skepticism in her voice.

"Yah- I should be able to wear a small," I told her, feeling defensive.

187

"Look at this!" Casey held up a chart.

Across the top were the words, "If she's still ugly, keep drinking." Beneath it was the silhouette of a slightly chubby woman with small breasts, no waist and large hips. Next to it were the words, "After 1 Beer." As you went down the chart, the woman's silhouette became more like that of a super model with every additional beer consumed.

"That's awful!" I groaned. "They're so shameless about judging women only on appearances. Cup size, mostly."

"Maybe we should show them what it's like to be in our shoes," she said mischievously. "I think I know how to make them feel insecure and objectified!"

She disappeared down and aisle and reemerged several minutes later, holding a yard stick. We paid for the dress and the yardstick and made our way home, in hysterics, thinking about how we'd use the yardstick.

We got home just in time for dinner. Erin had just stepped out of our room and closed the door behind her. Brian was already waiting in the hallway and Sarah was just emerging from her room on the other end of the hallway.

"Where are your roomies?" I asked Brian.

"Sean's just finishing up in the shower and I don't know where Chris went."

Just then, the door to the boys' bathroom flew open and Chris came running down the hall with a towel and some clothes slung over his arm. We looked at him, puzzled. A minute later, Sean started bellowing. "WHO TOOK MY CLOTHES?!"

That was when it dawned on everybody what just happened. Everybody burst out laughing. Chris was laughing the hardest of us all and he was already breathless from running the length of the hallway. Brian walked past Chris to the boys' bathroom and opened the door.

"Come on, man! We're waiting on you to go to dinner," Brian yelled, throwing fuel on the fire.

"BRIAN! BRING ME SOME CLOTHES, DAMMIT! IT WAS THAT BASTARD CHRIS, WASN'T IT?" Sean yelled, his voice echoing off the tile walls in the bathroom.

"I can't!" Brian lied. "Chris ran down the stairs. I think he's going to run your underwear up the flagpole. I locked myself out!"

We heard expletives coming from the bathroom and the cranking of the paper towel dispenser.

Sean, dripping wet, emerged from the boys' bathroom with nothing but a brown paper towel wrapped around his boney hips. Water was dripping down his skinny legs. He was scowling as he stormed down the hallway towards us.

"Oh my God," Erin said, burying her head into my shoulder. "I don't want to see this!"

I screwed my eyes shut as well. Casey whistled a cat call. Brian and Chris were in a heap on the ground, laughing their tails off. Sean was glaring at everybody, but by the time we got to the dining hall for dinner, he was laughing as well.

*****

After dinner, I revisited my study list again and freaked out. What had seemed like enough work last night now felt like a drop in the bucket. I hadn't expected shopping with Casey to take so long, and dinner ran late as well. I hit a key on my computer to wake it up and saw that I had a message from Lauren, but she had since signed off for the night.

LoreNsMyth: Call me when you can. Boy trouble.

Ohhhhh, Laur! It was too late to call her tonight. I didn't have time to talk anyway. I made a mental note to call her when my midterms were over.

"Casey, can you clean your stuff off the ground?" Erin asked. "I've asked you at least twice already!"

"I'll get to it!" Casey snapped. She was already pulling outfits out of the closet and transferring her cell phone, wallet, keys and accessories into a soft lemon colored handbag. "I have a date!"

Erin stiffened. Turning towards her so Casey couldn't see, I put my finger to my lips. I couldn't deal with any drama from them tonight. I had to get through most of calculus sections on my list tonight so that I could ask questions tomorrow in discussion and study group.

I worked the whole night until bedtime, barely noticing when Casey strutted out of the room an hour later. A few hours later, Erin began picking up the remaining things off of the floor and throwing them onto Casey's bed. When she finished, she walked out of the room and returned, dragging the clunky, communal floor vacuum. The roaring, wheezing contraption from the seventies grated on my already-raw nerves. I was already trying to read my Anthropology reader at twice the speed I usually read and absorbing only half of the material. But then I reminded myself that I should be grateful Erin was vacuuming because hell if I wanted to do it. After that, it was easy for me to be in the zone again and I didn't look up from my work until past one o' clock in the morning.

When I returned from the bathroom, I finally saw the result of Erin's cleaning. Casey's bed was piled high with clothes, shoes, handbags, papers and books.

"Thanks for vacuuming," I said to Erin, admiring our spotless carpet.

She gave me half a nod, without taking her eyes off of her computer screen. I climbed into bed and was glad to know sleep would come quickly.

As if on cue, Erin got up and turned out the lights, then sat back down at her computer.

"She'd better not be loud again tonight," I said, closing my eyes.

"Seriously. That was awful last night!"

"Gya," I agreed, drifting off. Sweet slumber came swiftly, as promised.

Unfortunately, it didn't stay long. Casey had trouble being quiet again tonight. This time, it was at 3 AM when she came home, turned on the light and exclaimed, "Shit!"

I deduced she saw her possessions piled on her bed, and pulled the covers over my head.

"That sucks. What should we do?" a male voice asked, startling me, just as I was drifting back off to sleep.

My body tensed up. She did *not* bring one of her boy toys home. This was too much!

"Whatever," Casey whispered fiercely. "I'll deal with this crap later. Let's sit outside so we don't wake my roommates."

I heard her go to her desk and scribble something. She slapped it on Erin's desk, not very quietly. . Then she turned out the lights as she and the boy walked out in the hallway and shut the door. I thought the disturbance was over, but I was wrong again. They sat outside and started talking. I wouldn't have thought I'd be able to hear them through the door, but in the silence of the night, their voices were quite clear.

Casey and her boy toy talked at length about the party they had just attended and compared it to a party that they attended last week. Then they started discussing Spring Break and how cool it would be if their fraternity and sorority went on a joint trip. Then the conversation moved to the drunk antics of some of his frat brothers. Not to be outdone, Casey threw a few of her pledge sisters under the bus and talked about someone flashing a police officer. I was in insomnia hell. I watched the clock change from 3:59am to 4:00am and wrestled with whether to burst through the door and yell at them both.

"Are you sure your roommates can't hear us?" the boy asked all of a sudden. "Because I know that I can hear my roommate when he talks to his girlfriend in the hallway."

"No, they can't hear us! Plus, they're asleep, so they even more can't hear us!"

"Are you sure?" asked the boy, teasing.

"Watch," Casey said. "Amy? Can you hear me?"

It didn't take long for me to jump on this opportunity.

"Yes," I said loudly. "I can."

There was silence on the other side of the door. Then there was some whispering. Then I heard the guy get up and leave. Casey came into the room.

"Sorry," she said.

I rolled my eyes and turned to face my wall, not even dignifying this feeble attempt at an apology.. Casey got ready for bed. As she climbed into her bed, she stopped mid-creak and said, "Shit!" again.

Then she started tossing things off of her bed. The shoes hit the short carpet with several dull thuds. When she threw the first book off the bed, it hit the ground with a very loud "Bang!" Erin woke with a start. When she saw it was Casey, she turned toward the wall and pulled her pillow over her head, grumpily.

"Casey," I hissed, no longer able to contain my exasperation.

She finished moving the rest of her things off of her bed quietly, but her sulking was loud and clear. I knew there was going to be drama later, but I could handle it better any other time but right now. Midterms were upon us. I sighed, nestled in my comforter and went back to sleep.

*****

The next morning, I was confronted by the same beast again. Rather than suffer the embarrassment of wearing an oversized sack to school, I dug for a dirty shirt that at least looked good and the second cleanest pair of dirty socks I could find in my laundry bag. After a couple of quick sniff tests, I emerged with my second favorite fitted black shirt and some generic white socks that could now be classified as charcoal colored. When I opened my underwear drawer, I saw one lone pair of sky blue bikinis. The situation was dire. I couldn't reuse underwear. My Mummy taught me better than that.

Digging through my coin purse, I extracted nine quarters. $2.25. I needed five more quarters to do a load of laundry. I stacked the quarters neatly on my desk right next to my laptop to remind myself to do laundry after class, hell or high water. Then, I grabbed a pen and wrote a "Q" on the back of my hand to remind myself to get the remaining quarters at some point. Without further ado, I headed off to class to confront the bigger problem of flunking out of school.

After class, I stopped by the arcade to get more quarters. Thank goodness for the change machine. I opened my purse and found a single dollar and a twenty. I fed the dollar into the bill slot. The machine spit it back out like a spoiled baby. Impatiently, I pulled the dollar out, rubbed it back and forth across the edge of the machine to smooth out the wrinkles and fed it back into the machine. It hesitated suspiciously for a moment, trying to determine whether or not I was feeding it the same crap as last time, and finally acquiesced, swallowing the dollar bill and releasing four quarters that clanked noisily into the metal tray at the bottom.

The machine only took fives and ones. I wondered if it was worth it to go find change for my twenty. I decided against it. It was after school snack time and there were lines everywhere. I took my quarters and decided to bum the last one off of a neighbor. Chris still owed me quarters from the last time he did laundry.

On my way back to my room, I stopped by the laundry room to see if the machines were in use. Fortunately, the washer was idle, but the drier was still in use. No problem. I hurried back towards my room. The door to the boys' room was open and Chris was sitting quietly at his desk, staring at his computer monitor intently when I walked by.

"Chris!" I said.

Chris jumped out his chair with a start. When he saw me, he deliberately moved his mouse to the corner of a window on his screen and clicked to close it. I didn't even want to know.

"What's up, Amy?" he asked, doing a poor job hiding his guilt.

"I need those quarters back for laundry," I told him, sparing him some awkwardness.

He pulled out his desk drawer and poked around for a minute and picked one out. He continued to dig around for a few minutes, but clearly couldn't find any more.

"I only have one," he said. "Can I give you the rest later?"

"You're lucky," I told him. "I'm just short one this time. Yah, get me the others when you can."

He walked over to me and handed me the quarter.

"Anything else?" he asked.

"No," I replied. "You can go back to… whatever it is that you're doing."

I unlocked the door to our room and dumped my backpack on my chair. I grabbed my laundry bag and the bottle of detergent out of the closet and tossed them by the door. Then I walked to my desk to collect the rest of the quarters.

They weren't there.

Where did they go? I remembered putting them in a stack by my laptop, but they weren't there anymore. A frantic search through all of my drawers and under my laptop turned up nothing. Then I got on all fours and crawled beneath my desk to see if they'd fallen or been swept off my desk on accident. The only thing I found was a half eaten Rice Krispy treat in cellophane and a movie stub.

I was getting desperate. People would be getting home soon and someone might beat me to the washing machine. Looking around the room, I spotted two quarters on Casey's desk. Then, I spotted her empty laundry bag sitting on her bed.

I jogged down to the laundry room and pried open the dryer door. The lacy thongs and stylish blouses were Casey's alright. Slamming the dryer door shut, I stormed back to our room. A month ago, I wouldn't have wanted anything to get in the way of our becoming friends, but now I just needed to get my laundry done. I picked up my cell phone and dialed Casey.

"Amy?" Casey's voice was surprised. There was a lot of noise on her end of the phone.

"Hi Casey. Quick question.I'm trying to laundry now, but I can't find the quarters I left on my desk this morning. Have you seen them?"

There was a pause.

"Casey?"

"Yeah, I borrowed them to do my laundry," she said.

"*Casey!* You *knew* I had to do laundry. Remember? You asked me about the ugly t-shirt yesterday?"

"Sorry, I forgot!" she said, not sounding sorry at all.

There was another pause. The lack of helpfulness on her part was appalling.

"You should have asked first!"

"Well you weren't around and I needed to do laundry! I didn't want to call you during class."

I clenched my fist. *Infuriating!* "Where *are* you?"

This was terrible. I was supposed to be her roommate, her pal, not her mother. But I needed to do laundry and she was acting like a child.

"I'm back on campus," she said. "I have a review session in a few minutes."

"Well can you stop by the arcade or somewhere and pick up some quarters on the way back?" I asked.

There was another pause.

"Yeah." I could hear the sulking even over the din on her end of the phone.

"Thanks!" I tried to inject some humor into the situation. "Listen, I really need to do laundry- I can't keep wearing ugly t-shirts to school!"

"Yeah," she said and hung up the phone.

I stared at the phone for a moment, unbelieving. *She* was trying to make *me* feel bad? *She* was the one who stole my quarters and *I* was the one who was put out! I snatched a quarter off of her desk and glanced at the coins in my hand to be sure I had six. Then I grabbed my laundry bag and the detergent, and dragged them down the hall to the laundry room.

Casey wasn't home by dinner time. I took my clothes out of the washer and stacked them in a wet heap on top of the drier before someone else could do it. The idea of someone touching my undergarments was disturbing to me. I considered calling her again, but decided against it. She would have to come home eventually. If worse came to absolute worst, I could walk around the hallway and bum them off someone else.

"Where's the princess?" Sean asked when Erin and I locked the door behind us.

"Not home yet," I answered.."Why?"

Sean didn't respond.

"Hey Red!" he called down the hallway.

Sarah poked her head out of her door, disappeared for a minute and came back out with her keys and her wallet. Chris and Brian ambled out of their room and locked the door behind them.

*****

I looked at the time. 7:53pm. I had a few minutes before walking over to DeNeve, the dorm complex across the street, to meet up with my study group. By this point, I had gone through all the homework problems again. Of the forty problems we'd been assigned over the last four weeks, I felt comfortable with about thirty of them. I had circled the four that I really couldn't make sense of. Hopefully we would all have the same issues and maybe we could work through them together. I threw my pencil case, my stack of problem sets and my notebook into my backpack. After looking distastefully at my textbook, I put that in as well. I might as well have put bricks in my backpack.

A few hours later, I was headed back to my room, more stressed than ever.

"Wow, that good?" Erin asked, her words too sarcastic for her big, innocent eyes.

I stormed into the room and flung my backpack to the ground.

"It was a complete waste of time! " I sputtered, tearing open my backpack and pulling out my Calculus notes as fast as I could. "No one was prepared! I spent the whole time explaining all the easy problems to them and no one could figure out the hard problems. I'm screwed!"

"Look on the bright side. You'll do better than all of them."

"I guess. Or maybe I just happened to be studying with the bottom of the class and all of the smart people are studying on their own."

I turned to my notebook. In my head, I counted how many hours I had between now and the exam.

"Wassup," a low voice growled from the doorway. It was Sean

"Studying," was my terse reply.

"Are you stressed out, Callaway?" Sean asked. "It's not like you to be rude."

"I have a Calculus midterm that's going to kick my ass and I'm running out of time to study for it."

"Who cares?" Sean asked, wandering into the room to my dismay. "It's just a grade. Caring about grades is so… high school."

He sat down on Erin's bed.

I didn't bother to dignify this with a response or tell him that my scholarship was dependent on my keeping above a minimum GPA.

Chris burst in the room, looking half embarrassed and half aggravated. His stout frame filled the doorway and his chest was heaving, like he'd been running. We all turned to look at him.

"Where's Casey?" he demanded.

Erin flung herself back in her seat and threw her arms up. "Why is everyone always asking where Casey is? Why can't you come in here and say, 'Where is Erin?' or 'Where is Amy?'"

"That doesn't make any sense," Chris said. "I would never ask, 'Where is Erin?' if you were in the room, so you would never hear me say that. Just like Casey will never hear me say, 'Where is Casey?'"

"You have a point," Erin said. "Casey is out being Casey. What do you want her for?"

Chris produced a crumpled poster from behind his back.

"Did either of you have anything to do with *this*?" he asked, uncrumpling the poster so that we could see it.

Erin took one look and burst out laughing. Chris must have seen the pride light up my face.

"YOU!" he said, coming towards me.. I stood up to meet him.

"What?" I asked, standing up from Erin's bed. "What are you going to do to me?" I asked, walking right into his shoulder, pretending to start a fight, as I'd seen guys do on the basketball court countless times.

I waited, amused, to see what would happen, ready to spring out of the way in case he chose to escalate it. He had sisters. I didn't know if this would make him more or less likely to deck me.

It didn't come to that. He backed down.

"This is *not* funny!" He slammed the poster down on my desk.

"What do you mean?" Erin cried. "It's hysterical! What goes around comes around! How does it feel to be on the other end of it?"

Chris was half-smiling, so I knew he wasn't truly offended. "You said it. What goes around comes around! You'd better watch out!"

With that, he backed out of the room, pointing at me. He mouthed the words, "I'm watching you."

I sat down at my desk and marveled at my work. Well, it was mine and Casey's work. She must have put it up next to the guy's urinals this morning if Chris just found it now.

It was a photo of Casey, wearing a skin-tight black cami with a plunging neckline and push-up bra. She wore a mocking smile on her face, raised one eyebrow and held out the meter stick that we purchased at Zoey's. I took the photo on my camera and then added large pink text on the top of the poster that read, "What's *your* cup size?"

9 "Experience the Walk of Shame"

Wednesday's calculus midterm was every bit as nasty as I expected it to be. But I had no time to mourn the loss of my self-worth because my economics midterm was right on its heels. Though it was easier than my calculus midterm, the professor threw in several tricky elements. I struggled as best I could with it and admitted partial defeat when I turned it in on Thursday morning.

My brain hurt from hours of intense concentration. I'd woken up at 5am to "warm up" for the exam by reviewing my notes and redoing a few of the nastier homework problems. The annoying thing was that most of the effort was wasted. The easier problems on the exam, I could have done without studying at all. The two hard problems at the end, no amount of studying could have prepared me for. I definitely didn't have it in me to start studying for Anthro, so I wandered out towards Bruin Walk and sat on the steps in front of Kerchoff to clear my mind of oligopolies and optimizing utility.

I watched as throngs of people walked by and marveled at how Bruin Walk in the morning was just a pale shadow of what it was later in the day. At 9am in the morning, it was busy, but quiet. Some people were speed walking and flipping through notes on their way to exams. Others poked along, half-asleep. A few were on cell phones, but the cell phones didn't come out to full capacity until about lunchtime. That was when you could be sure your fellow college mate was actually awake. Even the squirrels had not come out yet.

By lunch time, Bruin Walk burst into life. Clubs would be out in full force, enticing you to join with doughnuts or cookies. Political activists would be passing clipboards around with the latest petitions against offshore drilling and the banning of gay marriage. There'd be music blaring, adding to the audio chaos of people yelling into their cell phones in an attempt to locate their friends for lunch. Clumps of people would be lounging at the picnic benches, on every inch of stairs and sometimes in the grass as well.

I cupped my chin in my hands. People, people everywhere, but not a single confidant! I still felt so alone sometimes. There was no one for me to talk to about feeling unsatisfied with my Econ midterm. It wasn't important enough to call any of my old friends about it. And ironically, it wasn't important enough to talk to any of my new local friends about it. There seemed to be a lot of conversation topics that fell in this abyss. I drew a mental 2x2 in my mind like the ones we drew for the Prisoner's Dilemma:

	Good Friends	Casual Friends
Local Friends	None	Hallmates/Roommates
Faraway Friends	Friends from Home	Useless Anyway

Ah. My trouble was that I needed local friends who were familiar enough that I could talk to them about mundane troubles, like bad exams, minor boy trouble and feeling lonely. Somehow, I didn't feel like I could talk to Casey or Erin about those sorts of things yet. Was it because I didn't feel like they were good friends yet so I didn't want to talk to them about it? Or were they not good friends *because* I didn't want to talk to them about it yet? I laughed at myself for being a nerd. It had to be mental exhaustion.

A shadow fell over me. I looked up and saw Jeff smiling down at me, looking as hot as ever.

"What's so funny?" he asked, grinning.

"Nothing," I replied.

"No class?" he asked, still standing so I had to shield my eyes against the sun when looking up at him.

"I just finished an Econ midterm," I said. "I have a break until my next class."

"Wow, 8am class! You must have missed the memo. You're not supposed to sign up for any classes before 10am!"

"Naw, I got it. I like taking chances sometimes. Want to have a seat?"

"I have to run to class," he said. "I saw you over here and thought, 'What a coincidence! I was just going to ask her to my date party tonight!' This saves me a text message. Want to come?"

"I'll think about it," I said coyly, but I'm sure he could tell from my face that I'd be there with bells on. "What's the attire?"

"Semiformal tonight. It's at eight o' clock. No dinner, but I think we're getting appetizers or dessert or something."

"I'll let you know," I told him, keeping up my facade.

He gave me a lopsided grin. "You'll come," he said, turning away. "You can't fool me!"

"If you're lucky," I called after him. I didn't feel quite so alone anymore.

*****

Casey was thrilled that I was going to Jeff's date party because she was dressing up for a date party, herself. We both skipped dinner so that we would look slimmer in our dresses.

"This time, you have to let me do your make-up," she insisted. I relented.

We marched into the bathroom and Casey did her own hair and make-up first. Then she applied her artistic talent to me. When she was through, I examined myself in the dingy bathroom mirror and was pleasantly surprised. The green eye shadow that she applied faded evenly as it approached my eyebrow. Whatever foundation she used on me actually *did* make my skin look glowy. And the lipgloss that she slicked on smoothed away the unevenness of my usually chapped lips. Most importantly, she did all this without making me look like a Kabuki doll.

"It's not overdone," I commented.

"Do you *think* I would make you up like a cheap hooker?" Casey asked, putting a hand on her hip and sounding insulted. "You know how writing is your thang? Make-up is my thang."

"You're right," I laughed. "I should never have doubted you."

She curled a few wisps of my hair with a curling iron and pin the curls on top of my head. She left the rest of the hair straight. I tried to ignore the scratchy tickling of my long hair between my bare shoulder blades.

"There won't be a sorority girl who has anything on you tonight," Casey said proudly when she was done with me. I thought of a sarcastic response to this, but decided it wouldn't be very gracious of me.

Erin applauded when we returned to the room. I gave an awkward curtsy. Then we packed up our purses.

"Purses are such pains," I muttered as I dumped receipts, coins, pens and other random little scraps and wrappers out of my "going out" purse. "You have to carry one because you don't have pockets, but then they're like an anvil attached to your wrist the rest of the night. No, they're worse than that because they're not actually attached, so you have to make sure you don't lose it the whole damn night!"

"So negative!" Casey chided. "Think of them as accessories. You use them to accent your outfit. And you can hide all sorts of things in them. Like, where else would you put your pills and condoms?"

Erin and I stared at her.

"Do you want to borrow that lip gloss that I used on you so that you can reapply it yourself later?" she continued, without even the slightest pause.

"Um... sure. Thanks."

When I approached the white colonial house of SIE, I grew nervous. Since the "incident" at the beginning   of the year, I'd been back here twice without being called out on it. But I'd come with my hall mates for the normal Thursday night beer fests, in jeans, with my hair pulled back, unrecognizable as "that girl". Here I was now, with no moral support, looking similar to how I did that cursed night, at a date party, where I couldn't rely on the cover of smoke, crowds and loud music.

Jeff must have seen me from inside. He came out of the front door and down the walk to greet me. We locked eyes for several moments before we got close enough to speak. My stomach flip flopped against my ribcage as I walked up the length of the front walkway. Something about the way he looked at me- like there was no one else in the world- was enough to make me forget how to breathe.

"You look gorgeous tonight," he said, bending down to kiss me on the cheek. Very few men could say it without arousing immediate suspicion ... or snickering.

"Thank you," I replied, blushing in spite of myself. "You don't look bad yourself."

We walked into the house and I was impressed with how nice it looked when it was clean. Had that chandelier always been hanging in the front entrance? And I guess I'd never noticed that the floor was made of dark hardwood. It was a rather elegant looking interior when there weren't beer cans strewn across the floor and strobe lights casting chaos everywhere.

We walked into the foyer.

"Can I get you a glass of wine?" Jeff asked.

I nodded.

"Red or white?" he asked. "We have a Pinot Noir and a Riesling."

"Whatever you're having," I replied, trying not to let on that the names meant nothing to me.

He poured me a glass of red wine, then led me into the living room to meet his friends. I took a sip of wine and tried not to wince. It was very tart and the taste of alcohol overwhelmed everything. It took me a minute to shake off the fumes.

People stopped to look at us when we walked into the room. I hadn't seen so many beautiful people in a single social gathering before. The boys cleaned up astonishingly well in collared shirts and khaki trousers. Some even wore blazers. I caught a glimpse of the frosty tip guy, who could almost pass as dignified in his button up red shirt. I could hardly believe these were the same bums that showed up to class in sweatshirts and torn jeans. The girls were all wearing bold colored, form-fitting dresses, with their hair done up and make-up shimmering on their fresh faces.

Something about dressing up always makes you feel special. It's as if everyone is dressing up for *you*, just as you're dressing up for everyone else. It was absolutely silly, but I felt about a foot taller and suddenly very pretty. At least for tonight, I was part of this club of the social elite.

Jeff took my hand and walked me around the room, introducing me to people.

"Amy, this is Ken. Ken, this is Amy."

Ken wasn't bad looking either. He was as tall as Jeff, with dark hair and dark eyes. "Nice to meet you," he said. "This is my date, Karen. Karen, you know Jeff and his date Amy."

Karen was adorable and she knew it. You could tell by the way she gazed up through her long, dark lashes at Jeff and flipped her dark, silky cascade of loose curls over her shoulder.

"Jeff, you haven't called me in ages," she pouted. "We need to get together and catch up some time."

"I've been so busy with rush this year. Is my man Ken being a gentleman?"

"Of course!" Ken replied for her. "Do you even have to ask?"

"Ken says that he can drink you under the table," she cooed, never taking her eyes off of Jeff. I felt a little badly for Ken.

"We'll see if he can walk the walk later," Jeff replied, winking at her.

Maybe it was customary to flirt with other people's dates at these things. What did I know? She turned to look at me and smiled- a little less adorably. Girls know when to cut the act with other girls. I was on to her and she knew it.

"I like your dress," she told me.

I decoded the statement. This was female-speak for either "Let's make peace- I'll stop flirting with your date" or "I'm only saying this to appear nice in front of the guys."

"Thanks!" I replied, taking a sip of wine to buy myself a moment. I wasn't sure of her intentions, so I took the safe route. "I like yours too."

"What year are you?" she asked me, staring at me with those enormous eyes.

"First year," I responded. "What about you?"

"I'm a third year," she replied. "You're lucky you got started on the cool frat parties early!"

"I guess all you need is a winning ticket," I replied, looking up at Jeff, trying to look cute. God, it felt weird, trying to be all cute. I hated myself for doing it.

"Let's have a toast," Jeff suggested, raising his glass.

"What should we toast to?" Ken asked.

"How about hot dates?" Jeff said, glancing sideways at me. I could feel myself turning as scarlet as my wine.

"To hot dates!" the boys said in unison and all four of us clinked glasses.

"Jeff!" A fellow in a forest green shirt call out from across the room.

"Oh, it's Tom." Jeff lifted his chin in Tom's general direction. "I should go over and say hi. See you two later."

Jeff took my elbow and led me across the room.

And so the evening began, with a dozen introductions. The frat brothers were all very easy going, though slightly ill at ease in semiformal. You could tell by the way they shifted around when they were standing and tugged on their collars and cuffs. Most of their dates were sorority girls of varying heights, but generally two shapes: thin and stick- skinny. In contrast to the guys, they all looked perfectly at home in semiformal.

It slowly began to sink in over the course of the evening that I was not cut from the same cloth as these girls. They didn't wobble when they walked the length of the room in impossibly high heels. They didn't touch their hair incessantly to be sure the curls were still in place. They didn't clutch awkwardly at their purses, but set them down and picked them up instinctively. They didn't retreat when it was time to tell war stories about drinking or compare notes on bars and clubs. And they certainly didn't keep looking over at the buffet table. A few munched on carrot and celery sticks. But, for the most part, they continued to drain glasses of wine in absence of sustenance.

I was in way over my head. It didn't help that periodically, someone would comment on my unemptying glass.

Jeff moved through the crowd expertly, bumping knuckles with his buddies and toasting their dates. We didn't stay to talk to any couple for any substantial length of time, but even in my small talk, I was careful to maintain my cover by uttering deplorable falsehoods like,

"I *love* clubbing on Sunset!" and "You know, they serve the *best* mudslides at Sharkeez in Hermosa Beach!"

I guess the second one wasn't a falsehood. I'd heard Casey tell that to one of her sorority sisters on the phone one time.

Conversation was pleasant enough. We talked about the latest movies, funny incidents that happened in our little bubbles of student life, and the guys in the frat told funny stories about one another. People moved casually around the room, conversing easily and breaking out into occasional laughter. It was all very nice, except that I kept getting hungrier and hungrier. Finally, when I could no longer force down any more wine and ignore the gurgling of my stomach, I excused myself to get some appetizers. I felt self-conscious with every step because I knew I risked looking like a total hog among these long legged, vegetarian alcoholics. But this was an emergency!

I served myself a bacon-wrapped scallop and stopped to glance around the room. No one seemed to be looking at me. So then, I gleefully filled the rest of my plate with spinach puff pastries, mini egg rolls and a chicken skewer with peanut sauce.

Jeff played his part perfectly and never went anywhere without me. When we stood, he kept one hand on the small of my back, which continued to have an electric and comforting effect on me at the same time. When we sat to talk with his friends, he kept a warm hand on one of my knees. That was reassuring. Several girls around the room shot disapproving glances in my general direction.

I plastered on a smile that dared anyone to flirt with him.

As the night wore on, the alcohol began to flow more freely. Couples decoupled, someone killed the lights and they began to play house music. The high society date party dissolved into the rowdy drunkenness that I was accustomed to. Pairs began grinding on the dance floor, which was tantamount to having sex with their clothes on. That didn't help the state of my stomach, which was already unsettled.

Jeff and I moved around the room, participating in a few of the drinking games.

We sat down at the kitchen table, where several of Jeff's frat brothers were playing Quarters.

"How do you bounce it?" I shouted at Jeff, across the table and over the music.

"It's all in the wrist!" Jeff shouted back. "Watch!"

He rolled up his sleeve and pulled a quarter out of his pocket. His frat brothers whooped and hollered all around us, when Tom sat down next to him to race him.

"Ready?" Tom yelled? Jeff gave a chin thrust. "Go!"

They both appeared to take careful aim and went through a few slow motion practice gestures before hurling the quarters against the table hard. Tom's quarter rolled off the table on my side. His date Jen picked it up off the floor and handed it to him. Jeff's quarter landed a few inches from where it bounced, so Jeff was able to recover it quickly and try again. The guys shouted encouragement and ridicule at both contestants. I did my part and cheered him on. This went on several more times until Tom was eventually able to bounce his quarter into his glass. He gave high fives all around, while Jeff sheepishly drank the beer in the center of the table.

"Now the girls! The girls!" several of his frat brothers began yelling. I held my breath, hoping they would find something else with which to amuse themselves, but Tom and Jeff had already stood up from the table so that we could sit in their places.

Jeff handed me his quarter.

"You have to snap your wrist like you're shooting a basketball!" he told me, wiping his brow.

"You have to keep your wrist stiff so that you don't lose control of it!" I heard Tom tell Jen, as if lives depended on it.

"Ready?" Jen asked me. I nodded.

"Go!" Tom shouted. The frat boys yelled encouragement to both sides.

I flung my quarter on its edge, forgetting all about the instructions on how to hold my wrist. The quarter bounced too high and roll off the edge of the table. Jen's quarter didn't bounce high enough.

Someone retrieved my quarter for me as I tried to stare down my empty glass.

"Snap your wrist!" Jeff reminded me.

This time I did, and I got closer, but didn't hit the shot. The adrenaline was pumping as it did every time we had shooting contests during basketball practice. I could see the appeal of this. Jen finally got her quarter into her glass when I was on my fifth or six try. Everyone cheered.

"Good job!" I told her. She smiled, looked at the glass on the table and back at me.

Great. A whole glass of beer. With everybody watching.

I picked up the overflowing glass of cheap, pale beer and began to drink it. It *still* tasted bitter, washed out and nasty. Who said this stuff grew on you?

"Chug it!" someone yelled, when I stopped to take a breather. I looked at the glass and was dismayed to find it still two-thirds full.

"You got it," Jeff told me, putting a hand on my shoulder. I will never know how I got through the rest of that beer, but somehow I did, and as I staggered away from the table, trying to rid myself of that disgusting taste, there was a general roar of approval.

"Wahoo!" I hollered, hoping that I sounded halfway convincing.

Jeff sat down for a rematch with Tom, which gave me some time to recover before we moved on to beer pong. It struck me that all of these drinking games had two objectives. The first was to get everyone drunk as quickly as possible. The second was to reward people who could maintain the highest level of physical and mental agility while continuing to drink. Was maintaining acuity under the influence a skill that was necessary "in real life"? Or was this just a cultural phenomenon that occurred in college?

In beer pong, two teams stand across a ping-pong table from one another. In front of each team is a series if six cups, set up like bowling pins in a triangular formation. Each cup is filled with beer. The teams take turns trying to throw a ping pong ball into one of the cups on the opponents' side that still has beer in it. If they succeed, the opponents have to drink the cup of beer in which the ping pong ball landed. It was pretty nasty. The ping pong ball had been in everyone's hands, on the floor, under the couch and was generally filthy. But as a game, it was a big hit. .

After what seemed like hours, we wound up back on the couch, where I took two shots with Jeff, Tom and Jen to prove that I could. Then I excused myself to go to the bathroom.

On my way back from the bathroom, my knees buckled after a few steps, but I caught myself. The room was definitely spinning. I saw Ken sitting on the loveseat with two girls in his lap.

"How is a freshman girl different than a toilet?" he yelled above the music.

The girls on his lap giggled and draped themselves all over him.

"How?" Tom yelled back at him. Tom's hand rested on his date's ass.

"A toilet doesn't follow you around after you use it!" Ken boomed, laughing, spilling beer down the front of one girl's dress.

She continued to giggle and coo at him. Even in my current state of tipsiness, I was offended. *Way to set feminism back 80 years, ladies.* I took a scathing mental note for the article forming in my head.

When I got back to Jeff, I had decided I was done here. It was late and everyone was drunk. People were just loud and annoying. I got the feeling they were acting ridiculous because they wanted to, and they were using the alcohol as an excuse. The magic from before had completely disappeared. I touched Jeff's arm.

"Another shot?" Jeff asked me, holding up the bottle of Bailey's. I shook my head.

"Hey, I think I'm going home."

"What? Why?" he asked. "The party is just getting started!"

"I'm getting tired. I had two midterms in the last two days..." my voice trailed off. Jeff handed the bottle off to his frat brother and took my hand. I thought he was walking me to the door, but when we reached the foyer, he turned towards the stairs instead.

"Jeff, I need to head home. I want to go to sleep!"

"I know!" Jeff said. "You can sleep here."

Alarm bells went off in my head.

"I don't know if that's a good idea," I said, pulling my hand away. Jeff looked at me with big, earnest eyes.

"Don't worry! No funny business," he said, reading my mind and reaching for both of my hands again. "I promise. We'll just talk and go to sleep."

It was flattering that he wanted me to stay, even though I was so obviously not the life of the party. And it would be wonderful to have some alone time with him. On the other hand, was this not the classic set up for the night that you always regret?

I cursed my spinning head. It was all part of The College Experience, wasn't it? How could I write about it while I was running away from it? I made a quick pact with myself to go upstairs with him, but be firm about not getting too physical... tonight.

I looked up at him. "OK. You promised."

He smiled and crossed his heart. God, he was cute! Who wouldn't follow him up the stairs?

"I thought you didn't have a room here," I said when we reached the top of the stairs. There was a long hallway with several closed doors.

"I don't, but my buddy is the treasurer and he's out of town for his brother's wedding, so we can sleep in his room," Jeff said. It should have occurred to me that this arrangement seemed a little too convenient.

Jeff opened one of the doors and we stepped into the dark room. It was about the size of our dorm rooms, but there was only one full sized bed in it, which made it seem much bigger. You could tell it was a guy's room because it looked pretty Spartan. It was free of anything remotely frilly, like curtains, a bed skirt or picture frames. He had a bed, an austere looking oak desk, a computer and a beanbag chair. There wasn't even a rug on the wood floor. Moonlight streamed in from the window, giving everything a wintry glow. I shut the door behind me when I followed Jeff in.

Jeff sat down on the bed and patted the spot next to him. I sat down. I could feel the bed frame vibrating to the beat of the music below.

"Did you have a good time tonight?" Jeff asked, looking down at his feet.

"Yeah! The whole fraternity cleans up real well."

"Do you mean us or the house?" Jeff asked, looking up at me with a disarming grin.

"Both," I laughed.

"Well, we spent a lot of time on it," Jeff admitted.

He leaned in for a kiss and I acquiesced without a second thought. His lips tasted like red wine and his breath was warm on my cheek. For a moment, the world stood still. Even the house music faded into the background and it was just me and him in a moonlit room. Everything was fuzzy, insubstantial around us. I held his face in my hands and then ran one hand down his neck and onto his chest.

Slowly, he fell backwards onto the bed and I fell on top of him. His arms enveloped me. He began stroking my back in a very soothing way. We continued to make out for what seemed like a long time.

He kisses a little more aggressively than Eric, I thought. Then I gave myself a mental kick in the head. *Why are you thinking about Eric at a time like this?*

"I love holding you," Jeff said, when we came up for air.

"So don't stop."

"I don't plan to." He laid his cheek on the top of my head.

I shut my eyes and consciously relaxed my body. I hadn't realized how tense I was in my excitement.

"What did you think the first time you met me?" I asked, suddenly feeling bold.

"I thought you were so cute with your little ponytail and all your little boxes labeled." Jeff chuckled in a low voice.

"I can't believe you remembered how my *boxes* looked," I said, raising my chin to look at his mocking smile.

"It's a good thing I saw the boxes before I saw you because if it had been the other way around, they wouldn't have had a chance," Jeff said.

I laughed. The room continued to spin in the silvery light of the moon.

Jeff stroked my face with his thumb. "You didn't think I looked like a sweet guy when you first met me?"

"When I first met you, I thought you looked like a jock,. I don't know if a guy can *look* sweet."

"But I was good with your parents," he pointed out.

"You were!" I admitted. "So then I thought you were a well-mannered jock."

"I saved your box!"

"Fine, I thought you were sweet," I conceded. "Are you happy?"

"Yes," he replied, and kisses me again.

The next time we took a breather, my lips were raw and I was feeling the effects of sleep deprivation on top of the alcohol.

"Oh you're so tired," he observed, brushing a runaway curl out of my eyes. "Let me get you a shirt."

I rolled off of him and he produced a plain gray t-shirt from a duffel bag behind the bed.

"I wore it to school today," he said. "So it's not clean out of the wash."

I held my hand out for it. He tossed it to me.

"Can you unzip me?" I asked, knowing that I was playing with fire.

"Yeah, baby!" he said enthusiastically. .

"Don't get excited!" I warned him. I stood up and faced away from him so that he could access the back of my dress. "I really just need help with this zipper. Then I'm going to bed."

"Are you sure?" he asked, mischievously.

He lifted my long hair to one side, slid the zipper halfway down, then stopped. He bent down and kissed the back of my neck. He slid his lips partway down my neck and kissed my bare shoulder. I felt like my heart was going to flutter right out of my chest.

"You're so bad!" I proclaimed, once I could speak without giving myself away.

I spun around and finished unzipping myself. He watched me with keen interest.

"Turn around," I ordered him, suddenly feeling self-conscious.

"You're such a tease!" he protested, but he turned to face the wall.

"I'm not! You said we were coming up here to sleep!"

"I know," he admitted, reluctantly.

I slipped out of my dress and pulled his t-shirt over my head. It smelled like him. I used to have a t-shirt that belonged to Eric, which I loved because it smelled like him. *Dammit, focus, Amy!*

"All done," I declared.

I lifted the edge of the covers on the bed and slid into it, laying my head on the pillow. I produced my cell phone from my purse to set my alarm for six o' clock and saw that I'd missed two calls- one from Lauren, and one from Mum.

Thank goodness she couldn't see me now.

Meanwhile, Jeff had removed his shirt and slung it over his buddy's desk chair. He was in the process of unbuttoning his pants. I watched this was some apprehension.

I feverishly began making a list of reasons in my head for why we couldn't fool around tonight: I was tipsy. I had class tomorrow morning. I hardly knew him. I still had feelings for Eric. And maybe Brian.

Then I realized that in the College World, these were all completely irrelevant. I couldn't very well tell him the real reason: I was terrified because I didn't know what I was doing. I'd never been past second base! Even if I wanted to, I'd make a royal awkward mess out of the whole thing.

He finished removing his pants, shoes and socks. I tried not to stare at him, but it was hard not to. He had a really beautiful body- these thick, muscular arms and abs like a cobblestone boulevard. Eric had cobblestone abs. *Damn me!* He walked to the other side of the bed, got under the covers and moved over towards me. I laid on my side facing away from him. He draped his arm over my waist, so that we were loosely spooning. Again, I had to remind myself to breathe. I leaned back so that my head fit beneath his chin and shut my eyes.

"Are you comfortable?" he asked. I nodded.

"Are you?" I asked. I felt him nod.

"I'm glad you're staying over," he whispered.

"Me too," I replied.

"Let me know if you need anything, ok?"

"OK."

We made out for several more minutes. Finally, I yawned and said,

"Goodnight!"

'Night!"

Sleeping with someone for the first time is as awkward as it is sweet. We must have shifted positions about eighteen times during the night so that neither of us slept for more than half an hour at a time. After he removed his arm from my waist, I turned around and tried to lay my head on his chest, but this kinked my neck at a funny angle and the arm that was pinned beneath me began to tingle. It rapidly progressed to the pins and needles stage and I was forced to move.

I arrived at the conclusion that human beings were not meant to sleep in an embrace because *at least* one out of the eight limbs would fall asleep, and inevitably when someone moved, the other party would wake up. Near the end of the night, we gave up trying to hold each other and slept on separate edges of the bed. Sleep overtook me just as the sun was rising.

I woke with a start to the sun streaming on my face. Even though I was still exhausted, the strength of the sunlight indicated that it was later than I wanted it to be. I swung my legs over the side of the bed and sat up. My eye make-up was all smudged and that I probably looked heinous. Jeff wrapped a lazy arm around my waist.

"Morning," he said hoarsely..

"Good morning," I smiled. "I need to go home and change before class. Are you going to stay here and sleep?"

He nodded without opening his eyes.

"OK, see you later," I said, twisting around to give him a kiss on the cheek. When I took my cell phone out of my purse, I nearly had an aneurism. 9:30am! I had missed Calculus! Hadn't I set my alarm for 6? I mashed buttons. Yes, I'd set it to 6pm. *Shit!*

I stole a quick glance at Jeff and when it seemed like he was sleeping, I pulled his shirt over my head and slipped back into my black dress from last night, which had wound up in a silky puddle next to his trousers. I picked up my purse, slipped on my heels and looked around for anything else I might have left. Negative. Careful to close the door gently behind me, I exited the room.

When I turned to walk down the hallway, I was horrified to find several of Jeff's frat brothers staring at me. Some had just woken up and were headed to the bathroom. Some had already showered and were on their way back to their bedrooms. Some were dressed and ready to head down for breakfast.

After standing there, petrified for several moments, I held my head high and started The Walk of Shame. It all happened so slowly. First, I walked past Ken, who was wearing nothing but a bath towel. He glanced at me and back down at the ground with a knowing smile. He didn't say a word. Bastard! Then I walked past Tom, who'd just come out of his room in his boxers. He gave me an awkward chin thrust and said, "Hey." Two guys were headed down to breakfast. One raised an eyebrow and the other grinned at me impishly. It was infuriating!

The kicker was the guy with the frosted tips, paused at the top of the stairs. He looked me up and down, his eyes lingering for just too long on my chest. I brushed past him and started down the stairs.

Don't say anything, don't say anything, don't say anything, I told myself. I didn't want to make the situation any worse. I could feel my entire body smarting at the bitter irony of the whole thing. I didn't even do anything with Jeff last night and these smug jerks were treating me like a harlot. I heard Frosty Tips come down the stairs behind me.

"I hope you didn't forget anything this time," he said in a taunting low voice as I headed for the door. So he *did* remember.

I turned around slowly, fuming.

"Actually," I said through clenched teeth. "I did."

I crossed the floor between us in two steps and in one smooth motion, grabbed his shirt and kneed him in the crotch. His knees buckled and he gasped for air as if I'd knocked the wind out of him. As he sank to the ground, I held his collar for a second longer so I could stare him down before I headed out the door.

My satisfaction didn't last very long. If I thought it had been bad in the frat house, it was ten times worse on the way back to the dorms. For the second time in six weeks, I was limping back up the hill in high heels, totally humiliated, and angry with myself for doing something against my better judgment. Only this time, I wasn't saved by the cover of night. And there was no blending in with the jeans and t-shirt crowd, walking to school. I tried to keep my chin up as I passed other students, who couldn't help but to stare.

Who could blame them? I would probably stare at a girl in a rumpled black party dress, wearing smeared, heavy make-up and strappy heels at 9:30am as well.

As I turned and began laboring my way up the hill to the dorms, I began seeing people that I actually recognized. At that point, I gave up. I let my chin drop and kept my eyes on the ground, playing the part of the fallen woman. There just wasn't anything else I could do. I just wanted to get back to my room and pull the covers over my head

*****

Erin and Casey stared at me from their chairs as I recounted the horrors of the morning. They tacitly made peace with each other in support of my dilemma.

"They were totally taunting me, every one of them!" I said. "It was the longest hallway ever! I'll bet the whole frat thinks that I've slept with him now!"

"And he'll probably just play along with that story too," Erin said. I slumped down in my chair.

"I should have told you to bring a change of clothes!" Casey groaned, regretfully. "I always try to tuck a t-shirt and flip flops in my bag if I think I'm going to spend the night. I didn't think you would!"

"I didn't think I would either," I sighed.

"That makes me so mad!" Erin said, still very agitated. "I wish I could just punch them all in the noses! What a bunch of jerks!"

A renegade smile came to my lips.

"I kneed one in the crotch!" I said. Shock, then delight spread over their faces.

"You did? " cried Erin. "Tell!"

I told them about Frosty Tips and the well-aimed blow to his masculinity.

"Good for you!" Casey said, giving me a high five.

"He totally deserved it!" Erin concurred.

I beamed. But once again, the satisfaction was short lived.

"What are you going to do about Jeff?" Casey asked. The smile dissolved off my face.

"I don't know," I said. "I like him and all, but I don't want to set foot in his frat house *ever again*. And..." my voice trailed as I struggled with how to articulate my new thoughts.

"What?" asked Erin.

"I don't want it to get too physical too fast," I said, I looked at both of

211

them to gauge their responses as I continued. "I get the feeling he wants to move a lot faster than me. But... I don't want him to like me just for the physicality of it. I want him to like me for me. I feel like we haven't really gotten a chance to know each other yet."

"Well, do you like him a lot?" asked Casey. "I mean, do you think he could be the Love of Your Life or anything?"

"We-ell," I stalled. "He's hot, but like I said before, I don't really know him yet. I have to see how it goes."

"If that's the case, you should just have fun with it!" Casey said. "But that's just my opinion."

"Whatever," Erin said. "If you don't think he could be the Love of Your Life, you should just get rid of him. Boys are such distractions anyway. You don't need this headache!"

"But it's fun to be with him!" I refuted, though I completely saw her point.

"That's just it," Casey said. "Have fun with it and don't get invested then. That's what college is all about!"

As if she were reminded of something, she got up and looked in her underwear drawer.

"What's wrong?" I asked.

"I keep losing underwear!" she sighed.

"What?" Erin and I cried in unison.

"On accident! You know, in the heat of the moment, you fling them somewhere and you can't find them in the morning?"

We stared at her blankly. She looked entertained.

"Well, actually," she continued, "sometimes I leave it on purpose. Like last night, I planted a pair in a strategic location."

"Why would you do that?" I asked after recovering from my shock.

"To warn the lady of the house that's she's not the only lady of the house anymore," Casey said.

Before I could ask more questions, there was a knock at the door. I opened it since I was closest and there stood Sean.

"It's dinner time, yo!" he said, pointing at his watch. "Why did you close the door if you're all in here?" he added.

"We were having a private conversation!" Casey snapped at him. "That means no Sean allowed!"

"Well, I'm guessing you didn't want that Goth guy listening to what you guys were saying either," Sean said .

"Goth guy? What Goth guy?" asked Erin. "You're making that up!"

"I'm not," Sean said. "There was a guy hanging around your door for, maybe, five minutes."

"Weeeeird!" Casey yelled, drawing the word out.

"Which one of you is he stalking?" Sean asked us, amused. He looked at each of us in turn.

"I don't sleep with Goth guys," Casey said. "They're into weird shit."

"I don't know any Goth guys," Erin said. They both turned to look at me.

"It might be Jeff's roommate," I said, trying to pass it off as no big deal. "He looks... sort of Goth."

"Great!" cried Casey, throwing her hands up.

"Come on. He probably just wanted to say hi. I met him a few weeks ago and he seemed nice enough."

"Well, if he goes Columbine on our asses..." Casey said.

I cringed. I knew she wasn't being mean just to be mean. She was nervous. I guess I would be too if I weren't the one who knew him.

Without saying anything else, we grabbed our keys and cards, then headed out to dinner.

*****

It should not have been a huge surprise to me when I got my math midterm back with a big "68%" scrawled across the top of it in red crayon. Every minute of the exam was excruciatingly long, except for the final twenty minutes, which slipped through my fingers like sand as I was desperately trying to figure out a different way to integrate the torus, given the negative volume answer I was getting by doing it with polar coordinates. Nonetheless part of me died like when I got my first English paper back.

I don't know what I expected to get. Some part of me must have been holding out hope that the professor wouldn't be able to see through my mathematical blundering. It helped slightly when the professor wrote the mean score on the board: 66%. But not much. That put me at a B minus. I walked out of class in a stupor. What was happening to me? I had been an A student all my life, and here I was barely squeaking by in college. Was I an idiot? Was this the best that I could do?

Deep down, I knew it wasn't the best that I could do. There was a lot more that I could have done to get a better midterm score. I could have started my homework sooner, I could have gone to more professor's and TA's office hours, I could have found an alternative textbook at the library to supplement my own.

Being completely honest with myself, I knew that school had not been a top priority for me until this past week. I had been so concerned about getting the whole College Experience that all things social took precedence over all things academic. Was that really so bad? I mean, didn't I deserve a little bit of a break to enjoy the College Experience after over-committing, over-extending and over-achieving my way through twelve grades to get here? Didn't I?

In theory, I thought I should be alright with this, but I wasn't. I couldn't shake the nagging feeling that I really was not in control of my own College Experience. Rather, it seemed to be in control of me. Supporting this conclusion was the fact that I had continuously dropped the ball on calling Lauren, my family and other old friends back. I was "too busy". But there was something wrong with that. I was also so distracted these days and I couldn't seem to do anything about it.

I stopped by the library on my way out to check my email. I had one.

To: Amy Callaway <acallaway@ucla.edu>
From: The Daily Bruin <dailybruin@ucla.edu>

Thank you for your submission. We will review it and get back to you.

I slammed the mouse on the desk and an unseen librarian shushed me. All of my article submissions had ended with this same enervating email. I was discouraged and frustrated. This latest article was comprised of clever, I thought, observations that I'd made of social interaction at Jeff's frat party. I kept the name of the fraternity out of the article, but I thought the article would be interesting for non-Greek students. It looked like this article was also going to disappear into the black hole of Amy's articles.

I left the library and headed for the coffee house. Over the past few weeks, I had been successful in implementing part 1 of my economic plan to stay out away from overpriced, caffeinated beverages to prolong the lifetime of my anemic bank account, but this was an emergency. I stood in line and thought about all the distractions in my life.

First of all, I was sidetracked by my living arrangements. Casey was an endless disturbance, with her phone talking, her daily drama, plus my own efforts to try to stay on her good side. Erin was always in the room, cleaning or clacking away on her keyboard. Neither of them was silent, still or away, which is what I needed once in awhile.. And when the two were together, they drove each other (and me) absolutely batty. Chris and Sean came into our room frequently. Usually it was nothing important. They just didn't feel like doing work and they did their best to ensure that we wouldn't either.

The boy situation was more than just distracting, it was debilitating. For example, last night, I was supposed to read five chapters of *Ulysses* so that I could begin this week's writing assignment. And I was supposed to call Mummy back.

I had the book open on my desk and I read a few paragraphs. I didn't read them well because I could hear Brian   faintly through our wall, talking on

214

the phone to his girlfriend. I was straining to hear his gentle, encouraging voice.

"How was your day?... That's awesome. What did he say?... Are you up for going?... If you go, you know I will be there..."

Saccharine. Just sickening. I wished it were me on the other end of the phone.

I read another paragraph, but then noticed that Eric had signed on. I debated whether I should message him or not. It was the same debate I always had in my head. Half of me wanted to start a conversation with him to find out what he was up to, see if he was dating anybody, and try to extract a sentimental pronouncement. The other half of me said that I shouldn't message him because I would sound desperate and needy. My strategy du jour was to just play it cool and let him message me.

My eyes ran over another paragraph, then I glanced up to see if Eric messaged or if Jeff returned from being "@ flag football." Negative on both counts.

This dating thing was so weird. I felt like the night that Jeff and I spent together was very special and I waited for the Relationship Defining Talk that never came. We continued to flirt online and grab lunch once in awhile, but that was it. I wasn't going to bring it up, since I was the college newbie and he was the incumbent. But I wondered what it would take to become his official girlfriend.

I reread the previous two paragraphs because I just realized I had no idea what they said. A message window popped up from Eric.

Ericwolf45: hey u

I put my book down and sat up straight in my chair. I needed to be friendly, but cool; nostalgic, but getting on with life without him; flirty, but not desperate; and cute, confident and clever, preferably all at the same time.

Amyable7: how r u?

Ericwolf45: bz, same old. u?

Amyable7: same. lots going on.

Ericwolf45: like what?

Amyable7: u know: school, going out, trying to get back into writing

Ericwolf45: awesome- im glad ur doing that. i know it makes u ☺

Amyable7: thx. slow going tho. whats new w/ u?

Ericwolf45: walked on to the water polo team, so all practice & school now

Amyable7: no partying?

Ericwolf45: some, but mostly just w/ the team

Amyable7: happy?

Ericwolf45: 2 bz to think about it

Amyable7: home for thanksgiving?

Ericwolf45: yah, we shd get together

Amyable7: definitely

That little conversation took fifteen minutes. No joke. And I couldn't think about anything else while I was awaiting his responses and formulating my own to be sure I wasn't violating any of my own criteria. This was the most interesting part of the conversation too. It went on about nothing for another hour after that, and after we finished, I spent another twenty minutes analyzing it.

This was no way to live.

I was getting nowhere, and fast. If it was *this* much trouble just crushing on three guys, I couldn't imagine what it was like to *date* more than one!

Anyway, that was last night's distraction. Now, I stood in line at the coffee house, desperately wondering what else I could do to regain some control of my life.

"Amy!" A voice interrupted my thoughts. It was Autumn, who had strolled into the coffee shop and sidled up next to me. The man behind us cleared his throat loudly, but Autumn had happily lodged herself in line with me.

"Hey, what's happening?" I asked her, putting on a smile.

"You know what *I* heard?" she asked, in her signature chatty voice.

"What?" I asked, feigning excitement as best I could without caffeine.

"I heard that *someone* spent the night at SIE with a very cute second year," she declared. "What was it like? Are you guys official?"

"Shh!" I told her.

I didn't want to overreact, but it seemed kind of insensitive of her to be announcing to the world that I was some sort of sad fraternity floozy.

"Sorry," she said, lowering her voice. "So what happened?"

"Nothing happened! I mean, I spent the night with him, but we didn't do anything but make-out. And we're just dating."

Autumn looked disappointed. "I was hoping you'd make an honest man out of him. You know he has this reputation of being a player, right?"

I turned to look at her. "No, tell me."

"He brings a different girl to every date party," she told me. "My brother's friend is in that frat and he told me so. But I think that you are different. Ken said that Jeff seemed to be pretty smitten with you."

I felt like the time my feet flew out from under me when I went ice skating with Eric. After landing with a crash, flat on my back, it was excruciating to breathe.

"Next!" the lady called from the cash register.

I stepped up and ordered my cappuccino. Autumn came with me. Apparently, she didn't really want to order anything.

"Anyhow, I think you'd better call him. They had food poisoning at the frat house last night and it sounds like a lot of them are puking up their guts today."

As much as I resented her being nosy most of the time, she was good for information every once in awhile. We headed back up to the dorms and she caught me up on the general gossip on the floor.

When I reached my room, I called Jeff.

"Ring... ring... ring... Amy?" Jeff's voice sounded shaky and feeble.

"Jeff, how are you doing? I heard that some of you guys had food poisoning last night," I said, concerned.

"Yeah, it was pretty bad," Jeff mumbled. "A bunch of us... were sick all night."

"Are you alright?" I asked. "What did you eat?"

"We had dinner at the frat, but it was just chicken, rice and veggies, " Jeff replied. "I'm better. I mean, I haven't eaten anything all day because I'm afraid I won't be able to keep it down."

"Where are you?" I asked.

"I'm in my room," he replied.

"Want me to come up?" I offered. "I can bring you soda or crackers or something bland."

"That's so sweet," Jeff said. "But I don't want you to see me like this. I'm pretty gross. I think I'm just going to keep on sleeping and it will pass. I definitely want to see you when I get better. The Halloween party is next week. It's going to be awesome."

"Looking forward to it," I murmured, feeling trapped. I didn't want to face his frat brothers again, but I couldn't tell him that when he was puking up his guts.

"OK, feel better," I told him.

"Thanks, Cutie. Bye."

That was anti-climatic. I sighed and took out my econ homework that was due on Friday. It was mostly finished. I just had to plot one curve and then I was done with it. I sat down and tried to drown out Autumn's words. I had a player on my hands. But, she said that he brought a different girl to every party. Jeff was bringing me to two parties in a row. Maybe Ken was right. Maybe I *was* different. Maybe he was tired of the standard model that showed up to his frat's parties.

I carefully drew the axes and labeled them. Price and Quantity. Where was the demand curve? The higher the quantity of widgets produced, the lower the price because there would be plenty of widgets to go around. Widgets could be cute girls. Or they could be Amy. The price of cute girls around here was probably pretty low because the supply was high. You could spit and hit one, my grandfather would have said. What was the demand for Amy? High, just because there was one of me? Or low because I was just another undifferentiated girl. My Econ professor would be proud to know that I was applying what I was learning.

When I finished my homework, I opened my desk drawer but couldn't find my stapler. It didn't take long for me to locate it on Casey's desk. I blew my bangs up irately. This girl was such a princess sometimes. Was it really so hard to have some respect for other people's things? The least she could do was put it back where she found it.

After putting my problem set on the corner of my desk, I debated whether to go see Jeff. While I wanted to respect his wishes, I really wanted to see him and show him that I was girlfriend material. I decided that if I went upstairs to see him, I needed a good excuse.

I grabbed my wallet and headed to Hilltop, the dorm convenience store, to buy a bottle of Gatorade to bring him. Red or yellow? One of them was rumored to reduce sperm count, but I couldn't remember which one. I used to make fun of my guy friends in high school for how they engaged in death defying stunts without blinking an eyelash, wouldn't touch anything that might impair their "swimmers" with a ten-foot pole. I chuckled to myself as I gave up and bought the blue one. Then I made my way up to his room.

The door was ajar. I opened it slowly.

"Jeff?" I whispered, in case he was sleeping.

"Jeff's not here," Brandon said from his desk.

"I thought he was too sick to get out of bed," I said, confused.

"He was," Brandon replied. "I think he threw up all night. Then he slept all day today. About ten minutes ago, he left."

"Where did he go?" I asked, laying the Gatorade on Jeff's bed.

Brandon shrugged.

"Probably his fraternity," he said, bitterly. "He's there a lot."

I nodded.

"How are you?" I asked.

"Alright," Brandon replied. "Doing papers for class. Trying to figure out my purpose in life. You know."

I smiled. "Just your average school night, right?"

He also managed a smile. "Are you writing still?"

"Some," I replied, not wanting to talk about my pile of rejections from the Daily Bruin. "But school is keeping me pretty busy. I don't know where the time goes."

Brandon nodded. There was an awkward silence.

"OK, I'm going to head back down. I just wanted to drop off the Gatorade for him," I said.

"See you around, Amy."

"Bye, Brandon."

I went to bed that night feeling perplexed by Jeff. I was so attracted to him. Who wouldn't be? He was hot. And he was sweet, charming, and very... masculine. What was his deal? Was he just not taking applications for girl fiends? I had a hard time falling asleep that night, trying to figure it out. It didn't help that Casey was on the phone with her sorority sister until late, talking about the food poisoning incident at the frat.

"It would be different at the sorority," I heard Casey say, laughing. "Half the girls in the house are bulimic anyway, so it wouldn't be that much of a change for us. In fact, a few of us could stand to lose a few pounds."

10 "Gain 15 pounds"

Most of the horrors of midterms had faded by the time Halloween rolled around, though a new set of horrors set in when I tried on my French maid outfit.

I looked in the mirror after putting on my costume for the first time since I'd bought it. "Ohmygod, what happened to me?"

I guess I hadn't taken a good look at myself in weeks. Thinking back, my jeans *had* felt a little snug last week. I'd just attributed it to the dryer shrinking them. Denial at its best. But in my form-fitting costume, there was no question that I looked a little... chubby.

"What do you mean?" Erin asked, turning around in her chair to look at me. "It looks cute on you!"

"No! I have love handles! When did this happen? I've *never* had love handles!"

I pinched an unwanted addition to my body between my thumb and fingers- a squishy mantle that had laid itself evenly over my abdomen. This was appalling. I looked at myself straight on in the mirror and had a hard time locating my waist!

I turned sideways. Definitely thicker. I looked at Erin in despair.

"My thighs look enormous. See how the flab puffs out around the leg holes? And look at my chin! I liked this high neck because all of the other costumes had ridiculously low necklines, but now it makes me look like I have a *double chin*!"

"You're being overly critical of yourself! You look great, I promise!"

"I'm sorry!" I apologized, realizing that I probably sounded like the biggest whiner ever. "I *hate* it when girls do this. I never bitch about my body, but I guess I didn't really notice this happening and I really wanted to look good at Jeff's Halloween party on Friday."

"You look fine"

"Argh, I'm going to the gym! Do you want to come?"

Erin shook her head.

"Problem set," we said in unison. Then we laughed.

I shimmied out of the costume and threw on some sweats. There was a stack of work sitting on my desk and I'd resolved to be more diligent at my schoolwork, but I needed to do some damage control.

I walked rapidly down the hill towards the gym. There were four days until the party. A lot could happen in four days. My friends on the wrestling team in high school used to brag about how much weight they lost before wrestling matches to get into lower weight classes. They could lose up to five pounds in four days sometimes! Granted a lot of it was water weight, but even that should smooth out some of the bumps, right?

There was some sort of car smashing contest going on in Bruin Plaza. I walked carefully around the crowd. The Big Game with our cross town rival, USC, was coming soon. Lately, campus was obsessed with painting things red and gold, then demolishing them. They were currently taking a sledge hammer to an old school red VW Beetle with USC's Trojan seal painted on the hood. Glass, metal and cheers went flying.

I walked right by it and strode into the gym. I managed to procure an open treadmill. I jumped on and jacked the speed up to 6.0 miles per hour. That was a ten minute mile. No problem. Eight minute miles were my norm in high school.

Skinny divas rocked out on the TV monitors mounted above me. In front of me, a girl and a guy climbed the indoor rock wall. That would be a fun date idea, especially for an athletic couple. Maybe I would suggest it to Jeff at the Halloween party. My breathing began to get louder and my shirt was beginning to wick up sweat. I could feel pressure on my knees every time my foot hit the belt. After what seemed like hours, I glanced down at the timer.

3:40

I stumbled in my surprise, but caught myself. I'd only run a third of a mile? This was pitiful! How long had it been since I'd run? I tried to recall. I really hadn't been to the gym since Week 2, when I'd come with Chris, Sean, Erin and Sarah.

I slowed down the speed to 5.5 miles per hour and lengthened my stride to spare myself. For the sake of my self-respect, at the very least, I had to do this for thirty minutes.

"Thud. Thud." (gasp) "Thud. Thud." (gasp)

I sounded like an asthmatic elephant. Worse, I could feel body parts jiggling that didn't used to jiggle before. Most distressing was the bouncing of my ass. I had no idea things could get this bad in just six weeks!

I thought back to all the eating that I'd been doing. It wasn't uncommon for me to eat a slice of pizza, an enchilada casserole, a dish of fries and a dessert or the equivalent of that for dinner at night. I groaned inwardly as I recalled how I'd gorged myself with such joy and impunity! Now I was paying for it. I was well on my way to my very own personal Freshman Fifteen.

I glanced around myself for a diversion. Do you ever notice how the people you see in gyms are never the ones that look like they need to be in gyms? There were ripped guys in basketball shorts and soaked t-shirts, struggling with weights like it was a matter of life and death. The girls were less intense. They were generally lean and distracted.

I saw Karen, running daintily on a treadmill across the room. She hadn't even broken a sweat. This was Ken's date, the adorable one who had been flirting with Jeff at the date party last week. She looked amazing in spandex running pants and a stylish workout cami. Her long, dark ponytail bobbed jauntily behind her. There wasn't an ounce of fat on this girl. Well, if you didn't count her well-endowed chest.

Life was just not fair. Why couldn't my fat go to the "right" places? I bitterly wondered how much time she spent on upkeep every day.

I continued to thud and wheeze for another ten minutes. My lungs felt like they were going to collapse. My heart was pounding against my ribcage. I was soaked in sweat and my knees were growing sore from the abuse. I dialed down the speed to 3.0 miles per hour to catch my breath.

16:54

I allowed myself to walk for two minutes and then made myself run all the way to the thirty minute mark. Then I dragged my well-endowed, exhausted ass up the hill for dinner.

When I got back, I messaged Jeff.

Amyable7: dinner?

Jeffers56: already have plans with some buddies

Jeffers56: want to see you tho. can i stop by later?

Amyable7: sure- have good dinner

Jeffers56: thx, qt

I went to dinner with the usual gang and ate only a salad.

"Feeling alright?" Casey asked, glancing sideways at my anorexic dinner selection.

I nodded.

"Halloween costume," I whispered to her, so as not to draw attention to myself.

Erin gave me a sympathetic smile. Casey registered a look of understanding. The boys never stopped their conversation on the merits of the latest action flick they'd downloaded illegally online.

I left the dining hall famished. *How do girls do this to themselves?*

*****

After dinner, Erin got right back on her computer and began typing furiously.

I sat down at my desk and rubbed my temples. This work was never ending. My "To Do" list for the evening said that I needed to finish my Anthro and English reading. Progress *had* to be made on my math problem set as well, if I knew what was good for me. My instant messenger had to stay shut off for the evening so that I had a fighting chance of getting work done tonight. I grabbed my books and climbed up to my bed to further distance myself from temptation.

An hour or so into my reading about the matriarchal Trobriander tribe in Papua New Guinea, I noticed that Erin's typing seemed to be getting louder. She appeared to be pounding down on the keys. I glanced down in her direction and saw her shifting in her seat, like she couldn't get comfortable. I watched a new message pop up on her screen. She read it and clenched both of her fists, then dove at the keyboard with alarming ferocity to type back a staccato response..

"Everything alright down there?" I called from my penthouse.

"No! Jim's being a jerk!"

"What's wrong?" I asked, unable to shut off my curiosity even though I knew it was going to cost me some precious studying time.

"Remember how I told you there's this girl at MIT who is a family friend of his?"

"Yeah."

"Well, she's a second year and she's in a sorority. So she asked him to her date party."

"Does she know you guys are dating?" I asked, fascinated.

"I don't know! But if Jim were a good boyfriend, he would tell her that he has a girlfriend and probably shouldn't go with her. Right?"

Erin looked more belligerent than I'd ever seen her. I was afraid to answer her. It turns out that she didn't need an answer from me because she went right on.

"So he said yes! And when I told him that this made me kind of uncomfortable, he accused me of not trusting him! Can you believe that?"

"Well, *do* you trust him?"

"Not really!" she admitted. "Because why would he *want* to go to someone else's date party if he wasn't interested in her?"

"Maybe he feels like he should because his parents are friends," I pointed out.

"No way," she said, flinging herself back in her chair. "He's interested. He's just trying to turn this back onto me so he doesn't feel so guilty. Here, read this."

I climbed down from the bed and stood behind her so that I could see her computer screen. She scrolled the conversation up to the point where she wanted me to start reading.

Erin: what are you up to tmrw night? phone call?

Jim: can't- going to a party

Erin: what party?

Jim: just this party at one of the sororities

Erin: who are you going w/

Jim: so many ?'s!

Erin: just curious

Jim: genevieve asked me to go w/ her. her sorority's party

Erin: like a date party?

Jim: something like that

Erin: and you said yes?

Jim: sure, why not?

Erin: does she know u have a gf?

Jim: what's that have anything to do with anything?

Erin: i dunno. im kind of uncomfortable w/ this

Jim: why? we're just friends. im helping her out

Erin: she couldn't find someone else to go w/ besides someone else's bf?

Jim: come on, u r being dramatic

Erin: uh… ok

Jim: why are you getting all possessive on me?

Erin: i just think it's weird

Jim: don't u trust me?

Erin: yah

Jim: b/c if u can't trust me, how can we be in a relationship?

Jim: am i just supposed to sit around in my room for 4 yrs and not have any fun b/c ur "uncomfortable"? thats not fair.

Erin: ur not being fair! i never said u shouldnt have fun. i just think u shld respect my feelings

Jim: whatever

Erin: why do u want to go so bad anyway?

Jim: im not having this argument w/ u. ur being childish.

Erin: ur being selfish

I sucked in my breath. Wow.

"Don't you think if he really loved me, he would respect my wishes?" Erin demanded, her voice breaking into my thoughts.

"Of course!"

"I want to kick his ass," Erin said through clenched teeth. "Why are relationships so complicated?"

"You got me," I said, shaking my head. "I have no idea. I guess people are just complicated. Maybe he doesn't know what he wants."

"Or maybe he just wants too many things," Erin shot back. "Well he can't have his cake and eat it too. If he wants to have a girlfriend, then he can't be going to date parties!"

"Amen, sister," I said, thinking of Brian and his girlfriend. "If you're going to have a girlfriend, you shouldn't blur the lines with your female friends."

"Right. How do I tell him that?" Erin asked.

"Over the phone?" I suggested.

Erin began to look like she was losing her nerve. She bit her lip and looked less convinced.

"What if we break up?" she asked, her voice growing timid.

"Oh, Erin!" I said, not wanting to upset her. "You won't break up! He would be *stupid* to break up with you! But... if he insists on doing this dating thing, then... maybe you don't want to be with him anyway?"

I ended my sentence as a question so it wouldn't sound judgmental or prescriptive. I just wanted to suggest an alternative way of looking at it.

Erin thought about this and turned back to her computer. This was my cue to get back to my schoolwork. I had a hard time focusing on my book because I was thinking about Eric and me. If we had stayed together and done the long distance relationship, would we eventually have found ourselves in this predicament? Maybe one of us would want to go to a date party. And the whole thing would begin to unravel. It would turn into a bitter, ugly, drawn-out break up. I decided that I preferred the way we did it. We had no hard feelings towards one another. We had no chance to screw up our opinions of each other. The only problem was, we would never know if we would have made it. And I missed him. A lot.

Jeff IMed saying that he was going to stop by the room, but then never showed up that night. I sent a brief email to Lauren.

From: "Amy Callaway" <acallaway@ucla.edu>
To: "Lauren Avery" <lavery@princeton.edu>
Subject: Sorry!

L,

Sorry!!! So much going on! Everything alright??? Will call when I can.

Love, A

*****

On Thursday afternoon, Casey convinced me to go to step aerobics with her, in spite of my initial objection that it was pansy and from the 80's. I wondered how much good it would do the day before the party, but it was worth a shot.

"You can't wear that," Casey protested as she watched me pull on my mesh basketball shorts and an oversized t-shirt.

"Why not?" I asked, confused.

"Don't you have anything... tighter?" she asked.

"What? Why?" I asked. "I thought we were going to the gym, not clubbing!"

"So you can see how your body is moving in the mirror! That's how you make you're your form is right. Haven't you ever been to an aerobics class or a dance class?"

I shook my head. Then, I remembered that I had a stretchy yoga outfit that my aunt had given me last year. I dug it out of the closet. There was a black tank top with a yin-yang symbol on the chest and stretchy booty pants. They were already too small when I got them at Christmas. For sure they'd be miniature now.

I held them it up for Casey to see.

"That's good," she said,. She was putting on skin tight spandex as well, in pink and white.

I put my yoga outfit on and looked ridiculous. You could see every damn bump. I felt constricted in every direction.

Casey and I power walked down to the gym. We turned a few heads in our tight outfits. I felt incredibly self conscious.

"Make sure you stand between me and the instructor," Casey told me. "Because sometimes, we turn around and face the back, but the instructor stays at the front of the room and it might help you remember the moves if you watch me."

"I thought you said it wasn't that complicated."

"It's not… but just in case."

"That's very generous of you." I don't think she caught my sarcasm.

After swiping our ID cards at the front desk, we went upstairs to a part of the gym I didn't even know existed. I followed Casey into one of the dance studios, which had mirrors all along one wall and windows along the opposite wall. The sunlight poured into the room and reflected off of polished wood floor. Upbeat music played in the background, which added to this cheery picture. The petite instructor was already in the room. Even as she was looking through her binder of CD's, she had perfect posture and she moved gracefully, like a dancer.

"Hi Casey!" she called out when she saw us come in. "Who's your friend?"

"Hi Steph!" Casey replied. "This is my roommate Amy!"

"Nice to meet you, Amy! First time doing step?" she asked.

I should have taken it as a bad sign that she could tell that just by looking at me.

"Yes," I replied with a smile. "So go easy on me."

"You'll be fine," the instructor said.

I followed Casey to the back of the room, where we picked up a large, plastic plank and four hollow squares that Casey called "risers." I copied her as she stacked one riser on top of another twice. Then she laid the plank across the two mini riser towers.

"Make sure it's locked into place," Casey instructed me. I adjusted mine so that the plank sat snugly on top of the riser towers.

At this point, girls were streaming into the dance room and setting up their step benches up. Now I understood why Casey made me change. These girls were wearing brand spanking new tanks that were brighter and cleaner than some of my "going out" clothes. On the bottom, they wore cute shorts, leggings and capris in matching colors. I wondered if this was an LA phenomenon or if every aerobics class looked like this.

"OK, march out it," the instructor ordered, marching behind her bench. We all fell into lockstep, marching along to the beat.

"Deep breath in, arms overhead, bring them down and rest them on your thighs."

Everyone put their hands on their thighs with their knees bent and their backs arched down towards the floor.

"Roll it up, flatten back down, roll it up, flatten back down."

I observed that we were supposed to arch our backs down towards the floor and then up towards the ceiling, like a cat stretching. I had to admit that though I felt silly, the stretching felt good.

"Alright, for those of us who are new to step, I'm going to go over the basic moves. Everything we do in this class is just a combination of a few of these basic moves. Here's the basic. Right up, left up, right down, left down."

I copied the instructor as we did the basic eight times, starting with the right foot and then the left foot. We also learned corner-to-corner knees, lunges off the step, repeater knee and this move called a mambo cha-cha, which involved a step onto the bench with the right foot, an immediate step down off the bench with the right foot, then a fancy little turn while we cha-cha-cha'd away from our bench.

I caught Casey's eye on the mirror. She gave me a thumbs up. This wasn't so bad once you got over how strange it was that everyone was doing the exact same thing exactly at the same time, like pretty, dancing droids.

Then we got into combinations, which were a whole different story.

"V step, two, three, four. Good, now Mambo shasay!" the instructor called out, blithely. She stepped up on the bench and lifted her knee several times. I tried to imitate her, but was having a hard time both processing the words and watching her at the same time. I was beginning to pant.

"L step, now across the top," she called, lifting alternating knees deliberately at the end of her bench, and then skipping across the top of the bench. I was getting my left foot and my right foot all mixed up. I couldn't remember which foot to come down first. And I was totally off the beat of the music. I nearly fell off the top of the bench, tripping on my own feet.

"Step up, lunge left, lunge right. Knees around the world!"

Knees around the world? What world? What sort of instruction was that? I was completely flustered.

Everybody started doing single knee raises, but somehow moving around their benches so that they were facing a different corner of the room on every knee lift. Everyone was facing the back of the room, while I was still facing front, trying to figure out what on earth was going on.

"This is hard!" I mouthed to Casey.

When I finally got to facing backwards, everyone else was facing front. I blew my bangs up out of my face, in frustration. She gave me sympathetic look and tried to mouth something back, but I couldn't make it out. I kept catching sympathetic looks from the other girls in the class.

By the end of class, I was totally confused, stressed out and frustrated.

"How was it?" Casey asked.

"Terrible, Case!" I replied. "I had no idea what the heck was going on!"

"That's how everyone is their first class. In fact, you did really well compared to a lot of people on their first day," she said.

"Who in their right mind would go back for a second day?" I wondered aloud. "Hey, what were you trying to say to me during class?"

"Your yoga pants split open at the seam in the back," Casey said, wincing.

Of course they did.

I looked back behind me and saw a streak of my turquoise underwear down the center of my black yoga pants. How come these sorts of things never happened to her?

On the way home, I made Casey walk behind me to hide the big tear in the seat of my pants. I checked my cell phone and saw that I had missed a call from my Dad. I listened to the voicemail as we walked up the hill to Sproul, enduring the occasional cat call from a hormonal college boy.

"Hi, Honey. It's Dad. Listen, Mom's in the hospital right now."

I stopped dead in my tracks and Casey ran into me from behind. Mummy in the hospital? How could this be? My heart sprang two gushing leaks at once- one of fear and the other of guilt.

"What's wrong?" Casey asked me, concerned.

I turned around and put my finger to my lips to silence her.

"We think she's fine right now. She just fainted in the kitchen this afternoon and the doctor is running tests on her now. I just wanted to let you know. Give me a call back when you get this." Dad's voice was tense, but not panicked.

"My mom's in the hospital!" Then I held down the "4" button for my Dad's speed dial.

"Ring... ring... ring... Hi Amy." Dad's voice was calm. That was a good sign.

"Dad, what's wrong with Mum?"

"They're not sure yet, but all of her vitals are fine and she's awake now," Dad informed me.

"Can I talk to her?" I asked, anxiously.

"Well, no, they've got her on oxygen right now. She was just talking to me earlier. She said she was making dinner, felt kind of dizzy, and then just blacked out."

"Is she ok?" I cried.

"We think so," Dad replied. "I think she may have hit her head when she fell. She says it hurts."

I could hear my mother's voice in the background. "Amy!" That was enough to make tears spring to my eyes.

"Daddy, I want to come home!"

"Right now?" Dad was surprised. "It's Thursday. Don't you have class tomorrow?"

"It's fine!" I said. "I can get notes from someone else."

"Well, ok, Honey. I can come up there and pick you up tonight," Dad offered. "Can you be ready by 8pm?"

11 "Leave the nest"

Those two hours were a blur. I showered, threw some clothes in my overnight duffel and packed a few books. I tucked my laptop into my backpack. The last thing I did before I left was call Jeff to let him know I couldn't make it to the costume party the next day. It would be selfish to make my dad drive four hours in two days chauffeuring me back and forth between school and Irvine. I would have to stay the entire weekend.

"I'm so sorry to flake on you like this," I told Jeff over the phone, with a heavy heart. "I was really looking forward to this party."

"It's ok," Jeff replied. "Your mom is way more important. There will be lots more parties this year that we can go to."

I hung up and walked out to the turnaround at 8pm. Dad was already there waiting for me. We made small talk for the first few minutes of the car ride. I told him about my classes, a little bit about my roommates and about the food in the dorms. But I left out boy troubles and roommate issues. Dad was an engineer. He had little use for problems that you couldn't solve with equations or cold, hard logic.

I watched the dashed lines on the road blur into continuous, glowing lines and my mind drifted to my mother. The first memory that came to mind happened when I was five years old. We drove up the coast of California for spring break that year and stayed at this little bed and breakfast near San Francisco. On the day that we left, we'd driven about two hours down the coast towards home when I realized that we'd left Franklin, my bear, at the inn. My family recounted later that I let out a yelp that made all three of them jump. My Dad nearly killed me for causing him to drive off the road. Mum interrupted his lecture, turned around and asked me what was the matter. She was confronted with a quivering lower lip and eyes glazed over with the promise of tears.

"Franklin," I half whispered and half wailed.

"Honey, turn around," Mum said to Dad.

"Absolutely not," I remember Dad saying, stomping on the fragile heart of a five-year-old. "It's just a stuffed animal. That's going to add four hours to the trip and I have to get up for work tomorrow morning. Amy, Daddy will buy you a new bear when we get home, ok?"

I remember shaking my head wildly. A new bear?! To replace my lifelong companion. The idea! Mum understood. She didn't even need to look at me to know what had to be done.

"Honey, turn the car around. Or else get out and I will drive. You can sleep in the car if you have to," she said. My father looked at her,

231

dumbfounded.

"Are you serious?" he almost yelled.

"Pull over. It's important to her."

Those words echoed in my head now. I remember how grateful I was when Franklin was safely in my arms again. Mum was my angel. And how many times those words came out of her mouth over the years. "It's important to her." When I *had* to get new basketball shoes so that I wouldn't be the nerd with the cheap shoes. When Meg needed to get contact lenses before her eighth grade graduation dance.

All of my life, Mum had been taking care of everyone else. I searched my memory and couldn't think of a single moment when she complained about it or asked for anything in return.

And how did I pay her back? By being an ungrateful, spoiled brat. I couldn't even make time in my "busy" schedule to call her once in awhile. When recalling the amount of time I was spending thinking about stupid boys, I felt nauseated.

By the time we reached the hospital, the knot of guilt that sat in my stomach had grown to the size and weight of a cannonball.

"Dad, come *on!*" I begged, as he took his time locking the car.

"I'm coming!" Dad replied, sounding tired.

I followed him in through the automated doors. We maneuvered our way around the occasional wheelchair and gurney through the sterile white hallways to the back of the hospital.

"Here," Dad said, pointing to the door as we approached it.

I rushed in. Mum was lying on a wide hospital bed. She looked pale and fragile, with tubes and machines around her.

"Mummy!" I cried and ran to her bedside.

She held out her arms for me. I fell into them, feeling both relieved that she wasn't mad at me for not calling and anxious about her condition.

"You didn't have to come home, Amy!" she said. My cheek was smooshed against her neck and I could feel it vibrating as she spoke. "It's probably nothing. I feel fine. I think the only problem was that I hit my head when I fell."

"Mum, I was so worried!" I said, into her pillow, hugging her tight.

"I didn't want Dad to call you at school because I was *afraid* he was going to worry you," Mum said, ever the martyr.

"Jeez, Mum!" I cried. "I can't believe you wouldn't call me! You're my mom! I'm *supposed* to worry when things happen to you! Did you guys call Meg?"

"Meg's in Germany on a business trip," Dad replied.

"But did you call her?" I persisted.

No one said anything.

"You guys!" I said in exasperation. "She's going to be so mad!"

"Well, there's no sense in worrying her when she can't do anything about it," Mum said, practically. "It's no big deal. We can tell her over Christmas."

I rolled my eyes. I wanted to say that Meg would never forgive them if something terrible happened while Mum was in the hospital, but I refrained from suggesting such a thing.

"So what's happening now?" I asked, looking around the room for any sign of something more serious than a fainting spell.

"The doctor is running some blood tests just to be safe. The CT scan, MRI and EEG came out fine," Mum said. "The doctor wanted me to stay here overnight to be sure that my brain isn't swelling or bleeding slowly. If I'm fine in the morning, he says I can go home."

I nodded. I could feel my brows furrowing together.

"You guys should go home and get some rest," Mum continued, looking back and forth between my Dad and me. "You've got work tomorrow."

"Are you sure, Honey?" my Dad asked. I was struck by the tenderness in his voice.

Mum nodded, but I sensed that she was putting on a brave face for us. *I would not have wanted to stay in this plain, impersonal hospital room by myself, not knowing if my brain was alright.*

"Yeah, there's nothing else to do here. Go on, Baby," she said to me. "Go home with Dad. Thanks so much for coming to see me."

"I'm going to go home with Dad to get your car," I told her. "Then I'm coming back here."

"What? Why?" Dad asked.

"I'm going to spend the night here with Mum," I replied, bracing myself for the argument that I knew was coming. Both parents gaped at me.

"Amy, I'm *fine*," Mum insisted, as I knew she would. "Go home and get a good night's rest. You can come over in the morning!"

"No," I replied, ready to stand my ground. "If it were the other way around, you'd stay here with me too. I want to be here in case you need anything. You would do it for me. Why can't I do it for you?"

They couldn't argue with that. Dad opened his mouth to protest again.

"It'll be fine!" I interrupted him before he could begin. "I'll stay here and we'll have a sleep-over! It'll be fun! I'll bring my pajamas and everything. We can catch up... and gossip! I'll tell you about my classes and my roommates and everything!"

Mum couldn't help herself from smiling and I knew I'd won. I bent down to kiss her on the cheek.

"OK, I'll be right back," I said, as Dad and I headed out the door. We traced our steps back out to the front entrance of the hospital and out into the chilly fall air.

"This is really nice of you, Amy," my Dad said to me, as we got into the car.

"Dad, 'nice' has nothing to do with it," I told him. "This is Mum we're talking about. I've only got one."

"You know, she'd be fine here by herself for a night. You don't have to come back."

"Dad, it's important to her."

*****

The doctor came in around 9am to take her vitals again. She said that everything looked fine and that the lab results were clear. Mum might have just been stressed or dehydrated. We thanked her and I drove her home.

"What are you going to do today?" Mum asked me, in the car.

"I should probably do some schoolwork," I replied, keeping my eyes on the road. "I have so much to do for the end of the quarter. What about you?"

Mum shrugged. "I don't know. I should probably do some grocery shopping, laundry and stuff."

*****

On my way back to UCLA, I realized that I'd left my Econ problem set sitting on top of my desk at school and didn't turn it in. Damn me for being so careless. It was just stupid to miss easy points on trivial things like turning in my homework. I wondered if I could at least get half credit for turning it in late. My TA in that class seemed like an easy-going person, but I wasn't sure.

I said bye to Dad in the turnaround and bounded up to my room. After saying hi to Erin, who was working at her computer, I headed straight to my desk. There was a note on it.

Missed you at the party. Call me when you get back. –Jeff

I smiled for a moment, then continued to rifle under books and through various stacks of papers, but I still couldn't find my homework.

"Are you looking for your Econ homework?" Erin asked. She had twisted around in her chair to look at me.

"Yeah, how did you know?" I asked.

"I saw it on your desk after you left on Thursday night and turned it in for you on Friday," she replied.

I looked at her, amazed. Gratitude was welling up in my heart.

She shrugged.

"You left your class schedule up," she pointed out. "It was easy enough to do."

I walked over to her and hugged her, hard. "That was above and beyond, man"

"What are friends for?" she asked. "How's your mom?"

"She's fine, thanks for asking," I told her. "She fainted while she was cooking dinner and hit her head on the counter. But it looks like everything is ok now."

"That must have been so scary for you," she empathized, her dark eyes solemn.

"Yeah, I can't even imagine what I would have done if something had happened to her," I replied, my voice cracking. "I feel like such a schmuck for taking her for granted."

"We all do it. I know I do it too. You just get caught up in life sometimes."

"I know," I sighed. "Isn't it weird how we try so hard to impress random strangers sometimes and we don't use a fraction of that energy being nice to the people we love?"

"It's because we know they will always love us. Or that's how it's supposed to work, anyway."

We were both silent for a minute, contemplating the weight of her words.

"How's everything around here?" I asked, changing the subject.

"Jeff ended up taking Casey to the Halloween party," she said, looking at the ground.

"Oh?" A stab of compunction struck me, then jealousy. It took a moment for the feeling to pass.

Erin looked back up at me, trying to gauge my expression.

"What did she go as?" I asked, picking at an imaginary splinter in my bed post.

"A slutty pirate wench."

*****

The next few weeks flew by. I was juggling classes, midterms, and papers, while counting down the days until Thanksgiving.

I got home from the library late one afternoon, feeling particularly stressed about my last English paper. It just wasn't coming together like I wanted it to. I needed to develop stronger arguments supporting my claim that Hamlet's inaction sprang from his need to optimize his moral utility, not fear.

I stalked down the hallway towards my room, shaking my head and nearly ran smack into Chris.

"Whoa, there! You look intense."

"Sorry, man. I'm thinking about my paper. How's it going?"

He held up a dusty basketball. "Gonna go shoot some hoops. Need to clear my head."

I nodded. "Have fun."

"Hey, come with me. You look like you need to clear your head too."

"Naw, I got a lot to do."

"Come *on*," Chris cajoled. "Brian told me that you used to be a baller. Why don't you come out and show me what you got."

He held the ball out to me. I reached out to take it, but he moved it away. A spark of competitiveness ignited somewhere in my head and I pounced on him to wrestle the ball away.

"Oof! That's what I'm talking about," he laughed as I ran to my room with the ball.

"Give me two seconds," I called back to him.

I let myself into my room and pulled on my mesh basketball shorts and a ratty t-shirt. As I was lacing up my shoes, I realized that I had not played ball since I had gotten to college. It used to be such a big part of my life. No wonder I felt lost some days. Entire pieces of my past life had gone completely missing. I emerged from my room with the ball tucked under my arm.

"Wow, you mean business," Chris observed.

"I don't mess around." I grinned.

We played a fierce game of one-on-one. Chris won, but I took satisfaction in his breathless collapse on the court when he made his eleventh shot.

"You're good, for a girl!" he commented, splayed out on the asphalt, his t-shirt soaked through and his chest heaving.

There were two ways to take that statement. I gave him the benefit of the doubt.

"Thanks," I replied, holding my hand out for the ball.

He passed it to me and I positioned myself on the free throw line to practice shooting. I was also panting. My muscles felt weak and wobbly, foreshadowing tomorrow's pain. But in my physical turmoil, I found a mental calmness that I also hadn't experienced since summer. I was in my element. I was home.

Why *hadn't* this been a priority for so long?

Chris stood up and gestured for the ball. I tossed it to him and we took turns shooting, comfortable with each other and comfortable in our silence. I love playing sports until you're too tired to do anything but exist. It strips away everything but your focus, discipline and will. All that matters is physical. Everything else just sort of melts away.

"So how's life?" I asked, as Chris set himself up for a shot.

He shrugged. "Midterms."

"How do you like college so far?"

"It's alright," he said, after missing his shot and trotting to get his rebound. "Different than I expected, I guess."

"How?"

"I dunno," he replied. "I guess I expected everything to be easier."

"Like what?" I asked, holding my hand out for the ball.

"School... dating... partying... the friend thing," he replied, very honestly.

Ever notice how guys open up to you when you play sports with them? It boosts your credibility. Like if you can play sports, then somehow, you're less alien.

"I totally agree." I flicked my wrist and the ball sailed, but the arc was too low. I could tell as soon as I released it. "No one ever tells you that part. They always tell you about how it's fun and great and there are so many opportunities. I mean, there *are*. But you have to work for them."

"Yeah. But you seem to be doing ok. You're dating that one guy, right?"

"I guess," I replied. "This dating thing is so weird. We have this thing going on, but he could also have this thing going on with other people and I don't really know how I feel about it. I'm trying to be open- minded and use this freedom to find other people to 'try out', but... I don't know. It's not really working that way."

I passed Chris the ball. "Are you seeing anyone?"

"No," Chris answered, looking discouraged. "There's this girl that I met at Orientation who I think is hot and we keep running into each other, but she's totally out of my league, so I haven't been able to ask her out."

"What does that even *mean*?"

"What?"

"That she's out of your league."

"It means that she's too cool for me. We wouldn't have hung out with the same crowd in high school. She would have been with the, you know, uber popular kids, and been Homecoming queen and all that."

"Yeah, but we're in college now," I pointed out. "There *are* no crowds. Or, there are a thousand crowds. But I don't think there are leagues anymore. I hope we've outgrown that."

Chris sent the ball sailing through the hoop. I gave him a high five. He thought for a minute.

"You don't think that Erin and Casey are in different leagues?" he asked.

I shook my head. "Erin and Casey have different priorities and they might hang out in different crowds, but I really think that neither one of them is better than the other. If someone like Casey found someone like Erin to be attractive, why couldn't they date?"

"Is the guy that you're dating in your league?" Chris asked, still working it out beneath his furrowed brow. I retrieved his rebound and gave him his change.

"It's the same thing as what I just said. I think in high school, he would have been with the 'popular crowd', but there is no 'popular crowd' here. It's just him and me and we like each other. It's so much nicer to not be under the oppression of these labels here."

Chris looked more convinced. He flipped the ball at the hoop, but missed. I caught the rebound and began to make lay-ups.

"So you don't think she would think that I was... not good enough?" he asked, struggling to find the words.

"No. You're the only one who can make yourself feel 'not good enough'."

"You're like some kind of Yoda," Chris laughed.

I grinned. "Good guy, you are," I replied, playing the part.

"Seriously," Chris said. "You're, like, the nicest person in our group."

"Don't get mushy on me, man," I replied, banking a shot in off the backboard.

*****

I had lunch with Jeff in the student union the Wednesday right before Thanksgiving.

"You're glowing," Jeff noticed, before taking an enormous bite out of his pizza.

"I'm just *so* glad it's Thanksgiving. I feel like I've been holding my breath for a long time and finally I can exhale."

"What are you talking about? Speak English."

I rolled my eyes at him. "I just mean that I've been so busy these last few weeks, I haven't had a moment to just chill out."

"Seriously! Getting a date with you is like trying to get an audience with the Dalai Lama!"

"Whatever! Who is the one who is at the movies or at the frat house or out with the guys or playing football…"

"Ok, ok," Jeff laughed, holding his hands up in defeat. "We're *both* bad."

"Thank you!" I dug into my taco salad.

"Let's pinkie swear that when we get back from Thanksgiving, we will make more time for each other," Jeff proposed. He held out his pinkie as if he were sipping high tea with the Queen of England.

"I haven't done a pinkie swear in years," I told him, hooking my pinkie with his, awkwardly. "How old are you?"

"Old enough to know that you have to seal a pinkie swear with a kiss," Jeff replied, leaning across the table to kiss me.

It took me a few minutes to exhale.

*****

When Dad and I arrived home later that evening, I was ecstatic. I threw my arms around Mummy's neck and kissed her on the cheek. Then I ran upstairs to *my* room, flung my bags on the floor and catapulted myself into *my* bed.

I laid still for a moment and reveled in being surrounded by things dear and familiar to me. My gang of love-worn stuffed animals welcomed me home from my beat-up armchair in the corner. They seemed to be looking back at me, assessing whether and how I had changed. The posters of Monet's Bridge Over Water Lilies and Charles Barkely looked more faded than I remembered on the wall. My old swimming trophies, school awards and photos from what seemed like eons ago brought back a flood of happy memories. *Anne of Green Gables* was even sitting on my nightstand, just as I'd left it before I went to college.

I was thrilled to be home, but something felt different now. I think it was the realization that what used to be my entire world was really just a tiny sliver of the entire world. Home couldn't protect me from everything out there anymore, and this made it seem more fragile, somehow.

Meg made a grand entrance, as usual, when she arrived home the next evening, in time for turkey. She rang the doorbell several times, even though we knew she had a key to the house. We all dropped what we were doing and rushed to the front door. Dad opened the door and she waltzed in with her duffel, kissing Dad on the cheek.

"How do you feel, Mum?" she asked, giving Mum a kiss on the cheek.

"I'm feeling great," Mum replied, to everyone's satisfaction. "How do you feel?"

"I'm home!" she said. "And I don't have to answer another midnight call until Sunday! So I feel like a new person!"

She motioned me over and rubbed her palm back and forth across my head, like she used to do when we were kids and she used to be taller than me. I grabbed her in a bear hug.

"You'd better not be doing work!" I said. "I hardly get to see you ever!"

"The turkey smells amazing!" she exclaimed. We all sat down at the kitchen table and admired Mum's Thanksgiving dinner. Aside from a golden brown turkey, there was a savory boat of gravy, a plate piled high with yams, a baking dish of corn bread, and a bowl full of Mum's special sourdough stuffing.

Between bites, Meg told us about her consulting job, which sounded awful.

"So, the client meeting is at nine o'clock in the morning way out in the Valley," she said, waving a chunk of turkey on her fork around as she spoke. "We've been working all night on this presentation because the stupid research company that we hired didn't get us the data in time. At seven o'clock in the morning, the partner on the case is like, 'We can't take this to the client. This data doesn't back up the assertions that we're making and the deck looks sloppy, etcetera, etcetera.'"

"The partner 'is like'?" Dad said, disapprovingly. "The partner 'said.'"

"Whatever," Meg replied. "And we all look at each other because we have to get the thing printed and bound by eight o'clock if we have any hope of getting it to the client site on time."

"So what happened?" I asked, amazed that in real life, bosses could ask you to do something that is physically impossible and get away with it.

"So, he tells us to get in the car and clean up the deck on the way to the client site. We brought the binders and the hole punchers with us and we called the client's secretary to make sure we could use a color printer at their office!"

"You used the client's printer to print out a presentation that you were supposed to print for them?" I asked. "Doesn't that seem sort of unprofessional. Then they know you put it together last minute!"

Meg shrugged.

"I guess it was the lesser of two evils.... So the three of us are crammed in the backseat of the car, looking at my laptop and making corrections to the deck. The other associate is driving, while the partner and the case team leader are arguing over what changes to make. I'm right in the middle, trying to make the changes in a moving vehicle, which is really hard in PowerPoint on our little scratchpads with no mouse. Meanwhile, my laptop is running out of juice and the traffic is bumper to bumper."

"Did you make it?" my mom asked, eyes wide.

Meg leaned forward and stalled to be dramatic. "Barely," she said, setting her mug down loudly. "We arrived at 8:50. The partner and the case team leader started the meeting without me. I had the file on a memory stick, so I had to run it to the secretary, who had to print it out on the color printer. Then we found a typo on one of the slides, so I had to fix it and we had to reprint that page. Then I had to re-collate the pages because of this one that wasn't right. And then, I had to hole punch them. And then I had to put them into binders for twelve executives, and *then* I had to walk into the meeting and hand each executive their binder. This happened at 9:15am."

"Jeez, I'm tired just listening to you!" I declared. " How much do they pay you to do this job again?"

"Not enough," my dad answered for her. "What's the appeal of this job again?"

"I get to help executives make high level strategic decisions for their companies," Meg replied, as if reading off of a brochure. "If I worked at a normal company, executives wouldn't even know who I was for at least twenty years!"

*****

I heard Meg plodding down the hall in her slippers towards me. She poked her head into the room.

"Good night, Babyhead!"

"Hey Meg!" I said, my nose barely above my comforter. "Come in here a sec."

She came in and sat on the bed. "What's up?"

"Did you have a hard time your first year of college?"

"Why? Are you?"

"Well, no. I mean, it's not horrible or anything," I said, not wanting to be dramatic about it. "I guess I'm just not comfortable at school yet."

"Well, yeah. You're still adjusting. I think that's normal."

"Well, I don't feel like I'm really connecting with people and other people are. I feel like people are connecting over stuff like drinking and other 'bad' stuff," I continued, making little quotes in the air. "I tried drinking. It was fine, but I just wonder about whether I try other stuff or not, you know?"

She got my hint and looked thoughtful.

"This probably sounds so juvenile to you, huh?"

"It's not juvenile. Any time you go to a new place, you feel like a fish out of water. And you have to figure out what parts of your personality and your old life you take with you to your new life. I felt that way after I graduated college and went to work too."

Meg sat for a minute on the edge of my bed. I could almost see the wheels turning in her overactive brain.

"Yeah, the beginning of college was hard, I remember. At first, I was all excited to be in a new place and meet different kinds of people. But when that novelty wore off, I remember just feeling like the different-ness just made it hard for them to understand me. I did go through this whole identity crisis for awhile. In high school, I was smart, I was swimming, I was in student council... I had this special niche in high school society. But when I went to college, I couldn't find my niche for the longest time because I wasn't doing any of that stuff anymore and everyone was smart. So then, I was struggling with what made me special."

"I totally feel the same." I felt relieved. If she had the same problem, then I would do what I always did, and mooch her solution off of her. "So what did you do about it?"

"I didn't do anything," Meg said. "I guess my mentality just shifted. You inevitably make friends, even if they're different and nothing like your home friends. And you just learn to be comfortable without this niche thing. It's like a security blanket that you have to learn to live without. You learn to be alright not being defined by what you do or who you are with. You learn to be comfortable just being yourself."

"That's so cliche. What does it mean to 'be yourself' anyway?"

"I dunno. You have to decide what you care about and what you're interested in. You sort of have to let those things be your focus and not get caught up on what you *should* do or what other people *want* you to do."

"It's exhausting to care about that."

"Totally," Meg agreed. "You have to set your priorities straight or else you'll just be lost."

"Yeah, I was thinking about that the other day," I said, propping myself up on an elbow. "I played basketball with one of my neighbors the other day and it was the first time I did it since I left for college. Then I wondered why I hadn't done it sooner. It used to be such a huge priority in my life."

"But someone else enforced it for you," Meg pointed out. "If you didn't have a coach and teammates pressuring you to be there every day, do you think you would have made yourself do drills and suicides every day in high

242

school?"

I thought about this.

"Same with grades. Do you think you would have busted your ass in school the way that you did if you didn't have teachers and parents who cared? When you get to college, it all goes away. No one cares anymore about what you do or how you do. It's like your training wheels have just been taken away. You need to pedal faster or fall over."

Normally, by now, I would have been irritated by her condescending big sister attitude, but I really felt like I needed her guidance this time.

Meg continued. "About whether to try stuff or not...You also have to think about what lines you just won't cross and be totally comfortable with that. I mean, no one can tell you where the line should be. It's different for every person. But I guess you see where other people have drawn their lines, you see how it's working out for them and you decide where you are drawing yours."

"Hmmm..." I replied, mulling it over. "OK."

"It's better to draw them conservatively first. I've heard more people regret 'trying' some things before they're ready than trying them too late. No girl ever says, 'Shit, I should have given it up earlier.'"

We both laughed at this last observation.

"Are you sure?" I asked. "*Everyone's* doing it. There must be something to it!" I didn't ask her about her own experience with that last point, in a rare show of self-restraint on my runaway curiosity.

Meg shook her head, disturbed. "Hold on, let me bring you some books that will make you think twice," she said. She walked out of my room and returned after a few moments, carrying four books: *Memoirs of a Geisha, Gone with the Wind, The Secret Diary of Anne Boleyn,* and *A Thousand Splendid Suns.*

"You should read these before you get into... any of that," she said, distastefully.

"I've read *Gone with the Wind* and *Anne Boleyn,*" I told her, running my fingers over their worn covers.

"Well read them again, then read the other two," she advised. "I feel like we get such a warped view of sex these days. The media makes it seem so romantic and amazing and glamorous."

She exaggerated the words "romantic," "amazing" and "glamorous" for comedic effect.

"It's good to read about it from a more realistic point of view too."

"Thanks, Meg!"

Meg gave me a chin lift. "What are you doing tomorrow?"

"Having coffee with Eric."

"Is this the first time since you broke up?" Meg asked, looking at our Prom photo on my dresser. We looked so deliriously happy.

"Yeah."

"That will be interesting. How do you feel?"

"OK," I shrugged. "I mean, it will be good to see him. I miss him. It's going to be kind of weird. The last time I saw him, we made out for half an hour."

Meg laughed.

"It'll be fine. 'Night!"

"'Night!"

*****

I met Eric at our favorite coffee shop, a little mom and pop place called Allegro, with fading paint on the cottage-like exterior. He was already standing inside, studying the menu over the barista's head. His sandy brown hair still ended in fluff, his sunglasses were hooked in the pocket of his shorts, and his arms were crossed over his broad chest. He looked tanner than I remembered and something was different, though I couldn't put my finger on why.

When he saw me walk through the door, his face lit up into my favorite dimpled grin. I melted, as I had melted a hundred times before at this greeting.

He gave me a huge hug, which was at once very familiar, but also very alien because that was as far as he could go, now that we were just friends.

"Can I get you something?" he asked, looking back at the menu. "Chai latte?"

"Yeah, that'd be great!" I was pleased that he'd remembered my favorite drink.

"How are you?" he asked, studying my face, after he ordered and paid for our drinks.

"Great!" I said, too brightly. "My roommates are great. My roommate Casey is your standard Beverly Hills princess. Erin is an electrical engineer and she's always working. We're getting along alright, for the most part. School is fine. Everything is great! How about you?"

"Yeah!" he replied, receiving his mocha from the barista. "It's good! I'm at practice a lot. And when I'm not doing that, I'm hanging out with my neighbors and my teammates."

He handed me my chai latte and I followed him to a small round table for two.

"Tell me about your teammates," I suggested.

He launched into a description of his teammates. His voice was easy, though his posture was sort of anxious. He fiddled with his coffee cup using the hands that used to hold mine and sit comfortably on my knee.

As the conversation continued, I felt my spirits sink. I didn't want to talk about my classes or my roommates. Who cared about internships or summer jobs? I wanted to talk about us. I longed to hear that he missed me and that he was wrong to break up with me. We could relive our wonderful past and explore the possibility of a future, as we used to, in our honest and comfortable way. This petty parlor chat seemed to belittle our entire history.

Is the phrase "we're just friends now" a euphemism for "our deep and meaningful relationship has devolved into small talk"?

I thought about bringing up our relationship myself, but the words caught in my throat. Pride prevented me from telling him that I missed him. That would appear desperate. He had to do it. It had been *his* idea to break up.

When he asked if I was seeing anybody, I found myself telling him that I had started dating this guy that lived upstairs.

The expression on his face seemed cheerful. "That's awesome, Amy! He's a lucky guy!"

I didn't ask him the question back. It was taking all of my energy trying not to cry.

I kind of wished we hadn't met for coffee.

12 "Experiment with Sex"

Was it bad that I didn't want to go back to college after being at home for Thanksgiving?

Dad dropped me off in the turnaround on Sunday morning. I probably looked very unhappy because he nudged me on the shoulder. "Buck up there, soldier! You'll get used to it."

I managed half a smile. Then I took my backpack, laptop and bag of clean laundry out of the trunk. I waved as he disappeared from sight and made my way up to my dorm room.

Erin was already there. She had a textbook open on her desk and was working on a problem set.

"Hi Amy!" she said, looking up, then looking back down at her paper.

"Hi Erin! How was your Thanksgiving?" I asked, as I began to put my clothes away.

"Was fine," she murmured, her eyes glued to her textbook. There was silence. I stopped to look at her. After four days away, I thought she would have more to say to me. At least ask me how my Thanksgiving had been.

"Whatcha working on there?" I asked, trying again.

"Physics problem set." Again, she didn't look at me.

"Is everything alright?" I asked after a moment's silence. " Are you mad at me?"

She looked up at me with startled almond eyes, her pencil poised above her paper. "I'm not mad at you. Why?"

"Because you aren't talking to me! I haven't seen you since Wednesday! Aren't you going to tell me how your Thanksgiving was?"

"It was great!" Erin said rapidly. "We had a big turkey stuffed with sticky rice. That's a Chinese thing. And we saw a bunch of relatives and I saw some high school friends...."

She was still agitated about something. I took a stab at it. "Did you get to see Jim?"

"Yeah," she said, too quickly.

"Is everything alright between you?"

"Um, yeah," she said, not looking up. "We're back together, I think."

"You think?"

"Um, yeah, we are."

I sensed that I'd hit the target, but I could tell she didn't want to talk about it, so I continued to put my clothes away in silence, focusing my energy on my to-do list for the evening. There was work to be done on my final English paper for the quarter. The topic I'd come up with was exciting. And I felt clever for being able to read the same books for two different papers. I needed to finish reading *Memoirs of a Geisha* and review the other two books. It would probably behoove me to talk to Ethan about it first, so that I could be certain he wouldn't hate it.

A delicious thought struck me from out of the blue. What if I could write one paper for both classes? The paper that I was thinking of for my English prompt could be easily adjusted to address the Anthro prompt as well. The English prompt asked us to compare and contrast three different literary works from a feminist, political, allegorical or psychoanalytical perspective. The Anthro prompt was to compare and contrast the treatment of one of themes we discussed in lecture in three different cultures we didn't hadn't yet read about for class. I could write about the treatment of women/sex in the three different cultures represented by the three works of fiction that I was reading! That would certainly count as a feminist reading of them.

Erin let out a long sigh and I turned to look at her. She was staring through the wall, unblinking. Even her long, black ponytail seemed to droop.

"Erin! What's *wrong*? You're going to drive me crazy!"

She looked at me for what seemed like a long time. Then she got out of her chair and I thought she was going to walk out the door, but she shut it. Then she sat down on her bed, continuing to look at me as if trying to make up her mind about something. Finally she spoke. "You can't tell anybody!"

I nodded and straddled my chair backwards so that I could face her. "What's wrong?"

"I... I did it with Jim," she said, in a pained voice.

"Oh." I was at a loss for words. Never in a million years would I have bet Erin would have given it up before me.

"I shouldn't have done it," she continued, sorrowfully.

"Why did you do it then?"

"I... don't know!" Erin said, grabbing her teddy bear and resting her chin on its head. "I just missed him so much and ... I thought I was losing him. I thought he might be interested in... that girl... at MIT."

"Well, did you ask him?"

"Not explicitly. He kept saying that our relationship was stalled and we should try to see other people. College is a time to experiment. All that crap. I put two and two together and figured he was either interested in someone else or he wanted to fool around with someone because I wouldn't fool around with him, so…"

Her voice had begun to get hysterical, so she took a breath to calm herself.

"… so I thought maybe if I slept with him… oh my God, this is going to sound so dumb … maybe if I slept with him, I would have the power in the relationship again, like Sean said," she finished looking down between her teddy bear's ears.

"And?" I asked, leaning forward, overcome with sympathy and curiosity.

"I just felt awful," she said, her eyes filling with tears.

I had never seen Erin cry. She was always so rational. I handed her a tissue. She dabbed her eyes. I found myself chewing on the edge of my sleeve cuff. I wanted to say something comforting, but I didn't know what to say. She sat with her head buried in her teddy bear for several long moments.

"Erin, it's ok," I said, trying to be soothing.

"It *hurt*," she said, choking up. "And it's *so* awkward. I don't know how anyone could think that was fun! And the worst part was… it didn't change a thing! I don't think he really even cared that he was doing it with *me*! I think he just wanted to do it with somebody!"

"Don't say that! Of course he wanted to do it with you! You guys love each other, right?"

"What's love got to do with it?" she asked bitterly, chucking her tissue in the direction of the trash can and missing.

She didn't wait for an answer.

"That's just it! The one has nothing to do with the other! Afterwards, he was still aloof."

"Well, why are you still together then?"

"Oh, I don't know!" She rocked her bear back and forth. "Maybe we're not! I don't know. He thinks everything is fine. But I don't feel right. I feel… used. Cheap, or something."

"Oh, Erin!" I cried, feeling tears well up in my own eyes. "You're being too hard on yourself. It's all in your head! No one else would judge you that way."

"It doesn't matter. That's how I feel and I can't change it!"

"Why don't you look at it like… you both experimented and… that's all?"

"Because that's not what happened!" she insisted, tears welling up again. "I didn't want to do it in the first place. I just wanted him to love me, and I couldn't make him love me, so I gave it up for *nothing*. Who's the fool?"

"You're not a fool! How could you have known it was going to turn out this way? Come on, everywhere we look, we see sex, mixed up with love, passion… and all that froo froo crap," I added, quoting Meg.

I went over to the bed and sat next to her. She was not the hugging type, so I just laid my hand on her back and felt like an inadequate friend.

"You're ok, you're ok," I said over and over again, like my mother used to say to me when I fell off my bike and came screaming back to her with cuts and scratches. Slowly the tears subsided. She composed herself and looked at me with puffy eyes.

"Thanks, Amy," she said, wiping her eyes. "Thanks for listening. Don't tell Casey."

"I won't tell anybody. Are you ok?"

"I guess," Erin sighed. "I'm just hurt… and disappointed at… myself."

"Well, stop being so hard on yourself. The V-Club is losing five members every minute around here. I wouldn't worry about it too much," I said, trying to be humorous. She gave me half a smile.

"I can't take it back, anyhow." She put her teddy bear next to her pillow again and stood up.

I stood up next to her and handed her the washcloth dangling from her shower caddy. "Go wash your face, hon. Someday, you'll look back and it will only be a little oops, not a big one."

"Thanks, Mom," she said with a wavering laugh. She took the washcloth and headed to the bathroom.

I thought about the irony of this. The one time you *really* need your mother in college involves the one thing you can't talk to her about.

*****

Monday, I stayed after class to talk to my Anthro and English professors about my papers. They both approved.

Next stop, Ethan's office.

I burst in, all smiles. Ethan was sitting at his desk, Indian-style in his chair. When he turned to look at me, I sobered up quickly because of the stormy look on his face.

"Should I come back another time?" I asked, stopping dead in my tracks.

He shook his head. "No, this is as good a time as any. What's on your mind?"

"I just wanted to discuss my final paper with you before I started writing hardcore," I said, sort of wishing that I had opted to come back another time.

"Shoot," he said, his mind clearly elsewhere.

"I wanted to do a feminist reading of *Memoirs of a Geisha, Gone with the Wind*, and *The Secret Diary of Anne Boleyn* for my comparison. Maybe have a

249

discussion of how the authors' treatment of women and sex reflects differences in the cultures and societies?" I asked, suddenly uncertain.

Ethan tried very hard to look at me and pay attention to what I was saying, but I could tell he wasn't focused.

"Sounds interesting. You'll have to show me your outline once you start putting some main points together."

"Ethan, what's wrong?" I asked, cognizant of the fact that I was probably crossing the student-TA line, but I needed him to pay attention before I started pouring serious energy into this paper.

He shook his head. "I'm twenty-nine years old," he said. "And I feel like I'm never going to graduate."

"Why not? What more do you have to do to graduate?"

"I can't graduate until my committee says my dissertation is good enough."

"Well, how much more do you have to write?"

"I don't know. That's the problem. I write a chapter, they reject it. I rewrite it, they reject it. It's almost like they don't want me to graduate."

"Who rejects it?"

"Professor Barnard, mostly," Ethan muttered, glaring at the table. "He's my advisor."

"Why wouldn't he want you to graduate?" I asked, truly confused.

"For one, I'm cheap labor," Ethan pointed out. "And for two, he's kind of bitter. I think he wants me to suffer because he's suffering."

"Why is he suffering?"

"I shouldn't be telling you all this," Ethan said, sitting up properly in his chair.

"I won't tell anyone," Curiosity killed the cat, my mother always told me. But somehow, I couldn't cure myself of it.

"He's bitter because he hasn't published anything noteworthy in years,. He's getting a lot of pressure from the university. I guess he thinks that if I can publish something notable, he will get some credit for it, so he's keeping me around."

"Is he *trying* to publish?" I asked, my journalistic tendencies still getting the best of me.

"I don't even know. He spends a lot of time writing for private literary circles instead of general publication. I think he's pretty much living off his wife's fortune at this point."

"I'm sorry he's not letting you graduate."

"I'll figure it out," he said, shaking his head. "It'd be less of a problem if he wasn't such a grouch. I don't know why he's a professor if he hates college kids."

"Well, he was pretty cordial to me earlier today," I said, to be fair.

"Maybe he just hates guys. He is always nicer to women."

I laughed, uncomfortably. ."OK, I'll come back to you with an outline soon. Thanks for your time."

"No problem," Ethan said, and he went back to looking troubled before I'd even turned to leave the room. Poor guy.

13 "Be open to new ideas"

Two weeks before the end of the semester, several of us were smacked over the head with a second wave of midterms and final projects or papers. Everyone was busier and more stressed out. There were no more midnight walks or impromptu movie nights. Long, lingering hallway discussions became less frequent. Professors were beginning to mention the dreaded F word. Our carefree freshmen days were behind us.

"Oh my God, guess who I saw going to the library?" Autumn asked at dinner last night.

"Britney Spears," I suggested.

"Nooooo. Try again."

"Just tell us," I said, not in the mood to humor her.

"I saw *Sean* walk into the library this afternoon," Autumn announced proudly.

"Desperate times," Erin said, shaking her head.

I had my second calculus midterm at the end of the week. Even though the material was harder, I found it easier to study for it because I started earlier and there were fewer distractions. Everyone was studying more and partying less. I had an easier time saying no to people as well. It had finally begun to sink in that missing one party or movie or dinner would ultimately not change the course of my life.

The two days before my calculus midterm, I practically lived in the TA's and professor's offices. I made sure I could do every homework problem forward and backward. If I couldn't, I made them walk me through it until I was sure I understood what was going on. They were probably ready to kill me, but I decided I wasn't going to get a B minus in calculus. I learned so much in that eleventh hour. I couldn't believe I had missed so much the first time I tried to learn it.

I proceeded to the library to construct my cheat sheet. We were allowed one sheet of notebook paper, front and back, filled with whatever we could squeeze on there. I painstakingly copied equations and theorems from the textbook onto my cheat sheet. To maximize the amount of information I had on there, I wrote as small as possible, but the lines were beginning to run into each other and I couldn't distinguish exponents from the rest of the equations. Then I got smart and started using different colored pens to write adjacent lines.

After what seemed like hours, I couldn't sit still any longer. I felt like my nerves would just explode out of my body. So, I gathered up my textbook, notes and homework, laid them carefully into my backpack and headed for home. I walked quickly. It was getting chillier these days. After we set our clocks back, it was dark before dinner and always felt later than it actually was.

When I got home, I slung my backpack to the floor and breathed a sigh of relief. My math textbook was as heavy as a brick in there. I pulled my textbook out of my backpack and started off right where I'd left off.

I hadn't been at it long, when I realized that Erin was sniffling. It wasn't a sick sort of sniffling, but rather a soft, rhythmic sniffling… Oh dear, she was crying.

I turned to look at her. She was bent over her desk and she was heaving rhythmically. The two sides of my brain went to battle again.

She doesn't want to talk about, just get on with your work.

How can you be so insensitive? She needs you!

She would tell you if she needed you.

No she wouldn't. You wouldn't tell anyone either. You need to reach out to her.

You don't have time!

If you don't have time to be nice to your roommate, there's something wrong with you.

I shut my textbook with a bang and Erin jumped from the noise. She turned around, saw me looking at her and whipped around to look at her computer monitor again. But not before I caught a glimpse of red, puffy eyes.

"What's wrong?" I asked, trying to be sensitive.

"Nuffing," she said in a watery voice.

"Come on, Erin. I know it's not nothing."

"You probably think I'm the biggest cry baby *ever*"

"Whatever!" I cried indignant on her behalf. "Just because I saw you shed a few tears after Thanksgiving? Tell me what's wrong."

"Wow, you're like my personal shrink," Erin said, managing a little smile.

"That's what roommates are for. Isn't it in the contract?" I joked. "Just wait until I have a meltdown. It will make yours look like peanuts."

She smiled appreciatively. "I got my physics midterm back today,. And I bombed it."

"Bombed it like F or bombed it like B minus?"

"Bombed it like C minus."

I grimaced.

"Yeah, I know," Erin said.

"Well, was it a total shocker?"

"Well, no. I knew coming out of it that it didn't go great. But you know how you keep hoping?"

"Totally. I bombed my first calc midterm. And I felt terrible about that. I made myself feel better by thinking, 'What's the worst that can happen? So I get a bad grade. I'll make it up next semester.'"

"The worst that can happen is I turn out to be a failure."

"One midterm won't make you a failure."

"What if it's not just one midterm? What if I just can't cut it here?"

My brain shuddered with deja vu. It was strange to hear my own thoughts being uttered by someone else.

"I'm worried that I won't make the honor roll and my parents are going to be so disappointed" Erin continued, after watching me struggle to open my mouth.

"Come on, Erin. They love you for you."

"No, they only love me when I'm successful. You don't understand."

I found myself unable to rebut again. "I'm *sure* it's not true."

Erin just shrugged and turned back to her computer. I turned around to look at my cheat sheet. How could she think that? How could anybody's parent *let* her think that?

Dinner was somber. Everyone seemed to be in their own worlds, worrying about exams to come.

"Hey, did you guys see that they're offering ten minute massages in the lounge this weekend to help us relieve stress?" Casey informed us, breaking our anxious silence.

"That's cool!" I exclaimed, doing my part to ignite conversation. "I could use a ten minute massage!"

"What else can you do when you're stressed out?" Chris wondered aloud.

"Shoot hoops," I replied.

Chris put his hand up for a high five. I gave him one.

"Dance," Casey said, definitively. "Never fails."

"Dancing would stress me out *more*!" Brian commented. "Tall white guys have no business dancing."

We all laughed.

"I listen to classical music," Erin suggested. "And meditate."

"Along those lines, praying makes me calmer," Sarah added.

"Awww, that wouldn't work for me," Sean replied.

"Why not?" asked Sarah. "Have you ever tried?"

"Praying?" Sean asked. "No. I don't believe in organized religion."

"You can pray without being involved in organized religion," Sarah pointed out.

"Pray for what?" Sean asked, stabbing his fork into his pork chop. "Good grades? Even if there *were* a God, He couldn't help me with that now. I'm pretty sure I'm on my own."

"You could pray for guidance," Sarah suggested. Her freckles were beginning to stand out more against her alabaster skin. "You could pray for the strength to make hard decisions and take some responsibility for your life."

"I'm not buying it," Sean said, shaking his head.

"Hey man," Chris protested. "Everyone is entitled to their own beliefs, right?"

"You want to talk about responsibility?" Sean continued, energized by the controversy. "How is it responsible to be asking God for help all the time? If you were truly responsible, you'd do it on your own. It even says in the Bible that 'God helps those who help themselves.' Maybe God's got nothing to do with it. Maybe even the Bible is telling you that you've just got to help yourself!"

"I'm not going to waste my breath trying to explain it to *you*," Sarah said, icily. "I have a beautiful relationship with God that you will never even *try* to understand."

"Of course I understand it," Sean pointed out. "It's like my relationship with pot. You're depending on something else to give you hope, happiness, comfort, whatever. If you and I were really strong, Red, we wouldn't have to rely on something else or someone else. We could struggle through this miserable existence ourselves."

Sarah had already stood up, her hands balled up in fists. "You are horrible!" she announced, picking up her half-eaten tray. "I can't believe you would compare God with pot! You are a jerk and a nihilist. I hope, for your sake, that you're just being a contrarian, and that you don't actually believe what you're saying. It would be *really* sad if you did."

"Sarah, wait," I implored. "It's just Sean. Finish your dinner."

"No!" Sarah said, shaking her head. "I'm not even hungry anymore. And I can't believe the rest of you all can sit around listening to the crap that comes out of his mouth!"

With that, she stormed off, her curly red ponytail whipping indignantly from side to side.

"You didn't have to go piss her off like that!" I scolded Sean, when Sarah was out of earshot.

"Listen, she's entitled to her beliefs, so how come I'm not entitled to mine?" he asked, calmly cutting his pork chop into little squares.

"You are, but you didn't have to go out of your way to provoke her!" I was annoyed.

"I didn't go out of my way," Sean pointed out. "I happen to think that people arrive at truth through debate and discussion. You put out one view and I put out an opposing view. We bang on each other's views for awhile to see which one holds water, and we both get one step closer to truth. I thought we were mature intellectuals. Did I get off at the wrong exit and miss college?"

This made sense.

"But some things are sacred," Chris objected. "Some things are just out of bounds and off-limits."

"Like your mom," Brian suggested, trying to be funny. "You wouldn't want us to discuss the pros and cons of your mom, would you? She's sacred and out-of-bounds."

"That's a bad analogy," Sean said. "My mom is a person. There's not much to debate about her. I'm talking about ideas. You can debate ideas."

"Well, God is like Sarah's mom," Erin added. "He's just not up for debate with her. It's faith."

Sean shrugged. "I don't think so, but she left, so we're clearly not debating Him anymore."

That night, I stayed up late making my cheat sheet and I thought about what Sean had said. As much as I wanted to wring his neck for causing everyone to get angry or uncomfortable, I decided that he was right. It *was* important for him to challenge our assumptions or else we would never be forced to really think about why we believed them. If Newton hadn't challenged conventional wisdom, we never would have had calculus.

*****

The midterm on Friday was excruciating. I was better prepared for this one than the first one, but in some ways, this made it harder because I had higher expectations for myself. I arrived at the classroom fifteen minutes before class. Already, several students had claimed their seats and were looking over last minute notes. I sat down in the front row.

The exam started promptly at 8am and every seat in the classroom was occupied, which was funny because after the first day of class, the classroom was only about half full. The professor and the TA's passed out the exam, while I checked to make sure that I had a back up pencil and my big chunk of an eraser in my pencil case.

My knee jiggled up and down nervously, as it did during basketball games when I was on the bench. Everything seemed amplified. The faintest noise reverberated in the quiet lecture hall. I was hyper-aware of every minute that ticked by. My desk suddenly seemed too small and there was nowhere to put my calculator.

I jumped on the exam as soon as I got it, which was a better use of my nervous energy than twitching and worrying. I wrote my student ID number carefully across the top and double checked it. Then I glanced over the entire exam before starting. Five of the six problems looked like homework problems that I could do. The last one would take some time. I dove straight into the first problem.

*****

"Wow, I can't believe these meal vouchers are only worth three dollars!" I exclaimed, as I dug through my purse to find cash to make up the balance on my turkey, bacon, avocado and tomato sandwich. I ruefully handed the lady a large percentage of my cash.

"Yeah, there's no way that's right," Sarah agreed from behind me in line. "I eat way more than three dollars worth of food in the cafeteria for lunch."

We were talking about the meal vouchers that we got at the dorms, which allowed us to skip a meal in the dining hall and instead use that money to purchase a meal on campus.

"Where do you want to sit?" I asked, squinting as I looked around the sunny, crowded terrace.

Sarah put one freckled hand up to shield her eyes as she scouted out our prospects.

"There!" she announced, pointing to a table, whose occupants had just stood up. "And it's even in the shade."

"Good eyes!" I replied.

We sat down at the table and began unwrapping our sandwiches. Sarah ripped open her bag of pretzels and popped one in her mouth right away.

"Oh, I need to get a cup of water," Sarah said, standing up. "Can I get you one?"

I shook my head, eager to get started on my sandwich. The first bite was heavenly. I chewed blissfully and stared off into space, barely noticing the students buzzing around me like bees in a clover field.

"Hey, shoo!"

Sarah's voice brought me back to earth with a start. A very large squirrel was perched on the edge of our table   and   had   already   stuck   its   paw halfway into Sarah's pretzel bag. It saw Sarah approaching the table, flicked its tail impudently, and jumped off the table onto the tree.

"Unbelievable!" she said, shaking her head as she sat back down across from me. "These squirrels are brazen. They aren't even like normal squirrels. They're like ground hogs! They wouldn't survive a day in the wild."

I grinned.

"Sorry," I apologized. "I was a bad custodian for your pretzels."

Sarah smiled.

"It's fine. I'm surprised he got so close even with you sitting here."

"I was totally spaced out," I confessed. "A 787 could have landed right here and I probably wouldn't have noticed."

"Wow, everything ok?" she asked, unwrapping her egg salad sandwich and biting into it carefully.

"I had a calculus midterm this morning. So my brain is kind of fried."

"How did it go?"

"Better than the last one, that's for sure!" I replied, cheerfully. "But that's not saying much."

"You'll be fine," Sarah said, reassuringly. "You've been studying a lot for it."

I shrugged modestly.

"I hope so. How are you doing?"

"Good," she replied, leaning back in her chair and stretching out her long runner's legs. "I have a chem midterm next week and then I'm done until finals."

"You seem really calm about it," I observed, enviously.

"I'm working as hard as I can," she replied. "And whatever is meant to happen will happen."

"But then, why study at all?" I asked, confused. "If you don't study, whatever is meant to happen will happen, right?"

"Well, no," Sarah replied, pulling an olive out of her sandwich and setting it on her tray. "I believe that if I work hard, one set of outcomes is meant to happen. If I don't work hard, another set of outcomes is meant to happen. So it's still in my interest to work hard. 'God helps those who help themselves.' Even Sean knows that."

I looked up to see her smiling, good-naturedly.

"So you're not mad at him?" I asked, relieved.

"No," she said slowly. "I talked about it with my youth group that night and decided that I overreacted. First of all, if I have faith, then I shouldn't care what anybody else says. Second of all, if I don't have faith, then I *do* need to question and doubt and struggle in order to convince myself to believe again. I think that I was lashing out at Sean because I was having doubts and I was angry at myself for having them. So when he verbalized them, I took out my frustration on him instead of trying to work it out for myself."

I listened carefully. No one close to me was religious and I found this to be very interesting.

"So the Church encourages you to question and debate?" I asked.

"Absolutely," Sarah replied. "Christians believe that you need to convince yourself fully that God exists and you need to work on your relationship with God."

"Sean was saying something like that after you left," I explained to her. "He was talking about how you can only arrive at truth through questioning and debate."

"Ha!" Sarah scoffed. "Who would have thought I would agree with Sean?"

I smiled.

"I think that the other reason that I was miffed at him was because I felt like he was judging me," Sarah continued. "I mean, I know I shouldn't care, but for some reason, it just gets under my skin to think that he thinks that I am weak or stupid or whatever."

It was my turn to lean back in my chair, pensive.

"What does it mean to 'judge' someone?" I wondered aloud. "I hear that word being thrown around all the time. But what does it actually mean? If Sean was judging you, does it mean he had a different opinion than you? Or did he *think* badly of you because you have a different opinion than him? Or did he *treat* you badly because you have a different opinion than him?"

"I think it's the last two," Sarah replied thoughtfully. "People can have different opinions. I think that judgment comes in when you are condescending towards someone with a different opinion. Or you don't even attempt to look at things from the other person's perspective."

"It's tricky though," I said, looking down at my half-eaten sandwich. "Because if you are convinced that you're right about something, religion for example, how can you be open to the other perspective? I mean, how can you help thinking the other person is missing something?"

"Well, for example, I am not judging you even though you're not religious," Sarah replied, serenely. "I respect you as a person and I understand how you might come to your conclusion."

"But you still think I'm wrong."

"Well, yeah. But I'm not *judging*."

This was not a very satisfactory answer.

*****

Jeff IMed after dinner.

Jeffers56: brandon left for a mtg- wanna come visit?

He didn't need to ask twice. After brushing my hair and throwing on some make-up, I was on my way up the stairs.

"Hey, Cutie!" He greeted me with a huge grin when he threw open the door.

It didn't take long before we were making out on his bed. His strong hands held my face close to his and his breath was loud in my ears. When we came up for a breather, I asked the question that had been nagging at me since the frat party.

"Are we still seeing other people?"

"Sure." He reached across to tuck a strand of hair behind my ear. We were lying on our sides, facing each other in the narrow, twin dorm bed, his black sheets balled up in a heap at our feet..

I studied his face. He looked back at me.

"Why? I thought we were just dating. I think of dating as getting to know someone. And I feel like you can get to know more than one person at once."

"But at what point do you decide to be exclusive with someone?"

"Why do you have to be exclusive with someone?" Jeff shot the question back at me.

It was my turn to hesitate. "Well, someday, don't you want to get married?" I asked, also being careful with my words.

"Someday, I probably will, but not for, like, ten years. Until then, I don't see the point."

"But, isn't it more special when you're with one person?" I asked, trying another angle.

"Does your relationship with one friend make your relationship with another friend any less special?"

"I only have one best friend."

"But you have a lot of friends, who you have a good time with. I don't

260

see how this is any different. We're enjoying each other's company."

"It's different," I replied, cursing my inarticulateness.

"No, it's not fundamentally different. It's just a different way of thinking about things than you're used to. Anyway, this is what college is about. We're experimenting. We're meeting new people. We're trying to figure out who we want to be with. Right?"

"I guess," I muttered, turning away from him to look at the ceiling.

"Where are you going?" His hand found his way to my hip and he pushed down with his thumb under my hip bone.

I squealed and began writhing and laughing. "No fair!"

And then his mouth was on mine and we were making out again.

*****

You know how on those TV game shows they speed up the music when the time is about to run out and you feel your pulse quicken in time to the music? That's how I felt at the end of the quarter. There were just not enough hours in the day. On my desk, I had taped a list of things that I needed to do before time ran out this quarter:

- finish Eng/Anthro paper
- choose next qrter's classes
- create Calc cheat sheet for final
- redo all Calculus hw probs
- make summary of Econ notes
- redo all Econ hw probs
- stop by Daily Bruin office- articles unpublishable- why???
- LAUNDRY!!!!
- email Bookstore to confirm start date
- call Lauren, call Mom, call Meg, call Eric

At the moment, I was working on my paper. Erin was sitting at her desk, working on a physics problem set. Casey was at a party.

My paper was coming along. I was glad I'd spent some time with Ethan discussing the major themes I wanted to address before I started writing. He had been helpful, asking if I had evidence for assertions that I was making and pointing out counter-arguments that I should address.

One of the main themes of my paper was that sex was women's source of power and money in all three of these societies: Elizabethan England, the post-Civil War South and Japan after World War II. The women who were successful in each society used sex strategically to their advantage. While sex was necessary to get ahead, it was not sufficient. I pointed out that they had to

261

be clever in other ways to secure ultimate success. However, in all cases, they knowingly jeopardized their chances at love as soon as they chose to put the "sex" card into play. No one could honorably marry a woman who had sex with someone else. Of course, no one cared if the man had.

I read and re-read the last paragraph I'd just written and tried to think of any unsupported claims that I was making. My back and neck were sore from bend sitting tensely on the edge of my wooden chair. My eyes felt dry and prickly from staring at the computer screen for so many endless hours. I moved my head from side to side and my neck cracked, which felt good. I decided to take a quick break and check my IM messages, which I had chosen to hide.

Jeffers56: heading out to the frat- want to come along?

I looked at my clock. He'd sent the message half an hour ago. I typed a quick response in case he was still around. My computer was being slow and the words appeared a second after I had finished typing them.

Amyable7: can't tonight- working on paper…. come say hi?

I hid my messages again and began writing the beginning of my final section, which talked about how each of the societies punished all of the heroines for two sins- for using sex as leverage and for being clever. I also wanted to argue that they had no other alternatives. I wonder what choice I would have made in their situations: sex, ostracism and possibly a better life for my children or chastity, honor and poverty?

Halfway through my paragraph, there was a knock at the door that made me jump. It was Jeff, who leaned against the doorway.

"Hey Cutie," he said, coming in.

"Hey yourself," I replied. "I wish I looked as relaxed as you."

"When you get to be as old as me, you won't care about school anymore," he said.

"Shut up!" I laughed, swatting at him. He put his hands on my shoulders and began kneading with his thumbs.

"Wow, you *are* tense!" he commented.

The massage was painful, but it felt good. "I've been hunched over this laptop forever," I told him.

"Come out with me," he suggested. "It's not due tomorrow, is it?"

"I can't. It's not due tomorrow, but I want to finish it tonight because I have a whole list of other things I need to do before finals."

"You're so *responsible*," Jeff said, as if it were a bad word. He kissed me on top of the head.

"OK," I yawned, unable to suppress it.

"Oh I see how it is!"

I shook my head and pushed him out the door.

"Bye bye, see you later!" I called down the hall after him.

I sat back down and tried to get back into my writing frame of mind. Just as I picked up my hands to begin typing again, there was another knock on the door.

"I thought you were going..." I stopped when I looked up to see that it was Brandon, not Jeff at the door. His long, dark hair fell over his pale face and he managed half a smile.

"Hi Amy," Brandon said, quietly. I didn't want Erin to be scared of him, so I tried to act as normal as possible.

"Hey Brandon. I haven't seen you since..."

"That day that Jeff had food poisoning," Brandon said, finishing my sentence.

"That's right! Boy, that was a rough day for them."

"They probably deserved it," Brandon said, lugubriously.

"Well, I don't know about that!" I said, slowly, a little puzzled. I wondered if Jeff wasn't being nice to him, as a roommate.

"Are you writing?" Brandon asked, with interest.

"For class," I told him. "A feminist reading of some historical fiction."

Brandon nodded. Then there was an awkward pause.

"Well, I'd better go," he said, looking down the hallway. "Just wanted to come by and say hi."

"Have a good night!" I said. He turned and walked away.

"Amy!" Erin whispered. I turned around to look at her.

"Who was that?" she mouthed.

"Jeff's roommate," I whispered back.

"What are you guys whispering about?" Casey asked, as she burst into the room.

"Jeff's roommate came by," I told her.

"The Goth guy?" Casey asked.

"Casey, what is that smell?" I asked, sniffing in her direction.

Casey took off her jacket and hung it nicely on the back of her chair, where it continued to permeate the air with the smell of beer and smoke. I rolled my eyes at Erin when Casey wasn't looking.

"What did he want?" Casey asked. "Is he acting weird? Maybe he's a sociopath and we should report him."

"No. He's harmless. Just awkward. Maybe we shouldn't jump to conclusions."

"Whatever," she replied. "I'm going to jump in the shower."

I turned back to my paper and tried to remember my train of thought. When I couldn't recover it, I looked on my to-do list and remembered that I had to select my classes for next quarter. I double clicked on my browser. My computer made mechanical churning noises, indicated that it was "thinking." It was taking a lot longer to "think" these days, I'd noticed. I drummed my fingers.

I navigated to the course catalog online, which took several seconds to appear completely. It was difficult to choose classes for next quarter. I still wasn't ready to commit to a major, but if I wanted to keep pre-med or engineering as a potential major, there was no sense putting off physics and chemistry any longer. I selected one section of each using the software application. Then, I selected "Computer Science I." After watching Erin work on some programming projects, I decided that computer science seemed interesting because it was so different than anything I'd ever seen before. It would be a good way for me to learn more about technology. I resisted the urge to take another English class because I had just taken one. Political science or psychology? I selected "Psychology 101" from the list and then hit the button "Show Schedule."

My computer began making mechanical churning noises again. The bar at the bottom of the browser that shows the progress of the page loading was stuck. I hit "Refresh" impatiently and the browser obediently resubmitted the data. The progress bar got stuck again and I clicked "Refresh" several times in a row, out of frustration.

Then my computer froze.

I sucked in my breath. I tried to move my mouse, but the mouse on the screen wouldn't move. I pounded the "Enter" key a few times and then the "Esc" key a few more times. The fan at the back of my computer began to blow. The mechanical clicking and the fan together made it sound like my computer was wheezing and coughing.

By this point, Erin had turned around.

"Control, alt, delete," she instructed me.

"Oh my God, I don't remember the last time I saved my paper!" I told her, in a panic.

"Hopefully, it will auto-recover most of it," Erin said, but she sounded unsure of herself.

"Control, alt, delete- are you sure?" I asked. I positioned my fingers over the keys, but I couldn't bring myself to press them.

"You have to do it, Amy. It's probably not going to unfreeze itself at this point."

"OK, you're the electrical engineer."

I took a big breath and pushed down on the Holy Trinity. Nothing happened. The screen stayed the same.

"What do we do now?" I asked, truly shaken by the alien behavior of my formerly trusty sidekick.

"Hold down the power button," Erin suggested.

"Really?" I asked anxiously.

"Do it."

I held down the power button. Nothing happened.

"This is bad," Erin said.

At this point, I was in a full blown panic. The last time I could recall explicitly saving my paper was hours ago, before we went to dinner. The thought of having to recreate all that work made me dizzy. Then a worse thought entered my brain.

"What if I can't get *any* of it back?" I asked, voicing my ultimate fear. "What if it totally crashed?"

"Did you back up your paper anywhere?" Erin asked. She could read the answer from the look of horror on my face.

"It's ok, Amy," she said. "Move over."

Erin sat down at my computer. She held the power button down again for a few seconds and nothing happened.

"We have to cycle power," she told me.

"What does *that* mean?"

"We have to cut off the power supply"

"You're going to pull the plug?" I was horrified.

"Yes, I'm taking it off life support," Erin said, glancing at me sideways. "And I might have to pull the battery too because that's the auxiliary power."

"I can't watch!" I wailed. But I couldn't take my eyes off my sick, wheezing computer.

First, Erin pulled the plug out. The screen dimmed immediately, but continued to stay on. Erin lifted it up and turned it upside down. She found a panel at the bottom with a latch on it. She unlatched it and pulled out the panel. The computer died immediately. The screen went black and all sounds ceased.

"You killed it!" I whispered, looking at its lifeless shell.

Erin held up a finger, signaling me to wait. She put the panel back in. Then she reinserted the plug in the back. She set the computer back on my desk gently and pushed down on the power button. It beeped obediently, as it did every time I started it up.

I held my breath and watched as it completed its normal boot-up sequence. Everything proceeded smoothly and I could scarcely believe it. I clicked on my user name and it continued to load all of my personal settings. I glanced over at Erin, who looked very proud of herself. When my desktop was fully loaded, I gave her an enormous hug.

"Oh my God!" I cried. "I don't know what I would have done without you!"

"Open your paper before you thank me," she warned.

I did as I was told and found that the auto-recover function had indeed saved all of my work, except for the half paragraph I'd started to write. I breathed a sigh of relief. For the second time that night, I felt the tension loosen in my muscles.

"Now back that thing up in eighteen places," Erin instructed me. "Email it to yourself, put it on a memory stick, upload it to the school server..."

"Yes, ma'am!" I replied and did everything that she said. I felt my heart still pounding in my chest and my head was still spinning.

"It's like a pet," Erin observed. "When your computer dies, it's like a pet dying."

"Totally. Or worse. It's like part of you dying because it's all of your creations and possessions on there."

After backing my paper up as many ways as I could think of, I no longer had the mental fortitude to write anymore. I stood up as Casey came back in the room.

"I'm going next door," I announced. "I need some comic relief. Do you guys want to come?"

"I'll come with you," Erin said, stretching out her arms and yawning. "I can't do another problem tonight. I think I'm saturated."

"Let me get in my pajamas," Casey replied. "I'll be right over."

*****

Erin and I walked next door. We peered into the boys' room. It was dim because the room light was off. There were clothes slung over the bed posts, on the chair backs, even on the corner of a half-open wardrobe door. The room smelled faintly of beer, sweat and mud. All three boys were sitting motionless at the computers, with only their desk lights on.

"Wow, what's going on in *here*?" I asked, breaking the silence.

"We're working- can't you tell?" Chris asked, breaking into a grin.

"Never saw it before, so couldn't tell what you were doing. I was afraid you might be dead!"

"I'm surprised *you* aren't working! What's your name again?" Sean said to Erin.

"Oh, shut up!" Erin pretended to be annoyed.

"We're taking a study break," I told them. "Want to come out here and join us?"

"Kookie King ?" asked Brian, hopefully..

I shook my head. "Can't afford that long of a study break."

Brian pouted, but he stood up to come out.

"Any excuse to not study!" Sean said, standing up.

"I'll be right out. I need to finish this paper." Chris turned back to his computer.

I sat down in the hallway, with my back up against the wall. Everyone sat around me.

"So how's it going?" Brian asked. "We heard some commotion coming from your side of the wall."

"Yeah, we had a scare," I told him. "My computer froze and I was afraid I was going to lose the paper that I was working on."

"F-ing technology," Sean muttered, shaking his head.

"Erin saved the day though!" I grinned at Erin. "She 'cycled power' and it came back to life!"

Erin beamed.

"Ah, but after that, you will never be able to trust that crap again," Sean said.

We all stared at him.

"The computer, not Erin!" Sean clarified. We laughed.

"Why is school so hard?" I asked, heaving a giant sigh for all of fall quarter. "Wasn't it supposed to get easier after high school?"

"It's only hard if you care about grades," Sean pointed out. "Why the hell do you care so much? It's not like grades count for anything anymore."

"That's not true!" Erin cried. "If you want to go to grad school, grades totally matter."

"More school?" Sean looked appalled at the idea. "No thanks. I'm getting a J-O-B after this. No more studying. I'm going to go out there and *do* something."

"People do all sorts of important things after grad school!" Erin said indignantly. "Doctors, nurses, lawyers, professors and scientists all need to go to grad school!"

"I suppose," Sean conceded. "I'm not opposed to other people doing more school. *I* just don't want to do it. Look at how stressed you guys are over grades! More school is not worth four more years of freaking out. We just got done with that!"

"I think we're partly conditioned to care about grades. It's, like, ingrained in me," I observed.

"Pavlov-ian response," Brian suggested.

"What's that?" Erin asked.

"This guy Pavlov did this experiment with dogs. He rang and bell, then fed the dog. After he did it over and over again, just the ringing of the bell would make the dog salivate. They began associating the sound of the bell with food."

"Just like we hear the word 'finals', and we freak out." I added, connecting the dots.

"Well you shouldn't," Sean said. "Plus plenty of people do fine with just a college degree. Look, Bill Gates didn't even graduate from college! I'm going to go out there and make buckets of money."

He rubbed his hands together with a maniacal grin. Casey emerged from the room in her red silk pajamas. She looked like a Victoria's Secret ad.

"Money is overrated," Casey told Sean.

"Says the devil who wears Prada!" Sean scoffed.

"Don't get me wrong, it's nice!" Casey clarified. "But I think it's more important to do something that you love than to chase money in a job."

"What does that even mean?" asked Sean.

"Well, I want to be a public relations spokesperson," Casey said. "Because I want to be the public face of a large corporation. But I probably won't get paid that much."

"Would you forego all of your nice clothes, shoes and handbags for it?" asked Sean.

Casey hesitated. "Yes."

"No you wouldn't!" Brian said, calling her on her bluff.

"I can get money from my husband or my dad!" Casey pointed out.

I slapped my forehead.

"Why is making money such a bad goal?" Erin spoke up. We all looked at her, surprised.

"I don't think it's a bad goal if you want to be a doctor to help people, and making good money happens to be a side effect of being a doctor," I mused aloud. "But I think it's not so admirable if you just want money for money's sake."

"Why?" Erin persisted. I stared at her.

"It's like you're selling out!" Brian replied. "Like those Wall Street guys. They can't love what they do! They just want a lot of money."

"How do you know?" asked Erin. "Maybe they love making money!"

"Right, but that's not really admirable is it?" Brian asked, gently. "I mean, they're not helping anybody but themselves."

"I'm with Nerd Girl!" Sean said, enthusiastically, looking at Erin. "I can't believe you're arguing this side, but I like it! It gets lonely being right by myself all the time."

We all snickered.

"Why is making money for money's sake dishonorable?" Sean repeated, taking up Erin's flag.

"It's shallow to just want money!" I protested. "Don't you want to make a bigger impact on society... than just being a consumer?"

"First of all, I don't think that being a consumer is dishonorable," Sean said. "Every thing that you buy is creating a job for someone else in the world."

"More importantly," Erin added. "I think that it matters what you want the money *for*."

"What do you mean?" Brian asked her.

"I think it is dishonorable if you want money just to buy nice cars and spoil yourself."

I saw Casey sit up straighter.

"But I don't think it's dishonorable to want money to so that you can send your kids to any college they want or to make sure your parents have health insurance when they get old," Erin continued.

"That's true." I nodded.

"In fact, I think it's irresponsible to do something you 'love', like go work for the Peace Corps, if you can't really afford it." She made quotation marks in the air around the word "love."

"It means that your parents have to worry and work over-time to support you," she continued. "Or you're going to have to take out a high interest loan, and your future family will have to tighten its belt to pay it back."

"I hadn't really thought about it that way," Brian said, nodding.

"But if you do the Peace Corps, you're helping people that are probably less fortunate than your parents or your kids," I pointed out. "Isn't there honor in that?"

"Maybe," Erin replied. "So do you help strangers first or do you help your own family first? I choose to help my own family first, and if I have money left over, I will help others. By the way, Bill Gates is single handedly immunizing all of Africa with the money he made helping himself first."

"That's true," I conceded. I still thought the Peace Corps was cool.

"Look, at the end of the day, a job is a job," Sean said, not willing to share his Devil's Advocate spotlight with Erin for too long. "I think this idea that an altruistic job is somehow better than a money making job is absurd. You get paid for both kinds of work, just in different currency."

"No," Casey protested. "People who do altruistic work do it out of the goodness of their hearts."

"What does *that* even mean?" Sean asked, exasperated. "People do it to feel good about themselves, to get attention, to get to Heaven. Is that honorable? It's just a different form of payment!"

"You're arguing that altruistic people are also selfish." Casey looked at Sean.

"Yes, that's what I'm saying. Why should someone be put on a pedestal for preferring praise to a paycheck? Where's Red? She'd love this discussion."

"Leave her out of it," I groaned. "You pick on her enough."

Sean held both hands up.

"I didn't know that having an intellectual discussion qualified as 'picking on' somebody." Sean stood up. "Now if you will excuse me, I need to make up for a midterm that I slept through."

"You *slept* through a midterm?" Casey asked, aghast.

"It happens." Sean shrugged it off. "I didn't hear my alarm."

I stood up and followed Casey and Erin back towards our room.

"Amy," Brian said from behind me.

I stopped and turned around.

"How's it going?" he asked. We hadn't talked one-on-one since I found out about his girlfriend.

"Good. You know, busy with school and stuff."

"I heard that you were dating that guy Jeff," he said, looking down at the stubby blue-gray carpet.

"Yeah."

"Well, I just wanted you to know that I saw him kiss another girl on campus the other day." He continued to stare down at the carpet.

"We're just dating." I tried to sound calm, even though I felt my stomach cramp up. "He's not my boyfriend."

"I see," Brian said, still looking concerned. "Is that what you want?"

"I'm fine, as long as we're open about it. Anyway, I don't see how it's any of your business."

"As a friend, I just thought you should know," he said, looking at me.

"Thanks. Goodnight," I said and turned on my heel.

"'Night."

*****

I found that pressure was not limited to the classroom at the end of this first quarter of college.

The next afternoon, Jeff had again invited me up to his room. We chatted briefly about our day before diving into the standard course of making out. He was laying flat on his back and I was lying on top of him when his hands slid from on my back, to around my waist, to the front of my jeans. He wedged his hands between us and began fumbling with the button. I continued to kiss him, but my body stiffened. My breath caught in my throat, and my mind began to race. I was panicked, but I wasn't sure what to do.

He began to pull the waistband of my pants down with one hand, and he slid the other hand down the back of my jeans, along my bare cheek.

One part of me was wildly curious about the passionate love-making that could follow, but the practical part of me won out. I pulled his hand out of the back of my jeans.

He stopped kissing me and looked at me with heart-melting eyes. "What's wrong?"

"I'm just not that comfortable doing... that... right now." I looked away from him.

"Doing what? I was just exploring."

"Yeah... I don't know if I want you in my pants just yet." I was officially ruining the moment.

"Why not?" Jeff persisted, looking confused.

"I want to... err, explore... with someone special... who thinks I'm special too," I stammered, beginning to feel like a Puritan, an alien, or both.

"I *do* think you're special," Jeff replied, reinserting his intrepid hand down my pants.

This time, I yanked it out with unmistakable force.

"I'm not comfortable doing this with you if you are also doing this with other people," I forced myself to say.

I looked him square in the eye and he looked back at me without jest or resentment, but some sort of curiosity.

"I can respect that," he said, evenly, zipping up my jeans, as if to prove it to me.

We continued to kiss for a few more minutes before I made an excuse about having to work on my paper.

When I reached my room, there was a message from him on my computer.

Jeffers56: hey, cutie. i'm really sorry about that. i don't want u 2 b uncomfortable. we can go at ur pace. r u mad @ me?

I sat down and tried to focus my mind. I typed back.

Amyable7: no, im not mad. its fine. thx for understanding.

Then I tried to get in the mindset to work on the part of my paper discussing the imbalanced consequences of having sex for men and women in three different periods of history. All periods of history, was more like it.

*****

As luck would have it, both of my non-paper finals were on the very last day of Finals Week. So I had to hang around campus until the bitter end of the quarter. Casey was done by Tuesday and had taken off without so much as a goodbye. Erin was done on Thursday morning. I found the following note on my desk late Thursday night, after an 8am to 10pm mega session at the library.

Amy,

Good luck on your finals. You'll do great. Have a nice vacation and call me if you're bored. I'll miss you!

Erin

I was grateful to have the option of getting good sleep the night before my finals, though my body didn't cooperate. Even though I set my cell phone alarm and my regular alarm clock, I woke up every hour, sure that I had missed my wake-up call. As a result, I was running on pure adrenaline.

I don't know if it was the adrenaline or just the way the room was set up, but I found myself even more aware of everything during finals than during midterms. I was aware of where the proctors were standing in the room; how many kids were actually enrolled in the class; exactly how many minutes were left; how sloppy my handwriting became when I was nervous; if I was too hot or cold; if I had to go pee; and if I had to go pee in twenty minutes.

Paradoxically, I was also able to focus like my life depended on it. Every damn second that I was banging my head over how to solve a difficult problem felt like an eternity. Time ran out faster when I couldn't solve a problem.

When it was all over, I rushed back to my dorm. I had not been so excited to go to sleep since I-don't-even-remember. With the burden of finals lifted from my mind, my body physically craved my bed. I walked down the deserted hallway towards my room. It was strange to see everyone's door shut. The hallway seemed much smaller this way. I didn't dwell on it too much. I was looking forward to taking a hot shower and curling up with some of my girlie magazines. At some point, I would drift off to heavenly slumber.

That's about how it worked out, except that I was rudely awaked by someone knocking at the door in the middle of the night. *Who on earth could that be?* I wondered. With a lot of effort, I turned my head to look at my alarm clock. 1am. I turned back around, preparing to go right back to sleep. The knocking persisted.

"Guys, lemme in. I forgot... my keys."

Oh my God. It was Brian. And he was drunk.

"Come on guys," he called out, banging on the door. "Lemme in!"

He must have been really drunk. Chris and Sean had both been gone since Wednesday. I climbed down my ladder and opened the door. The light from the hallway was blinding.

"Amy, what are you doing in our room?" He looked totally disoriented.

"Sh!!!" I whispered, in case anyone was still around. "This isn't your room. This is *our* room. Your room is over there!"

I pointed next door.

"Don't be ridiculous!" he said thickly. " Don't you think I know my own room?"

"Here, read the door!" I said, pointing to our names on the door. "Casey. Amy. Erin."

He looked stumped for a minute and then a smile spread across his face. "You switched them," he said proudly, as if he'd solved a very deep mystery.

"Brian, that's your room over there. Want me to call security so they can let you in?"

"I am in!" he said, as he pushed past me into our room. "We don't need to call security! They'll find Sean's pot stash and we'll all be busted."

"Hey! Hey!" I whispered, tugging on his sleeve as he began to ascend the ladder to my bed. "What are you doing? That's my bed!"

"It's my bed too! We can share."

"No we can't share!" I whispered fiercely. "What would your girlfriend say?"

This seemed to trouble him. He paused for a minute, halfway up the ladder and shook his head slowly. "She wouldn't like that. No, she wouldn't," he said sadly. "But I like you a lot, Amy. You're so cool. And she may be gone soon…. I'm a terrible person"

Interesting.

He faltered for a second and rested his forehead the top of my mattress. He reached the top of the ladder, swayed a second, then fell face first into my bed.

Please don't let him puke, I prayed. I didn't know what to do. He was too heavy to move on my own. I guess I could let him sleep there. I could sleep in Erin's or Casey's bed.

I shivered. It was a cold night. I climbed onto my chair to get eye level with Brian. He was curled up with his arms crossed and his eyes closed. I tried in vain to get my comforter out from under him, but he was too heavy. I used two hands, braced my feet into my chair and yanked hard on it. The comforter came loose so suddenly that I lost my balance and toppled backwards, hitting my head against the bunk bed and finally landing flat on my back on the floor. Everything hurt.

"Ohhhhhh…" I groaned, touching the throbbing spot on my head.

"Whahappened?" asked Brian, peering down from my bed.

"I fell," I said. "Don't worry about it- go to sleep."

"I wanna help," Brian said, sitting up with some difficulty.

"I'm fine, go to sleep."

"Just stay there, Amy. I'm coming to rescue you."

I rolled my eyes as he fell down the ladder and knelt by me. A gentleman, even in his drunken state.

"What hurts?" he asked, reaching out to me.

"Nothing, I'm fine!" I tried to stand up, but my leg was still caught in the chair and I fell down again.

Brian slid his arms under my knees and my back and lifted me up as a groom lifts a bride over the threshold. I looked up at him and he was looking very earnestly at me. A month ago, I would have hoped he would kiss me. But curiously, I just felt confused. A few moments later, he lost his balanced and we both pitched into Erin's bed, tangled together.

"See?" Brian said after we'd sorted out which limbs were ours. "It's not so bad to share."

With that, he closed his eyes and fell asleep, one arm still slung across my stomach. I gaped at him, disbelieving. But at this point, it hurt to move too much and I was exhausted, so I shut my eyes as well and decided to deal with this whole situation later. I couldn't reason with him when he was drunk.

*****

Somewhere, an alarm went off. BEEP BEEP BEEP… BEEP BEEP BEEP…

I cracked an eye and looked at Erin's clock. 6:30am. Who would set their alarm for 6:30am on a Saturday morning? I groaned and turned over, coming face to face with Brian, who was lying awake, staring at the bottom of Casey's bed.

"Morning," he said awkwardly.

"Not yet," I muttered, pulling Erin's comforter over my head.

"What happened last night?"

I chuckled in spite of myself, but continued looking straight up at the underside of Casey's bed.

"I was fast asleep after a long day of finals and someone knocked on the door," I began, recounting the story in a way that would generate maximum guilt from Brian. "You kept insisting that this was your room and my bed was your bed. So I let you go sleep on my bed."

I paused for a second as a tremendous yawn overcame me.

"How did we wind up here?" he asked, concerned. "I think I remembered that you fell, but I don't remember how."

"I was trying to cover you, but you were lying on the comforter. So I tried to pull it out from under you and I fell. Then you tried to pick me up and we both fell into Erin's bed," I explained. "And I was so tired and everything hurt, so I just stayed here."

"But we just slept, right?" he asked, still concerned.

"That is correct, sir."

He looked relieved and put his head back down on the pillow. "I'm sorry, Amy," he said after some time. "I got wasted with the guys I play soccer with. I don't remember what happened after that, but I think I left my keys in my room."

"You get in a lot of trouble that way," I laughed.

"Always with you," he added. "I'm really sorry- I didn't mean to intrude on you this way."

"What way?" I asked innocently. "You mean by barging into my room in the middle of the night and tackling me into bed?"

I grinned at the horrified look on his face.

We heard heavy footsteps and the jangling of keys in the hallway.

"These damn kids always forget to turn off their damn alarm clocks when they leave for vacation!" A man's voice was annoyed. The beeping on the other side of the wall finally stopped.

"Hallelujah!" I said, closing my eyes again.

"Amy?"

"Hm?"

"Do you want me to go back to my room?" Brian asked, raising his head again.

"You told me last night that Sean had a stash of pot that they would find if they let you in the room," I reminded him.

"True," he winced and lowered his head again. "Do you mind if I.."

"Just be quiet!" I wailed in mock distress. "I don't care what you do, but I need to sleep!"

14 "Hang on to old friends"

Winter Break was nothing short of glorious. When I got home, I flung myself on my bed and rolled around on top of my comforter again. It was becoming a homecoming ritual. My dorm room still didn't feel like home, even after three months. I was beginning to wonder if it ever would.

"Amy! It's dinner time!" Mum called from the kitchen. I didn't need to be told twice. I could smell mom's seafood fried noodles and flew to the dinner table.

"Don't they feed you at college?" Dad joked, as he watched me heap my plate with Mum's cooking.

"It's not the same as Mum's," I said, with my mouth full.

"Well, they certainly aren't teaching you manners," Dad observed. I rolled my eyes at him.

"So, what's your plan for the week?" Mum asked.

"I'm going to see Lauren and the girls tonight. Oh, I have to bake some kind of cookie. We're having our cookie exchange tonight. Other than that, nothing, really. Hang out with whoever is around. When's Meg getting home?"

"She'll be home tomorrow night," Mum said. I could hear the emotion creeping into her voice. "It will be so good to have you both at home for more than a day."

"Aww, it's good to be home, Mum."

"So what's happening at college these days?" Dad asked, clearly uncomfortable with the underlying love-fest that could explode at any minute.

"Did I tell you about the guy who forgot to take the chapstick out of his pocket before he did the laundry?" It was the start of a very fun dinner.

*****

Lauren's house looked exactly the same. In fact, I was sure that Lauren herself probably looked exactly the same as well. The question was whether our relationship would be exactly the same   Our lives had degenerated into complete chaos since we'd left for college and neither of us had any sort of predictable schedule or privacy. The last few phone conversations had been brief. Was our relationship deteriorating or was I being paranoid? How ironic it was that I now had to worry about whether our relationship was alright, when it was precisely this relationship that was supposed to carry us through hard times.

Lauren opened the door and her face lit up. "You're the first one," she said and held her arms out for a hug.

"I wanted some Amy-Laur time," I replied.

"We need it!" She agreed enthusiastically.

I followed her into the house that I'd spent so many hours in during high school. We walked into the kitchen where we had drowned our high school sorrows in ice cream and brownies. Funny how that sounded great compared to vodka or Ecstacy now. I hoped the memories would remain vivid long into the future.

"How *are* you?" I asked, laying my lemon bars on the counter and sitting on one of the stools.

Lauren sat down next to me and helped herself to a lemon bar. "Where do I even start? What did I tell you last?"

"You were dating the hot soccer guy and then you broke up... by the way, I'm so so sorry that I couldn't talk longer when you guys broke up. I was right in the middle of midterms and..."

"Oh yeah, I was pissed at you about that," she said, a shadow passing over her face. "I needed you."

"I know," I replied. I couldn't look her in the eye, so I looked down at the counter and started playing with a misplaced rubber band. "I felt terrible. I will do a better job next quarter. This quarter, I was just so... overwhelmed. I feel like I don't have a lot of control over my life or my schedule anymore for some reason."

Lauren continued to chew. That was a good sign. "Yeah, I felt that way too. You know... you're still my best friend in the whole wide world and I want you to be that always. But we've got to figure out how we're going to make this work because we can't help each other if we don't talk and if we can't help each other then how can we be best friends?"

"You're right. We just have to make more of an effort. My parents don't want me using daytime minutes on the cell phone, but when nighttime minutes start, it's so late on the East Coast. My roommates are always around and I don't want them listening in on our conversation. And emails take too long to write."

"Yeah, it's hard. What if we have a designated time every week that we talk?"

"That would work. Let me know what your schedule is when you know it for next semester."

"OK," Lauren replied.

"So the break-up?" I got back on track.

"Right. The break-up. It was horrible, Amy. I'd never felt like that before. It was like my heart had been ripped out of my chest, bound up with a rope and put back in my chest, all bound up still. It *physically* hurt."

"Why did he break up with you?"

"No idea. I've been trying to figure it out. It's not like he's dating anyone else. At least, not that I know. He just said he thought we weren't right for each other and he needed to take some time to think about it. Just like that. Out of the blue one day. Up until then, it was going amazingly. We spent all of our free time together, I stayed over at his place almost every night because he has a single..."

"Did you... you know?"

"No," she replied without flinching. "But I thought about it."

"Did he want it?"

"Of course! But he said he understood and that I shouldn't do it until I was ready to."

"Do you think he got tired of waiting?"

"I don't think he's that kind of guy. I mean, we seem to connect on so many other levels. At least, I thought. I mean, this guy could talk about literature, politics, music, travel... you name it. We used to stay up half the night talking when we first started dating. We would talk about how our families influenced our development of a social conscience and all of these philosophical conundrums and stuff. That's why I totally fell for him. He's different. He's not like all of those other guys."

"Hmmm. That's so bizarre. Why would he just dump you like that? Are you guys still talking?" I asked, growing more upset by the minute on her behalf.

"He wanted to still be friends. I tried it for about a day, but it was so painful to see him and not be able to kiss him or stay over with him, I just told him that I needed my space for awhile. It's hard because he lives in my building. In a way, it makes it worse that he wants to be friends. If he were mad at me for something or if there were someone else involved, I could understand what happened to us. But it's so hard for me to see him every day, not be able to be with him *and* not understand why he doesn't want to be with me."

"That's ridiculous. I can't even imagine how hard this must be. I'm so sorry, Laur," I said sadly. "I wish I could make it better."

"Like the time you kicked Mike in the shin and told him to give me his tux jacket after Winter Formal." Lauren laughed.

"Oh yeah!" I joined in the laughter. "I forgot about that. I wish it were easy like that still. Oh my God, did I tell you about the guy that I kneed in the crotch?"

"NO!" she gushed. "Tell me!"

I proceeded to tell her about the night at the fraternity and the Walk of Shame the next day. We were both in stitches by the time the other girls began to arrive. I was glad I could laugh about it now.

The cookie exchange was fantastic. Erika made these incredible dark chocolate covered orange rinds. Morgan brought her Aunt Karen's meringues "because why not go with a classic?" Emily made strawberry cupcakes from scratch. She whipped the cream herself.

We stayed up late talking about our college adventures so far. We talked about our roommates, our professors, the oddballs we were meeting and how we felt about them. I listened contently as Morgan told us the story of how this poor guy kept dropping hints that he wanted to spend more time with her and how she totally misinterpreted them, to his frustration.

"Oh my God," Abby exclaimed after Morgan finished her story. "Do you guys feel like we were so sheltered growing up?"

"Totally," Kate agreed. "I'm one of *three* virgins on my floor."

"Seriously?" I cried. "No way!"

"How many virgins are on your floor?" she asked me.

I scrunched my brow and tried to think of who might or might not be and began counting silently on my fingers. Everyone burst out laughing.

"Maybe you're on the skanky floor," Emily told Kate. "I know there are more than three virgins on my floor. But I agree that we were totally sheltered here. It seems like everyone at school is a raging alcoholic."

"Do you think they really are or do you think they just talk like they are?" Morgan asked, skeptically. "Because I find that people *talk* about hooking up and getting wasted way more than they actually do it. There's this guy on my floor that is always asking if we want to get wasted and usually my roommates and I say no because we have practice in the morning or class or whatever. Well, one night, we finally took him up on it, and he wouldn't even drink that much! And the girl that he liked was there and getting toasted and he didn't even make a move!"

"My roommate talks about sex all the time," I piped up. "That one, Casey, who I was telling you about. It seems like she's pretty experienced in that department and it seems almost like... recreation for her. At night, she's always on the phone talking to her friends about who she's hooked up with lately."

"So weird!" Emily said. "I mean, obviously there's nothing wrong with having sex, but I can't imagine being so casual about it."

"Argh! Some people are having sex all the time!" Kate said. "One

Sunday morning a few weeks ago, my roommate and I woke up to this moaning coming from next door. I was like, 'What the hell is that?' Crystal says, 'It's probably their TV. Go back to sleep.' So we start to go back to sleep, but then I remembered. I was like, 'Crystal, they don't have a TV, remember? They came in here to watch the Oscars with us?' Then we both were totally grossed out. We put our pillows on our heads and everything, but we couldn't block out the sound. It was disgusting!"

"Ewwwwwww!" we cried, imagining the horrors of having to hear our own neighbors doing it.

"Want to know how I knew we were sheltered?" Erika asked, once we'd recovered.

There were emphatic "yes's" all around.

"I live next door to this guy named Jordan. He's cool. He comes from downtown LA and he's pretty cute. Well, he came over one day after class with a bag of tea. He's like, 'Do you want some?' I said, 'Oh! You brought tea. That's so nice of you!' He looks at me all weird for awhile. I'm telling you, it was so quiet you could hear a pin drop. He keeps looking at me like I have three heads and I'm looking at him, wondering why he's looking at me that way. Finally he says, 'This isn't tea. Haven't you ever seen pot before?' I told him that I hadn't and he walked out of the room shaking his head. He comes back ten minutes later to ask if I want to try some. I'm like, 'No, thank you!' and he walks back out of the room shaking his head. Things haven't been the same between us ever since."

Under the solidarity of our hearty group laughter, there was shared insecurity. I could feel it. In the World of College, there are the have's and the have nots. Those who *have* already had sex, gotten drunk, tried drugs and experimented with things that you wouldn't tell your parents about. *They* were the experienced, the seasoned, the wise. Then there was us. The "Just say No" kids, who had grown up straight-laced, getting good grades, participating in all the requisite extracurricular activities and going to the movies when we said we were going to the movies.

It was hard to hold the battle line that we were doing the "right" thing or the "smart" thing, when we had no idea what it was like to do the "wrong" thing. Everyone knows that in a debate about the pros and cons of drinking until you puke, the person who has never tried it is at a severe disadvantage. And yet, should that person cave or hold on to faith that they're doing the "smart" thing? I suspected that some of us would crack on some of our stances and some of us wouldn't. I wondered how it would divide us. I wondered if we would judge each other.

"Who wants another brownie?" I asked.

"Only if you have ice cream!" Emily replied.

"Brownie a la mode, coming right up!" Lauren said, jumping up and heading to her freezer.

*****

The next night after dinner, Mum, Meg and I got into our jammies and piled onto the couch to watch TV. We caught the end of one of the spy action movies, starring Angelina Jolie.

"Why is she so bad-ass?" I asked, in admiration.

"I don't like her very much," Mum said. "She has this arrogance about her."

"She doesn't care what anybody think," Meg added "She makes no apologies. She lives life totally on her own terms."

"She can probably get away with it because she's gorgeous," I said, hugging a pillow to my chest.

"I don't think that's it, though," Meg said. "I think that she's decided what matters in her life and she doesn't care about all the rest of it. Like, she honestly doesn't seem to care whether people like her or not."

"That's pretty ironic, considering she's in a business that relies on people liking her," Mum pointed out.

"But I think that the more she doesn't care whether people like her, the more people like her. You know?" Meg said. "She sort of reminds me of our one woman partner at work. This woman is incredible- she's really smart. She had to work really hard to get up to partner-level. But the thing is, she doesn't seem to care what people think of her. She's a bitch when she has to be to get things done and she always delivers. That's why the clients like her, but she's not really sweet or nice or any of that. She just has her priorities and she makes sure she can deliver on them. She has this same sort of confidence about her, like Angelina."

"Does she have kids?" Mum asked.

Meg shook her head.

Mum gave her a look that said "she-doesn't-even-know".

We watched as Angelina's character shot two villains simultaneously without batting a single long, luxurious eyelash.

"It must be so nice to stop caring what people think," I said.

"I think it happens when you find something you really want to do and you focus on it," Meg says. "Then the rest of it- all the other petty stuff- just sort of fades away."

I looked at her doubtfully.

"Well, maybe not totally," she admitted. "But I think it does some. Since I've been consulting, I literally haven't had time to worry about what anybody thinks of me except for my bosses and my clients. My life is a lot simpler now that way, and I kind of like it."

I hadn't really thought explicitly about how my caring what other people thought actually stressed me out until just now, but it made sense.

*****

As soon as that last final was over, Motivation packed its bags again, probably with all of the knowledge I'd gained studying, and was off on its next adventure, leaving me sitting at the kitchen table in my jammies at 11am, merrily eating Cheerios, while Mum was cutting coupons across from me. I felt deliciously free, without a care in the world.

"What are you up to today, Honey?" Mum asked.

I shrugged. "No plans. Emily is having a party tonight with high school people, so I'll go over to that after dinner."

"Want to go shopping?" Mum asked.

"Oh yef!" I cried enthusiastically, through a mouthful of Cheerios.

"Don't talk with your mouth full," Mum chided me.

"I need new jeans. Mine are getting tight," I confessed, reluctantly.

"It's all that dorm food," Mum clucked, shaking her head. "I'm sure your cookie party didn't help."

"Do I look fat, Mum?" I asked.

"You don't look fat," Mum replied carefully. "But you have put on a little weight. Your face is a little rounder."

I poked resignedly at my Cheerios with my spoon. If Mum said it, then there was no chance I could blame it on the old imagination anymore. I sighed.

"Should we wake Meg up and take her shopping with us?" I asked, changing the subject.

"Let her sleep. She needs it," Mum said, picking up her coupons again.

*****

Jeff called to ask if I wanted to go to Tahoe with him and a few friends for New Years. I should have been thrilled to be his main New Year's squeeze, but I wasn't all that disappointed when my parents said I couldn't go.

I spent New Year's Eve with my high school friends, at Morgan's house. It was comfortable and familiar. Eric had gone back up to Berkeley early. I didn't ask why.

I made my New Year's Resolutions the next day:

1. Study better
2. Lose 10 pounds
3. Finish "Freshman Fifteen" article
4. Find some community service to do
5. Forget Eric- really
6. Be more comfortable in my own skin

15 "Study"

Winter quarter started with the same bacchanal gaiety as the beginning of the school year. In some ways, it was even better. One quarter wiser, we freshmen could now appreciate the lifecycle of the academic quarter monster, and could therefore party smarter. The first two weeks, the beast lay largely dormant. We could dance, drink, watch movies and go out to our heart's content and it wouldn't bat an eyelash. By the third week, it began to open its eyes and become aware of its surroundings. At this point, it began singling out foolish or brazen college students who did not construct adequate defenses in the form of problem sets and reading lists.

By midterms, any college student still left defenseless would be snatched up in the jaws of the monster and mauled to death over the course of the quarter.

Armed with this new understanding, we took full advantage of the first two weeks of the quarter with slightly more caution. We filled our social calendars with movie nights, dinners out and frat parties. There never seemed to be enough time for everything. Lauren was going to kill me. I owed her a phone call, but every night there were activities more fun than the night before, and that got in the way.

Monday was the first night everyone was back from Winter Break and we all had dinner together. We found out that apparently, Sean was one of the last quarter's more damaged victims.

"It's so weird to be back," Erin observed. "Everything looks the same, but it *feels* different."

"*I'm* glad to be back," Sean replied, dumping salt onto roast chicken. Health-conscious Sarah goggled at him.

"New quarter, new video game to beat," Casey suggested.

"Naw, I have to be good this quarter," Sean replied, without any sarcasm in his voice. We all looked at him.

"Who are you and what have you done with Sean?" Chris asked, , elbowing Sean, as he took a sip of soda. It sloshed all over him.

"Watch it, jackass!" Sean yelled.

"There's the Sean we know and love!" Brian commented. We laughed.

"Why do you have to be good this quarter?" I asked, my curiosity unsatiated.

"I f-ed up my classes last quarter," Sean said, calmly, taking a bite of his saline chicken. "So the Dean wrote me an email and said that I have to meet with him on Thursday or else I might be expelled."

We all stopped eating.

"Expelled?!" Sarah asked, disbelieving.

"Wow, Red!" Sean said, good-naturedly. "Would you miss me?"

"Don't flatter yourself," Sarah replied, bristling. "Of course I wouldn't."

"But you're talking to me again."

"No I'm not."

"Expelled? How badly did you do?" I asked.

"Well, I got a D in everything except for Sociology. I got a C in Sociology."

"They can expel you for that?" Brian asked.

"Well, it sort of depends on how this meeting with the Dean goes on Thursday." Sean salted his pepperoni pizza. "If he decides I'm trying to 'change my ways', then he will put me on academic probation this quarter. If he decides I'm not, then he can kick me out right now."

After dinner, we went back to our rooms. After living at home for three weeks with my room all to myself, I felt oppressed when I looked at the three beds within feet of each other. I got on my computer to see who was around.

Amyable7: hi u!

Jeffers56: hey beautiful

Amyable7: howz it going?

Jeffers56: good! u?

Amyable7: great... wanna hang out?

Jeffers56: can't tonight- headed to the house in a few. ltr in the wk?

Amyable7: sure, let me know

Jeffers56: 'night!

That was disappointing.

"Let's go get coffee and cookies!" Chris voice broke into my thoughts. He and Sean were standing in the doorway expectantly.

"OK!" Erin replied. I was pleasantly surprised. Maybe she'd made a New Year's resolution to be more social.

"Naw, I have to go to the sorority tonight," Casey replied.

Sean made an obscene gesture at her.

Casey rolled her eyes.

"I'll come," I offered, looking for my sweatshirt. "Go get Sarah?"

And we were off for a lovely evening, wandering around Westwood. As we were walking back from a Kookie King , we heard an ambulance wailing near Dykstra. I insisted on closer inspection. As we walked up towards the concrete block of a dorm building, we saw an unconscious girl, pale and limp like a rag doll, being wheeled into the ambulance. There was a hushed buzz in the crowd forming around the ambulance.

"What's going on?" Sarah asked a girl who looked like she'd been watching for awhile.

"She's got alcohol poisoning," the girl replied. "They're taking her to the hospital to pump her stomach."

Who had told me that college was without consequences?

*****

Tuesday was my first day of work. After a very manageable chemistry class with a soft spoken bespectacled man, and a less manageable physics class, with a rapid-talking Russian, I was done with thinking for a couple of hours. I was excited to start work. It would be great to get a paycheck, albeit a small one. I grabbed a quick lunch at the Coop and showed up to the bookstore at 12:55pm with a big smile on my face to impress my new boss, Pam.

I walked up to the check-out counter, which was bustling with beginning-of-the-quarter book sale activity.

"Where's Pam?" I asked one of the girls standing at a cash register. "I'm Amy. I'm starting work today."

The girl waved me off without even looking at me.

"Can't you see I'm *swamped?*" she asked, clearly stressed out. She punched the cash register buttons, agitatedly. "I don't know where Pam is!"

"Pam is in the back room," said the guy next to her. He looked worried, fearful almost, but he had his wits about him. "Next!"

"Thanks," I replied, beginning to wonder what I'd gotten myself into.

I walked to the back of the bookstore and saw an unmarked door. I knocked. A large, red-faced woman opened the door. Like all of the other employees in the store, she wore a navy blue polo shirt over khaki pants and a black apron.

"Tell me you're Amy," she demanded, not smiling. Her course silver hair was pulled up in a stark knot at the top of her head.

"I'm Amy," I replied, wishing that I weren't.

"Good, now get in here!" She pulled me into the back room. I looked around the room at the hundreds of massive boxes in stacks of three or four against the wall. There was a big open space in the center of the room.

Pam didn't waste any time.

"First, you're going to have to change into your uniform. I have that for you in the locker room. Then, you will need to punch in your time card. The time machine is back there. Then you will need to restock the bookshelves. When things slow down around here, I'll have time to train you on the cash registers."

She was like an army commander, firing battle orders at me. Even as she was instructing me, she continued to pile books onto a cart at a dizzying pace. I could feel tension everywhere, even emanating out of the walls.

"I hope you're strong," she continued. "You need to go out there and see which books are running out. Then you need to come back here and get more of them. There's a cart you can use over there."

"How are the books organized back here? By author, by class?"

"They're not," she replied, looking me square in the eye. "That's your job."

I sucked in my breath. I was going to have to look in every one of these boxes, figure out what was in it and then move the boxes around to organize them in some searchable way. Each one of them probably had forty textbooks in them. They had to weigh a hundred pounds each!

I suddenly felt dizzy and wanted to sit down, but I was afraid to because Pam looked like she might snap me in half if I did.

"Well, what are you waiting for? Kids are out there complaining."

"Where's the locker room?" I asked.

In no time, I was doggedly running back and forth between the store and the backroom.

"Elements of Chemistry!" Pam yelled at me from across the room.

That was a new one. I hadn't seen that one yet. When I got back into the back room, I began tearing open boxes in search of the book. I groaned after I had gone through the large boxes at the top of the stacks. Now I would have to look at the boxes underneath them. I tried to lift a box off of the top of a stack and nearly broke my back as I staggered and pitched around under its weight.

"What's taking so long?" Pam's voice cut into the silence. I nearly jumped out of my skin. I deposited the box back on the top of the stack where I found it and I turned around in time to see her face disappear back out the door.

"I'm looking!" I called back. I decided that I couldn't lift the box from the top of the stack, so I pushed it off. It fell with a loud thud onto the bare, concrete floor. The thud echoed.

Pam's face reappeared in the doorway. "What the hell was that?"

I pointed to the fallen box on the floor.

Rage clouded her face. "Be careful! You're scaring the customers! And if we damage the books, we have to sell them at a discount!"

"I can't lift them from the top! They're too heavy."

"Well, *try!*" she said, her large chest heaving. She disappeared out the door.

I wanted to cry. I looked inside the newly revealed box and there was *Elements of Chemistry.*

"Found you!" I said wearily. I took out several of them and stacked them on the cart. I heard the door open behind me. My arms and back were beginning to ache from lifting all of the heavy books. Their sharp corners and edges cut off circulation to the tips of my fingers when I carried them in stacks.

The door creaked open again.

"Political Economy in the 21st Century!" Pam's voice was sharp like the crack of whip. I didn't jump quite as high that time.

I nodded without turning around. I heard the door shut again. *Political Economy in the 21st Century* was somewhere on the other side of the room. I located it and dumped several copies onto the cart as well. Then I opened the door, pushed the nose of the cart out of it and continued to try to maneuver the cart out of the door.

I restocked *Elements of Chemistry* and *Political Economy in the 21st Century.* There were students waiting impatiently at the shelves for them. They snatched them off my cart, without even waiting for me to put them on the shelves. I was annoyed at them for being annoyed at me. They had no idea! On my way back to the backroom, I noticed that two other shelves were empty. Students would be complaining soon. Neither of the books were books from the boxes at the top of their stacks.

"Excuse me!" a girl called. "There are no more biology books."

"What's the book called that you're looking for?" I asked.

She shrugged. "It's the book for Life Science III."

That meant nothing to me.

"Can you show me where it is?" I asked.

She heaved an impatient sigh, but led me to the shelf, where I noted the name and author of the book. Again, this one was not a top-of-the-stack book.

"Can you hurry?" she asked. "The line for the cashier is getting long!"

I bit my tongue and started toward the backroom. I caught Pam's glower from across the room. She headed ominously towards me.

Great. Another lecture.

Upon entering the backroom, I looked frantically at the stacks of books. I *had* to push the boxes off of the top, even if it might damage them because I couldn't get to the bottom boxes otherwise, and there was bound to be a riot soon if these shelves didn't get restocked. My arms strained as I pushed one off.

THUD.

I began tearing open the newly exposed box with a box cutter and my throbbing hands. The door opened behind me. I couldn't look at Pam. Every muscle in my body was aching and my nerves were wrought, but I couldn't let her see me capitulate. I needed to be stronger than that.

"Pam, I'm *sorry*," I began, trying to control the shaking in my voice. "I'm trying *really* hard not to damage the books, but I really can't lift them off the top of the stacks by myself and I'm trying to hurry so that I can restock them fast...."

"Let me help then."

It was a calm, familiar male voice. I turned around to see Brian standing in the doorway, wearing the requisite blue polo shirt and khakis.

Relief washed over me like a warm wave and melted some of the tension from my body. I heaved an overdue sigh.

"Am I glad to see you!" I said, wiping my forehead and managing a feeble smile.

"That's what a man likes to hear!" Brian laughed, coming into the room.

"I would have said it to anyone who walked in that door and was willing to help!" I told him, feeling the need to keep things clear between us.

"Did you have to add that part?" he asked, wincing.

"Can you help me unstack all of these boxes?"

"Let's do it," he said, rubbing his hands together.

We worked like mules for the rest of the afternoon with minimal conversation. Brian tried to make small talk a couple of times, but I responded abruptly each time. It was mean, and I don't like being mean, but I wasn't in the mood to be pleasant today. My shift ended an hour earlier than his and I made my way up the hill by myself, wondering if I could survive this new job.

When I got home, I was surprised to see both Casey and Erin in the room, talking. Erin was sitting at her desk, her long, silky hair draped over one shoulder. She leaned back in her chair. Casey was lying on her stomach on Erin's bed. I sat down on Erin's bed next to Casey.

"We're thinking about doing a Girls' Night tonight," Casey told me, cheerfully. "Are you in?"

"Yes!" I replied, "Today has been the longest day ever! I could use a girls night out!"

"It's the second day of the quarter," Erin said, confused. "How are you so busy already?"

"I started my job at the bookstore today.It's *hard*."

"What do you have to do?" Casey asked, turning onto her side so she could look at me.

"I have to restock the books," I said.

Both girls looked at me, confused.

"It's a lot harder than it sounds," I told them."Alright, so what are we doing for Girls' Night?" I asked, ready to think about something fun for the first time today.

"We're going down to the frats," Casey said, taking her scrunchie off and shaking out her golden mane. "They're all having parties this week, so it will be great."

I was hoping for something lower key, but I couldn't really tell Casey that. *I am a college girl. I am supposed to want to go to frat parties,* I thought to myself sarcastically.

"Cool," I replied.

*****

I remember when I first watched Casey get ready to go out at night, I thought she was so glamorous. She was like a princess getting dressed for the ball or like a movie star preparing for a red carpet debut. But now, after watching her several times and knowing what she did after she "put on her face", a darker analogy came to mind. She applied her make-up with the intensity of a warrior preparing for battle.

Even at the beginning, I noticed that when she was getting ready to go out, she grew quiet and thoughtful. She dug through her make-up bag thoroughly and deliberately, gauging the effectiveness of each of her weapons. I could imagine the thoughts running through her glowing blonde head. The black mascara or the brown? The black was more blunt, good for the surprise attack on the unsuspecting victim. The trade-off was that it was more recognizable by the competition as a cheap tactic. The brown mascara was definitely more subtle and could be used on a more savvy victim with a trained eye. Then came the question of which eye shadow to use. This depended on the method of attack. Some guys were best captured by the smoldering, sexy look, which required bolder, dark colors. Others were dazzled by the flirtation of sparkles and shimmers. Still others were best caught by the "natural look" which ironically took the most skill to pull off. This was the idea of wearing make up in a way that made you look like you were just born with glowing cheekbones and luminous peepers. It required the adroitness of a veritable Monet of make-up. The lip color had to be consistent with the eye shadow or else the whole disguise could be foiled.

Casey applied her war paint systematically with the precision of a seasoned veteran. She stared intently at her face during this entire process, unblinking. It was almost as if she were afraid that her reflection might draw a sword and kill her if she looked away for longer than just the time she needed to load her next weapon. First came the foundation, which she even applied with the same even strokes every time. A big dot of foundation on her forehead, her nose, each cheek and her chin. She blended it in with a spongey wedge to create a flawless canvas on which to lay out her battle plan. She would then apply her eye shadow. A lighter base color from her eye lashes to her eye brows. Then the other color, also applied with the steady hand of one who has mastered her weapon since childhood. It went on like this with her eye liner, her mascara, her highlighter, her blush, her lip liner, her lipstick and her lip gloss. After this, she would put finishing touches in her hair. The guys didn't stand a chance.

Everyone looked beautiful when we were ready to head out.

"Let's take pictures!" Casey commanded. All of us produced digital cameras from our purses and piled into the hallway. We made Chris come out and take several posed, internet-bound photos, so we could show our friends how cool we were.

"You guys look great," Chris said, and he meant it.

"Amen to that," a male voice said from behind us.

We all turned around. It was Jeff, who was dressed to go out as well.

"I was just coming down to say hi to Miss Amy, but it looks like she's busy," he said, his eyes dancing.

I walked over to give him a hug and was delighted at how perfectly this scene unfolded. I was all dressed up, looking my best. And I was going out with an awesome group of girls, not sitting at home, waiting for him to show up.

"How *are* you?" I asked, giddy.

"Great, now! I don't want to hold you up if you're headed out."

"What are you up to?" Casey asked, batting her luxurious, black lashes at him.

"Just heading to the house, nothing special," he replied. "Want to come?"

"Naw, we're having Girls' Night," Casey said, winking. "We can't commit ourselves to anyone tonight."

Everyone laughed. Jeff turned back to me.

"Do you have plans for Saturday night?" he asked, lowering his voice.

I felt all eyes on me and relished the envious looks I was getting. I thought for a moment and shook my head.

"Want to go out to dinner with me?" he asked.

"Would love to."

"Great, I'll come by around seven," he said.

I nodded, feeling on top of the world. Then, we headed out.

"What a *hottie!*" Autumn commented, when we were safely out of Sproul.

"Thanks?" I replied, unsure of how to respond. Everyone laughed.

"It looks like things are going well!" Sarah observed.

"You can say that again!" Lindsay chimed in. "It's *so cute* that he asked you out in front of all of us! He must really be into you!"

"I hope so," I replied.

"OK, no more relationship talk tonight," Casey declared. "It's Girls' Night. Chicks before dicks, right?"

We walked down to the frats with our chins held high, giving ourselves a point for every head we turned, and two for every cat call. I couldn't help recalling Sean's comment last semester that girls *wanted* to be objectified. It was indeed fun to feel attractive and wanted. We were undeniably enjoying being objectified. The irony of our earlier indignation did not escape me. I could see how this dichotomy of thought might confuse the male mind. A psychology course was definitely in order.

We drifted from one frat house to another and the pattern of behavior was pretty much the same at each. We would fight our way onto the dance floor. Some of us would go locate the alcoholic beverages and return with nasty, cheap beers for the rest of us. We would dance for awhile, alternately staring blankly off into space or yelling trivial comments at each other over the deafening music. Inevitably, a few of us would get groped by some faceless mystery boy and be (or pretend to be) indignant. The walls were lined with frat boys sizing up the girls, and girls pouting over any number of slights that could be considered "drama". After some time, we would declare this house "tired" and go on to the next house.

*****

Thursday, after work, I agreed to shoot hoops with Chris again. He was already dressed and waiting for me in the hallway when I got back to the dorms, mentally and physically exhausted.

"Come on, Callaway," Chris said, passing me the ball. "Let's go!"

"Alright. Give me five minutes to change."

"I'm going to head up there and reserve a court for us," Chris said.

"OK, I'll be right up." I passed him the ball back.

Erin wasn't home yet, so I let myself in and shut the door behind me so that I could change into sweatpants and a sweatshirt.

Just as I was pulling on my sweatpants, I heard a knock at the door. I opened it and Sean wandered in, half-dressed. He was pulling up the waistband of khaki's that were too nice to be his.

"I have a horrible headache," Sean said, sitting on Erin's bed with his head in his hands.

"Are you hung-over?" I aske, even though it was unlikely. It was the middle of the afternoon.

"No," he mumbled into his hands. "I think it's like a migraine or something. Do you have any medicine? I can't go to the Dean's office with this kind of headache."

"I don't keep any meds," I replied, glancing around the room. "Did you ask the RA?"

"I already knocked on her door, but she's not in. I thought one of you girls might have something. I don't know why it hurts so bad..."

"Hold on," I said, stepping over a mountain of Casey's shoes and prying open her closet door. I looked through her stash of pills and pulled out a white bottle with a red cap.

"Extra strength aspirin?" I asked.

Sean nodded without looking up and held out his hand. It took me a minute to figure out how to get the child-proof cap off.

"Wow, they make aspirin a lot smaller now than I remember," I commented as I handed Sean the small, white pill. "Listen, I'm going to shoot some hoops with Chris, but I hope you feel better. What time is your meeting?"

Sean popped the pill in his mouth, tilted back his head and swallowed it without water.

"In two hours," he said, still wincing.

"You're getting dressed early," I noticed. "No one but Casey starts dressing up two hours early!"

"I don't want to screw up this meeting," he replied, in a rare moment of vulnerability. "I don't want to leave."

I didn't want him to leave either, even though I would never admit it to him. He followed me out of the room, dragging his feet, and I made sure it locked behind us. I made the peace sign bunny ears with my fingers and walked briskly down the hall.

***

Chris passed me the ball as I arrived on the basketball court. I took a practice shot and missed.

"Sean's really nervous about this meeting with the Dean, huh?" Chris commented.

"Yeah, looks like it." I focused on keeping my right elbow tucked into my body so that my forearm was perpendicular to the ground.

"You have really good form."

"Thanks. It's not doing me much good right now, though."

"You're not warm yet."

"So how's life?" I ran around the three-point perimeter and took shots from the outside.

"Sweet," Chris replied, nodding his head. "So, remember that talk we had last time we shot hoops before Winter Break?"

"Yeah,"

"Well, I asked that girl out and now we're seeing each other!"

I was just setting up a shot, but I stopped and looked at him. "Chris, that's awesome! I'm so excited for you!"

"It was all *you*, baby!" Chris said, pointing at me with both index fingers. "Let me see the ball."

I passed him the ball and he began shooting. He hit a beautiful three-point shot. It sailed through the net without touching the rim at all.

"Nice shot! What do you mean?" I asked, retrieving the ball for him and passing it back.

"If you hadn't had that talk with me about no one being 'out of my league', I never would have done it."

"Aww! I'm glad I could help," I replied. "So how is it?"

"Well, we haven't done it yet, so I don't know how…"

"No no no! That's not what I meant. I mean, how is the relationship? What is she like, as a person?"

"Oh, I thought you were being one of the guys. You know, we're shooting hoops and all."

I shook my head and held my hand out for the ball.

"She's a cool chick. She wants to be a nurse. She spends time with her

295

family. Oh, she even knows Casey! They were in class together last quarter and they went to Vegas for a few days over Winter Break."

I stopped and looked at him.

"That's weird. She didn't tell me about that."

Chris continued to tell me about Serena, but I was stuck on Casey taking a trip to Vegas without inviting me, or even mentioning it to me. I felt betrayed, somehow. Weren't we supposed to be roommates and pals, by default?

I played a game of H-O-R-S-E with Chris and we played one-on-one up to thirteen points. He beat me by two points, but it was a good, close game. And we walked home together, dripping sweat, wobbly legged, and better friends. It was a gratifying feeling.

I came home to an odd sight. At first, it was just a pair khakis protruding from the lower bunk, motionless. Erin was perched at her desk, typing away, with music playing in the background, as if nothing were out of the ordinary. I walked into the room and saw that the khakis belonged to Sean, who was sitting on Erin's bed, slumped against the wall, his long legs stretching halfway across the small aisle between the bunk bed and the dresser. I bent down to have a better look at him.

That's when things got weirder. He was gazing at Erin, lovingly rubbing my bear Franklin between its soft brown ears. Alarmed, I snatched Franklin from him. He continued to rub the air where Franklin's fuzzy head had been for a second or two before he reacted. He looked confused for a minute, and then looked up at me. His eyes were glazed over and he had a goofy smile on his face. He held his hands out the way my cousin's baby did when he wanted "up".

"What's wrong with you?" I asked, handing him back the bear.

"Hi Amy," he said, with the same silly smile. He took Franklin back and began rubbing its tummy.

"How's your headache?" I asked.

"What headache?" he asked, dreamily.

"Jeez, Erin. What's wrong with Sean?" I was beginning to get concerned.

Erin finished the thought she was typing. "I don't know. I came home and he was standing outside of our door, so I let him in. He was all goofy like that, so I thought he was drunk and let him sit on my bed. He watched your screen saver for a long time, then he wanted me to play music."

"I'm not drunk," Sean declared. "I feel really good. Great, in fact!"

Erin and I exchanged a look.

"Sean, are you high?" I asked. I couldn't smell any pot on him though.

"No," he replied after some time. He began to rub Franklin across the top of his own tussled head. I snatched Franklin back, not wanting him to smell like a cross between sweat and hair gel. Sean laid down on the bed and began to trace the pattern on the underside of Casey's mattress with his finger.

"It's like he's drugged!" Erin declared, puzzled. "Sean, what did you take?"

"Nothing. Just that aspirin that Amy gave me."

A terrible feeling came over me. I picked up my backpack and dug around the cluttered pocket frantically for my cell phone.

"What the hell kind of aspirin did you give him?" asked Erin, alarmed. Her dark eyes grew large in her small peeked face.

I found my phone and started scrolling through my address book.

"I'm about to find out," I told her. After a moment, her expression resolved into a look of understanding.

"Ring... ring... ring... Amy, what's up?" Casey's voice was loud over the noise of a crowd in the background.

"Case, Sean came in here with a headache this afternoon and I gave him a pill out of your aspirin bottle," I said, cutting through the chase.

There was a pause.

"Case, are you there?"

"Yeah, I'm trying to remember what I put in the Tylenol bottle. What color was it?" she asked.

"White,"I replied. "Small, round white pill."

After another pause, she burst out laughing.

"You gave him e," she said,gasping for air.

"Sorry?" I yelled into the phone, not understanding what she'd said.

"E, Amy. You gave him Ecstasy," she said, enunciating so that I could understand her. I could hear the people around here burst into laughter.

"Well how do I fix it?" I exclaimed, alarmed.

"What are you talking about?" she asked. "There's nothing to fix! He's probably having the time of his life! Wow, I forgot I had it- I haven't dropped e in awhile. Just rub him a lot."

"Excuse me?"

"Rub his head and his arms and stuff. It will feel good. He's also going to want to look at flashing lights and colors and stuff. Music is good too," Casey said.

"I don't have time for..." I protested.

"I can't hear you! See you soon!" Casey yelled over the music.

And then she was gone.

I stared at the phone, disbelieving. I'd drugged somebody. That had to be illegal. What would my mother say?

"Well?" Erin's voice cut into my panicked thoughts.

"I gave him Ecstasy," I said, still trying to work it out in my head. "Casey put E in her aspirin bottle and I gave it to Sean."

"Well, what do we do about it?" Erin asked, leaning back in her chair, also panicked. Blinking instant message windows flashed like silent sirens next to her.

"Casey says to rub his head and his arms and stuff," I said.

"Yeah!" Sean's whole face brightened. He looked at me, then at Erin.

"I'm not rubbing anything," Erin said, recoiling in her chair.

"Awwww, please?" Sean asked.

I glanced at him and was met with the simple gaze of a child.. He held out his arm. I bent over and rubbed one arm with the very tip of my index finger, feeling ridiculous. Sean smiled in a delighted sort of way and closed his eyes.

"Amy, I *can't* believe you are rubbing Sean," Erin said, as if I were peeing on the carpet or something to that effect.

"Don't remind me," I muttered. "This is going to be the story of the year. I slipped Sean a little white pill so that I could rub him while he was drugged."

Erin laughed so hard, she nearly fell out of her chair. Sean giggled.. Finally, I found myself wanting to laugh at the irony of the whole thing. My whole life, I'd always been the safe, dependable, controversy-free boring person. What was happening to me?

"Sit here!" Sean commanded, pulling me down onto the bed with him. I continued to rub his arm. Erin stopped gawking and went back to her blinking IM windows, shaking her head.

"Sean, what does it feel like?" I figured I ought to learn something out of all of this. I was fairly sure I wasn't going to try E myself, especially after seeing the disgraceful condition Sean was in, but I was curious about it.

"It just feels good," he said.

"That's not a very good description. What does it feel like? Like a massage? Are you sleepy?"

He looked as though he had to concentrate very hard to answer my question. "It just feels really good when you touch me. Like you're giving me lots of super-hugs. Here, rub my head."

I began rubbing his head. Suddenly, I remembered. "Sean! Don't you have an appointment with the Dean soon?"

"That's right!" Erin said, snapping her fingers. "I was wondering why he was all dressed up. Now I remember!"

"Oh yeah. At five o'clock," Sean said.

I glanced at Erin's alarm clock. "Sean, that's in twenty minutes! Where is the meeting?"

"Some office on campus," he murmured, now focusing his attention on petting Franklin again.

"Focus, man!" I yelled. "Where is the meeting? You can't go like this! What are we going to do?"

"It's in my email," Sean replied, after thinking for awhile.

I sat down at my computer and navigated to the email site. "Sean, come here and log in."

He sat down next to me on the hard wooden seat and entered his log-in information. He scrolled through his inbox and retrieved the email from the Dean.

I fidgeted in the chair. "You can't go like this! They will expel you on the spot! Is there a phone number on there? Let me call and try to reschedule your appointment."

Sean looked at me, puzzled. I called the number at the bottom of the email. A woman answered.

"Dean's office," she said.

"Hi. My friend has an appointment with the Dean in twenty minutes, but he just… got back… from the dentist and is still… groggy on… Novocain."

I heard the woman click around on her keyboard.

"This is for Sean Alexander?" she asked.

"Yes, is there any way that we can reschedule him?" I asked, trying to keep my voice steady. Sean had started petting my arm and I shook him off with a warning look.

"I'm afraid not," the lady said, not sounding afraid of anything. "You see, the Dean has to pardon him in order for him to be allowed to remain at school. But the Dean has to give his pardon to the Registrar before the end of this week. And the Dean has no more appointments available this week. So if Mr. Alexander doesn't come in and talk to him now, then he will be asked to leave by the Registrar's office."

"I see," I stammered, trying to think as fast as I could. "Well, can I come with him then? He's not very… well right now."

"These meetings are confidential. We can't just let other students in."

"I'm his long-time girlfriend," I blurted out, in desperation.

Sean's glazed eyes lit up and he gave me a goofy thumbs-up. I slapped his wrist down and rolled my eyes.

"Well, alright," she said, uncertainly. "I suppose these are... unusual circumstances. You know you have to be here in less than fifteen minutes, right?"

"Yes, ma'am! Thank you, we'll see you soon!"

I hung up the phone and jumped out of my seat. I was still in my sweats and felt filthy.

"Erin, could you go with him?" I begged. "I'm disgusting. I can't show up to the Dean's office all sweaty."

She gave me a pleading look. "I would do it for you. But I won't risk my academic career for Sean. Whoever goes with him could wind up being in huge trouble if they find out that he's on E and you tried to cover it up."

"Sean, look out the window," I ordered him. He obeyed. I peeled off my sweaty workout clothes. I quickly put on a pair of nice black dress pants and a sweater.

"Amy, you don't have to go either. You don't need to risk yourself," Erin said as she watched me dress. "You don't owe Sean anything."

"I do," I replied, my voice as heavy as my conscience. "I drugged him up in the first place. Come on, Sean!"

I pulled him out of my seat by his arm. He stumbled a few steps forward.

"Let's go. See you soon, Erin!" I called over my shoulder. The last thing I saw was Erin's worried face, which was growing paler by the second. She was wringing her hands.

I had never walked so fast in my life. Sean tripped along behind me as I was dragging him by his sleeve and issuing instructions the whole way. I had no idea if he processed any of what I was saying.

"Sean, you have to be really polite to the Dean, ok? Don't try to be a smart ass. And if he asks you what happened last semester, don't tell him you were playing video games, getting drunk and smoking out all of last quarter. You hear?

Tell him that you had a hard time adjusting to college life. Tell him that you felt lost in classes because you weren't used to the big lecture halls and no personal attention. But make sure you follow up by saying that you've figured out how to study now. Tell him that you're sorry and you've got all of your personal issues sorted out.

Speaking of personal issues, I'm supposed to be your long-time girlfriend. We met at... basketball camp... the summer after sophomore year. We went to senior prom together and the whole deal. You got that? Well, he probably won't ask about me that much."

I heard him grunt behind me.

"And you just had a dentist appointment where they had to do a root canal. You can say you never had Novocain before, so you didn't realize how bad off you were going to be. If you'd known it was going to mess you up this badly, you would have done the root canal another time. Well, but you can say it was hurting you so badly. Are you getting all of this?" I asked, dragging him up the steps leading to Powell Library.

"We're almost there," I told him. We were both panting at this point. I glanced at my watch. We were cutting it close, but it looked like we were going to make it on time.

I heard him grunt something.

"What?" I asked, yanking on his sleeve so that he would hurry up.

"Thanks, Amy," he said so earnestly I stopped out of surprise for a moment to look at him. He looked back at me, the familiar disdainful smile missing from his face.

"You're welcome," I replied. And I jumped back into motion again.

"You're my girlfriend?" he asked behind me.

"Oh hell!" I replied, blowing up my bangs. "Just let me do the talking,"

*****

"I hate root canals too," the dean sympathized from across his giant desk. The heavy wrinkles in his leathery forehead deepened. "I'm glad they gave you anaesthesia. Your girlfriend is so nice to come down here with you."

I smiled and hoped he couldn't see how sick I felt inside.

"I'm very lucky." Sean was completely dead-pan. There wasn't a hint of sarcasm in his voice. The ecstasy was probably helping on this front.

"So, young man, what seemed to be the trouble last quarter?"

Sean fidgeted about in his chair. I stepped on his foot to make him stop.

"I was just having a hard time adjusting," Sean said, as I had instructed him to. "The big lectures were... intimidating and I didn't go talk to my professors when I didn't understand things."

Sean spoke slowly and continued to be dead serious.

"We are a public institution," the dean replied. "Large lecture classes are... inevitable, but I hope that you're figuring out a way to make the best of them."

"Yes, sir," Sean replied. "I'm working very hard at it this quarter. I've decided I want to be a professor of political science, like yourself."

"Well!" The dean looked very pleased. "That's an admirable goal. Do

301

you think that you will perform better this quarter?"

"Yes."

"Young lady, do you think that he will be able to perform better this quarter?"

"Sean is very smart," I told him honestly.

"Fine. Where is that form I need to sign?"

*****

Saturday night, Jeff took me to dinner at a little Italian restaurant on Gayley.

"I figured everyone likes Italian food," Jeff said, as we walked into the restaurant. Luckily, I did.

We sat down and the waiter brought us bread and water. I was happy to sit across from him and stare at him all through dinner.

"So how was the rest of your Winter Break?" I asked.

"It was cool," Jeff said, leaning back in his chair and stretching his legs out in front of him.

"What did you do?"

"I went up to Tahoe with some buddies from high school. One of my buddies has a cabin up there. Well, his dad does, I guess. We missed you at New Year's. We went snowboarding and snowmobiling. That was great, except for a few hours on New Year's Eve when the electricity went out and we thought we were going to die up there."

"Couldn't you just drive home?"

"It was snowing really hard, so some people thought it would have been bad to drive. *I* would have done it."

"Of course," I murmured, suppressing a smile.

"But it came back on after a few hours and we were able to watch the apple drop and all that. Luckily, we didn't need the fridge for beers or anything. We just left them out in the snow."

I laughed. "Convenient."

"Yeah, what did you do for the rest of break?"

"Saw friends, went shopping, did some writing."

"What did you do for New Year's?"

"I went to my friend's house. We had some of our high school friends over for champagne and desserts."

"Wow, you went all high brow on me," Jeff joked. "You didn't hang out with Casey or Erin over break?"

"Erin had a lot of family functions and I didn't hear from Casey much over break. She has a pretty busy social calendar."

"Right."

Our food appeared. Jeff's meat lasagna looked amazing. The spicy smell of sausage mixed with the lava flow of cheese oozing out the sides made my mouth water. I looked over at my garden salad. *I'm doing the right thing*, I told myself sternly.

Jeff began cutting into his lasagna and eating eagerly. I started on my salad, which was completely unsatisfying on a cold night like tonight.

"I thought about what you said before break," Jeff said. "And I think that we should date each other exclusively."

I swallowed my bite of salad, which hurt going down. "Really?"

"Yeah. I like you a lot and I think we could have something really great. Don't you think?"

"Totally," I agreed, recovering my composure. "It's just, I thought that you were all into dating other people and all."

"Well, I decided that it's not fair to you. You said that you felt like you couldn't get closer to me because of that and I don't want that. I want us to take it to the next level. *And*, when I saw you and your friends going out the other night, I got this, kind of, gut reaction. Like, I didn't want you dating other people either. I want you all to myself."

Suddenly, I wanted to stand up and hug him. I felt like all of the frustration, confusion and misery had all been worth it. *I* was worth it. It had all worked out. I sat still and just radiated.

Jeff must have seen the joy on my face. He reached across the table. I put my hand in his. He picked it up and kissed it. My heart stopped. Just stopped. For a beautiful still moment. It was like we *were* in a chick flick.

"I don't know what to say," I stammered, searching for words. "I'm really happy."

"Good! Let's eat! I want to take you somewhere cool after dinner!"

After paying for dinner with his dad's credit card, we got in his shiny black pickup truck and drove.

"Where are we going?" I asked, still glowing.

"You'll see,.."

"Not far, right?" I asked anxiously.

"No, we're almost there."

Somewhere cool ended up being Santa Monica beach, which I'd never been to, even though it was only twenty minutes from campus. We drove along Ocean Boulevard towards the pier. I stared, fixated on the enormous Ferris wheel, with flashing colored lights.

"That's beautiful!" I breathed. "And the lights are even more spectacular because there's just black behind it."

"I thought we could walk around on the pier and then maybe go sit on the beach," Jeff offered.

"That sounds very romantic. It might be kind of cold to sit on the beach though, no?"

"What are you? French?" Jeff joked.

I punched him playfully in the arm.

"I have a blanket in the back."

"Convenient. Must come in handy for beach dates a lot."

"Hey now!" Jeff objected. "I'll have you know I just bought that blanket this afternoon for this particular date!"

"I see," was my only reply. I was satisfied.

We parked in a big concrete parking garage that was dingy looking and the stairway smelled like urine. But I didn't care. I was walking on air, hand-in-hand with this gorgeous specimen of a human being. We walked passed restaurants and store fronts, commenting on possible venues for future dates.

We walked onto the pier, which housed this permanent carnival. We went into the ancient arcade and laughed at ourselves playing Dance Dance Revolution. Jeff climbed this swiveling rope ladder to try to win me a stuffed animal, but it flipped him upside down and he fell off. I won a very small stuffed panda bear, shooting a water gun at a moving target. And we topped off our night at the pier with a ride on the Ferris wheel.

"Stop swinging the bucket!" I demanded. Jeff laughed and swung it more.

The whole night, I felt like I was in a dream. It was the way I used to feel when I was with Eric. I wanted to tell the whole world, "He's all *mine*! Who's a rock star?"

Finally, we walked down the sandy steps of the pier onto the beach. The sand was freezing between our toes. We walked, hand in hand until there was no longer anyone within yelling distance of us.

"Want to sit?" Jeff asked.

I nodded.

He spread the thick, flannel blanket on the sand and we sat down. The wind whipped playfully through our hair, and the waves crashed insistently before us. The stars dodged in and out of the clouds floating above. We looked up quietly for awhile. Then we started making out. Jeff's lips were warm and soft on mine. He ran his fingers through my hair and behind my neck. Slowly, he laid me down on my back and positioned his body over mine.

He slid his hand up my leg. I was wearing jeans, but I could feel his touch acutely. After a few moments, his strong hand was alternately massaging the inside of both thighs and everything in between. I was miserably conflicted at this point. It was a delicious sensation and I wanted to see what would happen next. But at the back of my mind, my well-bred conscience was yelling with increasing frequency. *You're too young to be pregnant! Stop him right this second, Young Lady.*

I gave into Chastity. Playfully, I pushed back on Jeff, so he fell onto his elbows and I let myself fall top of him.

"I like it with you on top!" he joked.

I gave a nervous laugh.

We continued to make out. Either he got the hint or he already knew his boundaries because he didn't go any further than that, to my relief. We wound up staring at the stars for what seemed like hours before heading back to campus. It was a lovely evening.

16 "Experiment with Sex"

I got sexiled for the first time on Thursday of Week 2. It was a rare rainy day in Southern California and it seemed like the entire UCLA student population had crowded into Ackerman for lunch to get out of the rain. Sarah had commandeered a table for us. Sean, Chris, Sarah and I sat eating our Mexican food and observing the widespread devastation caused by the rain.

"Yeah, you SoCal people don't know how to deal with the rain," Sarah noted. "Everyone looks about as happy as a herd of wet cats!"

"I can't believe it rained!" I cried, indignant that the heavens had the gall to pull a fast one on me this morning. I'd been caught off guard when it started to rain about ten minutes into my walk to campus. It was too late to turn back for an umbrella. So I was condemned to sitting in wet jeans through classes all morning. My legs were cold and clammy.

"Seriously, who thinks to check the weather?" Chris said. He was in the same predicament. His usually well coifed hair stuck limply to his forehead.

"You are all hella spoiled down here," Sarah continued. "Back home, we check the weather every day."

"Aw, you're just *hella* jealous," Sean said, mocking Sarah's NorCal lingo. "You just wish it could be 76 and sunny every single day!"

"Actually, I don't!" Sarah retorted. "I like some variety in life, even in the weather."

"Hey, Autumn said that you and that frat guy are a thing now," Sean said to me, across the table.

How did she get a hold of these things?

"Officially?" Sarah asked, a big smile erupting on her face.

"Yeah," I admitted. "We're exclusive now."

"Amy and frat boy sitting in a tree," Chris started. I rolled my eyes at him, but couldn't help laughing.

"That's awesome!" Sarah said. "It's about time. And he's a cutie."

"Well, he's *alright*, if you can't have me," Sean said. We all groaned.

"Listen, I have an idea for what we should do after lunch!" Sean said, showing an uncharacteristic level of excitement.

306

"Huh-uh!" I preempted him, shaking my head. "I'm going straight home to change into some dry clothes."

"It will just take a few minutes!" Sean insisted. "It's going to be fun!"

"OK, what is it?" I asked, curiosity getting the best of me again.

"Well," Sean said, lowering his voice. We all leaned in so we could hear him. "There's this metal grate thing on the ground out behind the Coop. I guess it must lead to some underground storage or something. But this morning, I saw three people slip on it and fall on their asses."

I waited for the clever idea. But he looked like he was finished and took a bite of his burrito.

"And?" Sarah asked, echoing my thoughts. He looked at her like she was an idiot.

"And we should go out there and watch people fall on their asses!" Sean said, as if it were obvious. Sarah and I looked at each other. Chris shared Sean's enthusiasm.

"Hell yeah!" Chris yelled.

"I think it sounds juvenile!" Sarah cried.

"Well, Miss Holier-than-Thou," Sean said. "Do you have any better ideas?"

Sarah shrugged. After lunch, we followed Sean down the stairs, and out of the Coop. The rain was pouring down in sheets and I was chilled to the bone. Sean pointed out the metal cover on the ground, which I'd passed countless times before but never really noticed. It wasn't really a grate. It was a flat sheet of metal with a pattern of raised chevrons on it. The kind you see in cities just above underground storage. We crossed the street and hid under the overhang of the mathematics building. From there, we had a clear line of sight to the grate.

It didn't take long. Our first victim was an unsuspecting fellow in jeans and a hoodie. He'd pulled his hood over his head and shoved his hands in his kangaroo pouch. The second he set foot on the grate, he slipped, both legs came up from under him and he fell, SMACK, on his ass. He sat there, stunned for a minute. Then he looked around, embarrassed, got up and walked away.

Sarah and I looked at one another, pained that we should be party to laughing at other people's misery. Sean and Chris were doubled over, laughing.

"Come on," Chris gasped, slapping me on the back. "Have a sense of humor!"

But try as I might, I couldn't find anything funny about it.

"Wait, wait," Sean cried. "Here comes another one. This one looks like a professor!"

I turned around and saw Professor Brenner, my Anthro professor from last quarter, heading straight for the grate. My conscience overtook me. I ran out from under the overhang, yelling, "Professor Brenner! Professor Brenner!"

He stopped right before he stepped on the grate to look at me.

"Hi there!" he said. Couldn't remember my name, I noted. "How can I help you?"

"I...uh..." I gasped, searching for an excuse that would befit my running out in the downpour like an idiot without an umbrella. "I... uh... wanted to know what you thought of my paper from last quarter. I wrote about the treatment of women and... err... relationships..."

"...in cultures represented in literary works," he said, finishing my sentence. I was pleased that he remembered it. I waited for the verdict.

"I found it to be very well written," he said. "I didn't agree with every assertion you made. But overall, I thought it was quite good."

I beamed. Right behind me, I heard a crash and saw that the grate had claimed another unsuspecting victim. This time, it was a small Asian girl, who looked both embarrassed and flustered.

"Are you alright?" I cried, holding out my hand to help her up. Across the street, I could hear Chris and Sean howling with laughter. Professor Brenner turned and saw them across the street.

"Frat boys," he muttered darkly, shaking his head. "Someone should teach them a lesson..."

After I helped the poor Asian girl get back on her way, Professor Brenner took his leave of me. Sarah ran out from under the overhang towards me. I waited for her to catch up, so I could get under her umbrella and then we started walking back towards the dorms.

"That was ridiculous," she said. "Of all the stupid things...."

We heard another crash behind us and more laughter. I rolled my eyes.

"Seriously!" I concurred. "They'll never grow up!"

We walked slowly back to the dorms. Sarah and I parted ways at the top of the stairs and I headed towards my room. Initially, I thought I was the first one back because we usually left the door open if someone was in, unless we were sleeping. As I got closer, I noticed a white scrunchie on the doorknob. I found it peculiar, but didn't really get the picture until I inserted my key into the keyhole and heard the bunk bed through the door.

"SKEE SKAW... SKEE SKAW..."

A horrible thought crossed my mind. I listened more closely and heard Casey saying, "Yeah, baby" over and over again.

My stomach turned and I put my hand over my mouth, as I doubled over in disgust. In our room!? Did she *have* to?! And today of all days! Here I was, cold and wet, dripping rainwater all over the carpet and she was having sex in our room. I half wanted to just barge in there and embarrass her. But then again, I wasn't sure I was prepared to face the psychological consequences of that. I turned on my heel and walked down the hall to Sarah's room.

She had just put her backpack down and was booting up her computer. She saw me in the doorway and motioned me to come in.

"What's wrong?" she asked. "Did you see a rat or something?"

"Worse!" I cried. "I've been... sexiled!"

"Casey's got a guy in there?" Sarah asked, disbelieving. "That's horrible! You need to get in there and change before you freeze to death!"

"I know!" I exclaimed. She handed me her bathrobe, but I shook my head. I didn't want to get it dirty.

"Want me to go down there and break it up?" Sarah asked. I knew she would do it too. It didn't seem like Sarah was afraid of anything.

"I'm giving them twenty minutes to wrap it up," I said. "That's fair, right? I guess she has a right to privacy once in awhile. Do you and Amanda give each other privacy?"

"We post our class schedules on the door. We take our private time when the other person is in class," Sarah said matter-of-factly. "But I think when both people are out of class, they have equal right to the room. I'll totally go down there and bang on the door."

"I know you will," I said hastily. "And I really appreciate it, but I don't want to alienate Casey too much. She and Erin already don't get along and I don't want to get mixed into all that." I didn't want to admit out loud that some part of me was still in awe of her and still wanted her to like me.

"You're too nice," Sarah said. "I'd go in there and raise hell. I think you have it backwards. Who is alienating who right now?"

"Twenty minutes," I repeated, trying to sound firm about it. "Do you mind if I hang out in here for twenty minutes?"

Sarah shrugged. "Naw, suit yourself."

I swung my backpack down to the floor and pulled out my brand new physics book. The pages were beginning to get wavy from the rain that had seeped into my backpack. I opened it up to the first chapter and began to read. Sarah turned back to her computer and started checking her email.

My mind began wandering, even as I tried to focus on physics. Was I mad because I was cold and wet and Casey had picked an inconvenient time to lock me out? Or because I was disgusted she was having sex and putting me in a position where I had to think about that? Or because I felt like it was as much my room as her room and she was not treating it that way. Perhaps it was all of the above.

Sex. Did *I* want to have sex? How was I supposed to know? It's like being forced to choose a major when you don't know anything about it. Casey seemed to think it was the greatest thing after double chocolate white chocolate cookies at Kookie King . But after what happened to Erin and reading about women who didn't think it was all that pleasant, I had enough doubts to keep my curiosity in check. The question was: for how long?

Sarah interrupted my thoughts.

"It's been twenty minutes," she announced, looking eager to see what I'd do next. I put my physics book back in my backpack and stood up.

"I'm goin' in!" I said, like John Wayne did in the old Westerns.

"Alright," Sarah said, playing the part of Mississippi. "If you don't come out in thirty minutes, I'm goin' in after ya."

Her laughter gave me strength. I walked back to my room and the door was open. Casey was fully dressed, brushing her hair.

"Hi Amy!" she said as if nothing had happened. "How was your day?"

I guess she hadn't needed all of twenty minutes.

"Fine," I replied, trying to act as if nothing happened myself. "I didn't bring an umbrella to campus, so I got soaked on the way in."

"That's not good," Casey exclaimed. "You should change out of those clothes!"

"I think I will," I said cordially. I shut the door and changed into a sweat shirt and flannel pajama pants. I felt much better, though I was still mildly peeved at her. "Did you have a good day?" I asked.

"Fine. Didn't feel like going to class, so I stuck around here all day."

"Everything alright?" I asked, more to be polite than because I really cared. After all, she hadn't cared that I might want to come into our room after sitting in cold, wet jeans all day. Casey looked at me in the mirror and frowned, still brushing her hair.

"My period's late," she said.

"What?" I asked, thinking I'd heard wrong.

"Period's late. Makes me kind of nervous." I didn't know why she was telling me this.

"I thought you were on the Pill."

"I am. But accidents happen. Listen, will you come with me to Hilltop to buy a pregnancy test? I don't want to go by myself."

We put on our raincoats to walk out to Hilltop, the convenience store

310

nestled at the base of multiple dorms. We walked in silence down the stairs and out the doors of Sproul. The rain had stopped. In fact, the sun was fighting its way through the clouds. The question of sex was still top of my mind, especially in light of this recent development.

"Do you ever wish you were still a virgin?" I blurted out in spite of myself.

Casey stopped dead in her tracks and looked at me with a disdain I'd never seen before. "Are you judging me?"

"No! Not at all. I'm honestly just wondering... I think I may have to make the decision myself soon... is all."

Casey didn't look entirely convinced, but she turned and we resumed our walking. "You don't make that decision once. If you decide not to do it, you're going to have to make it over and over and over and over, and eventually it's going to wear you down," she said, as if recalling an arduous journey.

"It doesn't seem to be that hard for everybody. You know, to choose to be a virgin."

"It's easy to be a virgin if no one wants to sleep with you. I never understood why *some* girls act all proud of being virgins. If no one ever wanted to sleep with them, they didn't make any hard decision. The decision was made for them."

"So you're saying it's a greater feat when someone is *attractive* and a virgin," I repeated.

"Isn't it obvious? If you're attractive, your virginity doesn't stand a chance in college. Everyone on TV is doing it, your friends are doing it, the hot guy that you really like wants you to do it, your parents *don't* want you to do it... it's totally a recipe for losing your virginity."

"There are some attractive girls that are holding out! There are all these abstinence clubs, campaigns and stuff. I've seen them on TV."

"Wait until temptation hits. It's always the same story. You make up your mind that you're not going to do it until you get married. Then you see everyone doing it all around you. So you decide it's not so bad, but you want to wait until you find the perfect person."

I slowed unconsciously because I felt like I fit this description. Casey motioned me to hurry up.

"But then, you figure out that the perfect person doesn't exist, so you decide to settle for someone that loves you. If you can really keep to that, you're *already* doing pretty good. Before that point, most people figure out that love and sex have nothing to do with one other- at least from the guys' perspective. Or, they just figure out that sex is fun. Either way, they wind up where I am."

311

"Buying a pregnancy test," I finished, my mind still processing the pessimistic progression.

Casey stopped dead in her tracks again and gave me a look that would make babies cry. "Girlfriend, are you *judging* me?"

"Sorry!" I squeaked, holding both hands up. "Sorry! I wasn't judging you!"

Casey went straight to the aisle with the pregnancy tests and grabbed one marked with a "2 for the Price of 1" sticker. She also grabbed a pack of maxi pads and a notebook.

We left Hilltop as quickly as we'd arrived.

"I'm glad we didn't bump into anyone in there," Casey said, looking relieved, but still walking quickly. "Thanks for coming with me."

"You're welcome," I replied, shrugging.

"You're too damn nice," Casey said, looking at me as if she pitied me somehow.

"You're the second person who's told me that today," I informed her, not bothering to explain about the first one. "So do you ever wish you were still a virgin?"

"What's the point?" she asked, that hardened look coming back on her face. "I can't take it back."

*****

Friday, I floated through the day. I could scarcely focus in lecture. I had finally found someone that could make me forget Eric. I was as giddy as a little kid. In my mind, I kept playing the evening over again. I couldn't wait for the weekend, so I could spend more time with Jeff.

At 2pm, I met up with Erin at the statue of the Bruin Bear. We walked home together. Since her breakdown after Thanksgiving, Erin and I had become much closer.

"It's so weird to walk home when the sun is still up!" I commented, marveling at how blithe campus was in the afternoon.

"Oh yeah," Erin smiled. "You usually stay until dinnertime."

"Yeah, I think I work better in the library."

"Do you mind if we walk fast?" Erin asked. "I need to get on my computer and send my pseudocode to my TA before he leaves for the weekend."

"No problem," I said. "What's pseudocode?"

"You know how you write an outline before you write a paper?" she explained. "For computer programmers, pseudocode is the plan for the program before you actually write it."

I nodded, but was still confused.

"How was your night with Jeff last night? You must have gotten home late. I didn't even hear you come in!"

I sighed dreamily. "It was amazing! We went out to Beverly Hills and had this delicious prime rib dinner. Then we drove out to Malibu and watched the sunset."

"Wow! What a romantic! It used to be a good date if I could get my boyfriend to stop playing video games long enough to look at me. What are you going to do this weekend?"

I shrugged. "Who knows. But he's such a good planner, I think I'll let him plan it."

We had entered Sproul and climbed the stairs two at a time.

"Leave some time for the rest of us!" Erin complained. "We miss you at girls' night."

"Oh, you're attending now?"

"Yeah. I decided after I talked to you about that thing with Jim that I needed to have a few more close girlfriends."

"Chicks before dicks," I said, quoting Casey, and we both laughed.

As we approached our room, we heard the skee-skawing of the bunk bed again. Erin looked at me quizzically, but as we got closer and could hear Casey's moans mixed in with the bunk bed, a look of understanding replaced the confused expression. We stopped before the door.

"What should we do?" I whispered to Erin.

"I'm going in there!" Erin declared. "I've got to send this code out to my TA or he won't get a chance to look at it before the weekend and I'm hosed."

"Right now?" I whispered, dreading the confrontation.

"It's *our* room too."

Erin banged on the door. The skee-skawing stopped.

"Casey, open up!" Erin yelled through the door. "I need my computer *right now!*"

"Erin, is that you?" Casey called out. Anxiety lent an edge to her voice.

"Yes it's me. Open the damn door!"

She slapped the door for emphasis. I looked at her in awe. I had no idea she was capable of yelling.

"Can you come back in ten minutes?" Casey asked.

"No! I need it *right now.* I'm going to stand right here until you let me

313

in!"

We heard her squeaking around on the bunk bed, then we heard two people jump down and hit the floor. There was some more scuffling and I presumed they were putting their clothes back on. After a minute, a very red-faced Casey opened the door.

When she saw me standing there with Erin, a look of horror spread across her face. Erin pushed her way into the room and I heard her gasp. Casey tried to block my view into the room, but I ducked under her arm. And that's when I came face to face with Jeff, sitting on Casey's chair in his boxers.

I looked from Jeff to Casey and back again, not comprehending. After a moment of tense silence, they both started talking at once.

I didn't want to hear it, any of it.

I backed out of the room, then turned and walked down the hallway. I didn't know where I to go. Anywhere I went, I might see someone that I didn't want to face at this moment. The last thing I could stand was Sean's taunting or Brian's pity. I just wanted to be alone. But where could one be alone on a campus of 30,000 on Friday of Week 2?

Suddenly I walked with greater purpose. Where else? The library.

Campus, which had previously seemed so merry, now seemed to be mocking me. Throngs of students were walking up the hill back to the dorms, talking, laughing and looking forward to the upcoming weekend. Some glanced at me, bewildered, wondering who in their right mind would be walking to campus on a Friday afternoon. I was now well versed in ignoring people's stares. I hurried. Destination: isolation.

I ran up the steps through the grand doors. Instead of turning downward towards the stacks, where I studied, I walked up the ancient looking clay steps toward the great octagonal room, beneath Powell's famous dome. There, I found refuge in a cushioned chair, facing a window. I flung myself into the chair and tried to calm my breathing.

Don't cry, I told myself. There didn't seem to be any danger of it yet. During the fifteen minute walk back to campus, the feeling of being punched in the stomach gave way to a slow burning rage that made me smart all over. I didn't know which betrayal was worse. His or hers.

A million questions needed to be answered in order for me to understand what had just happened. Had he been playing me right from the start? Maybe he only told me that we were being exclusive so that he could get in my pants. Or maybe he had meant to be exclusive until he discovered that he probably wouldn't be getting any action anytime soon. Then he turned to Casey. Who seduced whom and when had this started? They had gone to Jeff's Halloween party together. Maybe it had started then. How could she look me in the eye every day, knowing that he was cheating on me with her?

Part of this was my fault. Kicking my backpack in frustration, I wondered how I had been so naïve. I might have seen this coming if I hadn't been so busy trying to be Jeff's girlfriend. If I hadn't been so boy crazy, I might have been more skeptical when Jeff had changed his tune about being exclusive with me. Maybe I had slighted Casey. Perhaps she wouldn't have fooled around with him if I hadn't antagonized her last quarter.

The worst part about it was how much time I had spent admiring them both last quarter. What a phenomenal waste of time! Just the thought of it seemed revolting to me now.

I continued to sit there as the shadows lengthened and the library grew quieter. The rage began to ebb slightly, making room for feeling like an idiot, which then gave way to sadness. I stared out the window, determined not to budge. I wondered if anyone missed me yet. I thought about calling Lauren, but I didn't feel like leaving the safety of the library yet.

In spite of my sulking (or maybe because of it), an idea began to form in my mind for another newspaper article. A short op ed piece on roommate courtesy in college. I opened my notebook to a fresh sheet of paper and began to write, pushing down on my pen so hard that I was engraving the words into my notebook paper.

"I find that the roommate contracts we wrote up with our RAs at the start of the school year are useless. If the purpose of a roommate contract is to keep the peace amongst roommates, then ours has failed us miserably. I'm glad that none of us smokes and that we've agreed not to play loud music after midnight. I suppose it's good that we don't leave food lying around for more than a day. But I feel like our roommate contract is still conspicuously mum about certain other contentious issues. I would make the following additions to ours.

- I will not sleep with my roommate's boyfriend, even if he is a sweet talking frat boy.

- I will not lock my roommates out under any circumstance, sex included, because when they are not in class, they have as much right to the room as I do.

- I will wash or remove anything of mine that emits an odor (like smoke-infused clothing or vomit) in a timely manner, acknowledging that my maid did not come to college with me.

- I will not borrow my roommates' things without asking first (like laundry quarters), and will replace them immediately after usage.

- I will not talk on the phone, play music or allow other people to enter my room if either of my roommates is sleeping or studying.

- I will confine my belongings to my designated areas of the room.

- If my roommate asks me to pick my things up off the floor so she can vacuum, I will comply and be grateful that she offered to clean.

· I will turn set my alarm clock for when I actually want to get up, then get up and turn it off after it goes off once. Furthermore, I will turn off my alarm clock when I go away on weekends or for vacation.

It's too bad that these have to be added to our roommate contract. I came to college naively thinking that most educated people were brought up to observe a certain level of consideration for others. But I have found that there are some in this college community that fall far short of the standard, my roommate being one of them."

I felt better after listing out all of my grievances. By this point, it was dark outside and I could see the poor kids stuck with late afternoon Friday classes scurrying back towards the dorms.

My cell phone vibrated in my jean pocket. I pulled it out and saw that it was Erin.

"Hello?" I whispered.

"Amy, where are you?"

"I'm in the library."

"Oh. Are you alright?"

"Eh," I responded, not quite sure myself.

"Will you come back for dinner?"

"Is *she* there?"

"No, Jeff and Casey left right after you left. No one else knows anything about it."

Jeff and Casey... their names together stung.

"OK, I'll come back for dinner," I sighed, packing up my things.

I was much calmer on the way back up to the dorms. My game plan was to let Jeff and Casey know how I felt about the situation. If they didn't show adequate remorse, I would go to the *Daily Bruin* with this op ed. I was not a revenge seeking person and I knew I should probably be mature about it and just let it go. But I couldn't for some reason. The hurt was too deep and I couldn't even stand the thought of letting them off easy. If the article didn't get published, I could just post it on our bedroom door so that the hallway would know. Some kind of punishment was in order.

Dinner was uneventful. I tried to act normal. Sarah dominated the conversation, ranting about TJ Collins, the three-point powerhouse on the UCLA men's basketball team. Apparently, he was in her sociology class and it was just sickening the way the professor (and the girls in the class) doted on him. She was up in arms about the privileges that the NCAA athletes were getting, from priority housing and registration to scholarships and other "perks."

"You know something is wrong when the athletes are getting better treatment than the scholars," she finished.

I nodded and took a big bite of my spinach rustica pizza. Usually one of my favorites, it tasted like sand tonight. I caught Erin looking at me and I looked away.

"It's not easy to be an athlete, you know," Sean told Sarah.

"I *know*, I *am* an athlete," Sarah responded. "I didn't say it was easy- I just don't think that athletics should be prized above academics. No, it's not even athletics, it's entertainment! To us, these athletes are entertainment!"

Chris was indignant. "They're not entertainment! We have pride in them! They represent us. They are our heroes!"

"Listen to yourself," Sarah cried. "You idolize them. Why don't you idolize the valedictorian of your high school the way you idolize TJ Collins?"

"There are lots of valedictorians here, but only *one* TJ Collins," Chris replied.

"You're not making an effective argument," Sarah said. "I could respond by saying there are lots of basketball players, but only *one* Erin Chen."

Erin beamed. She was very proud of being the valedictorian at her school. I lost track of the argument after that, as I began to think about what I was going to say to Casey.

I didn't have to wait long to say it either. She was waiting for me in our room when we returned from dinner. I walked into the room without looking at her and turned on my laptop.

"Amy, I need to talk to you," she said, in a voice that was both proud and pleading. "Alone," she added, glancing at Erin.

"Anything you say to me you can say with Erin here," I said

"Fine. Look, I'm sorry you had to find out this way…"

"You're sorry I had to find out or you're sorry you did it?" I asked harshly, interrupting her. "They're two totally different things."

To my surprise, Casey considered the question carefully, holding her golden head high. "I'd be lying if I said I was sorry that I slept with him. I'm sorry that you had to find out."

"What sort of apology was that?!" Erin cried from the peanut gallery. Casey and I both silenced her with a look.

"What do you mean?" I asked. "You're not sorry that you slept with my boyfriend?"

"First of, I didn't know he was your boyfriend. I knew you guys were

317

dating, but neither one of you said you were exclusively dating."

"That's just semantics! You knew I had a thing for him. Don't you think it would have bothered me just for that reason?"

"Well, I didn't think you'd find out! And if you didn't find out and you two didn't explicitly make it known that you were exclusively dating, then I didn't see anything wrong with getting involved with him."

"I can't believe he didn't tell you!" I cried.

"Not only did he not tell me. *He* came on to *me*. So he's not someone you want to be dating anyhow."

"That's irrelevant. If this incident had never happened, I'd still be dating him."

"Until you found out about him and some other girl," Casey pointed out.

I was so mad, I wanted to scream. I balled my hands into fists to contain myself.

"Case, I'm upset because I feel like both of you cheated on me," I found myself saying, trying to stop my voice from shaking. "How could you sleep with him if you knew that I liked him?"

She finally looked down and remained silent, her lithe arms, hanging at her sides.

"How could you betray me like this? How could you get involved with him and look me in the eye every day? How could you do something that you know might cause me pain?"

She looked at me with an expression that could have been apologetic or self-pitying. "My Dad cheated on my Mom when I was little. And she thought the same things as you. But then she realized that he still loved her. She realized that love and sex are not always related."

That was the third time I had heard her allude to this separation of love and sex. What was this all about?

"I had a little fun with your man," she continued, her voice quivering. "But I didn't have any feelings for him, and he didn't have any feelings for me. It was *just sex*. He likes you a lot. Maybe you should think about being open-minded and quit being so straight-laced."

I was dumbfounded. This was not the way I had expected the conversation to go.

She began packing her toiletries in her messenger bag.

"Open-minded?" I cried, jumping out of my seat and standing in front of Casey. "I *am* open-minded! Do you know how many times I *haven't* yelled at you for being an ass to Erin and me? Being open-minded doesn't mean excusing anything because someone, somewhere can justify it with twisted

318

logic."

Casey didn't look up, but continued packing. "Being open minded means accepting an idea that isn't mainstream or what's comfortable to you," she muttered, turning to walk out the door. "Besides, I have a right to have sex in my own room."

"It's not your room! It's *our* room! And we have a right to not be sexiled out of our own room. Maybe you should think about being considerate!" I yelled at her, my patience finally running thin. "Being considerate means taking into account someone else's feelings besides your own! Screw being open-minded! I have principles!"

"I'm going to the sorority house, where I won't be judged" she said under her breath, on her way out the door.

"Fine, *don't* take responsibility for any of your actions!" I yelled after her. I kicked the door shut behind her. The door slammed with a satisfying "Bang!".

I looked at Erin, who stood silently, blinking back at me. "She has issues," she said, shaking her head.

"How does that make any sense?" I asked, throwing my hands up into the air. I could feel tears smarting in my eyes, but I wouldn't let them fall. "Her Dad cheated on her Mom, so now it's ok to cheat on someone? I'd like to know how any rational person could come to that conclusion."

"Maybe she had to. I mean she had to choose between two scenarios. If she was convinced that love and sex were tied, then she would have to accept that her Dad didn't love her Mom anymore."

I could see what Erin was getting at.

"Maybe she's *still* convincing herself."

Erin nodded.

I got on my computer and began typing out my Op Ed. I didn't even care. I just hit "send" without looking it over.

*****

The next day, I was working my Saturday morning shift at the bookstore when the guy Matt I'd met at the *Daily Bruin* last quarter came up to the register with an anthology of Civil War era short stories.

"Amy!" he said, looking as if he hadn't thought of me in ages. "How are you?"

"I'm alright. Yourself?"

"Great!" he said, as he watched me fiddle with the cash register. It was giving me strange error messages. "Written anything lately?"

"Yeah," I said, looking confused as I manually entered in the price of the book. "I sent John something yesterday. Didn't he mention it?"

Matt shook his head.

"John who? I don't know if we have a John on our staff this year," he said, as he got out his wallet and dug around. He handed me a twenty, and as I got his change together, he wrote an email address on a post it sitting by the cash register and handed it to me.

"Send it to me again," he said, looking perplexed. "I'll ask around the office to see if anyone got it, but just send it again."

"Thanks," I replied, grateful that he was taking my writing more seriously than he had before. "Have a great day, Matt. Next!"

That evening, after dinner and after I'd sent my article to Matt, Casey returned to the room. When I saw that it was her, I turned back to my computer screen and ignored her.

Erin's gasp caused me to turn back around and take a closer look at her. Casey was covered in a bright red, splotchy rash. There were patches on her arms that had even begun to blister and ooze liquid. These were criss-crossed by long scarlet tracks, where she had been scratching herself.

"What happened to *you*?" I asked, so horrified, I momentarily forgot my anger.

"I don't know," Casey replied, through clenched teeth, throwing her things down. "I itch all over and now it's starting to burn."

"Did you go to the medical center?" Erin asked.

"No, they'd probably make me wait ten years," Casey said, with exasperation. "I called my parents and they're coming to pick me up. I'm going to see my family doctor right now."

"Maybe Sarah will know what it is," I suggested, trying to be hopeful. "She's pre-med."

Casey was preoccupied with scratching, so I ran down the hall to Sarah's room.

"Sarah, Casey's got a rash and I thought you might know what it is," I said urgently. Sarah got out of her chair and came back with me to my room.

"I'm not in med school *yet*," she reminded me, as we walked down the hall.

"I know," I said. "It can't hurt to look."

Sarah looked a reluctant Casey over.

"It looks like poison ivy," Sarah said, uncertainly. "Did you go hiking or running somewhere?"

"No," Casey replied. "I slept at the sorority house last night and just went to class today."

"Holy crap, what happened to *you*?" Autumn asked, peeking into our room.

"Nothing!" snapped Casey. "I'm not the goddam freak show at a circus."

"Jeez, sorry!" Autumn said, ducking back out of our room.

Casey's cell phone rang.

"Oh thank God!" she said into the phone. "I'll be right down."

She grabbed her purse and left.

Erin, Sarah and I looked at each other.

"Weird," Sarah said. I shrugged.

Sean walked into the room. "What's wrong with Miss America?" he asked, jerking his thumb over his shoulder at the door.

"Don't know," Erin said. "She's going to see a doctor about it right now."

"She seems pretty cranky," Sean said.

"Well, she itches all over," Sarah piped up.

Sean laughed. "Did some venereal disease finally catch up with her?"

"No," Sarah replied. "I think it's poison ivy."

"I'm going to tell Autumn it's a VD," Sean said. "That's better than publishing it in the *Bruin*."

"Don't!" Erin cried, giggling in spite of herself. "You're terrible!"

Sean grinned."Who wants to go to Westwood?"

Erin shook her head. "Nah, I have a lot of work to do."

"Where do you want to go?" Sarah asked.

Sean shrugged. "I dunno. There aren't any good movies out right now. Maybe we could just go to Kookie King or coffee or something."

"OK," Sarah replied. "I'll go get my wallet."

"You?" Sean asked, looking at me.

"I'm not feeling all that chipper tonight."

"Wow, you and everyone else," Sean said.

"Why? Who else isn't feeling chipper?" I asked, curious. After all, misery loves company, right?

Sean lowered his voice, in a move that was surprisingly tactful. "I think Brian and Heather broke up," he whispered, glancing over his shoulder. "He's been a total downer for the last couple days. They talked for, like, three hours

321

on Wednesday and they haven't talked since. And he's been all sad and shit."

"Is he ok?" I asked.

"Eh," Sean said indifferently. "He'll be fine. I think he doesn't want to talk about it."

That, I could understand. I didn't want to talk about my predicament either.

"So are you coming?" Sean asked.

"Yeah, I guess," I glanced at Erin, who was hard at work. If I stayed here, I would only distract her. Arming myself with my wallet and a sweatshirt, I set out with stepped out into the hallway.

"Erin, do you want anything from Westwood?"

She shook her head without looking up.

"OK, let's go," I said to Sean. We met Sarah and Chris in the hallway and headed out into the brisk night.

"How come Erin never comes out with us?" Sean asked.

"Yeah! I've noticed that too!" Sarah said.

"She told me once that she just didn't like going out," I said, shrugging. My breath became visible as I quickened my pace to keep up with the rest of the group. There were not many people out tonight.

"But it's not like she's not social," Sarah pointed out. "I mean, she's totally outspoken when we're at dinner and stuff."

"Yeah, I don't think it has anything to do with being antisocial," I replied, trying focus on the conversation. "I think she likes spending time with us. But I think that maybe she just feels guilty about going out when she has a lot of work to do."

"She *does* have a lot of work to do," Chris echoed. "Every time I go in there, she's working."

I nodded. "She's really serious about her classes. It sounds like the EE curriculum is pretty brutal."

We had arrived at Kookie King and the sweet aroma of freshly baked cookies soothed my nerves.

17 "Make New Friends"

My op ed was published Monday morning, almost verbatim. I was sitting in lecture, thumbing through the *Daily Bruin*, hope diminishing with every flip of the page. But there it was, on page 17, looking positively alien in columns on the gray newsprint, but oh so beautiful. After a year of being the editor, I'd forgotten how thrilling it was to see my writing in print, following an eternity of uncertainty.

The only thing that had been changed was the order of the contract line items, which the editor inverted. I agreed with the correction. "I will not sleep with my roommate's boyfriend" definitely belonged at the end of the list. I wondered how many people would see it, way back on page 17. I wound up being surprised.

At lunch time, Sarah and Autumn ran up to me at Covel Commons dining hall, where I was trying to decide between a chicken sandwich and a hamburger. Each was trying to talk over the other.

"This is awesome!" Autumn cried, shaking her rolled up newspaper at me. "We talked about it for half of my communications discussion! Everyone totally agrees with you that our roommate contracts are a load of crap. One guy wants to start a website for his final project to help roommates draw up their contracts specific to them and stick with it."

"You have more guts than I thought!" Sarah said. She was more blunt than my friends back home, who would have left out that pronouncement. "Here I thought you were too nice. This is public humiliation at its best!"

I beamed, though I couldn't squash the little seed of guilt that was germinating at the pit of my stomach. I felt vindicated in a way. The world could feel my pain and somehow this made things better. And it had seemed like the fitting punishment for Casey when I hit "Send" on my email. But after a few days, especially in light of her poison ivy incident, I began to get the sinking feeling that I had overdone it.

"It's too bad you didn't put Jeff's name in the article," Autumn pointed out, disappointed that I'd missed this opportunity to create scandal.

"I know," I said.

Because my name was on the Op-Ed, it was very clear that the contract was aimed at Casey, but Jeff had gotten off easy.

"I couldn't really put his name in there. Part of the reason I wrote it was because I was mad at them, but part of the reason was also to get people to think about being considerate roommates and to encourage them to speak up if their roommates suck."

Autumn and Sarah nodded.

"Has Casey seen this yet?" Sarah asked. "She's going to *freak* out."

"I don't know," I shrugged. "I haven't seen her yet today."

"How are her rashes?" Autumn asked. "Did they ever figure out what it was?"

"Well," I said. "They found out it *was* poison ivy. They don't know how it got into the sorority house, but everyone who took a shower that night and the next morning got it. They're scrubbing the whole place down this weekend."

"I thought so," Sarah said.. "But which one of those girls would actually go out into the woods and get her nails dirty?"

"The weird thing is that no one had gone camping," I replied. "Somehow, it got on their bath towels."

"What?" cried Autumn nervously. "How did it get on their bath towels?"

"No one knows! Maybe it was in their laundry detergent?"

"They don't all do their laundry together," Sarah said. "And I'm sure Casey brought her own towel that night."

"That's true," I agreed, as we sat down at a table and started eating.

"Someone must have sabotaged them," Autumn said, shaking her head. "It's too weird to be an accident."

"Wow, the Greek system is having some trouble this year! The speaker exploded at that one frat and didn't some frat have a case of mass food poisoning last quarter?" Sarah asked, then took a big bite of pasta salad.

"Yeah, that was SIE," I replied, my mouth full as well. "That's Jeff's frat."

"Did they figure out how that happened or was it just an accident?" Autumn asked.

"No, campus safety never figured out exactly what happened," I replied carefully. I didn't want to incriminate Brandon, though now I began to wonder if he had anything to do with it. After he had overheard me talking recounting my Walk of Shame to my roommates, the food poisoning incident had occurred and he wouldn't deny that he had something to do with it. Maybe he had heard my argument with Casey somehow and decided to avenge me again. That was creepy. Definitely too creepy.

*****

After lunch, I had two hours, so I headed back to my room. There was a small bunch of daisies on my desk along with a note that was barely legible. Thinking it was from Jeff, I had a good mind to throw it all in the trash, but I looked carefully at the signature on the bottom. I could make out an "S".

S-e-a... I was stunned. It was from Sean. I read the note eagerly, mostly out of astronomical curiosity. It took me a few passes, but it read,

"No man is worth your tears because the one who is will never make you cry." I'm sorry the dude was a dickhead. Let me know if you want to talk. Don't worry about ulterior motives- you're not my type. -Sean"

I chuckled. It was so Sean. I looked up and saw him standing in the doorway.

"You good, Callaway?" His voice was gruff. I nodded, but new tears welled up. I was touched by this uncharacteristic display of loyalty and empathy right when I needed it. It reminded me of what was missing from Jeff.

"Thanks for... this," I said, jutting my chin towards the flowers. "This was really nice of you. I was totally surprised."

"Aw, girls seem to like this crap from their friends," he said, shrugging and looking awkward all of a sudden. Compassion was ill-fitting on him.

"You said boys and girls couldn't be friends," I reminded him, raising an eyebrow.

"I changed my mind," he said, looking down at his feet. "You're a good person. You make my existence better. See, it *is* selfish in the end."

I smiled half a smile.

"Come here," he demanded, opening his arms.

I walked into them and wiped my residual tears on his hoodie.

"Don't get any ideas, though," he said. "I mean it- you're not my type. I only date bitches."

I laughed into his shoulder.

"You're not mine either. Wait, maybe you are. Apparently I date assholes."

"And put that note away- I don't want anyone else to know that I'm a closet nice guy."

"Yes, sir. Your secret is safe with me."

He gave me a final squeeze and sauntered out of the room. I put the note away in my desk drawer and booted up my computer. There were two emails of interest in my Inbox. The first was from Matt.

From: "Matthew Baker" <mbaker@ucla.edu>
To: "Amy Callaway" <acallaway@ucla.edu>

Amy,

Great Op-Ed. We were all impressed/amused. We've been receiving a lot of responses to it. Here are a few of them.

Keep up the great work!
Matt

****

Amy,
Thanks for writing that article on roommate contracts. My roommate is really inconsiderate too. She talks on the phone really loud, she leaves her stuff all over the room and she never thinks about anyone but herself. Your article inspired me to have a talk with her.
Thanks again,
Claire
P.S. I'm sorry about your roommate and your boyfriend.

****

The Op-Ed piece on page 17 entitled "Rethinking Roommate Contracts" was inane. The author was whining about things that plague every roommate relationship. She needs to communicate with her roommate more and not try to hide behind a contract. It also sounds like she's puritanical. Learning to live with those things is part of growing up. It's life.

****

The author of "Rethinking Roommate Contracts" hit the nail right on the head. I've also observed a widespread lack of consideration on this campus. I think our society places a deluded emphasis on making yourself happy and many people forget that they need to function in a way that maximizes the happiness of all of the people around them as well. Kudos to the author. I hope it works out with her roommate.

I was delighted. Up until now, most of my writing had been journalistic in nature. I loved the thrill of being the reporter that broke the story. But that was always about facts. Since the first day of Anthropology, I became more interested in generating discussion and provoking thought. This was the first article I'd written to that end, and I was thrilled that it had the desired response. I was inspiring people. I was prompting discussion.

The second email came from Jeff.

From: "Jeffrey Lewis" <jlewis@ucla.edu>
To: "Amy Callaway" <acallaway@ucla.edu>

amy,

i read your article today and i felt really bad about what happened yesterday. i don't know why i did it. i like you a lot. i think i just got scared. i know i can't ask you to forgive me right now, but maybe some day you can.

call me,
jeff

Part of me wanted to run to him and make him take it back. Take it all back and make it better again. But deep down, I knew better than that. His email was not good enough. He was not good enough. He wasn't.

His email reminded me that I should go talk to Brandon about the poison ivy incident. I would deal with him when the danger of uncontrollable tears had passed.

I called their room first, to make sure that Brandon was in and Jeff wasn't.

"Ring... ring... ring...click."

"Hello?" A lugubrious voice answered. It was Brandon alright.

"Brandon, this is Amy," I said. "Listen, is Jeff there?"

"No," he replied, sounding mournful again.

"Good," I said. "I have to talk to you. I'm coming up."

Before he could respond, I hung up the phone, grabbed my keys and headed upstairs. If there was any connection between the food poisoning incident at Jeff's frat and the poison ivy incident at Casey's sorority, I was going to break the story. I was on a high right now, having just seen my work in print and I needed another fix soon. I wasn't sure what I was going to do if the link was Brandon.

I burst into his room. He looked pleased to see me. Creepy.

"Brandon," I said, choosing my words. "There was an incident at Casey's sorority two days ago."

"Who's Casey?" he asked to my surprise.

"Casey's my roommate." I looked at him strangely.

"Oh. Delta Sigma Phi?"

"You've heard about it?"

He shook his head. "What happened?"

"Wait a minute. How did you know it was Delta if you haven't heard about it?"

Brandon shrugged and looked down. Now I *knew* I was on to something.

"Did you have anything to do with it?" I asked, pointedly.

Brandon looked up at me with his pale blue eyes. "No."

"But you did have something to do with the food poisoning at SIE?" I clarified.

"Maybe."

I glared at him.

"OK, yes, I did," he replied, squirming under my gaze.

"What about the speaker incident at Beta Pi?" I asked.

He shook his head.

"How did you know something happened at Delta?" I asked, going into attack mode.

"Guessed," he replied, looking down again, his stringy black locks falling in front of his face.

"You're lying," I accused him, straight out.

"What happened at Delta?"

"They had poison ivy introduced into the house, All the girls who used their bath towels got it."

Brandon seemed to be working very hard to prevent himself from smiling.

"What do you know? Do you know who did this?"

"No," he replied, looking up at me again. "I don't know who did it."

"Brandon, you know something about this. I can tell. Why can't you just tell me what you know?"

"Because I just can't! I'd be betraying people if I did."

"You can't just keep attacking fraternities and sororities!"

"I'm not! I only had anything to do with that one. And why are you defending them anyway? You're not in one, right?"

"No, I'm not. But I have friends who are and they don't deserve to live in dread."

"They don't think about that when they're socially oppressing people," Brandon said.

"What?"

"You know," Brandon continued. "They ban together and make everyone else feel like they're outsiders. Like they're not worthy. I find that socially oppressive."

"But that's no reason to attack them!"

Brandon shrugged. "To each, her own."

Not being able to pry any more information from him, I returned to my room to puzzle over Brandon's response. He had been involved in the food poisoning at Jeff's fraternity. He had not been involved in the speaker explosion at Beta Pi or the poison ivy incident at Delta. But he knew that something happened at Delta, though he didn't know what. There was a group involved. Greek haters.

At dinner that night, conversation revolved around my article. I can't say I wasn't pleased. I didn't know whether it was the article or the fact that I broke the story of Casey and Jeff that was the bigger hit.

"Wouldn't it be cool if your article changed the way we do roommate contracts at UCLA?" Erin asked.

I shrugged. "It would be cool, but I don't think it's going to happen. Mostly, I just wanted people to think about whether or not their roommate situations are working out for them and get them to do something if they aren't."

"But what can someone do if it's not working out for them?" Chris asked.

"What are you saying?" Sean demanded. "You don't like living with me?"

"Yeah!" Chris said, getting into it. "You stink!"

"I do?" asked Sean. "What part of me stinks?"

"Aw! I'm not going to smell you and tell you what part!" Chris said, disgusted. "All of you! Whew!"

"Well, if *someone* didn't use up all my laundry detergent, then I might be able to wash things!" Sean retorted.

Sarah rolled her eyes. "Clearly, you guys need a copy of the article on your door."

"Yes," Sean said, with a mischievous gleam in his eye. "I need to be reminded not to sleep with Chris's boyfriends."

We all laughed.

"Have Casey or Jeff commented on your article yet?" Sarah asked.

"Jeff wrote an email saying he was sorry. I still haven't seen Casey yet. I don't know if she cares about the article. I think the poison ivy is keeping her pretty busy right now."

"That was a good way to get back at her!" Sean exclaimed, giving me a high five across the table. "Way to stick it to her!"

"The article or the poison ivy?" asked Chris.

"The article! I had nothing to do with the poison ivy!"

I noticed that Brian wasn't saying much tonight. He didn't look up from his food.

"What did you think of it, Brian?" I asked.

"Good." Then he looked down at his stir fry again. Something was eating him.

When we returned to our room, Casey was lying in bed, with her hands clasped together on her stomach, staring at the ceiling, looking pitiful. It was enough to *almost* make me feel bad for her. When we walked in the room, she turned to look at us.

"Amy," she said quietly. "I've decided that I'm sorry."

"Sorry for what?"

"Sorry for sleeping with him. I read your article and you were right. I was being inconsiderate... and selfish. I shouldn't have assumed you wouldn't find out."

The change was remarkable. Casey, queen of the world as she knew it, was finally humbled. I took some satisfaction in the apology. She hadn't lost all her spunk though.

A minute later, she said with more gusto, "Did you *have* to publish it in the *Daily Bruin* though? You could have just told me instead of humiliating me in front of the whole freaking world. I can't walk down this hallway anymore without everybody and their mother judging me."

I considered telling her that humiliating her was precisely the point, but I thought that might cause unnecessary rancor, so I approached it a different way.

"You were the inspiration for the article, but it had a bigger purpose," I explained. "I wanted people to think about their relationships with their roommates and how they could be improved. You were just an example."

"Great," was all she said. I rolled my eyes at Erin so that Casey couldn't see.

We heard a knock on the door, even though it was open. Brian was standing there, looking at me oddly.

"Amy, can I talk to you for a second?" he asked.

"Sure," I replied, puzzled. I followed him out of my room. He led me down the stairs and into Sproul's deserted computer lab. We sat down at a terminal.

"First of all, are you ok?" Brian asked, looking down at the carpet.

"What do you mean?"

"I mean, with the whole Casey and Jeff thing... are you ok?"

"Yeah, thanks for asking. I was really upset the first few days, but today the article got published so I'm stoked and ... they're both jerks, and I'm glad I found out sooner than later."

Brian nodded.

"Did you write that article?" Brian asked me, looking me straight in the eye.

"Of course I wrote the article!" I cried, insulted that he would think otherwise. "Who else would have written it?"

Brian looked slightly relieved. He typed a URL into the browser window. A page began to load that looked like some sort of online newsletter. The words "Why Society" were written across the top in elegant calligraphy. When it was finished loading, I saw my article right beneath the banner bar, framed with a border of black and white Celtic knots. The author's name was M. Reed. I noticed two other differences between the *Daily Bruin* version of my article and this one. Here, the original order of the line items was preserved and there were a short paragraph tacked on to the end of the article that I didn't recognize.

"Who's M. Reed?" I asked aloud.

"I thought you might know," Brian said. I shook my head.

"How did you find this?" I asked him.

"I wanted to send your article to some of my buddies, so I thought it might be on the *Daily Bruin*'s website," he explained. "But instead of going straight to the Daily Bruin's website, I got lazy and just typed the first few words into the search bar. This was one of the search results."

I sat back in my chair, at a total loss of words. Who could have done this? It was such blatant plagiarism, how could they expect to get away with it? I leaned forward and studied the page again.

"They posted this article yesterday," Brian pointed out, as if reading my mind. "It wasn't published in the paper until today."

"True," I said, worried for a split second. "But I've got the emails to prove that I sent this article out before it was posted on this website."

Brian looked satisfied. "I'm glad, Amy. I was worried that ...."

I gave him a look. "What? That *I* plagiarized? I'm insulted!"

"No, no. Well, the thought had crossed my mind. But I knew you wouldn't do it. I was more concerned about other people accusing you and I'm

331

glad you've got proof that you wrote it."

I looked closely at the paragraph added to the end of the article.

"'Society has become overrun with selfish hedonists with no regard for the thoughts and feelings of others. My opinion is that it is time to show them that their actions are not appreciated,'" I read out loud. "Those aren't my words."

"Why would someone rip off your article and then add stuff to it?" Brian thought aloud.

"What *is* this newsletter?" I asked, scrolling down and looking at other articles. Brian read along, over my shoulder. I felt the familiar flutter of butterflies in my stomach when I felt the heat emanating from his nearby body.

"It looks like some sort of anti-society page," he said. He was right. There were several articles about the failings of society, the oppression of the majority on the minority and the lack of celebration for individuality. My article had to be the least eloquent one on the page. The contributors were writers. Good ones, at that.

"They reversed the order of your list," Brian pointed out. "That's weird, isn't it?"

"Actually, this was the original order of the list as I wrote it," I said, starting to fit puzzle pieces together. "But who would have known that? Only Matt and ..."

My voice trailed off. Things were beginning to make sense. I first sent the article to the mysterious email address that I thought was the *Daily Bruin* office, but I had   received no confirmation that it was.

"Who else knew?"

"Well," I said slowly. " At the beginning of the year, I went to the *Daily Bruin* office and met this guy Matt, who gave me an email address that I could submit articles to. But it was just some generic one. I gave him my email address too."

I began talking rapidly as I gained confidence in my theory.

"Then later that day, I got an email from a gmail account, telling me that this was the better email address to send articles to. So I've been sending my article ideas and articles to *that* email address. But I've gotten nothing but rejections from that one. On Saturday, I ran into Matt and he told me to send it to his personal email address, and then the article got published. But now I'm wondering who owns this mysterious email address is that I've been sending things to."

"We have to find out who sent you that email."

"Is there any way to figure out who an email address belongs to?"

"I don't think so," Brian replied, frowning. "But you should ask Erin."

Erin was very helpful. We couldn't discover who owned the email account, but we could see what IP address the email came from. She opened up Linux and tinkered around on an ancient looking black and white interface.

"Here," she said, moving over in her seat. "Put in your username and password." I obediently sat next to her and typed in my information. When my email came up on the screen, I pointed to the rogue email message.

"That's the one," I said. Erin continued to tinker.

"It came from somewhere on campus," she said, finally. "This IP address belongs to UCLA, but it's not from a dorm. I can't tell much more than that."

"Thanks, Erin." Brian and I looked at each other, but neither one of us had any fresh ideas.

*****

The mysterious email address was on my mind all the time. I had a hard time focusing on class. The professors' words went in one ear and out the other. I was hoping that the notes on the board would be sufficient when I had time to go back and read them later. But I'd noticed that it doesn't ever work out quite like that.

The only thing I could think of was how I had asked Professor Barnard for an inside contact at the Daily Bruin on the first day of class. I approached him about this.

"Professor Barnard?" I asked after the rest of the class had filed out of the room.

"Ms. Callaway?" he replied, standing up straight and peering at me with steel-colored, unblinking eyes.

"Do you remember when I asked you for a contact at the *Daily Bruin* earlier this year?"

He shook his silver haired head. "I don't recall." He put on his blazer and continued to stare at me. "Remind me again."

"I said I wanted to write for the *Daily Bruin* and you said you'd see what you could do"

"No recollection of it," he told me, furrowing his bushy white brows together. "I don't know anyone at the *Daily Bruin*."

"I see," I replied, feeling sheepish. "Sorry for bothering you."

"It's not a bother at all. Ethan tells me that your writing has improved dramatically this term."

"Thank you, sir." I knew it was supposed to be a compliment, but the implication that I was a poor writer before I showed up here was enervating.

As I wandered out of the classroom, I got back to thinking about this mystery plagiarizer. If it wasn't a student in the dorms, who could it be? A student in the apartments would not have a university IP address. So it wasn't a student at all. It had to be a professor, a grad student or staff. Maybe it *was* someone on the *Daily Bruin* staff that was double crossing the paper! I rubbed my forehead wearily. The problem was that I had told *everybody* that I wanted to write for the *Daily Bruin* when I first got to school. It could be anyone.

I was the first one back to our dorm room. I sat down to my computer and pulled up a browser to check my email. Instead of the usual myUCLA portal, a page of plain text came up that said, "Server Could Not Be Found."

Though I tried to remain calm, panic and denial struck at the same time. *Not now!* I needed to check my email and then revisit the "Why Society" page for further investigation. Shutting the browser window and opening it again didn't improve the situation, so I restarted my computer. While it was restarting, I checked to make sure my Ethernet cable was plugged securely into my computer and then crawled under the table to make sure it was plugged firmly into the wall. It was. To be safe, I unplugged Casey's computer and plugged my cable into her Ethernet jack.

My computer started up again, but in spite of changing the jack that I was plugged into, the page of plain text came up again. Denial progressed rapidly to anger and I pounded the desk in frustration. Grabbing my packpack, I prepared to go down to the computer lab. I would deal with the computer later, but now, I needed to get online.

I heard a knock at the door. My soft-spoken hall mate Ann was standing in the doorway.

"Is your internet down too?" she asked, a worried expression on her face.

"Yeah," I replied, relief washing over me. It wasn't my computer after all.

"I think the whole building is down," I heard Justin call from the other end of the hallway. "I just came up from the computer lab. You can't get online there either."

I put my backpack down and joined Ann out in the hallway. "What are you going to do?"

"I don't know. I don't know my reading assignment because the syllabus is online. Come to think of it, my problem set is online too. What about you?"

"There is some reading I could do. But there were a few things that I wanted to do online first."

As we were talking, a few more people walked out of their rooms, dazed and confused. Alex brought a deck of cards out with him.

"Poker anyone?" he asked. Justin, Ann and I sat down with him in front of the elevators.

"This is so weird," Ann said. "It's like we can't function without the internet now!"

"Well, we can't!" Justin asserted. "I don't even know what to do with myself now. I can't check my email, I can't read about sports, I can't get to my homework assignments... what the hell am I supposed to do? I can't even IM my friends!"

"What did people do before they had the internet?" I wondered aloud.

"They called people on the phone and interacted with them face to face," Alex said, laughing.

"I know, isn't that weird?" Ann exclaimed. "I never really thought about how dependent I was on the web. But I feel totally... lost without it!"

Chris and Sean burst out of the elevator together.

"Hey, what's going on?" Chris demanded, spying our poker game.

"Internet's down," Alex announced, with all the pomp and circumstance of a messenger bearing monumental news. Chris and Sean played their parts appropriately.

"The internet is down?" Sean repeated, incredulously. Chris's mouth hung open.

"How are we supposed to do anything?" Chris cried. "We can't even see what's for dinner!"

Alex nodded. "Hopefully they'll have it up by then."

"How long has it been down?" Sean asked.

"At least thirty minutes," I said. "That's how long I've been home anyway."

"I'm going to check," Sean said, climbing over us. He and Chris hurried to their room. We heard them go in. We continued to play poker. Two minutes later, they emerged from their room, as dejected as the rest of us had been.

"I'm in," Chris said, defeated, taking a seat next to me.

"Same here," Sean said, sitting between Justin and Ann.

Our spirits didn't stay low for long. Within the hour, the game had grown to seven people, and we were having a fantastic time.

"I'm going to see your ten and raise you one load of laundry," Alex said to Justin.

Amanda whistled. "This game is getting serious!"

We all laughed.

Sean, who was dealing, was beginning to have a hard time sliding cards to Chris and I, who were across the circle from him.

"After this game, we should play Mafia!" Justin exclaimed, also noticing that Sean was having some trouble.

"Ooooo," Amanda cried, clapping her hands. "I *love* Mafia!"

"Who's playing Mafia?" asked Pete, sticking his head out of his room.

"Wanna play?" Amanda asked. "We're going to play after this hand."

"I'm totally in," Pete said

Everybody was having such a great time. I suddenly realized that I knew very little about Alex, Justin, Pete, Amanda and Ann. We hadn't really hung out, even though we all lived only feet from each other.

It made me wonder what the price of technology really was. Were we shortchanging ourselves by choosing to socialize on the web at the convenience of our own schedules instead of participating in the "real world"? I tucked these thoughts away for a potential article later.

"OK!" Sean announced, rubbing his hands together. "Let's play Mafia! Does anyone not know the rules?"

Ann raised her hand.

"No problem," Sean said. "I'll explain it to you."

Part way through the game, Brian came up on the elevator. His hair was tussled carelessly and his backpack was falling off one shoulder. He said hi to everyone briefly, with a one sided smile, before retreating to his room.

"Want to play in the next game?" Sean called after him. "We're almost done with this one!"

"Next time," Brian called back as he let himself into his room.

At the end of that game, I excused myself and walked to Brian's room. I peered in. Brian had left the curtains drawn, so the room was dark and cave-like.

"Brian?" I called out, stepping into the room. His face appeared over the edge of his bunk bed.

"Hey Amy, what's going on?"

"Just stopped by to say hi. I was wondering if you had any thoughts on who stole my article."

Brian shook his head. "Someone who is anti mainstream society who knows you…."

To get eye level with him, I dragged Brian's chair over next to his bed and stood on it.

"Maybe it was my Social and Cultural Anthropology professor. He seems like a nice guy, but he does seem to have a chip on his shoulders about frat guys. He's really into socially constructed norms that he finds oppressive."

336

Brian sat up in his bed. He patted the spot next to him.

I climbed up onto the bed with him and we dangled our feet off the edge.

"So how can you find out if it's your Anthropology professor or not?" he asked.

"I guess I can go ask him if he knows anything about this 'Why Society' newsletter. Though if he did, he could just lie to me and say he didn't. That's what he'd probably do if he *did* steal my article."

"You could send a classmate, couldn't you?"

"I didn't really make any friends in that class."

Brian nodded and we sat there, stumped.

"How are you doing?" I asked after some time. "I heard you've been blue."

"Sean's a freaking busybody."

I grimaced. Sean would let me have it for giving him away.

Brian fell back in his bed and stared at the ceiling. "I'm doing ok, I guess. Heather and I broke up."

I fell backwards and lay next to him. "I'm sorry."

"It's fine. It wasn't like it was a surprise or anything. We were having trouble with the long distance thing. And she was really mad about that one night when I came into your room…"

"But you were so drunk! And nothing happened anyway!"

"Well," he said staring very hard at an imaginary spot above him. "I was pretty drunk, but it wasn't totally an accident."

I turned my head to look at him.

"She knew I thought you were a cool chick and she was already jealous."

"What do you mean it wasn't totally an accident?" I asked, still stuck on that point.

"I really *was* locked out. And I really *did* think it was our room at first. But some time before we fell asleep, I knew I was in your room."

I chuckled. Some part of me had known that all along. "So she broke up with you?"

"Well, it was mutual. I think the drunk incident was just a catalyst. I hadn't been sure about me and Heather for months."

"Then why did you stay together?" I propped my head up on my elbow to look at him.

Brian hesitated for a long time. "We thought she had cancer."

"Oh my God!" I exclaimed, sitting up. This was unexpected.

"It's fine now. They just took the tumor out and it wound up being benign. But all during fall quarter before the surgery, she was so scared. And she needed me. I couldn't break up with her *then*. I couldn't have lived with myself if I had."

I nodded in agreement. It all made sense now.

"That's why I went home almost every weekend last quarter. After the surgery when I knew that she was going to be OK, I wanted to stay at school some weekends to hang out with people and get work done. That started some tension because she thought I didn't want to hang out with her anymore. So she started getting all moody, and I didn't like it, so we decided to break up."

I was hit with an avalanche of mixed feelings. This poor girl thought she had cancer and then she had to deal with her boyfriend crushing on someone else. My heart went out to her. And he had wanted to break up with her, but couldn't because she needed him. It was at once sad and noble. I felt guilty for being "the other woman" because I now knew what it was like to be on the other side of that. The hurt was still raw. I also felt guilty for giving Brian attitude for having a girlfriend when he was having a miserable time as it was without my shenanigans.

"There was a time when I thought you might be interested in me," Brian started.

"Mmm hmm," I answered, twisting a lock of my hair, deep in thought.

"Do you think you might be interested in me again?" he asked.

Without meaning to, I heaved a big sigh. "I'm not ready to date anyone. I'm all messed up right now. To tell you the truth, I'm not too happy with your... gender... right now."

Brian laughed. "I understand. It's too soon. For both of us."

"And it's kind of weird, us having the same friends and being neighbors and all," I said, hoping he wouldn't get offended. He didn't.

"That's cool," he said. "But maybe someday..."

"Definitely. Definitely, maybe."

I headed back to my room, feeling like one part of me was beginning to heal. To make matters better, the internet was working again.

*****

At dinner that night, conversation started with the internet outage, but eventually migrated to the incident at Casey's sorority again when Lindsay pulled her copy of the *Daily Bruin* out of her backpack. The headline read, "Attack on Sorority Contagious."

"Who would try to attack a sorority?" Lindsay wondered outloud, twirling spaghetti gracefully around her fork.

"Maybe someone who is jealous," Amanda replied, tossing her long ponytail over her shoulder. She had narrowly escaped the same fate as Casey by being on a date that night with a surfer from Santa Monica City College. Casey was jabbing at her salad, which is how she generally was at the few meals she ate with us since the article was published.

"I've noticed that *you've* been hanging out at the sorority a lot less since the whole thing happened," Sarah teased her. "Aren't they cool enough for you anymore?"

"Ha ha ha," Amanda replied, drawing out the syllables. "You shouldn't make fun of them. They are really suffering!"

"I'm sure that the parties will be rescheduled," Sean said. He began eagerly digging into our favorite dessert of Captain Crunch cereal with peanut butter, strawberry soft serve and chocolate syrup.

"And some day, they *will* be able to starve themselves and wear make-up again," Chris chimed in.

Casey gave Chris the finger and muttered, "Jackass" loud enough for everyone to hear.

Amanda was fuming. She pushed the spaghetti around on her plate in an agitated way. "See! This is my point exactly! Everyone is just jealous because we have a reputation for being hot and popular. It could have been anyone in the whole school! It was probably one of those wannabe sororities. Or maybe it was some loser who got rejected by one of our girls."

"Don't flatter yourself," Sarah said in disgust. I admired her tell-it-like-it-is attitude.

"You know what *I* heard?" Autumn interrupted. We all turned to look at her, awaiting our daily helping of fresh gossip. "This girl in my politics discussion is dating a campus security offer and *she* said they found the parts used for the detonator used to blow up the speaker at Beta Pi in the Electrical Engineering lab. It was probably a student!"

Brian and I exchanged looks. This was an interesting bit of news.

"So the question is," Sarah said, "Whether these episodes link back to the same person or whether different people are attacking different fraternities and sororities."

"It has to be the same person," Sean said, furrowing his eyebrows. "If you had random, untrained people doing it, they would get caught. It seems like these are all premeditated and all planned out. I mean, you don't just show up to a party and decide you're going to blow up the sound equipment."

"Yah, Sean's right," Erin said. "You'd have to know there was going to be a party, you'd have to somehow sneak the explosives into the equipment without anyone seeing, and you'd have to have some sort of wireless detonation system so you could blow   it up remotely. This is totally the work of some organized... mastermind."

"This would make such a great story," Sean said, looking at me. "You could be one of those sleuthing journalists, like those guys who broke the Watergate scandal."

"It *would* be cool," I concurred, using my spoon to carve shapes in my soft serve and watching them melt slowly back into indistinguishable lumps. My mind was already going in a million directions. I had a hunch these attacks had something to do with the "Why Society" page that Brian had stumbled across earlier. It was some sort of organization that was against part of what fraternities and sororities had come to stand for. But it was a group that communicated online. Did they have physical meetings? Was my suspicion valid that it might be a professor leading up this effort? What would happen when they were through terrorizing the Greek system? Would they turn on other student groups too?

Meanwhile, Sean had moved on. He got that evil glimmer in his eye just before announcing, "You losers haven't given me a good debating challenge in awhile. Who wants to argue with me about abortion?"

"Hey, I'm Catholic!" Chris protested.

"Well, I suppose you're as good as anyone to start," Sean said, rubbing his hands together. I tuned them out as I thought about the attacks and being a writer.

*****

On the way back from dinner, Brian walked beside me.

"Amy, I got a response from that email address that you were sending your articles to," he said under his breath.

"You did?" I stopped for a second, but he put his hand on my back and pushed me forward gently. I continued walking.

"Yeah. I wrote that I'd heard about this group from a friend and I wanted to know if I could come to their next meeting. It's tonight. Want to come?"

I glanced behind me to make sure that no one else was listening.

"I don't know if I should come or not. I feel like whoever this is knows who I am if they keep stealing my work. They might recognize me and then they would know we were on to them."

"Good point. I hadn't thought of that. OK, I'll go and see what I can find out. At the very least, I'll see if I can figure out who stole your article. We can go from there."

"Where is the meeting?"

"The guy said to meet at Kerckhoff Coffee House patio at 11pm tonight."

"That sounds like a romantic, literary kind of place."

He chuckled. "Fitting, then."

"OK, well be careful. Text me if you need me."

Brian looked at me. I looked away quickly. Awkward.

***

Erin sighed and the clicking of the keyboard stopped. I looked up from my editing. She was sitting Indian style on her chair, hunched over. Her fingers were still poised on top of the keyboard, but they were uncharacteristically still now.

"What's wrong?" I asked.

Erin turned around. There were two little lumps in the middle of her forehead from her eyebrows furrowing together. She looked like she had the weight of the world on her shoulders.

"I'm talking to Jim. And I'm so mad at this whole situation. He changed his 'relationship status' to 'single' online and so all of our friends know we broke up. I keep getting these sympathy messages that I don't want to see or respond to. People are all getting their feelings hurt because they had to 'find out online' and I feel like he's just flaunting this in my face."

I nodded.

"I mean, I guess he has every right to, and maybe I should just get over it, but it just seems like I should have had more time to deal with it by myself before the whole world had to know about it and ask about it, you know?"

"Totally. It's awful that all of our business is up on the web now and everyone knows everything within five minutes."

Erin nodded miserably. "And the worse part of it is that I can't get over it. I still miss the f-ing bastard and I hate myself for missing him. I can't understand what the hell is the matter with me!"

"You're being too hard on yourself again. I think we're just creatures of habit. You're used to talking to him every day and thinking about him when you space out. Even if he's a bastard, you miss him because he was such a big part of all parts of your life."

I thought about the f-ing bastard that I missed as well. Erin must have seen it on my face.

"Let's not think about them, Amy. They're just going to make us sad and they don't deserve to have that kind of influence over us anymore."

"You're right," I said, shaking it my head. "It causes nothing but grief. How are you otherwise?"

"I don't know," she said, playing with a rogue thread unraveling from the hem of her jeans. "I feel like I'm working so hard here, but I'm not doing especially well and it's really frustrating. My parents will be disappointed."

"They're just grades." I wondered if I sounded convincing.

She shrugged.

"It's my job to get good grades, just like it's Dad's job to make money."

Touche.

"Maybe we need a break. Let's go next door and play video games!" I suggested, getting out of my chair. "I haven't done that since last semester."

Erin got up and we went next door. Chris was watching TV shows on his computer and Sean was chatting online. They both turned to us when we walked in. I couldn't help wrinkling my nose both because of the beer-sweat smell and because of the stack of porn magazines that had found its way back to the middle of their floor. I nudged it with my foot under the bunk bed.

"Hey are you guys up for playing video games?" I asked.

Chris ripped the earphones off his head and jumped out of his seat.

"We're always up for playing video games!" he said. He swatted cups and papers off of the top of the TV and began to hooking it up to the game console using a tangled nest of wires.

"Have a seat," Sean said, bunching his comforter into a ball and shoving it to the corner of his bed. "Please," he said, palm faced up, directing us to his bed.

"What should we play?" asked Chris.

"Your call," Erin said. "Why don't we play a game where we shoot men and they suffer a lot?"

I laughed outloud. Sean gave Erin a dirty look.

"I have a better idea," he said. "Why don't we shoot pizza dough at rats?"

"Yeah!" Chris cried. "You'll love it. My sisters love this one."

Within ten minutes, we were all in a heap on the bed, laughing.

"They don't even look like rats!" I cried. "They look like aliens with bad teeth!"

One of the buck-toothed aliens caught me right in the face with a squishy wad of pizza dough for my irreverence. Erin was laughing so hard, she had tears streaming down her cheeks.

"This is awesome! I don't know why we didn't do this sooner!" she exclaimed.

"Well it's not like we haven't been asking you every day for the last six months or anything," Chris said. "Oh! Watch out, he's about to... too late."

A rat riding a rocket found its way into our camp and blew it up.

"This is *hysterical*!" Erin said, in a new fit of laughter. "Who comes up with these games?"

Shooting rats lasted about an hour. After that, we moved on to a dance competition with a chicken, followed by various agility games and memory games. I only noticed it was late when I saw Lindsay walk by the room in her robe with her shower caddy. Lindsay was typically a late sleeper.

"What time is it?" I asked, emerging from the exuberance of our gaming orgy. I glanced around and saw Sean's clock. "Crap! It's already one o' clock. I was going to read a chapter tonight!"

"You're such a nerd, Callaway," Sean said. "I'm the one who is on probation and you don't see me freaking out, do you? Live a little!"

"You *should* freak out, if you want to stick around!"

Erin put down her controller and stood up, despite the manifold objections from Brian and Chris.

"No, I've got to go to bed," Erin said. "I have a meeting with my counselor tomorrow to decide what my concentration is going to be within Electrical Engineering. I can't be all sleepy."

The boys stopped their loud objections, but continued to grumble as they put their controllers away.

"Goodnight guys!" I called out as we walked out their door. "Thanks for playing with us!"

We heard muttering about people being straight-laced and squares in response. I looked back at Erin who was right behind me and we both giggled. On my way back to the room, I wondered how Brian was faring.

As we changed into our jammies and brushed our teeth, I thought about texting him, but that might get him into trouble if he was trying to be discrete at this meeting. I felt like I had to do *something*. I tried to rid myself of the thought that these people were potentially dangerous, but then I eased my mind by reminding myself that they couldn't do anything to him in Kerchhoff. Campus security regularly made rounds there at night. I brought my cell phone into bed with me just in case and laid it on Franklin's lap. This way, I could be closer to Brian if he needed help. After Erin turned out the lights, I tried to stay awake a little longer, but sleep overtook me.

18 "Save the world"

I was awoken by the lights being turned on and someone shaking me.

"Amy, wake up! Wake up!" Casey's raspy whispers were pleading.

I cracked one eye open and saw her silhouette against the ceiling light. She must have been standing on my chair.

"Case, what is it? What time is it?"

"It's three o' clock," Casey said. trying to be quiet for once in her life. "You have to wake up. I think I have a lead."

"What lead?" I asked, fighting to keep my eyelids open and trying to focus on Casey.

"I think I know who is attacking the frats and sororities!" she said.

I sat up slowly. "Talk to me," I demanded, mostly to buy myself some more time to wake up.

"I was at a party at Sigma Mu tonight. And I stayed over at the house because I was fooling around with one of the guys…"

"Skip that part," I said, exasperated, even in my sleepy state.

"Right, so I was getting ready for bed about an hour ago and as I was walking to the bathroom, I saw this little skinny guy who was dressed in all black. He was screwing around with the smoke detector."

I was awake now and very interested. "Go on," I said, reaching for my cell phone.

"So I started asking him what the hell he was doing and he tried to get away, so I grabbed his sweatshirt and kept asking him what he was doing and the guy that I was with came out of his room and pinned this guy down. And then a few other frat brothers came out and they threatened to beat him up if he didn't say what he was doing with the smoke detector."

"What did he say?"

"He said, 'The professor said to do it.' We kept trying to ask him which professor, but he said he didn't know. Then I freaked out because I think I know which professor."

"Ok, what's your theory?" I could hear Erin stirring in her bed below.

"I think it's Dan... I mean, Professor Barnard."

"How do you figure?"

Casey was searching my face for something.

"Well, how do you figure?" I asked louder.

"Promise you won't judge me?" she asked in a voice that sounded like a whimper.

"For crying outloud! This is hardly the time or place for that! I've judged you about as much as one person can judge another, so it's a moot point now!"

"Fine, whatever!" Casey said. Driven by her agitated state, she continued. "I think it's Dan... I mean Professor Barnard because... I was sleeping with him."

I felt myself reeling from this confession. Casey and Professor Barnard? She waited until I stopped being shocked before she continued.

"While I was sleeping with him, I hooked up with Trevor. Then there was that accident with the speaker. Then I fooled around with Jeff. SIE got food poisoning. I cut it off with the professor last week and this poison ivy thing happened. And tonight, I was at Sigma Nu and this thing happened. It's too weird to be a coincidence!"

I shook my head in disbelief. It seemed too simple, almost. Could all of these attacks really have revolved around Casey? As much as I didn't want to believe things could revolve around her, I had to agree with her that it was too much of a coincidence.

Where was Brian? We needed to lay out the puzzle pieces again. I looked down at my phone and saw the little envelop signaling a text message.

"Hold on a minute," I told Casey. I opened the text message. It was from Brian.

Help. Im @ 4153 W

I could feel myself panicking. He sent it an hour ago and got interrupted mid-message.

I hit "reply" and clumsily texted back:

R U OK? Where R U?

Casey shook my knee. "I think we should go to his house. I think we can find evidence of him plotting some of these attacks."

"What sort of evidence would you be looking for?" Erin asked from below.

We both looked down at her.

"I don't know exactly. But it's like you guys were saying at dinner. They're all premeditated and the guys who are carrying out the attacks haven't

345

seen Dan... I mean, Professor Barnard. So he must be emailing them or signaling them somehow..."

I thought of the webpage. "You're right. I think he might be communicating with them through this website that Brian found. Erin, if he's making webpages on his computer, that would count as evidence, right?"

Erin looked thoughtful. "Well, if the original html files are on his computer and the hosting company can verify that he owns the account or that he is uploading pages from his Mac address or IP address, then I think that is pretty good evidence, though I haven't had networks yet and I'm not entirely sure..."

"Well, first I have to make sure Brian is ok," I said, looking down at my phone. As if on command, the envelop appeared. I mashed at the keypad eagerly. The message said,

Thank you for ur concern. I am fine. Do not worry urself about me.

I read it over several times.

"This isn't from Brian," I said aloud, my hand shaking as I grew more panicked. "Someone took the phone from him."

Casey took the phone from me and looked at it. Erin climbed up on the chair beside her and looked as well.

"I need to find him! He's on this crazy hunt because of me!" I cried, throwing off my covers and scrambling down the ladder. I grabbed the phone back from Casey and went to his last message. He only had time to type out part of the address. I powered on my laptop.

"This is horrible. How are we going to find him with only half an address?" I moaned. Casey took the phone from me and looked at the numbers.

"I think I know where this is," Casey said.

"How could you?" I snapped. "It's only the number and one letter!"

"I think it's the professor's house," Casey replied, meeting my gaze evenly.

"Are you serious?"

Casey nodded. "The address is 4153 Wyton Drive. I've been over there a lot. Can we go now?"

Everything was happening quickly. I was having a hard time keeping all the pieces straight. I typed it into Google maps and saw that the house wasn't far off of the east side of campus. So we would have to cross campus and wander into the wealthy neighborhood just beyond it. I nodded and threw on a sweatshirt. I grabbed my keys and my phone. Casey changed out of high heels and put on brand new tennis shoes. All this time, Erin stood on my chair, watching.

"Erin, are you ready?"

"Why do I have to come?" she squeaked, alarmed.

"You're the computer expert!" Casey cried. "We need you to help us look for these files that you were talking about. Htkl or whatever."

"I'm not a computer expert. I'm barely better than average in my classes. I want to stay out of it!"

I took her hand and pulled her down off the chair, so that I could look her right in the face.

"Come on, Erin. We *need* you. I know you're worried, but if we can prove that this maniac is plotting attacks, then we could potentially save a lot of innocent people."

"And I can't go on living like this," Casey said. "I won't be able to date anyone ever again if he keeps this up."

"Tragedy of all tragedies," I muttered, keeping my eyes on Erin.

"Couldn't we do it tomorrow?" she asked, in a last-ditch attempt to dissuade us.

"No! When he finds out that tonight's attack wasn't completed, he'll be suspicious and he might destroy all the evidence. Besides, it's going to be a lot harder to break into someone's house during the day that it will be at night." Casey stamped her foot for emphasis.

Erin and I looked at each other for what seemed to be a long time. Then she went to her wardrobe to get a sweatshirt.

"OK, how are we getting there?" I asked.

"I'll drive," Casey offered, as she strode out the door. "That way, if we need to get away quickly we can."

"Right," I replied, on her heels. Erin came last, closing the door behind her.

I had thought that UCLA campus, like New York City, never slept. But that night, we didn't encounter a single person, except for the front desk guy, on our way out. We walked in the chilly winter night past Covel Commons to the elevator leading down to the parking garage. Once we were in the elevator, we felt like it was safe to talk.

"What's your plan?" Erin asked.

"Well, I know the back way into the house. There's a spare key under a flower pot," Casey said. Erin looked relieved.

"Once we're in, we just go to the study and get his files off his computer," Casey continued.

"What if there's a password?" Erin asked.

"Aren't you supposed to know how to crack those sorts of things?" Casey asked her.

Erin shook her head. "I can't crack a password without fancy equipment."

"Well then, we take the whole computer," Casey replied. Erin and I looked at her like she'd lost my mind.

"We can't take the computer!" Erin objected. "It's too obvious! We could get in serious trouble for that. If we just steal files, he might not ever know we did it. I've brought my external hard drive."

Casey threw her hands up.

"I don't know," she said. "I'm sure he has the password written down somewhere. He has a terrible memory and he writes everything down."

The elevator stopped and the doors opened. We followed Casey to her car.

"But we have to find Brian!" I reminded them.

"Well, if we get the evidence that we're looking for, then we can send the police in and *they* will find Brian," Casey said and climbed into the driver's seat.

"No!" I cried. "We have to save him! This man is clearly deranged. Who knows what he's capable of?"

"Fine!" Casey said. "Let's not panic. We should see what the situation is when we get in there."

Erin and I looked at each other. This was probably the best course of action.

We rode in silence for several minutes.

A question was tugging on my mind. Unable to suppress my curiosity any longer, I blurted out, "Why were you sleeping with Professor Barnard?"

"Does it matter?" Casey asked.

"Well, I think it would help me understand what's going on through his head and how to deal with him in case we run into him," I said. It wasn't a very good reason, but I read a psychological study one time that suggested any explanation was likely to get a better reaction than no explanation.

Casey gripped the steering wheel and took a deep breath.

Erin grabbed my arm. "Do you think we'll run into him?" she asked, her eyes widening.

"Well, I hope not," I replied. "But you have to be prepared for anything, you know?"

"Professor Barnard is married to a successful screenwriter," Casey started.

"I heard about this!" I replied. "My TA told me. She's worth a lot of money. Practically funding his entire existence."

"Right. Well, like ten years ago, my dad had an affair with this woman that lasted almost two years and it drove my mom into therapy and nearly wrecked our whole family. This woman is Professor Barnard's wife. Well, they weren't married yet, but she is now Professor Barnard's wife."

I was confused. "So you thought you'd sleep with him to...."

"To get even with her," Casey said with the unmistakable tone of pride in her voice. Erin and I exchanged a look. "I wanted to wreck her family like she almost wrecked mine."

"Well did it work?" I asked.

"Almost," Casey said. "I was leaving my underwear around everywhere and calling him during dinner and all sorts of obnoxious stuff like that. I know they got into a couple of fights. I would have kept at it except that he was starting to creep me out. When these things started happening at fraternities and my sorority, I was a little bit suspicious. Anyway, he's was starting to give me the jeebies. Has a serious thing for college girls."

I shuddered.

"And here I thought you were sleeping with him for a good grade," Erin said, half joking, but half not.

"What do you take me for?" asked Casey. "I would never sleep with a guy for a good grade."

"But you'll sleep with him for fun or for revenge?" I asked.

"Exactly," Casey said. "I don't do favors *for* them to get something *from* them. What do you think I am, some kind of whore? I do it for my own amusement. There's a difference."

Erin looked at me. I shrugged.

We were all the way on the other side of campus now and Casey turned off of Sunset Blvd onto a residential street. She turned off her headlights and began to slow down.

"OK, you guys," I said. "We won't speak until we're all the way in the study, ok?"

"That sounds about right," Casey replied.

She pulled up in front of a beautiful Tudor style cottage. Well, cottage wasn't the right word for it because it was enormous. The cream colored base glowed in the moonlight. The dark wooden beams that framed every facet and window of the second story stood out prominently. It was a fitting house for an English professor, I thought. It looked like what I imagined Shakespeare's house to look. One of the second story windows was lit up and I could see shadows moving inside.

"Crap!" I exclaimed. "Someone's awake in there!"

"It might be better that way," Erin said. "It might distract them. It would be worse if it was dead silent."

I didn't know whether she was trying to make us feel better or herself.

"True," I admitted.

We slipped out of the SUV and followed Casey to the back of the house. She produced a key from beneath a flower pot and let us into the house. It took a moment for my eyes to get adjusted. My heart was pounding in my ears and I could feel my palms getting clammy.

It was a good thing that Casey knew her way around the house. She motioned us to follow her and she began tip toeing through their enormous living room. I paused a moment to look at their grand stone fireplace with carvings of shepherds and sheep across the top. Erin nudged me from behind to keep me going. We walked past a grand staircase with plush cream carpeting leading to the second floor. We continued to creep past the kitchen and down a dark corridor. At the end of the corridor, Casey pushed a heavy wooden door. We all snuck inside and shut the door.

Casey flicked on a light. We found ourselves in a gigantic office. The furniture was all dark wood with green, patent leather cushions. It looked like the kind of office in which men from the turn of the century would smoke cigars and trade railroad bonds. Erin wasted no time sitting down at the massive desk and jiggling the mouse at the computer. The computer came out of hibernation and the desktop appeared.

Erin mouthed the word "Yes!" to us silently. She opened up an explorer window and began clicking around.

"What's the website called?" she asked.

"Why society," I responded.

"Spell that," she said, looking confused.

I punched it out in my cell phone and showed it to her. She nodded and kept clicking around.

Meanwhile, I began to hear a little jingling noise from down the hall. I put my hand on Erin's arm and put my finger to my lips. Erin stopped typing and we listened. The jingling was getting louder.

"What is that?" I asked, beginning to freak out.

"Shit!" Casey murmured under her breath. "That's Yeats! He's their black lab. He *loves* me."

I rolled my eyes. This guy was *such* an English major. Yeats?

"What are we going to do?" Erin asked, looking around, panicked.

"Have you found anything?" Casey hissed at her.

"I've found these folders called 'Project 1,' 'Project 2,' etc," Erin said. "Other than that, it doesn't look like he has much. He's got photos, music, school notes…"

"Just take it all!" I said, as the jingling got louder. Erin fumbled with the USB cable on her external hard drive. She got down under the desk and connected it to the CPU tower. Then she started clicking buttons on dialog boxes that popped up.

The jingling stopped in front of the door, and then the scratching started. We heard a whimper. Erin and I gave Casey a "Do something!" look.

"It will take nine minutes for me to lift all of the non-music, non-picture documents," Erin said. We looked at the status bar, which was just a sliver and barely growing at a noticeable rate. Nine minutes! It was going to be an eternity.

Casey went over to the door and cracked it open. A black snout pushed its way in. Casey didn't let the dog all the way in, but petted its head through the partially open door. The dog stopped whimpering and panted. The jingle of his tags echoed in the dark corridor as he shook his head from side to side. I cringed.

We watched the bar grow. 8 minutes left. I began opening drawers to see if I could find anything incriminating that we could take with us. In the top drawer next to the desk, I found several manilla file folders. I opened the first one. There were print outs of past editions of "Why Society" with the same Celtic knot frames around the articles. I flipped through them and definitely recognized some of my work in them. I pulled them out, folded them in half and shoved them in the marsupial pouch of my hoodie. The rest of the folders looked like papers published in academic journals.

7 minutes left. I opened another drawer. More folders full of bills and insurance papers. I took those out of the drawer and kept on digging. I pulled out a red colored folder and a wallet sized photo fluttered to the ground. When I bent over to pick it up, I found myself staring at myself. I froze and gaped. It was a candid photo in which I was talking, unaware that I was being photographed. I was more than mildly disturbed.

The folder contained an entire collage of photos, all candids of female students. Several were of my classmates, taken in the classroom. Some were of girls taking notes in class. Their faces showed a range of emotion from boredom to intrigue to concentration. One was of Casey, staring off into space, twirling her hair. I was appalled. When had there been a camera in class? I closed my eyes and tried to picture last semester's class. I could see Professor Barnard pacing back and forth across the floor, pontificating from his soap box and clicking that annoying pen.

The pen! I shuddered. This man was twisted. There was no better word to describe him. Well this would be great blackmail material! I could see it all over the *Daily Bruin* already. Erin brought me back to earth by peering over my shoulder and gasping when she saw the photos. I drew an imaginary circle around my ear with my index finger indicating that he was crazy and she nodded.

6 minutes left. Every minute seemed like forever. I looked around the room to see where we might hide should anybody show up. Two of us could hide beneath the desk. The three sides of it went all the way to the ground. We could hide behind the huge velvet curtains. There was a space in the corner of the room where the couch and the love seat met that was obscured from sight.

Casey pushed the friendly furry face out of the door and shut it. She shut off the lights and whispered, "Someone's coming! Hide!"

She ran to the desk. Erin looked at me in a panic and jerked her thumb at the computer.

"Just turn the screen off. Let it finish downloading!" I whispered. "You two hide under the desk. I'm going to hide in the corner." Erin turned off the computer screen as I scuttled across the room to the corner fortress I'd identified earlier.

We heard footsteps coming towards us and we could hear a man and a woman arguing. Yeats had begun whining and scratching at the door again.

"Damn dog!" Professor Barnard's voice was cranky. "What do you want in there?"

"Don't think the dog is going to save you," the woman's voice was menacing. "Are you having an affair or aren't you?"

"I told you, woman! It's just your damn imagination!" Professor Barnard's voice was annoyed.

"I didn't imagine up a pair of women's underwear under the bed," the woman said.

I heard Casey giggle and wanted to kill her.

"I told you that I don't know whose those are. Maybe the maid is messing around with someone when we're not home," Professor Barnard said in a you're-just-an irrational-woman voice, belittling her concern. Now I wanted to kill *him*.

"The maid couldn't fit into those panties if you paid her to," the woman cried. "Whoever owns those panties is scrawny!"

I could almost feel Casey bristling, even though I couldn't see her. I looked at my cell phone. Four minutes left. If they would just keep arguing in the hallway, we would be alright.

"Who the hell would I be having an affair with?" Professor Barnard asked..

"You tell me!" snapped the woman. "One of your students? One of your colleagues? How should I know what you do, or rather, *who* you do at school?"

Professor Barnard snickered. "You're just being paranoid!" he said. "I'm not having an affair and that's all there is to it."

There was a long pause.

"If you are," she said in a warning tone. "And I find out about it, it's the last straw, Daniel. I swear I'm going to divorce you and you won't get a penny. I'm going to throw your worthless, unpublishing ass out on the street."

Ouch! I thought. *Way to stick it to him!*

"Bullshit. I'd get half. It's California state law."

"I'm sure you haven't forgotten our pre-nup. I get everything if I can prove you're having an affair."

"Go to bed," Professor Barnard said, still annoyed. "I'll take the dog out."

They must have had another staring contest because it took a few moments before we heard her walk back down the hallway. The ever persistent dog continued to scratch at the door and whimper.

"Come on, Yeats! Do you have to go out?"

The dog whimpered.

"What is it, boy? Why do you want to go into the office? Did you leave a toy in there?"

The door opened and a widening cone of light spread over the carpet. I held my breath. The dog bounded in and went straight for Casey under the desk. I checked my cell phone. The download should be finished by now. The professor stood at the door, clapping his hands.

"Come here, boy! Come here!" he called to the dog.

Yeats continued to stay behind the desk. From where I was hiding, all I could see was his furiously wagging tail.

"Yeats, come *here*!" the Professor said, more sternly now. "What *is it*?"

The dog pulled his head out from under the desk long enough to give the professor a meaningful look and then disappeared under the desk again. The professor flicked on the lights and walked to his desk. I curled into a very little ball and screwed my eyes shut. Uh oh...

"What's *this*?" the professor said in an ominous tone. "Casey? Is that you? Come out from under there. And who is your friend here?"

I saw Casey stand up, red faced and defiant. Erin looked terrified. I saw the corner of the external hard drive in her marsupial pouch.

"This is my roommate," Casey said, after a long moment of silence. "I came back for my underwear, but I see your wife has it now."

353

"You could have just asked me for it," the professor said. "Why did you come here?"

"I didn't want to see you again," Casey said. She flipped her silky mane over her shoulder. "I just came to get what was mine and leave. I didn't think you would be up at this hour."

The professor looked back and forth between Casey and Erin.

"I could have you arrested for breaking and entering," the professor said.

Casey didn't miss a beat. "I could have you divorced," she replied. "If your wife needs evidence, I'm all the evidence she's going to need."

I saw Professor Barnard clench his fist. He looked conflicted.

"What do you want?" the professor asked, finally after the two stared at each other for some time.

"I want to get my … things and go," Casey said.

Yeats made a lap around the room and stopped to sniff me at me between the edges of the couch and the love seat. Professor Barnard glanced in my direction, but I don't think he saw me. I pushed Yeats' nose out of the crevice and I saw Casey slap her thigh to call him.

Yeats bounded to her. Professor Barnard didn't seem to notice.

I breathed a sigh of relief.

"Well, I can't get you your underwear," Professor Barnard told her. "Ann has it and she won't give it back. So why don't you just go home and we will just pretend this whole thing never happened. I'll buy you new underwear."

"No thanks," Casey said with disgust. "Come on, Erin."

"Be quiet," Professor Barnard reminded them as they all filed out of the room.

Casey went out first, followed by Professor Barnard and Yeats. Erin trailed behind and when she was the only one left in the room, she looked into my corner. I lifted my head up above the armrest of the couch and waved her out the door.

"I'm going to stay and find Brian," I mouthed.

She looked worried, but I waved her on again. She sighed and scurried out the door.

After a minute, the back door opened and closed. The jingling of Yeats' tags faded away. I waited a minute more to be sure no one was coming back in here and then crept out. When I stood up, the blood spread through my body again. My foot had fallen asleep because I'd been sitting on it and I shook it to loosen the cramp. When everything felt functional again, I tiptoed to the door, turned off the light, opened the door and looked down the hallway. The house was enormous. I had no idea where to begin looking for Brian. I could go back towards the kitchen and the living room, but he had probably hidden Brian in a more remote room that was harder to find, so I walked down the corridor in the other direction, opening doors on either side of the hallway quietly.

The first door opened to a small, florally decorated bathroom. I shut the door and moved on. The next door led to a beautiful vaulted library. It was one of those old school libraries that were two stories high, with a ladder on wheels to help you reach the books on the second story. The room had wood paneling all around it and through the darkness, I could make out oil paintings of sinister looking old men.

I pried my eyes from their hollow stares and stepped into the library to inspect the seams in the wall using the light from my cell phone display. *It might take me a long time to find Brian*, I thought to myself.

"Can I help you?"

Professor Barnard's gruff voice cut through the silence like a metal discharging in a microwave. I nearly jumped out of my skin. I turned around and there he was, not three feet away from me, with his arms crossed and looking ferocious. His eyes disappeared under the shadow of his bushy eyebrows in the dim lighting, making him resemble the ghoul that Sean had sent us over email.

I gulped and took a step back. I didn't know what to say.

"Ms. Callaway?" he growled, taking a step forward. "You're not the first nocturnal visitor to our humble abode tonight. But you probably know that already."

I looked around. There was literally nowhere to go. Professor Barnard stood in the doorway and I couldn't see any other way out. I began backing up more quickly.

"There's no need to be scared," he said, sounding almost insulted. "Let's be reasonable now. What is it you're looking for?"

I wondered if this was the time to confront him about the plagiarism, but decided against it. I stood a better chance of being set loose if he didn't know that I knew.

"I'm looking for my friend Brian," I said, squaring up to him. My voice sounded small and high pitched.

"Well let's go look for him then!" he said, turning around and walking out of the room.

I was taken aback. This seemed too easy. When I gathered my wits about me, I followed him out of the room. He signaled me to be quiet and I followed him back up the corridor, past the kitchen, through the living room and up the grand staircase. I stayed several steps behind him. Despite his slower gait, punctuated with a slight limp, he stood up as straight as a ramrod and held his head high.

We turned down the main corridor of the second floor and at the end of it, there was a much narrower, rickety-looking staircase made of unfinished wood. At the top of the staircase, there was a small door. Professor Barnard started up the stairs, but I hesitated at the bottom. He turned to look at me and raised a bushy silver eyebrow.

"Ms. Callaway, I said there was no reason to be scared," he murmured in a low voice. "I have no intention of harming either of you. Your friend is upstairs. We've been having a lovely chat about your writing. You should fetch him and be on your way. We can both pretend this never happened."

"How?" I asked him, unable to contain myself. "How can I forget that your little society has been plagiarizing my work?"

Professor Barnard stroked his chin.

"Why don't we make a pact then? You don't mention this to anyone and I will stop using your work."

"If I *did* mention this to the authorities, you'd be forced to stop using my work," I pointed out.

"You can't prove anything," Professor Barnard snarled. "And if you *did* mention this to the authorities, you might not ever see your little friend again."

I scowled, but remained silent.

"Now let's be reasonable about this. You take your little friend and we'll forget about this whole thing."

I grit my teeth together and nodded. Professor Barnard turned and started up the stairs.

He pushed open the small wooden door. Directly behind it, there was a second door, made of thick metal. It looked like the doors that I saw on aircraft carriers that Dad took me to see when I was little. The bottom of the door was still a foot off the ground and the top of the door was low, with rounded corners. All around it, the wall was made of metal. When the door was shut, it blended in and looked like part of the wall. On the door right above the knob, there was a widget that looked like the combination lock of a bicycle. There were five disks stacked next to each other like a roll of quarters laid horizontally. You had to roll each disk with your thumb until the letter that you wanted showed up in front of you. Beside it there was a small piece of paper taped up. I squinted to make out the words, "Above Royce's Main Artery".

Professor Barnard eyed me askance and stood directly in front of the lock so I couldn't see him input the combination. When he spun the final letter in place, there was an audible "click" and the door swung open. Inside, there was a room that looked like a miniature living room, complete with white leather arm chairs and a flat screen TV. He stepped inside and I followed. I saw the back of Brian's tousled head peaking over the top of an armchair. This was problematic. I needed to stay between Professor Barnard and the door, so that

I couldn't be locked in. But I wanted to go to Brian.

"Brian?" I called out to him, not moving from my strategic position on the floor.

I saw his head move.

"Amy?" he said, whipping around to look at me over the back of chair. "Get the hell out of here!"

Conflicted, I reacted an instant too late. As I turned on my heel, I felt Professor Barnard grab my hood with one firm hand. With the other hand, I felt him pull my cell phone out of my hand. Then I felt my legs being swept out from under me and I fell to the floor. He stepped over me and tried to pull the door shut. I stuck my foot in the doorway and he couldn't close it all the way. He opened it again briefly, kicked my foot inside and shut the door with a thud.

I sprung up and yanked on the doorknob, but it was no use. The door was locked tight. Oddly enough, the inside of the door looked exactly the same as the outside of the door. There was a cylindrical combination lock on the inside, also with five letters to it. There was a piece of paper taped up next to it that said, "Condition of Satan's Psychologist."

"Satan's psychologist," I murmured, scrunching my eyes shut. What on earth could that mean? Satan Satan? Or was this just representative of another evil person?

"It's a two-way lock." Brian's sober voice interrupted my thoughts. "That professor guy told me. You need a password to get in and you need a different password to get out."

"Brilliant. So you can lock people in *and* out."

"Exactly," Brian said. "This is their safe room. They would come in here if they needed to hide from intruders or something."

"And if they need to lock nosy college students in," I added.

I took one last look at the door. Then I walked around to the front of his armchair and saw that Brian's left wrist was handcuffed to coffee table next to the chair.

"Are you ok?" I knelt down and inspected the handcuffs, which were covered with leopard print faux fur. "Gross."

"I'm ok. Yeah, I don't know want to know where these have been," he said with a disgusted look on his face. He shook his left wrist so the handcuffs jingled. "I've been trying not to think about it."

"What happened?" I asked as I looked around for a key.

"Oh he put the key on that desk in the corner," Brian said, pointing to a desk at the far end of the room. I found it and came back to unlock him.

"I went to Kerchhoff patio like the email said. And there were three guys having coffee at one of the tables. I asked if they were there for the 'Why Society' meeting. They said yes and told me to pull up a seat. They said they were waiting for the van to come pick them up and take them to the real meeting spot. I asked where it was and they said they didn't know. It changes every week. So I waited with them. They seemed pretty cool. They play ultimate Frisbee on Wednesday afternoons..."

"Focus," I reminded him.

"Right," he said, rubbing his newly freed wrist. "Sorry. So I chatted with them for a few minutes and then this van pulled up. So we all got inside and I didn't think anything of it because everyone was so friendly. They started talking about your article. We pulled up to this house and they got me all the way into this room before I even suspected that *they* suspected. I was talking about how I agreed that fraternities encourage exclusivity and social oppression of others. One guy was playing with these handcuffs the whole meeting and he literally just reached over and snapped it on my wrist. The other guys started laughing and they all left the room. Then that professor guy came in and started interrogating me."

"What did he want to know?"

"He wanted to know how I heard about 'Why Society.' Apparently they interrogate all new members. The problem was that I couldn't tell a convincing story about how I found out about them and how I got the professor's email address."

I nodded. We stared at each other somberly.

"So what do we do now?"

"Casey and Erin know we're here, so they might show up with help. The problem is that police can't come in here without a search warrant and I don't know how long that takes or what the burden of proof is to get one. A lot of the evidence is in here with us."

I showed him the contents of my marsupial pouch. Brian looked aghast when he saw the folder of photos.

"Does this professor guy know that Casey and Erin know?"

"Yes. He found them under his desk. Erin was lifting files from his computer, but I don't think he saw that. He just kicked them both out."

"I'll bet he's trying to figure out how to dispose of our bodies *right now*," Brian said. He slid down to the floor, with his back against the base of the armchair. I sat down next to him.

"Satan's psychologist," I said, deep in thought. "Satan's psychologist, Satan's psychologist, Satan's psychologist..."

"Has a nice little ring to it, doesn't it?"

"This guy is such an English nerd."

"Takes one to know one."

I rolled my eyes at him.

"Are you religious?"

He shook his head.

"My mom is Catholic. So, I got to my First Communion, but stopped there," he said.

"What do you know about Satan?"

Brian got up and started pacing.

"Satan plays a couple of different roles in the Bible, if I remember right. He brings charges against sinners in God's court in one place. But then he is God's adversary a lot of times too."

"Isn't he also associated with the serpent in the Garden of Eden?" I asked, recalling a painting of Adam and Eve's expulsion from Eden that I'd studied in World History in high school once.

"Wow, I hadn't really thought about it, but I guess this guy *would* need a shrink. He has identity problems."

"Or maybe he was 'good' at one point and then went off the deep end." Where did I hear this story before? It seemed very familiar to me.

"Who would be a good shrink for Satan?" Brian wondered aloud.

"And who would also be someone who would catch the attention of an English professor. A very twisted English professor…"

"And a super control freak. I got the impression that none of these guys that are working for him has actually met him in person. He didn't come in here until after they all left. He's like the ruler of his own destructive little empire."

Reigning over his small, destructive anti-society kingdom, I thought to myself disdainfully, *instead of serving society in some constructive capacity*. Suddenly, the puzzle pieces clicked in my head.

"That's it!" I cried, jumping to my feet.

"You got it?" Brian asked, stopping his pacing and looking hopeful.

"I think it's Milton!"

Brian gave me a blank look.

"John Milton. The English poet!"

He shrugged.

"He wrote *Paradise Lost*. You must have read that in high school, right?"

He shook his head.

"John Milton wrote this long poem called *Paradise Lost* in which he describes the fall of man. The beginning of the poem is written from the point of view of Satan and his fallen angels. There's a really famous line in there where Satan says, '*it's better to reign in hell than serve in heaven.*'" I recounted, excitedly. "And he sort of describes how Satan cracked."

"Sounds vaguely familiar," Brian said, rubbing his head. "Now that you mention it, I think we read it, though it's ridiculous that you can actually quote a line from it. Let's put it in and get the hell out of here!"

We both raced to the door and looked at the combination lock.

"Milton is six letters," Brian said. "We've only got five here."

I looked at the clue again. "Oh, it says '*Condition* of Satan's Psychologist.'"

"What sort of condition do they mean?"

I mulled it over for a minute. "It could mean that he set a condition under which he would or wouldn't do something, but I think it means medical condition. Milton was blind."

I watched Brian turn the first little wheel until the letter 'b' came up. He then turned the adjacent wheels to spell out the word "blind".

We heard a click and the door swung open. We wasted no time racing down the hallway. The thick carpet muted the thudding of our footsteps. We tore down the grand staircase and then I took the lead, bringing us through the living room, where Yeats was sleeping. He jumped up and barked at us, his tail wagging.

"Be quiet, Yeats!" He paid no mind to my plea and followed us out the back door, yelping with excitement. Casey's SUV was right where we had left it.

"Thank God you're here!" I gasped as Brian and I collapsed into the backseat of Casey's car.

"Go! Go! Go!" Brian shouted at Casey, as we saw Professor Barnard emerge from the backdoor with a shotgun in hand.

Casey started the car and gunned the engine. We peeled forward, not a moment too soon.

"We didn't know how long to wait," Erin said, turning around to look at us. "We thought about calling the police, but we didn't have any evidence except the stuff we got off of his hard drive and I was afraid..."

"You did fine," I told her, breathlessly. "You probably would have gotten in trouble for breaking and entering. We can't go to the police without incriminating him with something worse than breaking and entering."

Erin gave me a tired smile.

"Speaking of which, what kind of loot did you get?" Casey asked. Our eyes locked in the rear view mirror. There was an absence of condescension in her gaze and for a moment, it was as if we understood one another. Just a moment.

"I have all of these photos of girls in his class. It's obvious that he took them without our consent. I don't know if that's a crime, but it at least paints a creepy picture of him to a jury."

Brian gave me a look that was half appalled and half doubtful.

"Yep. And then we have these 'Why Society' printouts. Some of them are my articles. I have to look them over and see if there is any connection between these and the attacks on the fraternities and sororities. If we can find that link and Erin can prove that he puts these pages together, then maybe we can get him busted for these attacks," I said.

"You're going to be the journalist that cracks this whole mystery," Erin said. "Just like Sean said."

"It's all just a theory right now," I told her. "I just have a feeling it's him, but who knows? Maybe he's someone else's puppet and we have to dig more."

We rode back to the dorms in silence. Casey's car clock said it was 5:45am. The sun would not come up for a few hours yet. When we got back to our dorm room, we all crept back into bed and slept until well after noon.

The flood of light coming into our window and the sound of a neighbors heading off to class woke me. I sat up and rubbed my eyes. After a few moments of reliving the long night in my mind, I climbed down the ladder without injuring anything. I sat down in my chair and stared at all the evidence laid out in front of me, focusing on the three "Why Society" printouts.

They were all laid out the same way, with a few pages stapled together. On the front page, there was always an article in the center that was the feature article, I guessed, by the way it was framed by Celtic knots. On either side of it and beneath it, there were three other articles. The second page contained letters from the editor and other readers, generally griping about society, mostly college kids. On the last page, there was a hodgepodge of events listed, like poetry readings, concerts, and meetings.

I mulled over the events on the last page of one of the editions. He could be instructing people to attack the fraternities and sororities at any of these events. He could be passing out fliers at these events or communicating through the performers. And what about these meetings? Surely these were planning meetings for the attackers. Would I have to sneak into some of these events to find out? My heart sank at the thought. That's precisely how Brian was trapped and now Professor Barnard would know who he was looking for.

I looked at the first pages of each of the packets again, mostly because he had ripped off another one of my articles- the observations of the frat party I went to last quarter with Jeff. I could feel my pulse quickening and frustration bubbling up in my chest. My words were being associated with this destructive human being. My words in this context, with all the other anti-society articles all around it, sounded far more venomous than I'd intended them to be. My night of irritation now came across as a condemnation of all college frivolity and that's not what I had meant.

Interestingly enough, Professor Barnard tacked on a short paragraph to the end of this article as well.

"By excluding others from their merriment, they are fracturing our community. Perhaps someone needs to bring their attention to those of us who are being excluded."

I logged on to my computer and looked at the latest "Why Society" page. I reread the final paragraph with two sentences in it.

"Society has become overrun with selfish hedonists with no regard for the thoughts and feelings of others. My opinion is that it is time to show them that their actions are not appreciated."

What was there some significance to these little paragraphs that were tacked on to the end of my articles? I looked at the feature article of the other edition that wasn't mine. It also ended with a short paragraph that was a battle cry for the troops to do something about the social elitist oppressors.

A knock at the door interrupted my thoughts. I opened the door and found Brian standing there in his sweats.

"Let's get to work!" he yawned.

"I'm all over it, sleepyhead!" I told him. I motioned him to be quiet and pulled Casey's chair over to my desk so that he could see look at the printouts with me.

"Check it out," I told him, pointing at the first article he stole from me. "I wrote this one too and the Professor tacked this short paragraph to the end of it too. I can't understand it. It doesn't quite fit with the article. It's always two sentences telling people to do something about the situation. What do you think?"

Brian looked at that one for awhile and then picked up the other two, reading them each in turn.

"Look at these dates, too," Brian said, pointing to one of the editions. "They're not evenly spaced. There are two weeks between the first two, then four weeks between the second and third. Then there's only one week between the third and the fourth."

"They roughly correspond to right before the attacks," I said after thinking about it for awhile. "Casey got poison ivy last week. There is an instruction somewhere in here telling people to attack. I feel like it's in these little paragraphs or it's being disseminated at one of these events in the back."

"You go to the next meeting," Brian suggested. I laughed.

"Words, words, words," I murmured, looking carefully at the most recent short paragraph. "Code words? Puzzles. He's into puzzles."

"Was the last frat that was attacked Sigma Mu?" Brian asked.

"How did you know?" I asked, startled.

"Look at this. The first sentence starts with 'S' and the second one starts with 'M.'"

"That's too easy!" I got out the one I had been looking at earlier. "B...P." I murmured. "Beta Pi. Wow, you're a genius!"

"No. You did all the sleuthing. If they hadn't been your articles he was stealing, we never would have even noticed those little paragraphs at the end."

I beamed at him. "We make a good team."

Brian got up. "OK, I'm going back to sleep. I'm guessing that you're going to be writing tomorrow's front page headline now?"

I nodded.

After he shut the door behind him, I opened up a fresh notepad document and started writing.

*****

The article was published on the front page of the *Daily Bruin* the next day. Among the tens of emails I received in my inbox regarding it, there were two especially of note.

The first was an official invitation to join the staff of the *Daily Bruin*. The first time I read it over, I was in shock. The second time, tears welled up in my eyes. And the third time, I convinced myself that I deserved it.

The other email that I received was from campus security in conjunction with the LA County Police Department. Because I had no phone number listed in the student directory, they emailed asking me if I would aid them in an investigation of Professor Daniel Barnard. They didn't have to ask twice.

After a fantastic dinner where I marinated in the praise of my dorm friends, I decided to take a walk by myself to think about my "Freshman Fifteen" article and give Lauren a call. She picked up after one ring.

"Talk to me, babe!" she gushed. "I hear you're a celebrity over there."

"Do you have an hour?"

"I'm making two. Start from the beginning."

"You will not believe this..."

Two hours later, I was still sitting in the corner of Northern Lights talking to Lauren when my cell phone started beeping, signaling a dying battery. The timing, for once, worked out fine, as I'd just finished telling her about my invitation to the staff of the *Daily Bruin* and the email from the authorities about an investigation of Professor Barnard.

"This is amazing," Lauren said at the end of it. "I'm so proud of you. I mean, I knew you were going to be a rockstar journalist, but I didn't know it was going to be so soon."

"Listen, Laur, my cell phone is beeping at me like it's dying, so I'm going to go. Anything new on your end?"

"No. I can't find anyone to crush on right now. I've also got to work on some articles for the *Princetonian*. But nothing to report for now. I'll call you if anything comes up."

"Love you," I said.

"Back atcha," she replied.

When we hung up, I felt really good. Not giddy, not exuberant, but content. I sipped on my mocha and leaned back in my chair. I felt more comfortable in my own skin now. When I first arrived at college, I was so anxious about people liking me, especially Casey. I wanted to seize this opportunity to be "cool". Somehow, it was something to cling on to in this vast ocean of students. I still wanted people to like me, but on my terms now, not theirs.

"We're closing, Miss," the guy behind the counter called to me, interrupting my train of thought.

"Oh wow," I said, looking at the clock. "Sorry!"

"No problem. You want any pastries?"

I looked hungrily at a bear claw in the pasty window, but a short mental calculation of how many hours on the treadmill it would take to burn that sucker off cooled me to the idea.

I shook my head. "No, but thanks."

"You sure? We're just going to dump them."

"You are?" I asked, surprised.

Wasting food had never been acceptable in my household growing up and I was amazed that they would throw out perfectly good pastries.

"Well, yeah. They're getting stale. We'll make new ones tomorrow."

"In that case, I'll take whatever you've got in the case," I said.

He filled up a brown paper shopping bag full and handed it to me over the counter. I walked home via South campus and made a detour into Westwood, where I found the man I was looking for sitting in front of Wendy's.

"Spare some change?" the guy called out to me as he saw me approaching.

His eyes were sunken in his dark, scruffy face. His long, stringy hair was matted with oil and dirt. I could smell him half a block away. Urine and sweat. Ugh.

"I can do better than that," I told him, as I approached him.

I dropped the shopping bag at his feet. He tore open the bag. He looked down at the pile of pastries, then up at me, speechless.

"Bless you," he said, after awhile, shaking his head.

"Share with your friends," I told him, and then I walked away.

I am ashamed to admit that I felt scared and uncomfortable spending more than a minute or two talking to him. But I felt good providing him with dinner.

On the way home, I thought how much food is thrown away at UCLA. Maybe this was a place I could contribute. Saving the world, a little at a time. It was definitely going on the list. I wondered if the *Daily Bruin* would let me borrow a photographer to take a picture of all the food that would have been wasted in a single night from a single coffee shop in campus.

*****

The next day, I asked to speak with the manager of the coffee shop between my classes. I had to wait thirty minutes for rush hour to be over before he could talk to me. He looked tired, but his eyes were twinkling.

"I'm Brett. How can I help you?" he asked, sitting down in the chair across the futuristic café table from me. He couldn't have been more than thirty years old, with a clean shaven face and black, spiky hair.

"Hi Brett, I'm Amy," I said, extending my hand. "I was here last night and one of your employees told me that you guys throw out the unsold pastries every night."

"We let the employees take home whatever they want and we throw the rest away," he corrected me. He stopped to smile at a customer entering the store.

"Well, the guy let me take home some of the leftover pastries and I gave them to the homeless guy down in Westwood."

"That was nice of you!"

"Well, I thought it might be nice if we could do that every night."

"Absolutely!" Brett replied. "Every few years, we get a student who suggests this. There are a few problems with it though."

"Oh?" I replied, taken aback. I thought my idea was original.

"The first problem is that we can never find students who are willing to take the food down to the food bank or the homeless shelter for more than a month or two. They get busy or tired of it and they lose interest. The other problem is that there are legal issues with us giving food directly to the homeless. If they choke on it or they are allergic to ingredients, then we are held liable for that. That's why some restaurants now lock their dumpsters."

Brett looked at me. "I don't want to discourage you, though. You're doing a really good thing."

"I'm not discouraged," I said, telling half a lie. "Let me try it a few days and see if I can get some volunteers. If you give me the food and I give the food to the homeless, then you're not liable anymore, right?"

"I'm not sure," Brett said. "I'll have to check. But you can take tonight's leftover pastries if you want."

"Can you save them for me so that I can pick them up tomorrow afternoon?"

"Sure. We'll put them in a shopping bag for you," Brett said, smiling. "I like your persistence."

"Thanks," I replied, then I headed out to the *Daily Bruin* office.

*****

"Hey, Rock Star!" Matt greeted me when I walked into the staff office.

"Hey Matt," I replied, blushing.

"What can I do for you? Your training doesn't start until third quarter."

"I know," I replied. "I'm trying to start this philanthropic... movement. Anyways, I was wondering if I could borrow a photographer tomorrow afternoon."

"Sure, what's the story?" Matt asked. "The photographers don't have a lot of work in the middle of the week."

"I'm trying to start a club or an organization or something to take leftover food from campus to the homeless."

"Wow, that's huge!" he replied, looking impressed.

"That's what she said!" a guy called from across the room.

I rolled my eyes.

"Tomorrow, I'm going to take the first batch of pastries down to Westwood myself and I wanted someone to get a photo of it. I want to put the photo in the paper along with a short article asking for volunteers."

"Sounds like a plan," Matt said, rubbing his hands together. "What time do you want one?"

"Six o'clock?" I suggested. "Just in front of Kerchhoff on the lawn?"

"You got it!" Matt said, pulling up a blank email and typing away.

"Thanks, Matt!"

"Take it easy, Amy."

*****

The next day, after class and a brutal homework session in the library, I went to Northern Lights to pick up the leftover pastries. Brett was there and he handed me two large brown paper bags full of them.

"That's a lot more than the last batch of leftovers I got!"

"Well, I went over to some of the other dining facilities and picked up some of theirs too," Brett told me. "I figured it was a good way to kick off your project."

"Thanks!" I was able to pick one bag up in each arm. They were large and unwieldy.

"Let me get the door for you," Brett said, running a few steps ahead of me. "Do you need help getting these down to Westwood?"

"Nah, my friend Sarah is going to pick me up at the turnaround and we'll go down to the homeless shelter together," I told him. "Thanks though."

"Let me know how it goes," he said, as he watched me waddle out through the door sideways.

I lifted my chin so that I could peer over the bags and see where I was going. It was already dark outside and the streetlights were on.

"Will do!" I called back to him.

I shuffled slowly past the English building, in front of Royce Theater, and down the steps leading to Bruin Walk. My shoulders began to ache and my arms tingled, not because the bags were heavy, but because they were hard to hang on to. The pastries inside were soft and shapeless, so squeezing the bags didn't add stability. The delicious scent of buttery croissants mixed with cinnamon buns made my mouth water. I had to remind myself that every pastry I ate was one less pastry for someone who really needed food. So I maintained self control.

Finally, I made it to the steps in front of Kerchhoff, which were deserted, like the rest of campus during the winter at dusk. I set the bags down and took a seat on the lawn. My cell phone indicated that I was ten minutes early and had a voice message.

"Amy. This is Agent Ryan Wilson from the Directorate of Operations at the CIA. We would like to speak with you about your recent activities in espionage and journalism. Please give us a call back at the following number ...."

I stared at my phone and replayed the message. I had indeed heard it right. What could the CIA want with me? A horrible feeling came over me about the breaking and entering, although the LAPD didn't seem to think it was a big deal.

I heard a chiding sound, "Tsk tsk tsk" from above me, and I looked up to see a very large squirrel sitting on the tree branch above me, eyeing the pastries.

"Don't even think about it," I warned.

It flicked its tail with impunity at me and began descending the trunk of the tree.

I looked down at the pasty bags and something gray caught the corner of my eye. How had the squirrel reached the ground already and gotten halfway across the lawn to me? My eyes flicked back to the tree trunk, where there was still a squirrel with its four limbs sprawled out and tense, edging headfirst down the tree trunk.

There were *two* squirrels after my pastries! I pocketed my cell phone and picked a bag up in each arm. Then I stood up.

The squirrel bounding across the lawn at me skidded to a stop to consider the change in the situation. It tilted its head and scolded me.

"Ch-Tsk-Ch-Tsk-Ch!"

"Ha!" I said, victoriously. "They're *my* pastries. Go home!"

I heard a rustle in the bushes behind me and saw a third squirrel, belly low to the ground, crawling towards me in stealth mode.

All three squirrels continued to creep towards me. I walked towards the one on the lawn and pretended to kick it. It scurried away for a second, but when it saw that I didn't chase it, turned around and came back. The one from the tree had already come right up to my left foot. I kicked at it, but it also jumped out of range quickly and came slinking back. They both seemed to sense that by holding these bags, I had lost the use of my arms.

"Argh!" I yelled, startled, when I felt something land on the back of my jeans.

The squirrel from the bushes was climbing up the back of my pants! I began flapping my elbows and a Danish flew out of one bag. One of the squirrels jumped on it, the other one looked up to see where it had come from. The squirrel that had jumped on me had already reached my back and was making its way up towards my shoulder.

"*Oh my God!*" I yelled.

My voice echoed off of the building. My skin was crawling and I was totally grossed out, but I wasn't going to let squirrels steal my pastries for the homeless shelter.

When the second squirrel began climbing up the front of my pants, I changed my mind and was ready to throw both bags of pastries to the ground and run. Before I did, I saw a big flash out of the corner of my eye.

"Say cheese!" the photographer called to me, unable to keep the laughter from his voice. "Or maybe pastreeee!"

Click. Click. Click.

"Get them off me!" I yelled, first shaking one leg, then the other leg, and twitching my head. "I'm going to drop these pastries!"

The photographer took a few more photos, quickly and then came trotting up to me, which was enough to scare the squirrels away.

I stood there, panting, heart pounding, with the two bags still in either arm.

"You'd better delete those photos!" I said, alarmed. "I'm Amy."

"Nice to meet you, Amy! I'm Josh. Let's take some photos!"

19 "Find yourself"

"Did you get a lot of volunteers from your article?" Erin asked me, the next afternoon. We were sitting in the golden afternoon sun which poured into Sproul's empty study lounge.

"One-hundred and thirty-seven," I replied.

"That photo was priceless! I can't believe the photographer got that shot."

"He had plenty of time to take it cuz he *sure* wasn't busy helping *me* out," I told her.

"Well, it was genius marketing," Erin replied, swinging her feet beneath her chair.

"Thanks," I replied, a little ruefully. "I guess my dignity is a small price to pay for getting a lot of volunteers to help with the homeless shelter."

Erin laughed her adorable, twinkling laugh.

"Are you Amy Callaway?" a deep voice asked from behind me. I turned around to see a man dressed in jeans and a blazer, which did a poor job hiding his very muscular arms.

"I am," I replied, feeling butterflies in my stomach. "This is my roommate, Erin."

"I'm Ryan Wilson," the man said, extending a hand to Erin and looking at her intently.

"Hi!" Erin squeaked, shaking his hand. "Sorry, I need to… go to class… right now."

She inched off her chair timidly, then shuffled out of the door.

"May I sit?" Ryan asked.

"Please," I said.

"Are we alone?" he asked. Even seated, he was an imposing presence. I felt like he could snap me in half.

I looked at him, confused. Of course we were alone. I don't think I'd ever seen a living soul in Sproul's study lounge the entire time I'd been here.

"I mean, there is a low probability that someone could overhear us, right?" Ryan clarified.

"Right," I responded.

"You must be wondering what this is about," Ryan surmised.

I nodded.

"I am from a special office within the CIA that does undercover work," Ryan explained. "In the past few years, it has come to our attention that our female special officers have been prodigiously successful in the field. No one seems to suspect them. They are able to access targets in situations that male officers would never be privy to."

He paused to inspect me. I tried to look sharp and nodded to signal my understanding. He continued, in a very rapid, clear voice, without one iota of emotion.

"When we ask our female agents what would make their jobs easier, they tell us two things. The first is that they wish there were more females in the department. This provides them more support. The second is that they wish they could have started their careers and their training sooner. Younger women also are privy to different situations than older women."

Logically, I could see where he was going, but I scarcely let myself believe it.

"We have been made aware of your recent work in espionage, code decryption and reporting," Ryan said. "And we think you have the qualities of a special agent for the CIA. Would you be interested in pursuing this career path?"

It took me a few moments to find my voice.

"Sir, I'm only a freshman. I don't even have a major yet."

"We know that," Ryan replied, looking at me as if it were an insult I thought he didn't know something. "We are starting our first top secret college program, in which we will begin training female secret agents. You can major in whatever you want, though we will require that you take a few core courses. We will train you in basic circuit analysis, financial analysis, firearms use, hand-to-hand combat, and espionage skills. You will also receive a few practice missions."

I continued to gape at him.

"When you graduate, you will decide if you want to become a secret agent. And we will decide if you are secret agent material. If either party doesn't think it will work, you can go on to do whatever you'd like. But under no circumstances can you tell people about this program or your involvement in it," he finished.

We stared at each other.

"What is the time commitment?" I asked.

"Training begins this summer. You will tell everybody that you are enrolling in summer school. We will train you on campus and at the FBI headquarters on Wilshire. We're running this as a joint program with them.

When school starts, your commitment will be an hour of physical training every week day in the morning, and the third weekend every month for special training and missions."

"Do I have to decide right now?" I asked, still overwhelmed.

"You have a week," Ryan said, standing up. He handed me his card. "This is a very prestigious program, Ms. Callaway. We are very selective about who we invite. I suggest you think hard about it. You seem hesitant."

"I just don't know if I could be a spy," I replied, in a stupor.

"You can be anything you want to be," he replied. "You determine who and what you are."

I took his words to heart.

"Remember, you can't tell *anybody* about it. Any of it."

I stood up and extended my hand.

"Thank you, Agent Wilson," I said. "I'll be in touch."

And then, he was gone.

*****

A few nights later, I was lying on Erin's bed with Erin and Sarah. We were all reading the draft of my "Freshman Fifteen" article. I'd asked for their opinions before I turned it in to Mr. Ives. For the first time all year, I felt at ease, maybe because I felt like I was beginning to regain control over my life again. My new friends were supportive and awesome, even though they would never be like my old friends. I was also beginning to feel more at home at school, even though it would never replace my home in Irvine.

"I think I would have been less stream-of-consciousness," Sarah commented.

"I like it," Erin replied. "It's very Amy."

I smiled. "Thanks, guys!"

The Freshman Fifteen-

What to Expect from Freshman Year of College

By Amy Callaway

College has been an amazing combination of gaining wisdom and having a great time! In this oasis between the stress of high school and the pressures of "the real world", everybody has near absolute freedom to do whatever their heart desires. There are countless opportunities to make friends and have fun. Just living in the dorms seems like a year-long pajama party. You are accountable to no one but yourself. This means that you can study or not, recreate yourself, discover what your passions are, and explore new ideas.

Notice I said that you *can*. I didn't say that you *would* and I didn't say that you *should*. This is because another side effect of this rule-less, boundary-less place called College is that no one will stop you from making poor decisions.

When Mr. Ives first asked me to write an article about what one could expect on entering college, I was a woman on a mission. Over the course of the entire first quarter, I was looking for the magical experiences and epiphanies that everyone would have in college. I thought that at some point during their freshman year of college, everyone would experiment with alcohol, drugs or sex. Everyone would dye their socks pink in the wash because they didn't know to separate the colors from the lights. Everyone would eventually "find themselves". Everyone would make great new friends and even meet their soul mate. And everyone would find a greater truth and purpose to life.

While some people did have a few of the aforementioned experiences, some didn't. Even the people who had common experiences had entirely different reactions to them and took away different "truths" from them. For example, of my friends who have tried drinking, some drink like fish now, while others totally condemn it. Some people have found their life's calling, while others are more confused than ever (I happen to fall in this category).

But the one thing that is true about college is that it is a place for you to test what you're made of. Here, you are exposed to so many ways of doing things and thinking about them. In this transition, I found out that for most of my life, I had based my identity on my family and my activities. I was Amy of Irvine, daughter of Bill and Jenna, a scholar, an athlete, and a writer. But when I arrived at UCLA, all of that context was stripped from me. No one knew me as any of those things. As I scrambled to explain to them who I was, scholar-athlete-writer suddenly became insufficient. When you're lying in the middle of the hallway at 3am, philosophizing with your neighbors, *who* you are suddenly takes precedence over *what* you are. When you fail a test for the first time in your life, you ask yourself why so much of your self worth has been based on your grades and not on the fact that you're a compassionate person.

College is the place to test out your ideas, values and belief. Sometimes, when you least expect it, someone will challenge a belief that you've always thought was unshakeable, and when you're forced to defend it, you may find that this person has a good point. Conversely, someone may bring up a random idea and you may find that it resonates with you. It's a place to figure out who you are and what you believe.

This has all been a very long introduction to The Freshman Fifteen, which is based on my first quarter and a half in college. Not everyone will have all of these experiences, but if you had mine, you might come away with these expectations of your freshman year:

1. **Gain 15 lbs**
   (even though you know you will)

2. **Get pumped about college sports**
   (but keep it clean)

3. **Party and drink**
   (in a safe environment)

4. **Date lots**
   (but for every person you date or think about dating, double the supply of aspirin)

5. **Get a job**
   (if you expect to have textbooks *and* a good time)

6. **Learn to live with roommates**
   (and be someone they can live with too; pranks help-sometimes)

7. **Experience the Walk of Shame**
   (hooking up, optional)

8. **Leave the nest**
   (but visit often)

9. **Experiment with sex**
   (then wish you hadn't)

10. **Be open to new ideas**
    (but don't assume that they are always better)

11. **Hang on to old friends**
    (but don't expect them to stay the same)

12. **Study**
    (or else bad things still happen)

13. **Make new friends**
    (but don't expect them to be like your old ones)

14. **Save the world**
    (little things count)

15. **Find yourself**
    (rather, redefine yourself)

Bibliography

1. Beckett, Samuel. *Waiting for Godot.* New York: Grove Press, 1954.

2. Faulkner, William. *The Sound and the Fury.* New York: Random House, 1956.

3. Golden, Arthur. *Memoirs of a Geisha.* New York: Random House, Inc. 1999.

4. Hosseini, Khaled. *A Thousand Splendid Suns.* New York: Riverhead Books, 2007.

5. Maxwell, Robyn. *The Secret Diary of Anne Boleyn.* New York: Simon and Schuster, 1998.

6. Mitchell, Margaret. *Gone with the Wind.* New York: Avon, 1973.

7. Montgomery, Lucy Maud. *Anne of Green Gables.* Boston: L.C. Page and Co, 1908.

8. Orwell, George. *Animal Farm.* New York: Signet Classic, 1956.

9. Orwell, George. *1984.* New York: Signet Classic, 1950.

10. *Playboy Magazine.*